the JOURNEY

WANDA & BRUNSTETTER

BARBOUR
PUBLISHING

ISBN 978-1-60260-681-4

All scripture quotations are taken from the King James Version of the Bible.

All German-Dutch words are taken from the *Revised Pennsylvania German Dictionary* found in Lancaster County, Pennsylvania.

This book is a work of fiction. Names, characters, places, and incidents are either products of the author's imagination or used fictitiously. Any similarity to actual people, organizations, and/or events is purely coincidental.

For more information about Wanda E. Brunstetter, please access the author's Web site at the following Internet address: www.wandabrunstetter.com

Cover design: Faceout Studio, www.faceoutstudio.com
Cover photography: Steve Gardner, Pixelworks Studios

Published by Barbour Publishing, Inc., P.O. Box 719, Uhrichsville, OH 44683, www.barbourbooks.com

Our mission is to publish and distribute inspirational products offering exceptional value and biblical encouragement to the masses.

ecpa Member of the
Evangelical Christian
Publishers Association

Printed in the United States of America.

DEDICATION/ACKNOWLEDGMENT

To Joe Thompson, who first introduced me to the Kentucky Amish and shared helpful information. To Lida Conkle and Patricia Thompson, who have also told me interesting facts about the area and answered many of my questions. And to our new Amish and Mennonite friends, whom we've enjoyed visiting during our trips to Kentucky.

I have learned, in whatsoever state I am, therewith to be content.
PHILIPPIANS 4:11

Fisher Family Tree

Abraham and Sarah Fisher's Children

Matthew
(m) Abby Miller
(Fannie's daughter)
_____

Stella
Derek
Joseph
Lamar
Brenda

Naomi
(m) Caleb Hoffmeir
_____

Sarah
Susan
Josh
Nate
Millie
Kevin

Norman
(m) Ruth
_____

Harley
Selma
John
Karen
Paul
Owen
Cora

Jake
(m) Darlene
_____

Doris
Diane
Delbert
Duane
Debra

Abraham and Fannie Fisher's Children

Titus
(single)

Timothy
(m) Hannah
_____

Mindy

Nancy
(m) Mark Stauffer

Mary Ann
(m) Abner Lapp

Stephen
Mavis
Lenore
Carl
Regina

Samuel
(m) Elsie

Lorie
Emma
Myron
Curtis

Zach
(m) Leona

Marla
Leon
Penny
Jared

Lucy
James
Jean

Fannie's Children from her First Marriage

Abby (Miller)
(m) Matthew Fisher
(Abraham's son)

Harold Miller
(m) Lena

Stella
Derek
Joseph
Lamar
Brenda

Ira
Katie
Raymond

Other Books by Wanda E. Brunstetter:

Indiana Cousins Series
A Cousin's Promise
A Cousin's Prayer
A Cousin's Challenge

Brides of Lehigh Canal Series
Kelly's Chance
Betsy's Return
Sarah's Choice

Daughters of Lancaster County Series
The Storekeeper's Daughter
The Quilter's Daughter
The Bishop's Daughter

Brides of Lancaster County Series
A Merry Heart
Looking for a Miracle
Plain and Fancy
The Hope Chest

Sisters of Holmes County Series
A Sister's Secret
A Sister's Test
A Sister's Hope

Brides of Webster County Series
Going Home
On Her Own
Dear to Me
Allison's Journey

White Christmas Pie
Lydia's Charm

Nonfiction
The Simple Life
A Celebration of the Simple Life
Wanda E. Brunstetter's Amish Friends Cookbook
Wanda E. Brunstetter's Amish Friends Cookbook, Vol. 2

Children's Books
Rachel Yoder—Always Trouble Somewhere Series (8 books)
The Wisdom of Solomon

CHAPTER 1

Paradise, Pennsylvania

Titus Fisher liked horses, dogs, and shoofly pie. What he didn't like was a cat that scratched, and a woman he couldn't trust. Today he'd dealt with both.

Gritting his teeth, he grabbed his horse's bridle and led him into the barn, wishing he hadn't gotten out of bed that morning. The day had started on a sour note when Titus had come to the barn to feed the horses and accidentally stepped on one of Mom's cats. Five of the irksome critters lived in the barn, and every one of them liked to bite and scratch. Whiskers, the smallest of the five, was the most aggressive. The crazy cat had been so miffed when Titus stepped on her tail that she'd clawed her way right up his leg, hissing and yowling as she went. When Titus had tried to push Whiskers off, she'd let him have it—leaving a nasty scratch on his leg.

Titus pulled up his pant leg and stared at the wound, still red and swollen. It reminded him of the time when he and his twin brother, Timothy, were six years old and had found a wild cat in the woodpile behind their barn. The mangy critter had bitten Titus's hand, and when the bite became infected, he'd started running a fever. Mom had taken him to the doctor's, where he'd been given a tetanus shot and an antibiotic. Ever since then, he'd had an aversion to cats.

"In my opinion, except for catching mice, cats are pretty much worthless," Titus mumbled as he guided his horse into one of the stalls. When he patted the horse's ebony-colored flanks, the gelding whinnied and flipped his head around to nuzzle Titus's hand. "Not like you, Lightning. You're worth every dollar I paid for you. You're dependable and trustworthy." He grimaced. "Wish I could say the same for Phoebe Stoltzfus."

Titus poured some oats into a bucket, and as his horse ate, he replayed the conversation he'd had with Phoebe on his way home from work that afternoon. . . .

"I'm not ready to join the church yet, and I'm too young to get married." Phoebe flipped the strings of her head covering over her shoulders and blinked her blue eyes. "Why do you have to put so much pressure on me, Titus?"

"I–I'm not," he stammered, "but I've been waiting a long time for you, and I'd thought that when I joined the church two years ago, you'd join, too."

"I wasn't ready then. I was only sixteen and had other things on my mind."

"How well I know that. You were too busy runnin' around with your friends and tryin' out all sorts of worldly things." Titus groaned. "Figured you'd have all that out of your system by now and would be ready to settle down."

She shook her head. "Maybe in a few years I'll be ready."

"You said that two years ago."

"Things have changed." She placed her hand gently on his arm. "My friend Darlene Mast is planning a trip to

Los Angeles, and she's leaving in a few days, so—"

He held up his hand. "Please don't tell me you want to go with her."

"I think it would be fun, and I've always wanted to see the Pacific Ocean." She looked up at him and smiled. "You're full of adventure and like to try new things. Wouldn't you like to see California?"

He shrugged. "Maybe someday, but not right now. What I want is for you to join the church this fall so we can get married."

She shook her head. "I just told you—I'm not ready for that."

"Will you ever be ready?"

"I don't know." She pushed a wisp of soft, auburn hair under her white organdy head covering and turned her gaze away from him. "I—I might not join the church. I might decide to go English."

"Are you kidding?"

"No, I'm not. I don't know if I want to be Amish."

Titus's jaw tightened as the reality of the situation set in. If Phoebe went to California, she might never come back. If she didn't join the church, they couldn't get married. Titus had been in love with Phoebe since he was seventeen years old, but she'd been four years younger than him, and their parents had disapproved. He'd waited patiently until Phoebe turned sixteen. Even then, his folks had been opposed to him courting her because she seemed so unsettled and ran with a wild bunch of kids.

Now Titus, at the age of twenty-two, still wasn't sure he and Phoebe would ever get married. If she did go English, the only way they could marry would be if he broke his vow to the Amish church, which he did not want to do.

"Can we talk about this later?" he asked. "After you've had a chance to think about this some more?"

"There's nothing to think about. I'm going to California." She tipped her head and stared up at him. "If you don't want to come, then I guess it's over between us."

"You can't do this, Phoebe. Are you just going to give up on us like this?"

She shrugged.

"Don't you love me anymore?"

"I–I'm not sure. Maybe we're not meant to be together."

Titus flinched. He felt like he'd been kicked in the stomach by one of his dad's stubborn mules. He had a sinking feeling that once Phoebe left home she'd never come back. All his years of waiting for her had been for nothing.

Titus's horse whinnied and nudged his hand, pulling his thoughts back to the present.

"Stop it, Lightning. I'm not in the mood." Titus kicked at a bale of straw and winced when Lightning whipped his head around and bumped his sore leg.

Lightning whinnied again and stomped his hoof. Then he moved to the other end of his stall and turned his backside toward Titus.

"It's all right, boy. I'm not mad at you." Titus stepped up to the horse and reached out his hand. "I'm upset with Phoebe, that's all."

As though accepting his apology, Lightning nuzzled Titus's neck.

Horses and dogs—that's about all that ever held my interest until Phoebe came along, Titus thought. *If there was only some way to get her out of my system. If I could just tell myself that I don't care anymore.*

―∾―

Pembroke, Kentucky

As Suzanne Yoder stared out the living room window, a sense of discontentment welled in her soul. She enjoyed living in Christian County, especially in the spring when the flowers and trees began to bloom.

I wish I could be outside right now, tilling the garden or even mowing the lawn, she thought with regret. It was too nice to be stuck indoors, yet she knew she needed to work on the quilt she'd started several months ago for her friend Esther Beiler's twenty-fourth birthday, which was less than a month away.

Suzanne's gaze shifted from the garden to the woodshop, where her grandfather and twenty-year-old brother, Nelson, worked. Due to painful arthritis, Grandpa's fingers didn't work well anymore, so he'd recently decided to look for someone else to help Nelson in the shop. Someone younger and more able-bodied. Someone who knew the woodworking trade.

Grandpa wasn't one to sit around or take life easy while others did all the work, but Mom had convinced him that he could still have a hand in the business by ordering supplies, waiting on customers, and keeping the books. Grandpa wasn't happy about it, but at least he wouldn't be sitting on the porch in his rocking chair all day, wishing he could be in the shop.

"I thought you were supposed to be working on Esther's birthday present," Mom said when she joined Suzanne in the living room.

"I was, but my eyes needed a break. I was thinking about going out to the woodshop to see if there's anything I can do to help out."

Mom's dark eyebrows furrowed as she slowly shook her head. "You'll never get that quilt done if you keep procrastinating, and

11

there's no need for you to run out to the woodshop, because I'm sure you and Nelson would only end up in a disagreement. You know how he feels about you hanging around the shop."

Suzanne frowned. No one in the family understood her desire to be in the woodshop, where she could enjoy the distinctive odors of wood being cut, sanded, or stained. It was a shame nobody took her interest in woodworking seriously. Not long ago, Suzanne had borrowed some of Grandpa's tools so she could make a few birdhouses and feeders to put in their yard. She'd never gotten any encouragement in making them, though. She guessed compared to the cabinets, doors, and storage sheds Grandpa and Nelson made, the birdhouses and feeders were insignificant.

Mom touched Suzanne's shoulder. "I'm going to plant some peas and lettuce this afternoon, so if you think you've worked long enough on the quilt today, I could use your help."

Suzanne didn't have to be asked twice. Any chore she could do outdoors would be better than being inside, where it was warm and stuffy. "I'll meet you outside as soon as I put away my quilting supplies," she said.

"That'll be fine." Mom gave Suzanne's arm a light tap and disappeared into the kitchen.

Suzanne glanced out the window once more and sighed as her gaze came to rest on the woodshop. "Guess I won't make it out there today—except to take the men their lunch."

—⚭—

Paradise, Pennsylvania

Titus left the barn and was about to head for the house, when a dark blue pickup rumbled up the driveway. He didn't recognize the vehicle or the young English man with dark curly hair who opened the cab door and stepped out.

"Is this where Zach Fisher lives?" the man asked as he approached Titus.

"Sort of. My dad owns this place, and Zach and his family live in the house behind ours." Titus pointed in that direction.

"Oh, I see. Is Zach at home?"

"Nope, not yet. He's up in Blue Ball, painting the outside of the bowling alley. Probably won't be home till sometime after six."

The man extended his hand. "I'm Allen Walters. I knew Zach when he lived in Puyallup, Washington."

"That was when he thought his name was Jimmy Scott, huh?"

"That's right."

"Zach's my half brother. My twin brother, Timothy, and I were born during the time Zach was missing. He was about six or seven then, I think."

"My mother and the woman Zach thought was his mother became good friends, so Zach and I kind of grew up together."

"Zach's mentioned that," Titus said. "Sure is somethin' the way he was kidnapped when he was a baby and never located his real family until he was twenty-one."

"I really missed Zach after he left Washington, but I'm glad he found his way home." Allen folded his arms and leaned against the side of his truck. "The last time I saw Zach was before he got married, and that was seven years ago. We've kept in touch through letters and phone calls, though."

"Did Zach know you were coming?"

Allen shook his head. "He doesn't know I've moved from Washington State to Kentucky either."

"You're welcome to hang around here until he gets home, because I'm sure he'll be pleased to see you."

"Thanks, I'll do that."

Just then, Titus's mother stepped out of the house and

started across the yard toward them, her slightly plump figure shuffling through the grass.

"This is my mother, Fannie Fisher." Titus motioned to Allen. "Mom, this is Zach's old friend, Allen Walters. He used to live in Washington."

Mom's brown eyes brightened as she shook Allen's hand. "It's nice to finally meet you. Zach's told us a lot about you and your family."

"He's talked to me about his family here, too."

"I explained to Allen that Zach's still at work and said he's welcome to stay here until Zach gets home."

Mom bobbed her head. "Why don't you stay for supper? I'll invite Zach and his family to join us. I think it would be nice for you to meet his wife and children."

"I'd like that," Allen said with an enthusiastic nod.

"If you need a place to spend the night, you're more than welcome to stay here." Mom smiled. "Since Titus is our only son still living at home, we have more than enough room to accommodate guests."

"I appreciate the offer, but I've already reserved a room at a hotel in Bird-in-Hand."

"That's fine, but the offer's open if you change your mind." Mom turned toward the house. "I'd better go back inside and get supper going."

As Mom headed to the house, Titus motioned to a couple of wooden chairs sitting beneath the maple tree on their lawn. "Why don't we take a seat?" he said to Allen. "I'm real interested in hearing why you moved to Kentucky."

CHAPTER 2

Pembroke, Kentucky

Everything sure looks good," Grandpa said as he seated himself in his chair at the head of the table. "Did you make any part of the meal tonight?" he asked, raising his bushy gray eyebrows as he looked at Suzanne.

"She cut up the cabbage and tomatoes for the coleslaw," Mom said before Suzanne could reply.

"What about the *hinkel*? Who fixed that?" Suzanne's nine-year-old brother, Chad, wearing an expectant expression, pointed to the platter of crispy fried chicken.

"I made the chicken," Mom said.

Chad pushed a hunk of flaming red hair out of his eyes and smacked his lips noisily. "That's *gut* to know, 'cause the last time Suzanne tried to bake a chicken, it came out of the oven chewy like rubber."

"That's because the chicken was old and tough," Suzanne said in her own defense.

The skin around Chad's blue eyes creased as his freckled nose wrinkled. "Wouldn't matter how old the bird was, 'cause you'da done somethin' wrong to it." He touched his jaw. "My

15

mouth was sore the rest of the night after chewin' on that horrible chicken."

Grandpa's pale blue eyes narrowed as he shot the boy a warning look. "That'll be enough. Let's pray so we can eat."

All heads bowed. Suzanne's silent prayer was short and to the point. *Heavenly Father, thank You for this food, and help my family to see that I have other skills that don't involve cooking. Amen.*

Suzanne heard Grandpa rustle his silverware, so she opened her eyes. Everyone else did the same.

"Would ya please pass the macaroni salad?" Suzanne's six-year-old sister, Effie, asked. She had the same red hair and blue eyes as Nelson and Chad, which they'd inherited from their father, who'd died in a farming accident two years ago. Suzanne's hair was more subdued, a combination of her mother's brown hair and her father's red hair.

Suzanne handed Effie the bowl of Mom's zesty macaroni salad, and then she turned to Grandpa and said, "Have you found anyone to work in the woodshop yet?"

He frowned as he shook his nearly bald head. "We'd thought about training Russell, but your uncle Dan needs the boy's help at his dairy, so we've decided to look for someone who already has some woodworking experience."

"There's no need for that," Suzanne was quick to say. "You can hire me."

Her brother Nelson's pale eyebrows lifted high on his forehead. "You're kidding, right?"

"No, I'm not."

"You're not experienced," he said with a shake of his head.

"I've made a few birdhouses and feeders."

"Those are small and don't begin to compare with the finely crafted cabinets, doors, and storage sheds we make in our shop." Nelson motioned to the window facing their yard. "Besides, you've got plenty to do taking care of the vegetables and flowers we grow in our garden and helping Mom in the house."

"But gardening is seasonal, and when I'm in the house for too long, I get bored." Suzanne picked up her napkin and wiped the juice from the chicken on her fingers.

"You wouldn't be bored if you spent more time in the kitchen," Nelson said. "How are you gonna find a husband if you don't learn to cook?"

Suzanne glared at him. "Why does everyone think a woman must marry? I personally don't care if I ever marry."

"You weren't sayin' that last year when you were hopin' James Beiler would start courtin' you," Suzanne's sixteen-year-old brother, Russell, chimed in. He was the only child in the Yoder family who had Mom's brown hair and brown eyes.

Suzanne clenched her fork so tightly that her fingers turned numb. She didn't need the reminder that she'd previously had a crush on Esther's older brother. For a while, it had seemed like James might be interested in her, too, but then he'd started courting Mary Jane Smucker. Last fall they'd gotten married and moved to Lykens, Pennsylvania.

From across the table, Russell squinted his coffee-colored eyes at Suzanne. "I'll bet the reason James dropped you for Mary Jane is 'cause she's such a good cook. About the only thing you can make is soup and sandwiches, and nobody wants that for supper every night."

"That'll be enough," Mom admonished. "Just eat your supper, and leave Suzanne alone."

Chad reached for a drumstick and plopped it on his plate. "Sure am glad Mom knows how to cook."

As much as it hurt to be reminded of her shortcomings, Suzanne knew that her brother was right. Unless she learned to cook, she'd probably never find a man willing to marry her. Well, she wouldn't worry about that until she found a man she was interested in marrying. Right now she needed to concentrate on finding some way to convince Nelson and Grandpa to let her work in their shop.

Until that day comes, she thought, *I'll continue to sneak out to the woodshop when no one's there and see what I can do on my own.*

―ᴍᴍ―

Paradise, Pennsylvania

"I'm so glad you're here, and I can't wait for you to meet my wife, Leona, and our three kids," Zach said as he, Allen, and Titus made their way across the yard to the picnic tables that had been set up on the lawn.

Allen grinned and draped his arm across Zach's shoulders. "I've wanted to do this for a long time. Just never got around to it until now."

Titus noticed right away the look of happiness on Zach's face. He was obviously pleased to be reunited with his childhood friend.

"So what brings you to our part of the country?" Zach asked, raking his fingers through the sides of his sandy brown hair. "The last time we talked on the phone, you said you were real busy at the carpentry shop in Tacoma and didn't know when you might get away."

Titus was tempted to jump in and share all that Allen had told him that afternoon, but he figured he'd better let Allen do the talking for now.

Allen moved to one of the wooden benches. "Let's sit down. While we're waiting for the rest of your family to show up, I'll tell you the other reason I'm here."

Titus took a seat on one bench, and Allen and Zach sat across from him.

"As you know," Allen began, "after the lumber mill where

I worked in Tacoma shut down, I began working for Todd Foster as a carpenter."

Zach nodded. "That's what Titus does now. He's been working for our brother-in-law, Matthew, for the past year."

"I told him that before you got home," Titus put in.

"Anyway, while I worked for Todd, I built a home that I thought would be for myself. I even acted as my own contractor." Allen leaned his elbows on the table and smiled. "Then before I had a chance to move in, someone offered to buy the house from me. So I sold that home and built several others, which I also ended up selling."

"Is that how you became a full-time general contractor?" Zach questioned.

Allen nodded. "Of course, I had to be licensed and bonded first. Even though I continued to do some of the carpentry on the new homes I built, I hired a paint contractor, an electrician, a plumber, and. . .well, you get the picture."

Zach glanced at Allen's pickup, sitting in the driveway. "The sign on your truck says WALTERS'S CONSTRUCTION, HOPKINSVILLE, KENTUCKY. Is that where you're living now?"

"That's right. After my girlfriend, Sheila, was killed by a drunk driver near the Tacoma mall, I felt like I needed a change."

Zach's eyebrows shot up. "I didn't know about that. I'm sorry, Allen."

"It happened six months ago, and it's my fault for not letting you know. I grieved so hard at first, and then when my cousin Bill, who lives in a small town near Hopkinsville, suggested I move there and start up my business, I jumped at the chance." Allen ran his fingers through his thick curly hair. "I've been working there for the last five months, and since I had some business in Pennsylvania this week, I decided to come see you."

Zach smiled and thumped Allen's shoulder. "I'm real glad you did. I've missed all the times we used to spend together."

"I've missed them, too," Allen said with a nod. "Which is why I'm hoping you might consider the offer I'm about to make."

Zach leaned forward with an expectant look. "What offer's that?"

"I was wondering if you'd like to move to Kentucky and work as a subcontractor for me, painting the houses I build."

Zach clasped his fingers behind his head and squinted his dark brown eyes. "That's an interesting idea, but I was away from my real family for over twenty years when I was living in Washington as Jimmy Scott. There's no way I could move away now and leave them all. Besides, our painting business is doing real well, and I sure couldn't leave Arthur in the lurch."

"I understand, and I'm not trying to pressure you." Allen tapped his fingers along the edge of the table and glanced over at Titus. "I'm also looking for a carpenter who'd be willing to work for one of the Amish men I know in Kentucky. The man has his own woodshop and does quite a bit of my work, but he's got arthritis pretty bad and can't use his hands for woodworking anymore."

"Allen's already talked to me about this, and I said I'd go," Titus spoke up.

"Go where?" Mom asked as she and Dad joined them at the picnic table.

"To Kentucky," Titus replied without hesitation. "Allen knows an Amish man there who needs a carpenter. He phoned the man awhile ago, and when he told him about me, the man said he'd be willing to give me a try."

Deep wrinkles formed across Mom's forehead as her dark eyebrows furrowed. "Why would you want to leave your job here and move to Kentucky?"

"Phoebe and I broke up today."

Mom's brown eyes widened, and her mouth formed an *O*.

"She's going to California with her friend Darlene," Titus explained.

Dad grunted. *"Em Phoebe sei belaudere mehnt net viel."*

"You may think Phoebe's talk doesn't mean very much, but I believe her," Titus said with conviction. "I don't think she's planning to come back, either."

Titus noticed the look of relief on Mom's face. She was obviously glad that Phoebe was leaving.

Dad's steely blue eyes stared intently at Titus. "Just because you and Phoebe broke up doesn't mean you should move to Kentucky."

"I'd like a new start—go someplace where I'm not reminded of Phoebe. I think moving to Kentucky's the best thing for me right now. Allen's agreed to rent a horse trailer so I can take Lightning along. We'll be leaving in the morning."

"You can't be serious!" Mom's voice rose to a high pitch, and her face tightened, making her wrinkles more pronounced.

"Jah, I am," Titus replied.

"What about your job with Matthew?" Zach questioned. "I wonder how he's going to take this news."

"After I made my decision, I called his cell phone and talked to him about it."

"What'd he say?" Dad asked.

"He gave me his blessing and said, since work's been a little slow in his shop lately, he thought he could get along without my help until he can find someone else to take my place."

"You won't make it in Kentucky." Mom shook her head. "You never stick with anything, Titus."

"I stuck with Phoebe—until she dumped me, that is."

"That's true, but sticking with her is nothing to brag about. Phoebe wasn't good for you," Dad said with a scowl.

"Well, I'm hoping Kentucky will be good for me, because I've made up my mind, and that's where I'm planning to go."

Mom planted both hands on her ample hips and whirled around to face Dad. "Abraham, don't just stand there; do something!"

CHAPTER 3

Hopkinsville, Kentucky

This town isn't as big as some, but I think you'll find everything you need here," Allen told Titus as he pulled his truck into a gas station in Hopkinsville. "There's a hospital, doctors, dentists, chiropractors, restaurants, and plenty of places to shop—including a big Walmart. Most of the Amish who live in the area hire a driver to bring them into town, and I'll make sure you get the names and phone numbers of a couple of people who drive for the Amish."

"I appreciate that." Titus yawned and stretched his arms behind his head. It had been a long drive, and he was tired.

Allen eased his truck up to the pumps and turned off the engine. "As soon as I get some gas, we'll head toward Pembroke, which is where Isaac Yoder's woodshop is located. Once you agreed to come here, I left a message on Isaac's voice mail, letting him know when we'd be leaving, so I'm sure he'll be expecting us soon."

"I hope so. Sure wouldn't want to barge in thinking I have a job and then find out that he didn't know anything about me coming." Titus would never have admitted it to Allen, but he felt nervous about meeting the man he hoped would be his new boss. Starting over in a new place with new people was an adventure, but it was also frightening. What if he messed up? What if Isaac Yoder didn't like his work?

Allen gave the steering wheel a couple of taps. "I've gotten to know Isaac fairly well in the short time I've been here, and I'm guessing that even if he had no idea you were coming, he'd roll out the welcome mat."

Titus chuckled, hoping his nerves wouldn't show. "He sounds like my twin brother, Timothy. He's about as easygoing and friendly as anyone I know."

"After we leave Isaac's place, I'll take you to the trailer I bought as an investment a while back—mostly for the property, though," Allen said. "My real estate agent said the place is fully furnished, but I've only seen the outside, and it's nothing fancy. So I won't charge you much rent, and at least you'll have someplace to live while you're getting settled into your new job and learning your way around."

"Sounds good." A sense of anticipation replaced Titus's nervous thoughts. He'd never been this far from home and realized that this was a good chance to prove his worth to his folks—and to himself.

While Allen pumped the gas, Titus leaned his head back and closed his eyes, letting his thoughts wander. He could still see the pathetic look on Mom's face when he'd said good-bye to her and Dad yesterday morning. She'd pleaded with him not to go, until Dad finally stepped in and told her that they needed to let Titus lead his own life and that he was a grown man and had the right to live wherever he pleased. Mom had tearfully hugged Titus, saying she wished him well, and then she'd said that if things didn't work out for him in Kentucky, he could always come home.

Mom doesn't understand that I need to get away from everything that reminds me of Phoebe, Titus thought. *Even though Phoebe will be in California, if I'd stayed in Pennsylvania I'd see her family, so it would be hard not to think about her. It's better if I make a clean break and start life over here where there are no reminders of the past.*

Titus's stomach growled. He opened his eyes and reached into his backpack, fumbling around for a candy bar. In the process of looking for it, he discovered a note that Phoebe had written him some time ago—when he thought she still loved him.

His stomach tightened. How was he ever going to get her out of his system? He couldn't stop thinking about her, and seeing her love note only made her rejection hurt all the more. He crumpled the note and pushed it into Allen's litter bag.

The truck door opened, and Allen climbed in. "All set!"

"I didn't realize you were done pumping the gas."

"Yep. Ready to meet the man who'll hopefully be your new boss?"

"Uh. . .guess I'm ready as I'll ever be."

"Are you nervous?"

"A little. I've never been this far from home, and starting a new job in a new place is kind of scary," Titus admitted.

Allen nodded. "I'll give you some advice my dad gave me when I left home: 'Those who fear the future are likely to fumble the present.'"

Titus groaned. "I sure don't wanna do that."

"Just do your best and try to keep a positive attitude, and I'm sure everything will work out fine."

"I hope so."

Allen drove out of Hopkinsville and turned left on Highway 68. After they'd gone a few miles, he pointed up ahead. "There's the Jefferson Davis Monument. It's just a couple of roads over to your right."

Titus whistled. "Wow, that building is sure tall!"

"You'll have to go inside the monument sometime and

take a look at the view from up there."

"Think I just might."

"What else would you like to do for fun?" Allen asked.

Titus turned his hands palms up. "Don't really know yet. Maybe some fishing if there's a nearby lake or pond. Oh, and I also like to ride horseback, so hopefully there are some good trails for riding."

"There are several ponds in the area, and I'm sure you can find lots of places to ride your horse. This community doesn't get near as much traffic as Lancaster County, so you can go most anywhere on your horse if you've a mind to."

Titus smiled. "Sounds good to me."

When they reached Pembroke-Fairview Road, Allen turned right. They drove a mile or so, and then he turned onto a dirt road. Titus noticed a sign by the driveway: YODER'S WOODSHOP.

As they continued up the lane, a large white farmhouse came into view. To the left of the house was the woodshop, with another sign above the door. To the right was a huge flower garden with some plants that were just coming into bloom.

As they drew closer, Titus saw a young, auburn-haired woman bent over one of the plants. He took a deep breath, trying to still the pounding of his heart. He couldn't see her face, but from the back, she looked like Phoebe.

—◆—

Suzanne lifted her head and turned when she heard a vehicle rumble up the driveway. Seeing the sign on the truck, she realized it was Allen Walters. The truck came to a stop, and both doors opened. Allen got out, and so did a young Amish man with dark brown hair whom she'd never seen before.

Grandpa stepped out of the woodshop just then and joined them on the lawn. Curious to know who their visitor was, Suzanne left the garden and hurried into the yard.

"This is Titus Fisher, the young man from Lancaster County, Pennsylvania, I called you about," Allen told Grandpa.

"Glad to meet you." Grandpa shook Titus's hand. Then he looked over at Suzanne and said, "Titus is going to help out in my shop, and if things work out, he'll be hired full-time."

That bit of news didn't set well with Suzanne, but she forced a smile and said, "It's nice to meet you, Titus."

"Same here," he mumbled, staring at Suzanne in a peculiar sort of way. It was almost a look of disgust.

"Titus will be staying in the old trailer I bought awhile back," Allen said.

"Oh, you mean the one Vernon Smucker used to own?" Grandpa asked.

Allen nodded.

"It was sad when the poor man died, because he'd never married and has no family that any of us know about. That old trailer has been sitting empty for quite a spell." Grandpa looked at Allen and slowly shook his head. "I'm surprised you bought the place. Haven't been inside it for a long time, but from what I remember, it was pretty run-down, even when Vernon lived there."

"I bought it as an investment," Allen said. "Figured since there are no homes for rent in the area right now, it'd be a good place for Titus to live."

Grandpa shrugged; then he looked over at Allen's truck and motioned to the horse trailer behind it. "Looks like you've brought a horse with you, huh?"

Allen nodded. "It belongs to Titus."

"I didn't want to leave Lightning behind," Titus explained.

"Didn't you bring a buggy for the horse to pull?" Grandpa asked.

Titus shook his head. "Figured I could ride Lightning to and from work every day."

"That's okay for now," Grandpa said, "but once winter comes, you'll need a buggy."

"I'll get one before then." Titus glanced at Suzanne, and a blotch of red erupted on his cheeks. He cleared his throat and quickly looked away.

Is there something about me he doesn't like? Suzanne wondered.

Just then, Esther Beiler came up the driveway on her scooter.

When Esther joined them, Suzanne introduced her to Titus and then added, "This is Titus Fisher. He's from Pennsylvania, and will be working in Grandpa's shop." Suzanne nearly choked on the words. It should be her working for Grandpa, not some stranger who wouldn't even make eye contact with her.

Esther smiled politely, and her milk-chocolate brown eyes shone brightly in the sunlight as she shook Titus's hand. "It's nice to meet you."

"Nice to meet you, too." Titus returned the smile and looked directly at Esther when he spoke. Apparently he found her more favorable to look at than Suzanne. Esther was an attractive young woman—dark brown hair, vivid blue eyes, and a dimpled smile that turned many men's heads. Suzanne felt plain compared to Esther.

"Where in Pennsylvania did you live?" Esther asked.

"Lancaster County, in Paradise. My oldest sister and her husband own a general store there, and several others in my family have businesses there, too."

"My folks lived in Strasburg when I was a baby, but Dad moved our family here before I started school," Esther said.

"Could be my folks and your folks know some of the same people," Titus said.

The sun-dappled leaves of the trees overhead cast a shadow across Esther's pretty face as she nodded. "I wouldn't be surprised."

"You all can get better acquainted some other time." Allen

motioned to the woodshop. "Right now, I think we ought to head in there and meet Suzanne's brother Nelson."

Titus gave Esther another quick smile. "It was nice meeting you." Then he glanced at Suzanne, looked away, and mumbled, "Uh—you, too."

As the men walked away, and the women headed for the porch, Esther whispered, "Titus seems nice, and he's sure good-looking, wouldn't you say?"

Suzanne shrugged. "I suppose so, but he acted kind of odd and would barely look at me."

Esther giggled. "Maybe he saw that smudge of dirt on the end of your *naas*."

Suzanne groaned and swiped her finger over her nose. "So that's what it was. Before you came, I was working in the garden. Guess I must have touched my naas with my dirty finger."

They sat on the porch swing, and Esther glanced at the woodshop. "I hope Titus likes it here enough to stay. We could use more available young men in our area."

"How do you know he's available?"

"You didn't see a beard on his face, did you?"

"No, but that only proves he's not married. It doesn't mean he's not courting someone in Pennsylvania. He could even have plans to be married."

"Are you going to ask?"

Suzanne pushed her feet against the porch to get the swing moving. "No way! If you want to know, you should ask."

Esther grinned, revealing the two deep dimples in her cheeks. "I might, if the opportunity comes up."

"How about now? Why don't you go to the woodshop and see what you can find out?"

Esther halted the swing. "*Ach*, I couldn't do that."

"Why not?"

"He'd think I was too bold. Besides, he and Allen are

29

talking business with your grandpa and Nelson right now."

"So how are you going to find out what you want to know?"

"I'll ask, but just not in front of anyone." Esther's elbow bumped Suzanne's arm. "Are you interested in him at all?"

"Of course not. I don't even know him."

"Then you wouldn't mind if I took an interest in him?"

"Not at all. I'm sure he'd be more interested in you than he would me, anyway."

"What makes you say that?"

Suzanne held up her index finger. "For one thing, you can cook and I can't."

Esther lifted her gaze toward the porch ceiling. "That's nobody's fault but your own. You're twenty-two years old, and you should have learned to cook by now. If you don't learn soon, you may never find a man."

"I've tried cooking a few things, but Mom has no patience with me in the kitchen. Whenever I mess up she gets frustrated and ends up doing it herself. Why, just last week I tried making some bread." Suzanne groaned. "The crust was so hard, I thought I might have to cut it with a saw."

Esther snickered. "I know you're exaggerating, but if you want to learn how to cook, I'd be happy to teach you."

"Thanks anyway, but there are lots of other things I'd rather be doing. Besides, I'm not interested in finding a man right now."

"Do you think you ever will be?"

Suzanne shrugged. "Maybe someday. . .if I can find one who cooks."

CHAPTER 4

W hat did you think of the Yoders?" Allen asked Titus as they headed down the road in his truck again.

"They seem nice enough. I think Nelson and I will get along fine, and hopefully Isaac will be pleased with my work and hire me full-time."

"What'd you think of Nelson's sister Suzanne?"

"I. . .uh. . .can't really say. Didn't talk to her long enough to form an opinion." Titus turned toward the window and spotted several horses grazing in the pasture of an Amish farm. *I came here to forget about Phoebe and start a new life, and what did I find? A woman who looks so much like Phoebe she could be her sister!*

Since Isaac's woodshop was on the same piece of property as the Yoders' home, he'd probably see a lot of Suzanne. Every time he saw her, he'd think of Phoebe, who'd be sitting on some sandy beach in California with nothing on her mind but sunning herself and having lots of fun.

Sure wish I hadn't wasted all those years waiting for her, he thought with regret. *Should have listened to Mom and Dad when they said Phoebe was too young and immature for me. I can't believe I was dumb enough to believe she'd be ready to join the church and marry me when she turned eighteen. She was probably leading me on so I wouldn't court anyone else.*

"Here we are. This is the trailer I was telling you about," Allen said, breaking into Titus's disconcerting thoughts.

Titus stared out the truck window in disbelief. The dilapidated, single-wide trailer had metal siding that was dented in places. Fake-looking shutters hung lopsided at the filthy windows, one of which was obviously cracked. The steps leading to the front door looked slanted, the screen door hung by only one hinge, and the porch sagged like an empty sack of potatoes. If the outside of the trailer was any indication of what the place looked like inside, Titus knew he'd be in for a lot of work to make it habitable.

As though sensing Titus's reservations, Allen offered him a reassuring smile. "Sorry about the condition of the place. Guess the outside needs a little more work than I'd thought. Let's go inside and take a look. Hopefully it's not so bad." He opened the truck door and stepped out. Titus did the same.

As they walked through the tall grass, a crow swooped down from the pine tree overhead, flapping its wings and screeching as though Titus were an intruder. At the moment, that's what he felt like.

"Watch out for that hole," Allen said as Titus stepped onto the porch.

Too late—Titus's foot slipped into the crevice, knocking him off balance. He grabbed the handle on the screen door to keep from falling over and pulled the door right off the hinge.

Oomph!—he landed on his backside with the screen door on top of him.

Allen picked up the screen and slung it into the yard. "Are you okay?"

Titus clambered to his feet, feeling like a complete fool. "I'm fine. Just never expected that to happen. Guess I should have though; I'm always doing something stupid to embarrass myself."

Allen studied him, then shrugged and opened the front door. "You might want to use the back door until we can get some work done to the porch," he said.

Titus stepped inside and halted. "Ugh! What's that disgusting odor?"

Allen's nose twitched like a rabbit's. "It smells musty in here. I think once we get some windows open and the place airs out, it should be okay."

Oh Lord, what have I gotten myself into? Titus silently moaned. *Maybe I should have listened to Mom and stayed in Pennsylvania. Maybe I'm not capable of making any right decisions.*

—⁓—

Paradise, Pennsylvania

As Phoebe tossed a few clothes into her suitcase, she thought about Titus and wished he'd been more understanding about her going to California. If he hadn't already joined the church, she was sure he'd have been willing to go with her. Maybe she could get him to change his mind.

Tap. Tap. Tap. "Phoebe, are you in there?"

"Jah, Mom. Come in."

When Phoebe's mother entered the room, she stopped short and stared at Phoebe's suitcase lying on the bed. "I—I was hoping you'd change your mind about going."

Phoebe shook her head. "I'll be leaving this evening after Darlene gets off work."

Mom pursed her lips, and her pale blue eyes narrowed. "If that young woman runs off to California, I doubt her job at the restaurant in Bird-in-Hand will be waiting for her when she gets back, and you might not have a job cleaning house for our neighbors either."

"It doesn't matter. We'll both find other jobs." Phoebe shrugged. "If we come back, that is."

Mom sank onto the edge of Phoebe's bed. "Don't tell me you're thinking of staying in California permanently. I thought you were just going for a short time—to see what it's like on the West Coast."

"I might stay there if I like it." *And even if I don't. Anything to get away from you and Dad always telling me what to do.*

"I guess that means you have no plans to join the Amish church?"

"I don't know yet. I need more time to think about it. I want to enjoy some of the things the English world has to offer. I want to see the Pacific Ocean and walk on the beach."

A few wisps of Mom's faded auburn hair, now streaked with some gray, peeked out from under her covering as she lowered her head. "You've been to a couple of New Jersey beaches with your friends. I don't understand why you think you need to go clear across the country to walk on the beach."

"It's different in California. Darlene's been there once, and she said I would like it."

Mom folded her arms and met Phoebe's gaze. "What about Titus? He's been waiting for you all these years, you know."

Phoebe grunted. "Like you care about that. You and Dad have never liked Titus."

"It's not that we don't like him. We just knew you were too young to think about courtship when he first took an interest in you. Once you turned eighteen, we had no objections to him courting you."

"Well, he shouldn't have been in such a hurry to join the

church. He should have given me more time to decide what I wanted to do." Phoebe closed the lid on her suitcase and zipped it shut. "I don't want to talk about this is anymore. I've gotta go."

"But if you're not leaving until this evening, what's the hurry?"

"I'm going over to the Fishers' to see if I can get Titus to change his mind and go to California with us."

―⟁―

"You look so *mied*, Mom. Why don't you have a seat while I pour us some tea?" Fannie's daughter, Abby, motioned to the kitchen table.

Fannie pulled out a chair and sighed as she sat down. "You're right. I am tired. Hardly slept at all last night."

Abby poured them both a cup of tea and sat down next to Fannie. "You look awfully sad, too. Are you still *brutzich* over Titus moving to Kentucky?" Abby's dark eyes revealed the depth of her concern.

"I suppose I am fretful," Fannie admitted. "I just can't believe he made such a hasty decision or that Matthew was okay with it. Titus hasn't been working for him very long, and he should have been more considerate about leaving Matthew in the lurch."

"Matthew's fine with Titus's decision, Mom. His business is slow right now, and when it picks up again, he'll hire someone else. Maybe one of Norman's boys will be interested in learning the woodworking trade."

Fannie blew on her tea. "Seems like everything was going along fine one day, and the next day, that English friend of Zach's showed up and whisked my *bu* away."

Abby chuckled. "Titus is hardly a boy."

Fannie sniffed, struggling to hold back the tears threatening to spill over. "Doesn't he care about us anymore?"

"When someone chooses to move away from home, it doesn't mean they don't care about their family. Remember, Mom, you left Ohio and moved here so you could marry Abraham. When you made that decision, I didn't take it personally or think you didn't care about me anymore."

Fannie plucked a napkin from the wicker basket in the center of the table and dabbed at her tears. "I realize that, but I wasn't running from something the way Titus is. Besides, it wasn't long after I moved to Pennsylvania that you came here, too."

"But when you left Ohio, you didn't know I'd eventually move. Only God knew that." Abby took a sip of her tea. "If you're really upset about Titus leaving, maybe you and Abraham should consider moving to Kentucky."

"And leave the rest of our family?" Fannie shook her head vigorously. "Never!"

"You're not living close to Harold and his family," Abby reminded.

"That's different. Your brother didn't move away when I was living in Ohio."

"No, you did." Abby set her cup down and placed her hand on Fannie's arm. "When I first came to Pennsylvania to help when you were pregnant, I never thought I'd move here permanently. It was only to be until after the twins were born and I was sure you could handle things on your own. If my boyfriend, Lester, hadn't died in that horrible fire, trying to save my quilts, I would have gone back to Ohio to marry him as soon as you were able to handle things on your own." Deep wrinkles formed across her forehead. "After Lester died, I saw no reason to stay in Ohio. So in a way, I was doing exactly what Titus has done. I left one place and moved to another in order to get away from unpleasant memories."

Fannie blew her nose on the napkin. "I know you're right, but it's more than just missing Titus that has me so upset."

"What else?"

"I'm worried that since one of my sons has left home, some of the others may decide to leave, too." Fannie nearly choked on the sob rising in her throat. "If more of the family goes, I don't think I could stand it. I really don't."

"As Abraham always says, 'Let's not put the buggy before the horse.' All the men in our family have good jobs here, so it's not likely that any of them will leave Pennsylvania."

"I hope you're right."

A knock sounded on the back door, interrupting their conversation.

"I wonder who that could be." Fannie dabbed at her tears again. "I really don't feel like company today."

"I'll go see." The chair scraped noisily across the linoleum as Abby pushed it aside and stood. "Should I tell whoever it is that you're not up to visitors today?"

Fannie waved a hand. "No, don't do that. It would seem rude. You'd better just invite whoever it is to come in."

Abby left the kitchen and returned moments later with Phoebe Stoltzfus at her side.

Fannie clenched her fingers so tightly that the damp napkin she held began to pull apart. The last person she wanted to see right now was the young woman responsible for her son's decision to move away.

"Is Titus here?" Phoebe asked. "I need to speak to him."

Fannie shook her head. "No, he's—"

"I stopped by Matthew's woodshop but it was closed, so I thought maybe Matthew had gone somewhere with his family and had given Titus the day off."

"Matthew had some errands to run in town, and as you can see, I'm right here," Abby said. "And of course, our *kinner* are in school today." She looked over at Fannie. "Would you like to tell her, or should I?"

"Tell me what?" Phoebe pulled out a chair and sat down.

Fannie's lips compressed as she tapped her fingers along the edge of the table. "Titus is gone—moved to Kentucky—thanks to you."

Phoebe's eyebrows shot up. "Are you serious?"

Fannie gave a nod. "Took all his clothes and even his horse."

"But. . .but I had no idea Titus was planning to leave Pennsylvania. He didn't say a word about it when I talked to him the other day." Phoebe wrinkled her nose, as though some foul odor had permeated the room. "Some people have a lot of nerve!"

"Jah, they sure do." Fannie stared hard at Phoebe. "And I'm looking at such a person right now."

Phoebe's face flamed. "You think it's my fault that Titus moved to Kentucky?"

"That's exactly what I think. He made the decision after you broke up with him and said you were going to California."

"I didn't actually break up with him. I just said—"

"It makes no never mind. Titus is gone, and he left because of you."

Phoebe sat with a shocked expression. Then with a loud *humph*, she jumped up, nearly knocking over her chair, and dashed out the door.

Fannie blew out her breath in exasperation. "I know it's not right to wish the worst for anyone, but I hope that selfish young woman is miserable in California and gets exactly what she deserves!"

CHAPTER 5

Western Pennsylvania

Phoebe leaned her head against the window in the passenger's side of Darlene's car and closed her eyes. They'd left Lancaster County earlier that evening, after a tearful good-bye from Phoebe's parents. Mom had begged her not to go, and Dad had given her a stern lecture on not becoming caught up in worldly pleasures.

I still can't believe Titus went to Kentucky without telling me, Phoebe thought bitterly. *What's in Kentucky, anyhow? Will Titus find someone else to take my place? Will he end up marrying someone there and stay in Kentucky for good? Should I have listened to him and stayed in Pennsylvania? Should I have agreed to join the church and marry him? But if I'd stayed in Pennsylvania, I might never have had the chance to see California. Besides, I have a lot more living to do before I tie myself down to a husband and kids.*

"I'll bet he doesn't stay in Kentucky even a year," she muttered under her breath.

"What was that?" Darlene asked.

Phoebe's eyes snapped open. "Oh, nothing. I was just thinking out loud."

"Thinking about Titus Fisher, I'll bet." Darlene flipped her blond ponytail over her shoulder. Dressed in a pair of blue jeans and a pink T-shirt, she looked nothing like the plain Amish girl who'd gone to the one-room schoolhouse with Phoebe for eight years.

Phoebe glanced at her own pair of jeans. Mom and Dad had never approved when she'd worn English clothes. They rarely approved of anything she did.

Darlene nudged Phoebe's ribs with her elbow. "Were you thinking about Titus or not?"

"Yes, and I still can't believe he moved to Kentucky."

"Maybe it's for the best."

"What's that supposed to mean?"

"If he'd stayed in Pennsylvania, you might have felt obligated to return home and join the church. This way, you're free to stay in California if you want to."

"I guess you're right." Phoebe yawned. "Sorry. I can hardly stay awake."

"Well, go to sleep then. I'll wake you when I'm ready to stop for the night."

Phoebe closed her eyes and rested her head against the window. She was bound to feel better once they reached Los Angeles.

—⁓—

Pembroke, Kentucky

When Titus woke up the following morning after a restless night on a lumpy bed, he hurried to get dressed, then made his way to the kitchen. As he passed through the small living room, he stopped and surveyed his surroundings, wondering if he'd been out of his mind for agreeing to stay here. The paneling on the living room walls had been painted an odd shade of yellow; the upholstery on the old rocking chair and sofa was torn; and the only throw rug on the floor was frayed around the edges.

He moved on to the kitchen to check out that tiny room. The hinges on the cabinets were rusty; only one burner on the propane stove worked; the porcelain sink was full of rust stains; the curtains were faded; and several places in the linoleum had been torn, revealing the wooden floor beneath it. Titus had left all the windows open last night, in an effort to air the place out, but he could still smell some mustiness. Obviously nothing had been done to maintain this trailer in a good many years.

Titus opened each of the cupboard doors and groaned. Not a stick of food in the house, of course. Allen had offered to take him shopping last night, but he'd gotten an urgent call from one of his contractors and said he had to rush off. Titus had assured him that he could survive for a while on the snack food he'd brought from home and would get to a store on his own after work today.

Think I'd better eat that granola bar in my backpack, saddle Lightning, and head over to the woodshop, Titus told himself. *It wouldn't be good for me to be late on the first day—especially since I haven't proven myself to Isaac Yoder yet.*

—w—

It was almost noon when Suzanne's mother suggested that Suzanne take the sandwiches she'd made out to the woodshop for the men.

"Can't you take them out?" Suzanne asked.

Mom's forehead wrinkled. "You take the men's lunch out to them nearly every day, so why not now?"

"I feel funny around Titus. I don't think he likes me."

"For goodness' sake, Suzanne, he hasn't had a chance to

get to know you, so why would you think he doesn't like you?"

"When he was here yesterday he looked at me in disgust, and then after that he would hardly look at me at all. Esther said it was probably because I had a dirt smudge on my nose, but I think it may have been something more."

"He's probably shy. Give him a chance to get to know you before making assumptions." Mom handed Suzanne the lunch basket. "Now would you please take the men's lunch out to them?"

"Are you sure you won't do it?"

Mom shook her head. "I need to get some baking done, but if you'd rather do the baking, then I'd be happy to take the sandwiches out to the woodshop."

"No way! If I did the baking, nobody would speak to me for the rest of the week because I'm sure I'd ruin whatever I tried to make."

"If you spent more time in the kitchen, you might have learned how to bake by now."

Suzanne didn't say anything in her own defense. She'd had this discussion with Mom before, and apparently Mom didn't realize just how impatient she could be when it came to working in her kitchen. Suzanne figured making excuses to stay out of the kitchen was easier than telling Mom the truth.

"I made enough sandwiches so Titus can have one, too," Mom said. "Unless he went shopping last night, he may not have brought any lunch with him this morning, because I'm sure there was no food in that old trailer."

Suzanne wrinkled her nose. "If there had been, it surely would have been spoiled by now." Lunch basket in one hand, and a jug of lemonade in the other, she turned and hurried out the door.

When Suzanne entered the shop, she found Titus and Nelson sanding some cabinet doors while Grandpa sat at his desk writing something in the ledger.

"I brought your lunch," Suzanne said, placing the wicker basket and lemonade on the desk beside him.

"*Danki.*" Grandpa smiled up at her. "Did you bring enough for Titus, too?"

"Jah." She cast a quick glance in Titus's direction.

"I appreciate that," Titus said, without looking at her. "I haven't had a chance to buy groceries yet, so I didn't bring a lunch with me today."

Suzanne frowned. *He still won't look at me. I wonder why?*

"No need for you to ever bring your lunch to work," Grandpa said. "I'm sure my daughter will be happy to provide your noon meals." He motioned to Suzanne and smiled. "And my helpful granddaughter will bring it out to us whenever she's home."

"What'd you bring today?" Nelson asked, moving across the room toward Suzanne.

"Ham sandwiches, lemonade, and some peanut butter cookies," she replied.

"Did you make the cookies, or did Mom?"

"Mom did."

Nelson's only response was a quick nod.

Suzanne was relieved that neither he nor Grandpa had said anything about her lack of cooking skills. It would be embarrassing to have that announced in front of someone she barely knew.

While the men ate their lunch, Suzanne looked at the set of cabinets Titus and Nelson had been working on. Her fingers ached to pick up a hammer and begin a project of her own. She knew that wouldn't be appreciated, though—especially by Nelson. He'd probably ask her to leave.

In no hurry to return to the house, Suzanne grabbed a broom and started sweeping up the pile of sawdust on the floor. While she swept, she listened to the men's conversation, occasionally peeking at Titus. It didn't take her long to learn that he had a twin brother named Timothy, who'd been married to Hannah almost two years, and that they had a one-year-old daughter, Mindy.

"Your *bruder* must have gotten married when he was pretty young." Nelson thumped Titus's arm. "You don't look like you're much more than twenty years old."

"I'll be twenty-three in October. Mom's always said that Timothy and I have baby faces." Titus's face sobered. "Timothy was twenty when he married Hannah, and she was more than willing to become his wife. But then things always seem to go the way he plans."

"How many other brothers and sisters do you have?" Nelson asked, apparently unaware of Titus's attitude when he'd spoken about his twin.

"Timothy's my only full brother, but we have three half sisters and five half brothers from my *daed*'s first marriage. Our *mamm* and her first husband had a girl and a boy several years before Timothy and I were born, so that gives us another half brother and sister. All my siblings are married except for me," Titus added with a frown. At least Suzanne thought it was a frown. Maybe he just had a case of indigestion.

"So your folks were both widowed for some time before you were born?" Grandpa asked.

"Jah."

Nelson whistled. "You have a big family. Ours is small by comparison."

"How many brothers and sisters do you have?" Titus asked.

"Besides Suzanne, there's Russell, Chad, and our little sister, Effie."

"I guess that is small compared to ours." Titus reached for a cookie and took a bite. "Umm. . .this is good." He glanced over at Suzanne, frowned, and then quickly averted his gaze.

Not this again. He's got that look of disgust. Does he think I was listening in on his conversation? Is he irritated that I'm still in the shop? Maybe he thinks like Nelson, that a woman's place is in the house.

When the men finished their lunch, Suzanne set the broom aside and gathered up the sandwich wrappings and empty jug of lemonade; then she put everything in the basket. "I'm going back to the house now," she said to Grandpa. "Is there anything else you'd like me to bring out to you?"

He smiled. "I think we're fine. If we get thirsty we'll drink water from the jug in the ice chest in the back room."

"Okay. See you at suppertime." Suzanne hurried from the shop. At least she'd learned a few things about Titus. She still didn't know whether he had a girlfriend or not.

Of course, she reasoned, *it's not my job to find that out. Esther's the one who's interested in him, and she did say she would ask. I just wonder when she'll do it, and what she'll find out.*

Chapter 6

Paradise, Pennsylvania

As Fannie stood at the kitchen sink, peeling potatoes for supper, her thoughts went to Titus. He'd used Allen's cell phone to let them know he'd made it to Kentucky, but she didn't know how often they might hear from him in the days ahead. She planned to write letters, of course, but knowing Titus, it was doubtful that he'd take the time to write back. Probably would just leave messages on their voice mail from time to time, and she'd never get to speak to him directly.

"What are you thinkin' about?" Abraham asked, touching Fannie's shoulder.

She whirled around. "Ach, you startled me!"

"Sorry."

"How do you know I was thinking about anything?"

He gave her arm a gentle squeeze. " 'Cause I said your name three times, and you just stood there, staring out the window without saying a word."

"I was thinking about Titus and how much I miss him."

"I miss him, too, but we still have the rest of our family living here."

She nodded. "Just doesn't seem the same without one of our special twins."

"The twins are special," Abraham agreed. "Havin' those boys was such a comfort to me after Zach was kidnapped."

"I know they were." Fannie set her potato peeler aside. "Let's sit down so we can be comfortable while we talk."

They sat across from each other at the table. "The twins didn't take the place of my lost son, but they sure filled an empty spot in my heart," Abraham said.

She nodded. "Even though I thought I was too old to have anymore *bopplin*, when the twins came along, it was a blessing to me as well."

Abraham smiled. "Remember when Titus and Timothy were teenagers, and how much they liked to joke around?"

"Jah. One of the things they did to irritate each other was to grab the other one's hat and toss it into a tree."

"And remember the time when the boys were fooling around and got too close to a pile of manure?" He reached for the plate of pickles she'd cut up before starting the potatoes and popped one into his mouth. "They ended up with that stinky stuff all over themselves."

Fannie crinkled her nose. "What a stench that was! It took two or three good scrubbings before I had the smell out of their clothes, and I don't know how much soap and water they used to get their bodies smelling good again."

Abraham chuckled. "Another prank those two often pulled was pretending to be each other. 'Course I've always been able to tell 'em apart, because Titus's left eye is a little bit larger than his right eye, whereas the shape of Timothy's eyes is about the same."

"It's the difference in their personalities that's always let me know which twin is which," Fannie said. "Timothy's easygoing and doesn't let much bother him. But Titus has always been impulsive and kind of headstrong."

Abraham gave a nod. "Timothy's a steady worker and has been satisfied to farm with me and work part-time as a painter for Zach. Titus has tried several different jobs and becomes easily distracted."

"Between the two of them, Titus is more immature." Fannie sighed. "Why, that boy couldn't even do his chores without being reminded all the time. I have to wonder how long he'll stick with the new job in Kentucky."

Abraham grabbed another pickle. "I think he'll do okay. Once he starts working, he works hard and does a good job. He just needs to be on his own so he can grow up. I believe Titus might be on a journey to discover himself, and we need to let him find his own way."

"Do you think he'll ever get over Phoebe Stoltzfus?" Fannie asked, going to get the coffeepot from the stove.

"I hope so. Maybe he'll find someone new in Kentucky— someone more mature and settled into the Amish ways— someone who'll make him a good *fraa*."

Fannie frowned. "I'd rather he came back here to find a wife. If he marries a woman from there, he'll probably never move back home."

"I know it's hard for you to see one of our sons move away," Abraham said, as she handed him a cup of coffee. "It's hard for me, too."

Fannie sniffed. "I never thought any of the kinner would decide to leave."

"As much as it hurts to have Titus gone, we need to accept his decision and realize that it's probably for the best."

"Why do you say that?"

"Think about it. If he'd stayed here and kept pursuing Phoebe, she may have hurt him again and again."

"But she's gone to California," Fannie said. "I don't see

how she could hurt him from there."

"She'll be back." Abraham grunted and slapped the table with the palm of his hand. "Mark my words, that girl won't last long out there in California among the English."

—ᴍ—

Pembroke, Kentucky

"We've put in a good day, but it's time to call it quits," Nelson said, setting his hammer aside.

Titus did the same. "Say, I need to stock up on some food. Can you tell me where the nearest store is located?"

"We do our big shopping at the Walmart in Hopkinsville, but there's an Amish-run store in the area, and they carry most of our basic needs, as well as some bulk foods."

"Where is it?" Titus asked.

"Just off Highway 115—the Pembroke-Fairview Road over near the Fairview Produce Auction. You probably went past the place when Allen brought you here yesterday."

"I don't recall. Just remember seeing the Jefferson Davis Monument."

"The store's not far from there."

Titus grabbed a pen and scribbled the directions on his arm.

Nelson's eyebrows lifted high. "There's no need to mark up your arm with a pen. I'll write it down for you." He quickly scrawled the directions on a tablet and handed it to Titus.

Titus smiled. "Danki."

"How you planning to get to the store?" Isaac questioned.

"Figured I'd ride over on Lightning."

Isaac grunted as he shook his head. "You're gonna need somethin' bigger than the back of your horse to carry groceries home. Why don't you go up to the house and see if Suzanne's free to drive you to the store? Tell her she can take my horse and buggy if she wants."

Titus hesitated near the door. He wasn't sure he wanted Suzanne to take him anywhere. But he guessed Isaac was right—he couldn't carry all the groceries he'd need on the back of Lightning. He grabbed his straw hat from the wall peg near the door, plunked it on his head, and headed out the door. "See you both tomorrow," he called over his shoulder.

When Titus stepped onto the Yoders' back porch, an orange, white, and black calico cat whizzed past his leg. Startled, he jumped back, nearly clipping the critter's tail.

"Go on! Get away! Shoo!"

The cat hissed at Titus, leaped off the porch, and bounded away.

"Stupid *katz*," Titus mumbled as he knocked on the door.

A few seconds went by; then Suzanne opened the door. "Can I help you with something?" she asked, tipping her head.

Seeing her again made Titus's heartbeat pick up speed. He sure wished she didn't remind him so much of Phoebe.

"I. . .uh. . .need to get some food and a few other things, and Nelson said there's a store nearby."

"That would be the Beilers' store. You met Esther Beiler yesterday."

Titus shuffled his feet, feeling more uncomfortable by the second. "Umm. . .your grandpa said I should ask if you'd mind taking me there. Said you could use his horse and buggy."

Suzanne's mother, Verna, stepped out of the house just then. Titus had met her briefly when he left the shop the day before. "I need a few things at the store myself," she said, smiling at Titus. "So Suzanne would be happy to take you to the store."

Suzanne shot her mother a questioning look, but she didn't offer a word of protest.

"You can tie Titus's horse to the back of the buggy, and then when you're done shopping you can drop Titus off at the trailer," Verna said.

"Oh, okay," Suzanne mumbled.

Titus suspected by the slump of Suzanne's shoulders that she wasn't happy about accompanying him to the store. Well, he could understand that because he wasn't thrilled about going with her, either.

—◊◊—

As Suzanne and Titus climbed into Grandpa's buggy, one of Suzanne's cats—a fluffy gray one—leaped in and jumped up on the seat between them.

"Get out of here!" Titus muttered as he pushed the cat out.

Suzanne ground her teeth. He obviously didn't like cats any more than he liked her.

As they headed down the road toward the store, Suzanne tried to make conversation, but that was hard to do when Titus didn't say much in response.

"What's that?" Suzanne asked, when she noticed some writing on Titus's arm.

"What's what?"

"That." She pointed to his arm.

Titus's face colored. "Oh, I. . .uh. . .started writing the directions to the store when your brother told me. . ."

"I can't believe you'd write a note on your arm."

"It's easier than carrying a tablet with me all the time. I've been doing it since I was a kinner." He'd spoken without looking at her again.

Suzanne didn't say what she was thinking, that writing notes on his arm was really strange.

When they arrived at the store, she left Titus to do his shopping while she went after the things Mom needed. She'd just started down the bulk foods aisle when Esther joined her, wearing a frown.

"I thought you weren't interested in Titus."

"I'm not."

"Then what are you doing here with him?"

"He needed to come to the store, and since he doesn't have a buggy, Grandpa volunteered me to take him."

"Oh, I see. Did you find out whether he has a girlfriend or not?"

"No, you said you were going to do that."

"I will, but I need to wait for the right opportunity. I can't just go up to him and say, 'Oh, by the way, I was wondering if you have a girlfriend in Pennsylvania.' "

Suzanne bit back a chuckle. "No, I guess that would seem too bold."

"Why don't you ask him?"

"Why me?"

"Because with him working in the woodshop, you'll see him more often than I will."

"I can't just blurt it out, but if the subject comes up, I'll ask. Does that make you happy?"

Esther's face broke into a wide smile. "I'll be even happier if he's available."

———⁂———

When Titus finished shopping, he found Suzanne talking to her friend. He said a quick hello to Esther and then told Suzanne that he'd gotten everything he needed and was ready to go whenever she was.

"Great. I'll be done soon."

A short time later, Titus and Suzanne paid for their purchases, said good-bye to Esther, and climbed into the buggy. They'd no sooner pulled away from the store, when it started to rain.

"Does it rain much here?" he asked.

"In the spring, mostly, but we can have showers any time."

They talked more about the weather and the kinds of trees and plants that grew in the woods along the road. Titus listened with interest as Suzanne told him that maple, cedar, river birch, willow, and pine trees grew in the area, and that a bush called crape myrtle could grow to be anywhere from fifteen to twenty feet high and six to fifteen feet wide.

"Crape myrtles put on a show all year long," Suzanne said. "Their long-blooming flowers come in pink, red, white, and lavender. In the fall, the leaves turn yellow or red, then drop off to reveal peeling gray and brown bark."

"Seems like you know a lot about flowers and trees," Titus commented, glancing briefly her way. At least he'd been able to make eye contact with Suzanne now that the shock of her looking so much like Phoebe had worn off.

"I enjoy doing almost anything that takes me outdoors, and I also enjoy—" Suzanne pointed to a rabbit skittering into the woods. "Do you like to hunt?"

He nodded. "I've gone deer hunting with my half brothers Jake and Norman a few times."

"I like to hunt and fish," she said, "but Nelson thinks women shouldn't do things like that."

Titus glanced at Suzanne again. She might look like Phoebe, but there were definitely some differences. Phoebe wouldn't go near a hunting rifle, or even a fishing pole. She liked adventure but not the kind that involved tromping through the woods or sitting by a pond for hours, waiting for a fish to bite.

"Do you miss your family?" Suzanne asked, changing the subject.

"I probably will, but I haven't been gone long enough to miss anyone too much yet."

"Not even a girlfriend?"

"Huh?"

"I wondered if you might have a girlfriend back in Pennsylvania."

"I did have one," he mumbled, wishing she hadn't brought the subject up. "But that relationship's over now."

"Oh, I see."

They rode in silence the rest of the way, with the only sounds being the splatter of raindrops against the roof of the buggy and the steady *clip-clop* of the horse's hooves on the road. Titus was glad when Suzanne didn't question him further about Phoebe. It wasn't something he wanted to talk about right now.

When they arrived at the trailer, Titus hopped down from the buggy, untied his horse, and led him to the barn, which wasn't in much better shape than the trailer. Then he returned to the buggy for his groceries. "Danki for the ride," he said, giving Suzanne a nod.

"You're welcome."

As Suzanne's horse and buggy pulled away, Titus hurried into the trailer. When he entered the kitchen, he screeched to a halt. A huge puddle of water sat in the middle of the floor.

CHAPTER 7

I t rained all night, and Titus had trouble sleeping, with the constant *ping, ping, ping* of the water dripping into the pan he'd set on the kitchen floor. No wonder the house smelled so musty. This probably wasn't the first time the roof had leaked. To top it off, he'd discovered some fresh mouse droppings under the kitchen sink and inside a couple of the cupboards. He figured he must have at least one mouse in the house. He'd have to see about getting a couple of traps to take care of that.

Guess I'd better climb up on the roof and see about patching the place where the water's been coming through before I leave for work today, Titus thought as he forced himself to crawl out of bed the next morning. He would have done it last night if it hadn't been raining so hard. So he'd put up with the dripping and spent the evening cleaning out the propane refrigerator, as well as the cupboards, before putting away his groceries. As soon as he got his first paycheck, he planned to hire a driver and go to Hopkinsville to get a new mattress for his bed. If his new job worked out well and he decided to stay in Kentucky permanently, he'd need to find a better place to live, because this trailer wasn't fit for the mice.

—⧓—

"I can't believe Allen would expect Titus to live in Vernon Smucker's old trailer," Suzanne said to her mother as they scurried around the kitchen getting breakfast on the table. "I didn't get to see the inside, but if it's anything like what I saw outside, Titus has a lot of work ahead of him to make that place livable."

"I never thought much about it, but you're probably right," Mom said, turning from the stove where she was frying some bacon. "Vernon's trailer has been abandoned for quite a while now, and it's probably not fit for anyone to live in. I think we ought to talk to my daed and Nelson and see about getting a crew of people together for a work frolic soon. The trailer might be livable if a group of us helped fix it up."

"Who are we helping?" Grandpa asked when he and Nelson entered the kitchen.

"Titus," Mom answered. "Suzanne said the trailer he's living in looks pretty bad from the outside, and I'm guessing it's going to need a lot of repairs inside as well. So I was thinking we ought to have a work frolic to help him fix the place up."

"That's a good idea," Nelson said with a nod. "Titus told me yesterday that the place is a mess."

"I'll talk to some folks in our area and see about setting a date for the frolic," Grandpa said. "If we'd known sooner that Allen was bringing someone to work in the woodshop, and that he'd have him stay in Vernon's old place, we could have had the trailer cleaned and repaired before Titus got here."

—⧓—

Titus was relieved when he found a ladder, a hammer, some

nails, and a roll of tar paper in the old shed behind the trailer. He would use the tar paper to patch the wooden part of the roof, and when he had the chance to buy some shingles he'd finish the job.

As he set the ladder in place and began to climb, a bird chirped from a nearby tree. "I'm glad someone's in a happy mood this morning," Titus muttered. "I'll bet you wouldn't be singin' so cheerfully if you had to fix a roof."

Titus usually wasn't so negative, but ever since he and Phoebe had broken up, he couldn't seem to find anything cheerful to think about. He needed something positive to focus on—something to get excited about and look forward to.

As the bird continued to sing, Titus stepped onto the roof and glanced around, looking for any low spots where water might be lying. He discovered one area, and was heading in that direction, when—*crack!*—a hunk of wood gave way and his foot went through.

His boot hit something, and he looked down through the hole. "Oh, great. I think I'm standing on the refrigerator!" Titus gritted his teeth and pulled his leg out of the hole. Now he'd have to look for a piece of plywood to repair that hole.

He moved cautiously toward the ladder, wincing from the pain in his calf. He leaned over and pulled up his pant leg. Blood oozed from scratches and a cut.

"Guess I'd better get my leg cleaned up and bandaged before I try to patch this stupid roof," he mumbled. It was a good thing he'd thought to buy a bottle of peroxide and a box of bandages when he'd gone to the store yesterday.

Titus limped his way down the ladder and moved slowly toward the back door. This was not the best way to start out his morning.

What a dummkopp *I am. This is so typical.* He gritted his teeth. *I'll bet this wouldn't have happened to Timothy. He'd have probably seen that rotten board in time to keep from stepping on it. If I hadn't been distracted by that stupid chirping bird, maybe I would've seen it, too.*

Titus shook his negative thoughts aside. He couldn't waste time being angry at himself. He needed to get inside and tend to his leg.

After cleaning the wound, Titus was relieved to see that the cut wasn't too deep and wouldn't require stitches. However, a large bruise was already forming, and it had begun to throb. Well, he couldn't let it stop him from getting the roof patched, so as soon as he'd put a bandage on, he grabbed the hammer from the kitchen counter and limped out the door.

—❦—

Sometime later, with the roof temporarily patched, Titus saddled Lightning and headed to work.

As he approached the Yoders', he spotted their phone shanty at the end of the driveway. *Since I'm already late, I may as well stop and make a phone call*, he decided.

Titus tied Lightning to a tree and stepped into the shanty; then he took a seat on the folding chair and dialed his twin brother's number. Of course no one answered, because it wasn't likely that anyone from Timothy's family would be in their phone shanty. He left a message on their voice mail, telling Timothy about the condition of the trailer, and asking him to tell their folks he said hello.

When Titus entered the woodshop, he found Nelson sanding a door. "Sorry I'm late," he apologized.

Nelson frowned. "It's a good thing Grandpa's not here right now. He's always believed in starting work on time. He'd probably say, 'No rule of success will work if you don't.'"

"Sorry," Titus mumbled. "I had a rough morning."

"What happened?"

Titus explained about repairing the roof.

"That trailer needs a lot of work." Titus slowly shook his head. "I didn't know the roof was bad until it rained yesterday and left me with a puddle in the middle of the kitchen floor. There's so much work to be done I hardly know where to begin."

"Not to worry," Nelson said. "Grandpa's out right now, spreading the word that the trailer needs repairs, and we're planning to have a work frolic there on Saturday."

"That'd be great." Titus felt relieved. It would be much easier to make the place livable if he didn't have to do it alone. "Is there anything special you'd like me to do today, or should I continue with the cabinets I was working on yesterday?" he asked.

"You can work on the cabinets, and if you're not done when I finish with this door, I'll help you with 'em."

"Okay."

Titus and Nelson worked in silence the rest of the morning. Shortly before noon, Allen showed up. "Thought I'd better come by and see how you're doing," he said, thumping Titus on the back.

Titus groaned. "With the exception of a leaky roof, a scraped-up leg, some problems with mice, and a trailer that needs lots of repairs, I'm doing great."

Allen's thick, dark eyebrows met at the bridge of his nose. "I'd let you bunk in with me, but my house is on the other side of Hopkinsville. With my job taking me all over the place right now, I wouldn't have time to bring you to work every day."

"It's okay. I'm sure the trailer will be fine once it's fixed up."

"My grandpa's out right now, telling folks about the work frolic we're planning for this Saturday," Nelson said.

Allen smiled. "That's good to hear, and I'll be there to help out, too. In fact, I'll go over to the trailer when I leave here and do some measuring so we'll know how much roofing material will be needed."

"That'd be much appreciated," Nelson said. "With your carpentry skills and ours, I'm sure we'll get the job done twice as fast."

"Speaking of carpentry skills, I've just contracted to build a new house on the other side of Hopkinsville, and I'd like you to make the cabinets and doors for it," Allen said.

Nelson nodded enthusiastically. "Sure thing. We're always glad for any work that comes up."

"Great. I'll be by to discuss the details with you as soon as I hear from the homeowners about what type of wood they'd like." Allen turned toward the door. "See you both on Saturday."

———

Suzanne had been working on Esther's quilt most of the morning, but she hadn't accomplished a lot. That was probably because she kept glancing out the window at the birds swooping down from the trees to get a drink of water from one of the birdbaths in their yard. She hated being cooped up in the house on such a warm spring day, but if she didn't work on the quilt, she'd never get it done in time for Esther's birthday.

Suzanne made a few more stitches, glanced out the window again, and was surprised to see Esther walking across the lawn toward the house. Not wanting Esther to see the quilt, she put her needle down and hurried outside.

"I hear there's going to be a work frolic on Saturday to fix up the old trailer where Titus is staying," Esther said when Suzanne joined her on the lawn.

Suzanne could tell from Esther's eager expression that she planned to go to the frolic. "When we found out that the trailer needed lots of repairs, Grandpa decided to schedule the frolic," Suzanne said.

Esther bobbed her head. "He came by our place this morning and told us about it."

"I assume you're planning to go?"

"Oh jah. My folks will have to work at the store on Saturday, but they said I could go to the frolic to help out." Esther smiled. "If I get the chance to speak with Titus alone that day, I may work up the nerve to ask if he has a girlfriend."

"You don't have to do that now," Suzanne said. "I already asked."

Esther's eyes widened. "You—you did?"

"I said I would, remember?"

"Oh, that's right. Guess I didn't figure you'd follow through."

"When I drove him home from the store yesterday, he was talking about his family, so I asked if he had a girlfriend in Pennsylvania."

"What'd he say?"

"He used to have one, but doesn't now."

Esther grinned. "So maybe he might take an interest in me."

"Could be. He's sure not interested in me."

"How do you know?"

"Because he doesn't say much to me, and when he does, he barely makes eye contact."

"Maybe he's shy."

"That's what Mom thinks, but I don't believe so because from what Nelson and Grandpa said at breakfast this morning, Titus had a lot of things to say to them yesterday when they were showing him around the shop."

The back door opened, and Mom stepped onto the porch. "I have lunch ready for the men, and I'd like you to take it out to them," she called to Suzanne.

"Okay."

Esther touched Suzanne's arm. "Mind if I go with you?"

"Suit yourself." She took the basket from Mom and headed for the woodshop, with Esther hurrying along at her side.

When they entered the shop, Suzanne set the basket on Grandpa's desk. "Are you ready for a break? Mom made you some lunch," she said to Nelson, who was sanding a door.

"We're more than ready," he said with a nod.

"Jah, me, too." Titus set the can of stain aside and reached for a rag to wipe his hands. "Things didn't go well for me this morning, and there was no time to make any breakfast," he said without looking at Suzanne.

"What happened?" Esther asked, moving to stand beside him.

He looked right at her, which only confirmed to Suzanne that he liked Esther but was repulsed by her. "My leg got banged up when I fell through the roof, tryin' to fix a hole."

Esther frowned. "That's *baremlich*. You weren't hurt bad, I hope."

"Just a cut, some scratches, and an ugly bruise, but I'll be okay."

"I don't think anyone ought to be living in that old trailer right now," Esther said.

Titus bobbed his head. "I can't argue with that, but the mice sure don't mind, 'cause I've seen evidence of 'em under the sink and in a couple of the lower cupboards."

"What you need is a cat to take care of the mice," Suzanne spoke up. "You can have one of ours if you like."

He shook his head. "Thanks for the offer, but I can take care of the mice by setting some traps."

Suzanne merely shrugged in reply. She couldn't believe he'd rather set traps than let one of her cats keep the mice away.

Maybe it's because I offered him the cat, she thought. *If Esther had offered, I'll bet he would have said yes.*

Suzanne didn't wait around for the men to eat their lunch. Instead, she turned to Esther and said, "I'm going back to the house. Are you coming?"

Esther's gaze went to Titus, then back to Suzanne. "I guess so."

When they stepped outside, Esther plopped her hands against her hips and glared at Suzanne.

"What's wrong?"

"How am I supposed to get Titus interested in me if I can't spend any time with him?"

"No one said you had to leave the shop."

"I wasn't about to stay there and watch Titus and Nelson eat their lunch after you announced that you were leaving." Esther's dark eyebrows drew together. "What's your hurry getting back to the house, anyway?"

Suzanne shrugged. "No hurry. I just didn't feel like watching the men eat. Besides, I'm uncomfortable around Titus. He makes me feel like I'm always wearing *dreck* on my naas."

"You don't have any dirt on your nose today." Esther snickered and touched the end of Suzanne's nose. "Unless he thought one of your little freckles was a speck of dirt."

"That's not funny." Suzanne hurried her steps toward the house. If Mom seriously expected her to bring lunch out to the men every day, Suzanne would just run into the shop, set the basket on the desk, and run back out.

Of course, she reasoned, *if I do that, I'll miss seeing what projects the men are working on, and I can learn a lot from watching. Guess I'll have to take one day at a time and hope Titus becomes a little friendlier once he gets to know me better.*

CHAPTER 8

Paradise, Pennsylvania

Timothy Fisher had just left the chiropractor's for an adjustment in his lower back, when he decided to stop by Naomi and Caleb's store to say hello before heading home.

"It's good to see you," Naomi said from behind the counter, where she had been reading a copy of one of their Amish newspapers, *The Budget*. It was hard to believe she was forty-seven, because she looked like she was in her thirties. There wasn't a speck of gray in her golden brown hair, and she could still see perfectly without reading glasses, which their younger sister Nancy often wore.

"Good to see you, too. Have you been busy here today?" he asked.

"We sure have, and this is the first chance I've had to take a break." Her cocoa-colored eyes showed no sign of fatigue when she smiled. "Of course, it's springtime, when the tourists start flocking to our area."

His brows furrowed as he leaned on the counter. "I know the tourists are good for business, but I wish they wouldn't stare at us Plain People or snap pictures right in our faces."

Naomi shook her head. "Not every tourist does that, and I think those who stare are probably just curious about our lifestyle and the way we dress."

"I guess you're right, but there are times when I'd like to pack up my family and move someplace where there aren't so many tourists."

"You're not thinking of joining Titus in Kentucky, I hope."

"The idea is kind of tempting, but I don't think Hannah would agree to move. She likes it here, and she and her mamm are really close." He rubbed his fingers along the edge of the counter. "Sometimes I think she and Sally are too close. Hannah goes over there almost every day, and she thinks she has to ask her mamm's advice about everything she does."

Naomi stared down at her paper. Timothy figured she was either bored with the conversation or agreed with him about Hannah being too close to her mother, but was too polite to say so.

"Titus left me a voice mail this morning," he said, changing the subject.

She looked up. "What'd he say?"

"Said he's not happy about the place Allen expects him to rent."

"What's wrong with it?"

"Just about everything, I guess. The roof leaks; the furniture's torn and saggy; the walls need painting; the yard's overgrown with weeds; and the place has *meis.*"

Naomi grimaced. "I could put up with a leaky roof and torn furniture, but I can't tolerate mice."

"A few cats would probably take care of his problem, but you know my twin. He hasn't liked cats since we were kinner and that wild cat bit him."

"He ought to be over that by now," she said.

"Titus doesn't get over anything too easily. Why do you

think he moved to Kentucky?"

"He's probably trying to get away from the pain of Phoebe breaking up with him, but moving away from a painful situation isn't always the answer. When I left home many years ago, it was to try and forget the pain of leaving Zach on the picnic table." Naomi sighed. "It didn't do a thing to relieve my guilty conscience, though."

Timothy knew the story well. Even though he and Titus hadn't been born when the kidnapping took place, they'd grown up hearing about how Zach had been taken right out of their yard after Naomi had gone into the house to get cold root beer for a customer. It turned out that the man who'd stolen Zach lived in Puyallup, Washington, and Zach had grown up there, not knowing his real family was Amish and lived in Paradise, Pennsylvania. By the time Zach found out about it and came to Lancaster County in search of his identity, Timothy and Titus were teenagers.

"The past's in the past," Timothy said, smiling at Naomi. "What counts is what we do with today."

She nodded. "I just hope Titus learns that and will make the most of each new day."

—m—

Pembroke, Kentucky

Soon after Titus got home from work, he decided to go out to the shed to put the ladder away, as he hadn't taken the time to do it when he'd come down from the roof that morning.

Once he put the ladder back, he went to the barn to see if he could find anything he might use to fix up the place. He spotted a canvas tarp, and when he pulled it back, he was surprised to see an old buggy in need of repairs. He figured with some new wheels, a new windshield, and lots of elbow grease, it would be useable. He pushed the buggy to the middle of the barn. Maybe after the frolic, he'd have time to work on it. Right now, getting the trailer livable was his first priority.

Titus's stomach growled noisily, reminding him that he hadn't eaten since noon. "Guess I'd better get in the house and see about fixing some supper."

He'd just stepped onto the porch when a horse and buggy pulled into the yard. He was surprised to see Suzanne get out and secure her horse to the hitching rail.

"I brought you something," she called.

Curious to see what it was, Titus joined her beside the buggy. He was even more surprised when she reached into the buggy and lifted out the same calico cat he'd seen at the Yoders'.

"This is for you," she said, holding the critter out to him.

Titus took a step back. "What makes you think I want a katz?"

"Her name is Callie, and she'll help keep the mice down."

He shook his head determinedly. "I told you today, I don't need a cat. I'm planning to set some traps for the mice."

"But Callie's a good mouser, and she'll keep you company."

"Don't need any cat company. I've got my horse."

"But horses don't catch mice."

"I appreciate the offer, but I really don't want a cat."

Suzanne's furrowed brows, and the droop of her shoulders, let him know that he'd probably hurt her feelings.

"I appreciate you coming by," Titus said, hoping to ease the tension. "I'll see you tomorrow." He turned and hurried into the house, eager to fix something to eat.

He'd just taken out a loaf of bread and some lunchmeat to make a sandwich when he heard a noise on the porch. He opened the door to step outside, when the calico cat zipped between his legs and darted into the house.

Titus glanced at the hitching rail and saw that Suzanne's horse and buggy were gone. "That's just great!" He gritted his teeth. "I told her no, but she left the stupid katz here anyway. Tomorrow morning I'm taking the critter back to Suzanne, and she'd better not try anything like that again."

CHAPTER 9

When Titus stepped out his front door the next morning, he nearly tripped over something furry on the porch. He looked down and groaned. The stupid calico cat was curled into a ball, purring loudly.

Before Titus had gone to bed last night, he hadn't seen any sign of Callie, so he'd assumed she'd left and hopefully found her way back to the Yoders'.

"Well, you're going back now." Titus bent down to pick up the cat, but she opened her eyes, let out a piercing howl, and leaped off the porch like she'd been hit with a bolt of lightning. Titus took after the animal in hot pursuit.

Round and round the yard they went, until Titus was panting for breath. Was it any wonder he didn't like cats? They were nothing but trouble.

Callie headed for the porch again, and Titus followed, his jaw set with determination.

Crouched in one corner of the porch, the cat's hair stood on end as she hissed at Titus.

"*Kumme*, kitty. Come here to me now." Titus reached out his hand, and was almost touching the cat, when she swiped the end of his finger with her needle-like claws.

"Yeow!" Titus drew back quickly, and frowned when he saw blood.

The cat continued to hiss as she hunched her back and eyeballed Titus as though daring him to come closer.

Titus stood still a few seconds. He lunged again. This time Callie lunged, too. She sank her teeth into Titus's hand, and he let out another yelp. The cat let go, gave one final hiss, and tore off into the woods.

Titus rushed into the trailer to get a bandage and some antiseptic. It was a cinch that he wasn't going to catch the cat this morning. Maybe he'd scared her badly enough that she wouldn't come back. Hopefully the critter had enough smarts to head for home.

—⁕—

Paradise, Pennsylvania

"Sure wish we'd hear something more from Titus," Fannie said to Abraham as they sat at the kitchen table, eating breakfast. "I went out to the phone shanty and checked our voice mail this morning, but there were no messages from him."

"He called when he got to Kentucky, and he's only been gone a few days," Abraham said. "Give him some time; I'm sure he'll call again soon."

"Maybe we should plan a trip to Kentucky to see him. I'd feel better if I knew what it was like and saw for myself that he was doing okay."

Abraham shook his head. "I don't think Titus would appreciate us checkin' up on him. He needs to make it on his own without our interference. Besides, Timothy and I are in the middle of planting season, and I don't have time to be making any trips." He patted Fannie's arm gently. "You know what your problem is?"

"What?"

"You're too protective of our kinner...especially the twins."

Fannie took a sip of her coffee and was about to say something more on the subject, when the back door swung open and Timothy stepped into the room.

"*Guder mariye*," he said.

"Mornin'," Abraham mumbled around a mouthful of toast.

"Help yourself to a cup of coffee and come join us at the table," Fannie invited.

"Don't mind if I do."

"How's your back doin'?" Abraham asked as Timothy poured himself a cup of coffee and then pulled out a chair at the table and sat down.

"Better. The adjustment Dr. Dan gave me yesterday really helped."

Fannie smiled. "That's good to hear. It's never fun to have a sore back."

"I'll be ready to join you in the field as soon as I've finished my coffee," Abraham said.

"No hurry. Take your time." Timothy looked over at Fannie and smiled. "I thought you might like to know that I had a voice mail message from Titus yesterday."

She perked right up. "Really? What'd it say?"

"He mostly talked about the trailer he's renting from Allen. Said it's a mess and will need a lot of work to make it livable."

Fannie frowned. "Didn't Allen know the place needed work when he suggested Titus move in there? What was he thinking?"

Timothy shrugged. "Beats me. Maybe he didn't know the place was so bad."

"He should have known since he owns the place," Abraham interjected.

"Well, I'm just glad Titus left a message for me, because it's strange having him gone, and I sure do miss him."

Fannie sighed deeply. It didn't seem right that the twins were separated. They'd always been so close. Now that Titus was living two states away, he and Timothy might drift apart.

She directed her gaze toward the window, focusing on two finches eating from the feeder hanging in the maple tree. She thought about how mother birds push their babies out of the nest so they can make it on their own and wondered if Abraham was right. Maybe she was overprotective where her two youngest boys were concerned.

—⁘—

Pembroke, Kentucky

Suzanne had just gone outside to hang some clothes on the line, when Titus rode into the yard on his horse. She found it interesting that he rode horseback, when almost everyone else in their community traveled by horse and buggy. But then, Titus seemed a bit different from the young Amish men she'd grown up around.

She watched as he dismounted and led his horse to the barn. A short time later, he reappeared and strode over to where she stood by the clothesline.

His eyebrows furrowed, and that same look of disgust she'd seen before settled over his face. "Would you mind tellin' me why you left your *dumm* katz at my place when I asked you not to?"

"I didn't, and Callie's not stupid. She jumped out of the buggy when I was driving away, and I figured she'd follow me home."

"Well, she didn't. She made herself at home on my porch, and then when I tried to catch her this morning, so I could bring her back here, this is what I got for my trouble." Titus held up his bandaged finger and frowned.

Suzanne felt concern. "Did Callie bite you?"

"Jah, and then she ran into the woods."

"I can't believe it. Callie never bites."

"Well, she bit me."

"I'm sorry. Does it hurt much?"

"It sure does, and it won't be easy tryin' to work with a sore hand today."

Suzanne was tempted to offer her help in the woodshop but knew Nelson would never agree to that, no matter how much work needed to be done.

"You'd better keep an eye on that bite," she said. "Cats have a lot of bacteria in their mouths, and the wound might get infected."

"I know all about that. It happened to me once when I was a boy." He held up his finger and waved it around. "I put some antiseptic on it, so I'm sure it'll be fine."

Suzanne was about to suggest that Titus go to the clinic and get a tetanus shot, but he started walking away.

"Wait! I wanted to say something else," she called.

He halted and turned to face her. "What?"

When she took a step toward him, her foot slipped on a rock, and she swayed unsteadily.

He reached out to catch her. "You okay?"

Suzanne's face heated with embarrassment. "I–I'm fine. Just lost my balance when my toe hit a rock."

"So what'd you want to say to me?"

"I was just going to say that if Callie shows up at your place again, maybe you should consider keeping her."

His eyebrows shot up. "Are you kidding?"

She shook her head. "She probably bit you because she was scared. If you'd give her a chance, you'd see that she'd not only keep the mice down, but would make a good pet."

He held up his hand again. "Would a good pet do this?"

Before Suzanne could respond, he turned and stomped off toward the shop.

Suzanne clenched her teeth. It seemed like she couldn't say anything right to Titus, and if she wasn't saying something to irritate him, she was doing something stupid to embarrass herself. Maybe the best thing would be to stay as far away from him as possible. But with the work frolic coming up on Saturday, that might be kind of hard to do. Unless she could think of some excuse not to go.

CHAPTER 10

Los Angeles, California

"D on't you just love it here?" Darlene asked Phoebe, as they flopped onto the beach towel she'd placed on the sand.

"It's okay, I guess." Truth was, California wasn't anything like Phoebe had expected, although she'd never admit that to Darlene. Jobs were hard to find, prices were high, and too many people crowded around. But she did like the beach access, and she sure couldn't have had that available to her at home. She also liked the warm sunshine and all the cute guys she'd seen on the beach.

Phoebe had been lucky to find a job at a local ice-cream parlor, but it was boring work, and her wrist hurt when she had to scoop out the hard ice cream to make a cone. Darlene was working as a waitress at a restaurant, which she said paid better tips than her wages. They'd pooled their money to pay rent on a small, one-bedroom apartment, but the place was run-down and not in the best part of town.

While Darlene stretched out on the towel with her eyes closed, Phoebe stared at the waves lapping against the shore, and her thoughts went to home. What were Mom and Dad doing right now? Did they miss her? If she decided to stay in California permanently, would they ever come for a visit? Did she want them to? If they came, they'd no doubt spend the whole time criticizing everything she did and complain about how overcrowded it was. It would probably be best if she didn't encourage them to come.

As a group of young men started a game of volleyball, Phoebe thought about Titus and how many times the two of them had been involved in volleyball games back home. Even when she wasn't one of the players, she'd enjoyed watching from the sidelines.

I'll bet if Titus was here right now, he'd be involved in that game, she thought. *He's always liked volleyball.*

Phoebe scooped up a handful of sand and dumped it on Darlene's bare toes.

Darlene's eyes popped open. "Hey! What'd you do that for?"

"Let's see if we can join that game of volleyball."

Darlene grinned and clambered to her feet. "Good idea. Let's do it!"

—⁂—

Pembroke, Kentucky

When Titus woke up on Saturday to the early morning light, he glanced out his bedroom window and was relieved to see that the sun was shining brightly. Having nice weather would make it easier for those coming to help him work on the trailer.

Titus stepped into the dim hallway, blinked, took a few steps, and stubbed his toe. "Ouch! Guess I should have put my boots away last night, instead of leaving 'em in the hall. If this place was bigger, I'd have more room for things."

He moved on to the bathroom to wash his face, and halted

76

inside the door. That stupid calico cat was curled into a ball, sleeping in the sink!

He frowned. "How in the world did you get in the house?" The cat's only response was a quiet *meow.*

Titus had given up trying to return the critter to Suzanne. Every time he'd made an attempt to catch the cat, she'd escaped his grasp. He'd resigned himself to the fact that he was stuck with her, and after seeing the remains of a few mice in the yard, he had to admit, she was a pretty good mouser. He figured as long as she stayed outside he could put up with her, but he wasn't about to invite the mangy critter into his house.

He glared at the cat. "So how'd you get in? I know I didn't leave the front or back door open, and I closed all the windows that don't have screens."

The cat continued to sleep, apparently oblivious to Titus's presence.

Well, he couldn't worry about how she got in right now. What he needed to do was find a way to get her outside without picking her up, because he didn't want to chance getting scratched or bitten again.

Maybe if I throw something over the cat, I can pick her up that way. Titus pulled a bath towel off the hook behind the door, and was ready to drop it over Callie, when she came awake, leaped into the air, and landed on his shoulder.

Her sharp claws dug into his flesh, and he let out a screech. Callie hopped off his shoulder and raced out of the bathroom like her tail was on fire. Titus followed, hollering, "Stupid katz! You're nothing but trouble!"

When he reached the kitchen, where the cat stood, hunched and hissing, he opened the back door, grabbed the broom from the utility closet, and pushed the animal out the door. "Get outside! You don't belong in here!"

Titus slammed the door behind Callie and drew in a deep

breath. If that crazy cat was going to stick around, she'd better learn her place.

He started making a pot of coffee, figuring it wouldn't be long before people began showing up for the work frolic. Beyond the benefit of getting the trailer fixed up, today would give him a chance to meet more of the Amish people who lived in this community.

Titus had just set a bowl of cereal on the table, when he heard a vehicle rumble into the yard. He moved over to the sink and peered out the window in time to see Allen step out of his truck.

Titus opened the back door cautiously, to make sure the stupid cat wasn't waiting for another chance to get inside. Fortunately, she was nowhere in sight.

"Come in for a cup of coffee," he said when Allen stepped onto the porch.

"That sounds good. I need something to wake up this morning."

"You're the first one here," Titus said, leading the way to his cramped kitchen.

Allen glanced around the room and released a low whistle. "I know I saw it the night I brought you here, but it looks even worse than I remember. If I'd known how bad it was, I would have found you somewhere else to stay until we could get the place fixed up."

Titus handed Allen a cup of coffee and motioned for him to take a seat at the table. "If my folks saw where I'm living, Dad would probably say it was the kind of challenge I need, and that it would do me good to rough it for a while. But if Mom saw the way the trailer looks, especially the kitchen, she'd get all worked up and insist that I come right home."

Allen chuckled. "Most mothers are like that where their kids are concerned. They don't want to see them go through any trials or deal with hardships." He blew on his coffee, then took a sip. "When I left Washington to move here, my mother fussed and carried on like I was moving to a foreign country where nobody spoke English and no one had indoor plumbing."

Titus grimaced. "When I first laid eyes on this place, I had my doubts about whether there was indoor plumbing. Figured for sure I'd be stuck using an outhouse and would have to take a bath in a galvanized tub."

"I guess in some parts of the country that's still how it is," Allen said, "but most of the Amish, as well as the Horse and Buggy Mennonites who live around here, have indoor plumbing. Although I do know of a few women in the area who do their laundry in a tub outside."

Titus's eyebrows furrowed as he stared into his coffee. "My mom wouldn't like that, and most of the Amish women I know wouldn't either." His thoughts went to Phoebe. He was sure that she'd never put up with such primitive conditions. She didn't even like using her mother's gas-powered wringer washer, which they kept in the basement. She'd sometimes taken her clothes to one of the local Laundromats in Lancaster County, saying it was easier, and that the clothes came out softer when they'd been dried in an automatic dryer, rather than on a line.

"Why the furrowed brows?" Allen asked Titus.

"I was just thinking about having to wash clothes in a tub outside. Since there's no gas-powered washing machine here in the trailer, I'll probably have to look for a Laundromat someplace nearby."

"There's none close that I know of, but there are a few in Hopkinsville," Allen said. "If you can't get to town often enough to keep clean clothes in your closet, you could always wash them in the bathtub, I guess."

Titus shook his head. "Not if I can help it."

"Then maybe you'd better find yourself a wife who's willing to wash your clothes."

"No way! I'm not interested in marrying anyone right now." He glanced out the window toward the barn. "I am interested in the old buggy I discovered the other day, though."

"What buggy?"

"Found it in the barn, under a tarp. It's in pretty bad shape, so it'll need some work to make it useable, but if you're willing to sell it for a reasonable price, I'd be interested in buying it from you."

Allen looked at Titus like he'd taken leave of his senses. "Why would I want to sell you an old, beat-up buggy?"

"Figured since you own this place, the buggy's yours."

"Legally it is, but I wouldn't think of charging you for the buggy. Especially since you've had to put up with this dump of a house for the last several days." He made a sweeping gesture encompassing the kitchen. "The buggy's yours to do with as you wish."

Titus smiled. "Thanks, I appreciate that."

The *clip-clop* of horses' hooves could be heard coming up the driveway.

"Sounds like the workers are starting to arrive." Allen pushed his chair aside and stood. "Guess I'd better get out there and hand out the supplies I brought with me today. Then I'm gonna roll up my sleeves and get busy with the others so we can make this place livable."

Titus glanced at his bowl of cereal, mostly uneaten and now turned soggy. He guessed he'd better not take the time to eat the rest of it. If the others were about to start working, it wouldn't look right if he didn't make an appearance right away. Besides, he was eager to get started and looked forward to seeing how much they could accomplish in one day.

When Titus stepped outside, he was surprised to see how many Amish men and women had come to help. Allen introduced him to Emmanuel Schwartz, the buggy maker, and Titus asked about getting new wheels and some other things for the buggy he wanted to fix.

"Jah, sure, I've got all kinds of wheels," Emmanuel said with a grin that revealed a couple of missing teeth. "You come by my shop anytime, and I'll let you choose."

"I'll do that as soon as I find the time," Titus said with a nod. He moved on and met the man who owned the lumber mill in the area, an elderly couple who owned a greenhouse, and a widowed woman who ran a bookstore, as well as several other people. It didn't take him long to realize that the folks in this community were friendly and eager to help out.

He was about to grab a hammer and join some of the men who were tearing off his old roof when he spotted Suzanne's friend Esther heading his way.

"Hello, Titus, it's nice to see you," she said.

He gave a nod. "Nice to see you, too."

She smiled, her cheeks turning a light shade of pink. "My folks couldn't be here today, but I came to do some cleaning inside and help feed everyone."

Titus's stomach rumbled at the mention of being fed. He should have gotten up earlier so he'd have had more time to eat a decent breakfast.

"I made some raisin bread, and Rebekah, who owns a bakeshop, brought doughnuts and cinnamon rolls, so whenever anyone needs a break, we'll have everything set up over there." Esther pointed to the tables that had been placed under the maple tree in the middle of the yard, where several women scurried about.

Titus was tempted to head over there, but he knew he really ought to get some work done before he took a break.

As if sensing his dilemma, Esther smiled and said, "Why don't you come over and sample some of my bread now? If you wait too long, it might be gone."

Titus's growling stomach finally won out. "Guess it wouldn't hurt if I had one piece of bread. Might give me more energy to work."

They walked through the tall grass and visited a few minutes while Titus ate, not one, but two pieces of her moist and tasty raisin bread. Esther not only had a pretty face, but she could obviously cook. "This is really good," he said, smacking his lips.

Esther smiled. "I'm glad you like it."

—⁓—

When Suzanne climbed down from the buggy behind her mother, she spotted Esther standing under a maple tree, talking to Titus. *I'll bet Esther's happy,* she thought. *She's finally getting to spend a few minutes alone with Titus. Once he finds out what a good cook she is, he'll probably want to court her.*

Mom handed Suzanne a container full of peanut butter cookies. "Would you please take these over to the food table? I'm going inside to see what needs to be done."

"Why don't you take the cookies to the table, and I'll go inside and see what needs to be done?" Suzanne suggested. She really didn't want to be here at all. She'd been hoping she could stay home so she could go out to the woodshop and fiddle around. With Nelson and Grandpa at the work frolic, they'd have been none the wiser. But no, Mom had insisted the whole family come to help out.

"I see Esther over there," Mom said. "Wouldn't you like to visit with her?"

Normally, Suzanne would have enjoyed chatting with Esther, but she didn't want to interrupt the conversation between her friend and Titus.

"Go on now." Mom gave Suzanne a little nudge. "When you and Esther are done visiting, you can come help with whatever needs to be done in the house."

Suzanne hurried across the yard, and as she set the cookies on the table, she heard Titus mention something about finding an old buggy in the barn that he planned to fix up as soon as he found the time. Esther seemed to be hanging on his every word, and Suzanne wasn't about to interrupt.

By this time next year, they'll probably be planning a wedding, Suzanne thought as she leaned against the table. *I, on the other hand, will probably never find a man willing to marry me. Why can't men see that there's more to a woman than a pretty face or the ability to cook? Why can't they be interested in someone who likes to hunt, fish, hike in the woods, or work with wood?*

Suzanne was about to head for the trailer, when Esther touched her arm. "Have you been standing there long?"

"Uh. . .no, not really." Suzanne motioned to the peanut butter cookies. "Just came over to add those to the rest of the baked goods setting out."

"Did you bake them?" Esther asked.

"No, my mamm did." Suzanne hoped Esther wouldn't say anything about her cooking skills—or rather, the lack of them—in front of Titus. From the way he sometimes looked at her, she figured he already thought she was stupid and incapable.

"How are things going with Callie?" Suzanne asked Titus, after he'd helped himself to a cup of coffee. "Since you haven't brought her back to our place, I take it you've decided to keep her?"

"Haven't been able to catch the critter. So I suppose I'll have to let her stay." Titus frowned. "She found her way into the house last night, and I discovered her sleeping in the bathroom sink this morning."

Suzanne bit back a chuckle. "Callie's always liked to sleep in strange places. Even when she was a kitten, I never knew where I might find her."

"I don't care where she sleeps, as long as it's not in the trailer."

"Don't you like cats?" Esther asked.

"Nope, I sure don't."

"How come?"

"They bite and scratch. One nearly took off my finger when I was a kinner, and I've tried to stay away from cats ever since."

"Not all cats bite and scratch," Suzanne said. "And those that do usually have a good reason."

"Humph!" Titus held up his hand. "There was no good reason for your stupid cat to bite me the other day." He set his cup on the table. "I'd better get to work. It was nice talking to you, Esther. Oh, and thanks for that great-tasting raisin bread."

As Titus walked away, Suzanne gritted her teeth. He'd worn a frown on his face throughout most of their conversation, but when he talked to Esther he was all smiles. He was obviously attracted to Esther, and Suzanne had no problem with that. What she didn't understand was what he had against her.

CHAPTER 11

The air rang with shouts and sounds of carpenters and roofers, the chatter of children, and the laughter of women who'd come to help at the work frolic. By noon, a good many repairs to the trailer had been completed. They had removed the old roof and put on a new one, repaired both front and back screen doors, replaced most of the boards on the porch, cut the overgrown lawn, and weeded quite a bit.

The inside of the trailer looked much better, too. Volunteers had given the home a thorough cleaning, replaced hinges on the broken cabinet doors, re-covered the living room furniture, and brought in a better mattress for Titus's bed. Someone had also given him two sets of sheets, as well as several towels and washcloths. His cupboards and refrigerator had been stocked with plenty of food. Titus was amazed at the generosity of these people, some of whom he hadn't met before.

As he sat at one of the tables on the lawn, enjoying the variety of sandwiches and salads the women served, he decided that he might have made a good decision moving to Kentucky. Things had gone well with his job at the woodshop so far; the trailer, while not in the best condition, was now livable; and he'd made some new friends. He'd show his folks that he was able to make it on his own. He'd show them, as well as the rest of his family, that Timothy wasn't the only one who could succeed.

Titus glanced over at Esther, as she poured him another cup of coffee and smiled. *I know I said I wasn't interested in getting married, but if I were to start courting a woman from Kentucky, and eventually got married, that would let everyone at home know I've settled down and made a life of my own. Of course,* he reasoned, *I'll have to get Phoebe out of my system before I can even think about marriage.*

—∭—

As the noon meal was being served, Suzanne noticed how Esther was conveniently pouring beverages at the table where Titus sat between Nelson and Allen. She'd seen Esther talk to Titus several times during the morning, making it obvious that she was interested in him. If Esther wasn't careful, she might chase him away with her boldness.

Suzanne plunked down on a bench next to her mother. "Sure has turned into a warm day," she commented.

Mom nodded. "I thought you were going to help serve the beverages."

"Esther's doing that."

"She's serving coffee but not lemonade. Since the weather's turned warm, I'm sure some of the men would rather have something cold to drink."

Suzanne shrugged.

"Why don't you carry the jug of lemonade around to the tables and see?"

"All right, but I'd better get a sandwich, before they're all gone." Suzanne plucked a ham sandwich off the platter closest to her and plopped it on her plate. Then she grabbed two of the peanut butter cookies Mom had made, as well as a handful of potato chips. "I'll be back soon," she said, rising from her bench.

Suzanne hurried to the table where the beverages sat and picked up the jug of lemonade. After she'd served the two tables nearest her, she made her way over to the table where Titus sat. "Would anyone like some lemonade?" she asked.

Nelson and Allen both nodded, so she poured some into their cups.

"How about you?" she asked Titus.

"Sure," he replied without making eye contact.

Not this again. Suzanne lifted the jug, and was about to pour some into his cup, when Nelson turned in his seat and bumped her arm.

Whoosh! Lemonade splashed all over the front of Titus's shirt.

"Were you trying to drown me?" Titus sputtered.

"I'm sorry. Nelson bumped my arm, and—"

Before Suzanne could finish her sentence, Titus abruptly got up and headed for the trailer, mumbling something about how clumsy she was.

That's just great, she thought with regret. *At the rate things are going, Titus will never look at me with anything but disgust.*

CHAPTER 12

For the next two weeks whenever Titus had a free moment, he worked on the old buggy he'd found. He still preferred to ride Lightning to work every day, but when it came to grocery shopping or hauling anything big, having a buggy was a good thing.

As Titus made his way to the kitchen one morning, he felt thankful once again for all the repairs and cleaning that had been done to the trailer. He'd met so many good people the day of the work frolic and again the next day when they'd met for church at the bishop's house.

This coming Saturday would be his day off, and he thought he might like to saddle Lightning and take a ride for a better look around the area. It would be good to do something fun for a change. His new job was working out well, and both Isaac and Nelson seemed to be pleased with Titus's carpentry skills. Unless he messed up and did something stupid, it looked like his position in the woodshop would be permanent.

A knock sounded on the door, and Titus went to see who it was. When he opened it, he was surprised to see Suzanne standing on the porch, holding a flat of primroses.

"I thought you might like to have a little color in your front flower bed," she said. "Even though the weeds are gone, it looks kind of bare."

"I guess it does." He scuffed the toe of his boot along the threshold, not knowing what else to say. By now he ought to be used to seeing Suzanne, since she often came out to the woodshop to sweep the floors or bring them lunch. But each time he saw her, she either said or did something to irritate him. Was it because seeing her still made him think of Phoebe?

"So, is it all right if I plant the flowers?" Suzanne asked.

"Sure." He turned and was about to step back into the house, when she said, "Have I done something to offend you, Titus?"

Titus whirled around and blinked a couple of times. The sunlight brought out the glints of gold in Suzanne's auburn hair. "Wh—what do you mean?" he stuttered.

"You usually don't say more than a few words to me, and when you do, you rarely look right at me."

He forced himself to meet her gaze. "I'm lookin' at you now."

She gave a nod. "I might think you were still irritated about the lemonade bath I gave you the day of the work frolic, but you've acted strangely toward me since the first day we met, and I'd like to know why."

Her piercing blue eyes seemed to bore right through him, and he quickly looked away. "I've forgotten all about the lemonade."

"See, you're doing it again. You're not looking at me when I'm talking to you."

Titus turned his head and looked her right in the eye. "Is that better?"

"Jah."

"Okay," he said, then drew in a quick breath. "You have

done a few things to irritate me, but the real reason it's hard for me to look at you is because you remind me of someone. Someone I'm trying to forget."

"Who?"

"Her name's Phoebe Stoltzfus—the girl I used to court in Pennsylvania." He frowned. "I thought she was going to marry me, but she took off for California with one of her girlfriends instead."

"Is Phoebe Amish?"

He pushed his hands against the doorjamb so hard that his knuckles turned white. "She was raised Amish, but she's never joined the church. Phoebe started running around even before she turned sixteen, and I'm pretty sure she's gonna go English."

"How old is Phoebe now?"

"Eighteen."

"She's still pretty young. Maybe she'll change her mind and return to Pennsylvania and join the church."

"I doubt it. She's been stringing me along since she was thirteen."

Suzanne's eyebrows squeezed together. "You've been interested in the same girl since you were thirteen?"

He shook his head. "I was seventeen when Phoebe was thirteen, and I waited for her until she turned sixteen, so we could start courting." He stabbed the side of the door with the toe of his boot. "For all the good it did me."

"It's no surprise that it didn't work out. She was practically a child when you became interested in her."

"That's what my folks and her folks thought, too. I figure she must be pretty immature even now if she ran off to California without caring at all what I thought."

"Maybe she wasn't the right girl for you."

"Now you sound like my folks. I don't think Mom or Dad

90

ever liked Phoebe. They tried to discourage me from the very beginning, and so did Phoebe's folks."

"I don't mean to sound like your folks. I just think you might need to find someone who's more mature and settled. Someone like—"

"I might do that if I can find the right woman. I'd like to make sure my job is secure and that I have a home of my own before I think about finding a wife and settling down, though. Need to prove to my family that I can measure up."

"Measure up?"

"To my twin brother, Timothy. He's been doing all the right things since he got out of school. Went to work right away for our older brother Zach; later bought a house with some land he could farm; then found a good woman and got married. He and Hannah have a daughter and another baby on the way." Titus tugged his left earlobe. "Timothy's way ahead of me. I might never get married, much less own a place of my own." He gestured to the trailer. "Might spend the rest of my days rentin' some place like this."

Before Suzanne could respond, Callie leaped onto the porch, darted between Titus's legs, and raced into the kitchen.

Titus grunted. "Stupid critter seems determined to get in. If you had to haul a cat over here, couldn't you at least have picked one that's content to be outside?"

Suzanne frowned. "Callie is usually content to be outside, but if you've been having problems with mice, then I would think you'd want to allow the cat in the house."

"Cats belong outdoors." Titus stepped back inside, grabbed the broom, and chased the cat out the door.

"You don't have to be so mean," Suzanne said with a huff.

"I'm not mean. Just don't want to pick the critter up and take the chance of getting bit again. Besides, a little push with the broom won't hurt her any."

"Maybe not, but I'm sure you scared the poor thing. You'll never make friends with the cat if you chase her around with a broom."

"Who says I want to make friends with the critter?"

Suzanne glared at him. "I don't have time to stand here and debate this with you. Do you want me to plant the flowers I brought or not?"

"Go right ahead." Titus quickly shut the door.

—◊—

"That man is so rude," Suzanne fumed as she carried the flat of primroses to the flower bed. Obviously Titus didn't know how to care for a cat.

Should I take Callie back? Suzanne glanced around but saw no sign of the cat. After Titus had chased Callie with the broom, she'd disappeared behind the barn. *Maybe when I'm done planting these flowers I'll look for her,* she decided.

Suzanne grabbed the shovel she'd brought along and stabbed it into the hard ground, twisting it angrily. *Callie isn't the only thing Titus doesn't appreciate. He obviously didn't appreciate me bringing over these flowers because he didn't even say thanks. Makes me wonder if his folks taught him anything about manners and how to treat other people. Is it any wonder his girlfriend ran off to California? She was probably tired of his bad attitude. Humph! I think I should speak to Esther about Titus and let her know what he's really like.*

Suzanne had just finished planting the primroses when she heard a pathetic, muffled-sounding *meow*. She glanced to her left and saw Callie rolling in the grass with her head stuck in a soup can.

"Ach, my!" Suzanne jumped up and rushed over to the cat. She tried to pull the can off, but Callie wouldn't hold still. It was going to take two people to free the poor cat—one to hold

Callie and one to pull on the can.

Suzanne hurried across the yard and knocked on the trailer door. Titus pulled the door open a few seconds later. "Are you done planting the flowers?" he asked.

She gave a nod. "But I need your help. Callie has a soup can stuck on her head."

He lifted his shoulders in a brief shrug. "What do you want me to do about it?"

"I want you to help me get the can off."

"If she got it on, she ought to be able to get it off."

"I don't think so, and we can't just leave her like that. Please, Titus, you've got to help me get that can off."

"Oh, all right." Titus stepped off the porch, and Suzanne followed him into the yard, where the pathetic cat was still thrashing about. He bent down, yanked on the can, and it lifted Callie right off the ground. Her claws came out, and he let out a shriek. "Stupid katz clawed a hole in my shirt, and now I think my chest is bleeding!"

"Set the cat down and let me see." Suzanne wasn't sure whom to be more concerned about: Titus, or the poor cat, stuck in a can.

Titus shook his head. "I'm fine. I'll tend to my scratches later." But he did place Callie on the ground.

"Have you got any metal cutters?" she asked. "I think we need some in order to cut the can off Callie's head."

"I think I saw an old pair of tin snips in the barn," he said. "You keep an eye on the cat and make sure she doesn't run away while I go look for 'em."

—⁓—

When Titus entered the barn, he found the tin snippers hanging on a nail. He pulled them down, and then slipped on a pair of heavy-duty gloves, as well as a jacket to protect himself.

"Sure don't know why I'm doin' this," he muttered. "I don't even like cats."

When Titus returned to the yard, he found Suzanne squatted down beside Callie, who was squirming around as she pawed frantically at the can that held her captive. "I've got the snippers," he announced. "I'll slip around front and try to cut her free."

Suzanne's eyes narrowed. "You're going to use that old rusty-looking cutter?"

"Sure, why not?"

"It really looks dull. Probably wouldn't cut a stick of butter."

"Well, it's the only pair I could find." Titus knelt on the grass in front of the cat.

"She's scared and might not cooperate with you," Suzanne said. "Maybe I should try and hold her."

Titus shook his head. "We know that's not going to work. She's too upset. Just leave her on the ground, put your hand on her back, and I'll see if I can cut the can off."

As Titus began clipping at the can, the cat flipped her head from side to side.

"Be careful; you might cut Callie's head." The panic in Suzanne's voice let Titus know how worried she was about the cat.

"I'm being as careful as I can, but it would help if she'd just hold still." He gritted his teeth as he continued to cut.

Finally, with one last snip, Callie was free. She shook her head a few times, and growled, crouching low to the ground. Looking up at Titus, she hissed as though threatening him. Then with a high-pitched meow, she darted for the barn.

"Stupid critter," Titus muttered. "She acts like I'm the one who put the can on her head." He stomped on the can and shouted at the cat's retreating form, "Don't play with cans, you ungrateful katz!"

Suzanne stepped in front of Titus and planted both hands on her hips. "If you didn't leave your cans lying around, she wouldn't have gotten herself into such a fix."

"I didn't. Don't know where that can came from. She probably got it out of the garbage." As Titus thought more about the whole situation, it suddenly seemed kind of funny. "Stupid critter put on quite a show for us, didn't she?" he asked with a snicker.

Suzanne glared at him a few seconds; then she looked down at what was left of the can and started to giggle. "She did look pretty silly with her head in that can."

Laughter bubbled in Titus's chest, and he leaned his head back and roared. Soon they were both laughing so hard tears ran down their faces as they held their sides.

Finally, Titus got control of himself and bent to pick up the can. "Sure hope nothin' like that ever happens again. That was downright stressful!"

She gave a nod. "I appreciate the fact that you took the time to free Callie—especially when you don't even like her."

"Couldn't let her spend the rest of her days wearin' a can on her head. Regardless of what you may think, I'm really not mean."

Before Suzanne could respond, he hurried into the trailer and shut the door.

—∾∾—

Paradise, Pennsylvania

"Hi, Mom, how's it going?" Samuel asked as he entered the kitchen, where Fannie sat working on a crossword puzzle.

"We're fine here. How are things with you and your family?"

"Everyone's doing well. The older kinner are looking forward to getting out of school at the end of April."

"That's just a few weeks away." Fannie motioned to the stove. "If you have the time, help yourself to a cup of coffee."

"Think I will." Samuel poured himself some coffee and took a seat beside her at the table. "Where's Dad this morning?"

"He had a dental appointment, so he headed to town right after breakfast."

"I'm surprised you could get him to go. Dad's always hated going to the dentist."

"I know, but he lost a filling the other day, and I talked him into going before the tooth started hurting." Fannie took a drink from her cup and filled in the next word on her puzzle.

"Have you heard anything more from Titus?" Samuel asked.

She shook her head. "He left a message for Timothy a few weeks ago, but he's only left one message here, and that was the day he got to Kentucky. I've written to him a few times already, but he hasn't answered any of the letters." She sighed. "Guess he's either too busy or is trying to prove that he's independent and doesn't need me anymore."

Samuel placed his hand over Fannie's. "I'm sure it's not that. Most likely, he's keeping busy."

"I thought I'd feel better about his move if your daed and I went to Kentucky so I could see for myself that Titus is doing okay." Fannie slowly shook her head. "But your daed says he's too busy right now with the spring planting and such."

The back door swung open, and Timothy rushed into the room with one-year-old Mindy in his arms. His face was red and beaded with perspiration.

"What's wrong, Timothy?" Fannie asked. "You look *umgerennt*."

"I am upset. Hannah's outside in the van with our driver and is hurtin' real bad with contractions. She started bleeding awhile ago, too, so we're taking her to the hospital." Timothy moved toward the table. "Hannah's mamm is going with us, so I was wondering if you could keep Mindy while we're gone."

"Of course." Fannie held out her arms, and the child went willingly to her. "Please call as soon as you know something."

"I will." Timothy leaned over and kissed his daughter's forehead; then he turned and hurried out.

Fannie sighed. "I hope Hannah's going to be all right. The *boppli*'s not due for several more months. I sure hope she won't lose it."

CHAPTER 13

Pembroke, Kentucky

As Titus ate breakfast that morning, he thought about Suzanne and how much she resembled Phoebe. He knew it wasn't fair to compare the two women when their personalities weren't the same, but it was hard to look at Suzanne without thinking about Phoebe, which only reminded him of her betrayal. Titus wondered if the ache in his heart would ever heal. He wanted to settle down and get married someday, but would he ever find a woman he loved as much as he had Phoebe?

He added a spoonful of sugar to his coffee and stirred it around. *I'll never find a wife if I don't get a grip on my anger toward Phoebe. And I won't make any points with Isaac if I don't start being kinder to his granddaughter.*

Yesterday, after Suzanne had come into the shop and made a nuisance of herself, he'd stupidly said something to Isaac about his granddaughter being a pest. The elderly man had shaken his arthritic finger as he looked Titus in the eye and said, "Suzanne may be a *pescht* sometimes, but she's my *grossdochder*, and I'd appreciate it if you kept any negative remarks about her to yourself."

A verse from Proverbs 15 that Titus had heard at church last Sunday popped into his head: *"A soft answer turneth away wrath: but grievous words stir up anger."* He knew he'd been unkind to Suzanne several times, and he owed her a thank-you for the flowers she'd planted for him. *If she's still outside, I should probably speak to her before I leave for work,* he decided.

He pushed his chair aside and opened the back door. Suzanne's horse and buggy were gone. "Should have come out here sooner," he mumbled. "Shouldn't have let her leave without saying thanks."

When he got to work, he'd stop by the Yoders' house first and talk to Suzanne.

Titus returned to the kitchen and halted. Callie was perched on the table, lapping milk from his bowl of cereal.

He clapped his hands and shouted, "Get down from there, you stupid katz! I should have left you trapped in that soup can."

Callie leaped off the table and raced outside. That's when Titus realized he hadn't shut the door when he'd gone out to look for Suzanne.

He groaned and set his bowl in the sink. This was not starting out to be a good day. Hopefully things would go better after he'd spoken to Suzanne.

—⁓—

When Titus arrived at the Yoders', he put his horse in the corral and went up to the house. Suzanne's mother answered his knock.

"Guder mariye," she said. "If you're looking for Nelson or my daed, they're already out at the shop."

Titus shook his head. "I'd like to speak to Suzanne."

"She's not here. Left right after breakfast. Said she was taking some primroses over to your place to plant. Didn't you see her there?"

He nodded. "She did come by, but she left before I did. Figured she'd be here by now."

"She may have stopped at the Beilers' store on her way home. Said something about needing a few things from there, too."

"Guess I'll have to wait and speak to her later on then."

"Maybe you can talk to her when she brings lunch out to the shop around noon."

"Okay. I'd better get to work now. Sure don't want to be late." Titus turned and sprinted to the shop.

He'd just entered the building, when Nelson rushed up to him and said, "There was a message for you at the phone shanty from your mamm."

"What'd it say?"

"Your sister-in-law's been taken to the hospital."

"Which sister-in-law?"

"I think she said it was Hannah. I didn't erase the message, so you'd better go out and listen to it yourself."

Titus opened the door and raced down the driveway to the phone shanty. Once inside, he took a seat and listened to the message.

"Titus, it's Mom. I wanted you to know that Hannah's in the hospital and may lose the boppli. Timothy left Mindy with us, and he's at the hospital with Hannah. He seemed pretty upset when he was here earlier. Please say a prayer for them, Titus."

Titus dialed his folks' number and was surprised when someone picked up the phone.

"Hello. Who's this?"

"It's Samuel. Is that you, Titus?"

"Jah. What are you doin' in Mom and Dad's phone shanty?"

"I dropped by the house this morning to visit with Mom and was on my way out when I heard the phone ring." There was a pause. "How are you? Is everything going okay with your new job?"

"Other than a few cat scratches on my chest, I'm fine, and so's the job."

"How'd you get the cat scratches?"

"Never mind. It's not important right now." Titus slid his fingers along the edge of the table. "I just listened to a message from Mom. She said Hannah's in the hospital and might lose the baby. Do you have any more information?"

"Not really. I was here when Timothy brought Mindy over. We haven't heard any news yet, but we'll let you know as soon as we do."

"I appreciate that." Titus frowned. "Sure wish there was a phone shanty at the place I'm staying. It'd be easier than having to check messages and make calls from the Yoders'."

"You ought to see about having one put in, or you might consider getting a cell phone."

"You're right; I'll do one or both."

"Is everything else okay?" Samuel asked. "You sound kind of down."

"I'm fine; just tired is all." Titus heard a buggy coming up the driveway and glanced out the open door of the shanty. The rig pulling in belonged to an Amish man Titus hadn't met.

"I'd better get back to the shop. Looks like we've got a customer coming in."

"Okay. Good talking to you, brother. We'll keep you posted."

Titus hung up and said a prayer for Hannah and Timothy. He knew how excited they were about having another child and was sure they'd be very disappointed if she lost the baby.

When Suzanne entered the Beilers' store, she found Esther behind the counter, waiting on Mattie Zook, who was married to Enos, one of the ministers in their church.

Suzanne found the items she'd come to get, stepped up to the counter, and waited for Mattie to leave.

"I'm surprised to see you here so early," Esther said when Suzanne placed two spools of thread and a container of straight pins on the counter. "Did you get up with the chickens this morning?"

"No, but I just visited a cocky rooster."

Esther tipped her head. "What are you talking about?"

Suzanne explained about taking the primroses to plant in the flower bed in front of Titus's trailer and how he hadn't even said *thank you.* "If I were you, I'd think twice about a possible relationship with Titus," she added.

"Do you mean because he didn't appreciate the flowers?"

"It's not just that. Titus has recently broken up with his girlfriend back home, who apparently looks like me." Suzanne grimaced. "I'm sure he's not over her yet, so you may as well give up on the idea of him courting you."

Esther's eyebrows squeezed together. "Are you sure the reason you don't want me to have a relationship with Titus isn't because you're interested in him?"

"Of course that's not the reason. I'm not the least bit interested in Titus." Suzanne leaned on the counter and pursed her lips. "Since I remind him of his old girlfriend, I'm sure that's at least one of the reasons I irritate him."

"Did he tell you that?"

"Pretty much."

"That's *lecherich.*"

"I agree, but while it might seem ridiculous to us, if Titus is still hurting because of his ex-girlfriend, then I guess looking at me makes him feel even worse."

Esther's forehead puckered. "If he's not over her yet, then I suppose he's probably not interested in beginning a relationship with me. . .unless I can make him forget her."

"I don't think that's a good idea."

"How come?"

"I just told you. He's trying to get over a broken heart. Besides, he hates cats."

Esther slowly shook her head. "Not everyone is crazy about cats the way you are."

"I'm not saying they have to be crazy about cats, but Titus doesn't even like them. When I was there this morning, he chased poor Callie with a broom. Of course, he did help me get a can off her head."

"What?"

Suzanne explained how Titus had cut the can off Callie's head. "Poor Callie was really traumatized, and I'm surprised she's still hanging around his place."

"Maybe she stays because there are so many mice."

Suzanne nodded. "That has to be it. She's certainly not staying because she's treated well. I think I'm going to head over there again and see if I can find her. If I do, I'll take her back to my house where she'll be safe."

CHAPTER 14

Paradise, Pennsylvania

I'm so sorry, Hannah," Timothy murmured as he sat beside his wife's bed, holding her limp hand in his. "I know how much you wanted this baby."

Tears welled in her soft brown eyes, and she sniffed a couple of times. "D–didn't you want the boppli, too?"

"Of course I did, but we still have Mindy, and if it's God's will, we'll have another baby sometime."

She pulled her hand away from his and turned her head toward the wall. "I. . .I can't even think about that right now."

"You're right. You just need to rest and get your strength back." He gave her arm a gentle pat. "Why don't you close your eyes and try to get some sleep? I'm going down the hall to phone my folks and let them know we lost the boppli. Your mamm's in the waiting room, and I'll tell her you're resting and that she can come in to see you after you've had a nap."

Hannah only nodded in reply.

Timothy left the room and hurried down the hall, where he found a phone booth outside the waiting room. After he'd called his folks and left a message, he dialed the Yoders' number and left one for Titus as well. He wished his twin was here now so he could talk to him about all this. They'd always been there for each other in the past, and it was hard to have Titus living so far away—especially now, when Timothy needed his support.

He gripped the phone so tightly that his fingers ached. *It's Phoebe's fault Titus isn't here. It was because of her selfishness in running off to California that he decided to leave home. Titus should never have gotten involved with that selfish girl. He should have listened to me and courted Sarah Beechy, who was older and more mature. Of course,* Timothy reasoned, *it's too late for that now. Sarah married Daniel King a year ago, and they're expecting their first baby. What my twin brother needs is to find a mature woman who can cook as well as Mom, is sweet-tempered like our sister Abby, and enjoys the outdoors as much as Titus does.*

—⁂—

Pembroke, Kentucky

When Suzanne pulled her horse and buggy up to the hitching rail in Titus's yard, it didn't take her long to realize that he'd already left for work, because his horse wasn't in the corral, where it had been earlier this morning.

Suzanne climbed down from the buggy and secured Dixie to the rail. Then she headed for the barn, hoping Callie might be there.

When she stepped into the barn, she blinked a couple of times, trying to adjust her eyes to the dimness there. "Here, Callie," she called. "Kumme, kitty. Come."

All was quiet, and there was no sign of the cat. *Maybe she's sleeping in a pile of hay somewhere.*

Suzanne clapped her hands. "Here, kitty, kitty."

Still no response.

Suzanne searched all around the barn, clapping her hands and calling Callie's name, but the cat was nowhere to be found.

Suzanne left the barn and wandered around the yard, continuing to call for the cat. Nothing. Not even a quiet *meow*.

Finally, resigned to the fact that she wasn't going to find the cat today, Suzanne untied Dixie and climbed back in the buggy.

When Suzanne arrived home sometime later, she found Mom outside hanging clothes on the line.

"Do you need my help?" she asked, stepping up to the basket of laundry.

"I appreciate the offer, but I'm almost done." Mom motioned to the paper sack in Suzanne's hands. "I take it you stopped by the store on your way home?"

"Jah. I needed more thread to finish Esther's quilt."

"Are you close to having it done?"

"I'm getting there, and since Esther's birthday is only a week away, I really need to work on the quilt for the rest of today. Unless you need me for something else, that is."

Mom shook her head. "You're free to work on the quilt."

"Okay, great."

"Did Titus like the primroses you took over to his place this morning?" Mom asked.

Suzanne shrugged. "I really don't know. He didn't even say thanks."

"Well, some men don't appreciate flowers that much." Mom smiled, although unexpected tears had gathered in her eyes. "Except for your daed, of course. He enjoyed the beautiful flowers we grow in our garden as much as I do."

Suzanne nodded. "I think you're right, and I sure do miss him."

"Me, too." Mom sniffled, as though trying to hold back her tears. "Last year was hard, losing first my mamm, and then your daed. But for all our sakes, I've tried to focus on the positive."

"You've done a good job of it, too." Suzanne gave Mom a hug. She was thankful they still had Grandpa with them, and hoped he'd live a good many more years.

—⚹—

A few minutes before noon, Verna Yoder came out to the shop with lunch for the men.

"Where's Suzanne?" Titus asked when Verna set the basket on Isaac's desk. "She's usually the one who brings lunch out to us."

"Suzanne's in the house, working on a birthday present for her friend Esther."

"Oh, I see. Maybe I'll stop by the house after work today because there's something I need to tell her."

"Would you like me to give Suzanne a message?" Verna asked.

"No, that's okay. What I have to say is best said to her face."

Nelson looked over at Titus with raised brows. "Is there something going on between you and my sister?"

Titus's face heated. " 'Course not. I just need to tell her something, that's all."

"What kind of sandwiches did you bring us?" Isaac asked, as though sensing Titus's discomfort.

"Bologna and cheese." Verna smiled. "There's also a jug of milk and some brownies in the basket."

Titus smacked his lips. "Brownies sound good; I like most anything chocolate."

"You wouldn't like my sister's chocolate pie," Nelson said. "She made it once, and—"

"You should get busy and eat so you can get back to work." Verna gestured to the stack of wood in one corner of the room. "Looks like you've got plenty to do."

"That's a fact," Isaac said with a nod. "Just this morning we got an order for a custom-made storage shed, and also a set of kitchen cabinets. If things keep going like this, I may need to hire another man."

Verna smiled. "I'm glad you're keeping busy. It's better to have too much work than not enough." She moved toward the door. "I need to check the clothes on the line, so I'll leave you three alone to eat."

After the men's silent prayer, Titus grabbed a sandwich and eagerly ate his lunch. Everything tasted good, and he found that he was even hungrier than he'd realized.

They'd just finished eating when an English man who lived in the area entered the shop, also wanting a storage shed.

While Isaac wrote up the man's order, Titus and Nelson started working on a set of cabinets that had been ordered last week. Titus was glad they were busy, because being busy helped take his mind off his concerns for his family back home. He wished he knew how Hannah was doing.

Shortly before quitting time, Verna returned to the shop and told Titus that she'd discovered a message for him on their voice mail.

"Who's it from?" Titus asked.

"Your brother, Timothy, and I think you should go out to the shanty and listen to the message yourself."

It must be bad news about Hannah, Titus thought as he hurried out the door.

When he entered the phone shanty and listened to the message, his suspicions were confirmed. Hannah had lost the baby, and Timothy sounded very upset. He said he didn't know what he could do to comfort Hannah, and asked for Titus to remember them in his prayers.

Titus let his head fall forward into the palms of his hands and said a prayer for them right then. Hearing the grief in his brother's voice made him wonder if he should ask Isaac for some time off so he could go home. But with all the work they had piled up in the shop, he knew that unless it was a real emergency, he probably shouldn't ask for any time off. If only he could call home more often and speak directly to someone, instead of leaving messages all the time.

Titus sat a few more minutes; then he lifted his head, picked up the phone, and dialed Allen's number. He was glad when Allen answered on the second ring.

"Hey, Allen, it's me, Titus. If you're not busy on Saturday, would you be free to come and get me? I want to go to Hopkinsville and see about getting a cell phone."

CHAPTER 15

"Are you sure it's okay for you to have that thing?" Allen asked as he and Titus left the cell phone store on Saturday morning. "I mean, isn't it against your church rules to own a cell phone?"

Titus shrugged. "It's different with every community. Some church districts allow cell phones if you have your own business, but I know of some that won't allow them at all."

"What about this district? Do they allow cell phones?"

"I don't know, but I think I'll keep it to myself for now."

Allen quirked an eyebrow. "You think that's a good idea? Wouldn't want to see you get in trouble with the church."

"I don't want to get in trouble, either, but I need a better way of keeping in touch with my family back home. Since Zach has a cell phone for his business, I'll be able to call him whenever I want. I can even ask Zach to set up a time for me to call Timothy or my folks."

Titus frowned. "Do you know how frustrating it was when I got the message that Timothy's wife had a miscarriage, and I couldn't speak to him directly? Had to leave a message on his voice mail, and that's so impersonal."

"I see your point."

"Are you hungry?" Titus asked as they climbed into Allen's truck. " 'Cause I sure am, and I'd like to treat you to lunch."

"That sounds good to me. Where do you want to eat?"

"I don't know any of the restaurants in town, so you'd better choose."

"All right then, we'll head over to Ryan's Steakhouse and eat ourselves full." Allen grinned. "I learned that expression from Zach after he returned to Pennsylvania to find his roots."

Titus smiled and thumped his stomach. "I'm definitely ready to eat myself full."

—⁂—

"I'm finally done with Esther's quilt," Suzanne said when she stepped onto the back porch and found Mom sitting in her chair, shelling fresh peas from their garden.

Mom looked up and smiled. "That's good news. You got it done in plenty of time for Esther's party next Thursday night."

"I draped it over the back of the sofa, in case you'd like to see how it looks."

"I certainly would." Mom set the pan of peas on the porch, rose from her chair, and followed Suzanne to the living room.

"You did a nice job on it," Mom said. "The dahlia pattern looks good with the red and gold material you used."

"I hope Esther likes it."

"I'm sure she'll be very pleased."

Suzanne glanced out the window. "Since I'm done early, I think I'll get my fishing pole and head to the pond for a few hours. If I'm lucky, I might catch a few fish, and we can have them for supper tonight."

"That'd be nice." Mom smiled. "Maybe I'll make a batch of cornbread while you're gone. That always goes good with fish."

Suzanne slipped the quilt into a cardboard box and hurried

out the door. As she stepped onto the porch, she spotted Grandpa sitting in his favorite wicker chair with his eyes closed and his chin resting on his chest. She thought about inviting him to join her at the pond, but didn't want to disturb him, so she stepped quietly off the porch.

As Suzanne approached the barn to get her fishing pole, she nearly bumped into Nelson, who was leading his horse out of the barn.

"What are you up to?" he asked.

"I'm going fishing," Suzanne replied. "What about you?"

"Need to run a few errands. Then I'm heading over to the Rabers' place for supper."

Suzanne smiled. Nelson had been courting Lucy Raber for a few months, so he spent most of his free time over there.

"Did Titus ever get a chance to speak to you?" Nelson asked as he led his horse over to his buggy.

"About what?"

"Don't know, but a few days ago he said he wanted to talk to you about something. Just curious what it was about."

Suzanne's brows furrowed. "The only time I've spoken to Titus this week was on Wednesday morning when I went over to his place with some primroses. I haven't seen him since because I've been busy working on Esther's quilt, and that's also why Mom has brought your lunch out to the shop the last few days."

"I'm guessing Titus probably forgot about talking to you because he has other things on his mind right now."

"What other things?"

"His twin brother's wife had a miscarriage."

Suzanne frowned. "I hadn't heard about that. When did it happen?"

"Sometime Wednesday morning. He seemed real upset about it."

On the way home from Hopkinsville, Titus called Zach. He was relieved when Zach answered right away.

"Hi, Zach, it's me, Titus."

"Hey! It's good hearing from you," Zach said. "How are things going?"

"Okay. I was calling to see if you've heard how Hannah and Timothy are doing."

"Hannah's home from the hospital now, but she's grieving pretty hard over losing the boppli. Timothy's upset, too, but they have the support of both their families, so I'm sure they'll get through it."

"Jah." Titus glanced over at Allen. "Guess who's sitting beside me?"

"Who?"

"Allen. I'm riding in his truck."

"It must be his cell phone you used to call me."

"Actually, I'm talking to you on my own cell phone. Just bought it today."

"Are cell phones allowed in the church district there?" Zach questioned.

"Don't know yet, but I'm hoping they are."

"Shouldn't you have asked someone first, before you bought the phone?"

Titus gritted his teeth. He might have known he'd get a lecture from his older brother. It seemed like he could never do anything without someone in his family questioning him. But then, maybe Zach was right. Buying a cell phone without finding out if it would be allowed was probably a stupid thing to do. However, he'd been desperate to make a more direct contact with his family.

"You still there, Titus?" Zach asked.

"Uh, jah. Just thinking is all."

"I'll be seeing Mom and Dad at church tomorrow. Is there anything you'd like me to tell them?"

"Just say that I'm doing okay and will call and leave them a message soon. Oh, and tell Timothy and Hannah I'm sorry about the boppli, and that I'm praying for them."

"I will. Nice talking to you, Titus. Take care."

Titus clicked off the phone. "It was good talking to Zach, but it made me feel kind of homesick, too," he said to Allen.

"That's understandable. This is your first time living away from your family, so you're bound to miss them." Allen tapped the steering wheel a couple of times. "With me being an only child, it was hard on my folks when I moved away, and it was hard on me at first, too."

"But you're used to it now?"

"Mostly, but that's probably because I keep so busy with my job. When I'm not lining out subcontractors to do the work I've taken on, I'm busy scouting around for land and homes to buy." Allen motioned to a large white house with peeling paint and blue shutters that looked like they were about to fall off. "See that old place?"

"Uh-huh."

"It used to belong to an elderly couple who I understand lived in the area for a long time. Guess the husband died a few years ago, and the wife was put in a nursing home last month. I've been waiting to see if the place comes on the market, because if it does I'm hoping to buy it as another piece of investment property."

"What would you do with it?" Titus asked.

Allen shrugged. "Don't know for sure, but from the outside it looks like it's in pretty bad shape, so I'd either tear it down and build a new house, or I might remodel and sell the place, hoping to make a profit."

Titus studied Allen a few seconds. For a young man just a few years older than him, Allen sure had a lot of drive and determination to succeed. Even more than Timothy, who'd always seemed to know exactly what he wanted.

Not like me, Titus thought. *I'm nearly twenty-three, and I'm still floundering with no real purpose or goals. Is it any wonder my family treats me like a boppli and tells me what to do? If I could only find a way to prove to them that I'm mature and successful in something.*

"Here we are," Allen said, as he pulled his truck into Titus's yard. He motioned to the trailer. "The place sure looks better since we had the work frolic. Are you more comfortable here now?"

Titus nodded. " 'Course, I'd like to own a home of my own someday."

"You're welcome to buy this place," Allen said. "I could lease it to you with the option to buy."

Titus lifted one corner of his straw hat and scratched the side of his head. "I'll give that idea some thought." Fact was, he wasn't sure he'd want to buy this old trailer, even though it was a lot more livable now. Still, if he bought it, he'd have a place he could call his own, and eventually he could replace the trailer with a real home.

"Would you like to come in for a cup of coffee?" Titus offered as he opened the truck door.

"I appreciate the offer, but I'd better be on my way. I'm taking a lady friend of mine out to supper tonight, and I don't want to be late."

"Didn't realize you had a girlfriend. Are things serious between you?"

Allen shook his head. "Not really. We're just friends right now, but I guess time will tell."

"Well, have a good evening." Titus lifted his new phone

and grinned. "I'll give you a call on this real soon."

Allen smiled. "Maybe we can go somewhere just for fun some Saturday. I'd like to show you the Jefferson Davis Monument if you're interested."

"That'd be great. Seeing that was one of the things I thought I'd like to do on one of my days off."

"Great. Let's make plans to do it soon."

Titus hopped out of the truck. "See you, Allen."

"Sure thing," Allen called as he got his truck moving.

Titus had just stepped onto the porch when he spotted Callie chomping on the remains of a mouse. He grunted. "You're gettin' fat, ya know that, cat? I think maybe you oughta slow down on the mice you've been eating."

The fat cat ignored him, just kept chomping away.

Titus rolled his eyes and opened the front door. When he stepped into the trailer, a blast of warm air hit him in the face. *This place sure gets stuffy when it's closed up for the day. Think I'll go out to the shed and get that old fishing pole I saw hanging on the wall. Then I'll head to the pond I discovered down the road a piece and cool off.*

CHAPTER 16

Paradise, Pennsylvania

I don't know what I can do to help Hannah," Timothy said to his mother, as the two of them sat on her porch, drinking a glass of sweet meadow tea. "She just won't stop talking about how she lost the baby, and now she's beginning to question God."

Mom placed her hand on Timothy's arm. "Would you like me to talk to her about this?"

"You can if you want, but her mamm's already tried, and she got nowhere, so Hannah probably won't listen to you, either."

"It's easy for our faith to waver when things don't go as we'd planned." Mom paused and took a drink of tea. "Since Titus left home, I've found myself questioning God several times, but your daed keeps reminding me that when we suffer disappointments and face difficult trials, that's when we need to pray more and open up the Bible and study God's Word."

Timothy nodded. "I can't force Hannah to do those things, but I can pray for her and share a few verses of scripture."

Mom gave his arm a light tap. "I hope Hannah appreciates what a good husband she has."

Just then, Zach came walking down the driveway, from

the direction of his house. "Thought you'd like to know that I talked to Titus earlier today," he said, stepping onto the porch.

"Did he leave a message on your voice mail?" Mom asked.

"Nope. Spoke to him directly." Zach took a seat in the chair beside Timothy.

"What did Titus have to say?" Mom asked.

"Said he's doing okay, and that he bought a cell phone so he can keep in better touch."

"Are cell phones allowed in the church district there?" Timothy questioned.

Zach shrugged. "Titus said he wasn't sure."

"Knowing my twin, he probably bought the cell phone without asking whether it was allowed or not," Timothy said. "Titus has many good qualities, but he often acts before he thinks."

"He is kind of impulsive," Zach agreed.

Mom nodded. "But he's a good son, and I sure miss him."

"We all do," Timothy agreed, "but I understand his need to move away and make a new start. Maybe the journey he's on will be good for him. Might help him grow into the man God wants him to be."

—⁓—

Pembroke, Kentucky

Suzanne had been fishing for nearly an hour without even a nibble. If the fish didn't start biting soon, she wouldn't have anything to give Mom for supper. She enjoyed the cool shade provided by the nearby trees, but it wasn't worth it if she wasn't getting any fish.

Maybe I need to move to another spot, she decided. *I could try fishing off the small dock that someone built on the other side of the pond.*

Suzanne gathered up her fishing gear, and had just gotten settled on the dock when she spotted Titus heading her way.

A look of surprise registered on his face as he approached her. "Sure didn't expect to see you here," he said, dropping to the dock beside her.

"What kind of a greeting is that?" she mumbled.

Titus looked directly at her. "You don't have to get so huffy. I wasn't tryin' to be rude. Just didn't expect to run into you here at the pond."

With a flick of her wrist, she cast her line into the water. "Didn't you think I knew how to fish?"

"It's not that. I just thought. . . Oh, never mind." Titus turned away. "Seems like I can never say anything right when you're around," he mumbled.

"It seems like I can never say anything right to you, either." Titus baited his hook and cast his line into the water.

"Nelson mentioned that you'd been looking for me the other day and wanted to tell me something," Suzanne said, changing the subject.

"Uh. . .jah, I did."

"What was it?"

He sat several seconds, staring at her.

"What's wrong? Why are you looking at me that way?"

"I just noticed that your eyes are a darker blue than Phoebe's."

"Phoebe?"

"The girl I told you about the other day. The one who looks like you."

"Oh."

"Her face is a bit thinner than yours, too."

"Are you saying that I'm fat?"

His ears turned pink as he shook his head. "Didn't mean that at all. Just was thinking maybe you don't look as much like

Phoebe as I'd thought."

"So why were you looking for me the other day, and what did you want to say?" she asked.

Titus pulled his straw hat off and fanned his face with the brim. "I wanted to apologize for the way I carried on when I was trying to get the can off your cat's head. Guess I acted pretty immature."

She gave a nod. "Apology accepted."

"I also wanted to thank you for those flowers you planted at my place. They do make the flower bed look nice."

Suzanne smiled. "You're welcome." Maybe Titus did have a nicer side. Maybe it wouldn't be so bad if he and Esther ended up courting.

"Is this a pretty good fishing hole?" he asked, leaning back on his elbows.

"It usually is, but today the fish don't seem to be biting."

"Really? Because I think I have a nibble."

Suzanne watched as Titus reeled in a nice-sized catfish. He took the hook out of the fish's mouth and placed the fish in the plastic bucket he'd brought along.

They sat quietly for several minutes, until Titus reeled in another catfish. "I'm two up on you now," he said with a grin.

"I don't need the reminder." She grimaced. "I've never had such bad luck fishing before. I should have caught several by now."

"What kind of bait are using?"

"Worms. What are you using?"

He held up a worm. "Same as you, only I think mine are fatter."

She snickered. "I doubt the fish are checking for the size of the worms. Guess it's just not my day for fishing, that's all."

"What other things do you like to do for fun?" Titus asked.

"Anything that has to do with being outdoors. Oh, and

I also like to work with—" Suzanne's hand jerked as a fish tugged on her line. "I've got one, and I think it's big!"

When Suzanne reeled in the fish, she was surprised to see that it was bigger than either of the fish Titus had caught so far.

"That's a nice one," Titus said. "I'm impressed."

She smiled, amazed at how well he'd responded to her catching a bigger fish. Maybe he wasn't the kind of man who liked to be ahead of everyone else. Maybe he was nicer than she'd thought.

"What are you doing next Thursday evening?" she asked.

"Probably not much. Why do you ask?"

"I'm planning a surprise birthday party for my friend Esther, and I thought you might like to come."

"That sounds like fun. Where's it gonna be?"

"At my house. Esther just thinks she's coming over for supper, and I'm hoping she'll be surprised when she discovers many of her friends there."

"I don't know Esther well enough to be considered one of her friends," he said. "Do you think she'll mind if I'm included?"

"I'm sure she won't. Esther's always been the friendly type, and I think she's open to making a new friend." *In fact, I know she's open to making you her friend.*

"What time's the party?" he asked.

"Six o'clock."

He pulled a pen from his pocket and wrote the time on his arm. "I'll transfer it to a notebook when I get home," he said when she stared at him.

Suzanne shrugged. *I hope Esther won't mind having a boyfriend who writes notes on his arm.*

CHAPTER 17

On Thursday evening, Titus headed over to the Yoders' place, using the old, gray, Lancaster-style buggy he'd fixed up. The buggy now had new wheels and battery-operated blinkers. He'd also reupholstered the seats and put new side mirrors on. It wasn't as nice as the buggy he'd had in Pennsylvania, but it would serve for most of his needs.

Titus smiled as he set the box with the birdfeeder he'd made in the back of the buggy. It was modeled after one of the covered bridges back home, and he'd stayed up late last night putting the finishing touches on it. Working with wood was one thing he did well, and he enjoyed it more than painting or any other job he'd done since he was a teenager. Since he didn't know Esther that well, he wasn't sure what her interests were, but he hoped she'd like the feeder.

He'd just stepped into the buggy when his cell phone rang. As soon as he saw Allen's number flash across the screen, he said hello.

"Hey, Titus. How are you doing?"

"Doin' fine. How are things with you?"

"Good. Say, I was wondering if you'd like to see the Jefferson Davis Monument with me this Saturday."

"Sure."

"I'll come by your place in the morning, around ten. Oh, and I'm inviting my friend Connie to go with us, so if there's someone you'd like to ask, feel free."

Titus slid his finger down the side of his nose as he thought about Allen's suggestion. If he went with Allen and his girlfriend, he'd feel like an intruder. If he invited someone to go with him, it'd be more like a double date. But who would he invite? He sure couldn't ask Suzanne. Being with her, on what would seem like a date, would only make him think of Phoebe. He thought about Esther, and wondered if she'd like to see the monument with him.

"You still there, Titus?"

"Uh. . .yeah. . .just thinking about who I might ask."

"There's no pressure. Don't feel like you have to invite anyone."

"Okay, I'll give it some more thought. See you on Saturday."

Titus ended the call and frowned. Why did Allen have to complicate things by inviting his friend?

—⁓—

Suzanne was glad all the guests she'd invited for Esther's birthday party had arrived early. This gave Nelson and Russell the chance to see that all the horses were put in the corral and the buggies had been parked behind the barn where they couldn't be seen. Titus had been the last person to arrive, so while they waited for Esther, Suzanne introduced him to some of the young people who'd come from another district in their area.

They'd only been visiting a short time when Russell spotted Esther's horse and buggy pull into the yard. "I'll go out and take care of her horse," he told Suzanne.

"Be sure she doesn't follow you out to the corral," Suzanne called as he headed for the door. "Tell her to come right to the house—that we've got supper ready and are waiting for her."

"Don't worry; I'll make sure she only comes here."

When Russell went out the door, Suzanne put her finger to her lips to let everyone know they needed to remain quiet. Several minutes went by; then the back door squeaked open and clicked shut. A few seconds later, Esther stepped into the room.

"*Hallich gebottsdaag*—Happy birthday!" everyone shouted.

Esther blinked and covered her mouth in surprise. "Ach, my!"

Amid squeals of laughter and everyone talking at once, Esther made her way over to Suzanne and gave her a hug. "You sneaky little thing. I thought you were just having a quiet birthday supper for me."

Suzanne smiled. "I wanted to do something special for you this year."

Tears welled in Esther's milk-chocolate brown eyes. "You're such a good friend. I really was surprised."

"Say, when are we gonna eat?" one of the fellows shouted. "I'm starved!"

"If you men would like to help Nelson and Russell set up tables on the lawn, we womenfolk will bring out the food," Suzanne's mother said.

"Why don't you go outside and relax on the porch until we're ready to eat?" Suzanne nudged Esther toward the door.

Esther hesitated, then took a few steps toward the kitchen. "I don't feel right about not helping."

"Go on now. Just enjoy," Suzanne insisted. Whenever Esther came over for supper, she always scurried around the kitchen, helping serve the food. Suzanne was determined that tonight her friend should just sit and relax.

Esther finally nodded and went out the back door.

A short time later, everyone was seated at the tables. After the silent prayer had been said, Mom passed the platters of food around: chicken fried to a golden brown, creamy macaroni salad with a bit of tangy mustard, pickles, several bags of potato chips, and olives.

"I forgot to bring out the potato salad you made this afternoon," Mom said to Suzanne. "I'll go get it right now."

Mom hurried away and returned a few minutes later with the potato salad, which she set on one of the tables.

Titus plopped a big spoonful of it onto his plate and passed it to Nelson.

"No, thanks," Nelson mumbled around a mouthful of chicken. "Think I'll pass on the potato salad."

"Not me. I've always liked potato salad." Titus shoveled some onto his fork and took a bite. "Yuck!" His face contorted as he looked at Suzanne. "What'd you do, pour a whole bottle of vinegar in there?"

Suzanne's cheeks burned like fire. She knew she shouldn't have made anything for Esther's birthday supper, but Mom had insisted she make the salad, and had even assured her that the recipe was easy to follow.

"It can't be that bad." Esther reached for the potato salad, spooned some onto her plate, and took a bite. Her lips puckered, and her nose wrinkled as she swallowed it down. "Whew...that's really strong!"

Suzanne scooped up the bowl and dashed for the house. It was bad enough that she couldn't cook well, but to be embarrassed in front of her friends was mortifying.

When she entered the kitchen, she raced to the garbage can and dumped the potato salad in. Then she grabbed a napkin from the kitchen table to dry her tears and flopped into a chair.

"I'm sorry if we upset you," Esther said, entering the room. "Your potato salad was so strong, it took me by surprise."

Suzanne sniffed. "I. . .I don't know why I even try to cook. I stink at it, that's for sure."

"You don't stink at it. You just need more time in the kitchen, and you need to sample what you make before you serve it. Maybe a bit of sugar would have cut the strong vinegar taste."

"I don't like being in the kitchen. I worry about messing up, not to mention Mom's reaction to it."

"You'll never find a husband if you don't learn to cook. Most men want wives who can fix tasty meals."

Suzanne moaned. "We've been through this before."

"But don't you want to learn to cook so that when you find the man of your dreams you'll be ready for marriage?"

Suzanne folded her arms. "I doubt I'll ever find the man of my dreams. You, on the other hand, have already found someone you're interested in, and once he finds out how well you can cook, I'm sure you'll have him eating out of the palm of your hand."

"Are you talking about Titus?"

"Jah."

"I may be interested in him, but so far, he's shown no interest in me."

"He's here at your party, isn't he? I don't think he would have come if he wasn't interested."

"Maybe he came because he wanted to meet some of the other young people in our area. Or maybe he came for the meal."

"He'll probably never come here for supper again if he thinks I might fix any part of it." Suzanne motioned to the door. "I think we need to get back outside. As soon as everyone's done eating, you can open your gifts. Then we'll have the cake Mom made, which I know will be good."

—⁓—

As Titus sat across from Esther, watching her open the gifts, he was filled with a sense of anticipation, wondering if she'd like the birdfeeder he'd made for her. She certainly liked the colorful quilt she'd just opened from Suzanne—even said she planned to save it for her hope chest.

"If Suzanne could cook half as well as she can quilt, she'd probably be married by now," Nelson said with a snicker.

Suzanne shot her brother a look of disdain. Even Nelson's girlfriend, Lucy, didn't appear to be too happy with him.

"You did a nice job on the quilt," Lucy said to Suzanne.

Suzanne smiled, although it appeared to be forced. "Open this one next," she said, pushing the box that held Titus's gift toward Esther.

Esther read the card Titus had taped to the box and smiled sweetly at him. "This is so nice," she said, removing the birdfeeder. "Did you make it, Titus?"

He nodded. "Made it to look like one of the covered bridges we have in Pennsylvania."

Nelson thumped Titus's back. "I'm impressed. Seems like you can make just about anything and do it well."

Titus smiled. It felt good to receive such affirmations. It felt good not to be compared to his twin for a change.

After the cake had been eaten, the young people visited until it was dark; then people started leaving. One of Suzanne's cats leaped into Titus's lap and swiped its sandpapery tongue on his hand. He shooed the cat away and stood. "I'd better go. Thanks for inviting me to the party," he said to Suzanne.

"You're welcome. I'm glad you were able to come."

Titus smiled at Esther. "Would you like me to get your horse?"

"I appreciate the offer," she said, "but Nelson's already gone out to get Ginger, and Russell's volunteered to carry my gifts out to the buggy."

"Okay. I'll walk out with you and hitch your horse to the buggy when he brings her out."

In the light of the full moon, Titus could see Esther's pretty face as she looked up at him and smiled.

They walked across the yard, and when they got to her buggy, he turned to her and said, "Have you ever visited the Jefferson Davis Monument?"

She shook her head. "I've driven by it many times but have never gone inside the gift shop or the monument."

"I'm planning to go there this Saturday with Allen Walters and his girlfriend. I was wondering if you'd like to go along."

Esther nodded eagerly. "That sounds like fun. What time?"

"Allen said he'd pick me up around ten in the morning."

"I'll ask my folks if I can take that day off."

"Great. I'll stop by the store on my way home from work tomorrow evening and see if you'll be free to go or not."

"I'll see you tomorrow then." She flashed him another dimpled smile. "Thanks again for the birdfeeder. I like it a lot."

"You're welcome."

Just then, Nelson showed up with Esther's horse, Ginger, so Titus hitched her horse to the buggy, said good-bye, and went to get Lightning.

—m—

When Titus entered his trailer that evening, he lit a gas lamp and headed down the narrow hallway toward his bedroom. As he approached the bathroom door, he halted. All the toilet paper had been pulled off the spindle and lay shredded on the floor.

He grimaced. "What in the world?"

Meow! Meow!

Titus kicked the toilet paper aside and followed the *meows* coming from his bedroom. When he stepped into the room, he screeched to a stop. At the foot of his bed lay Callie and four tiny kittens!

CHAPTER 18

As Titus headed to work on Friday morning, he thought about Callie and how she'd chosen his bed as a place to give birth to her kittens. He couldn't leave them there, of course, so he'd found a wooden box and lined it with rags. Then he'd put the cat and her kittens inside and taken the box to the barn. He'd checked on them before breakfast and fed Callie, knowing she needed plenty of nourishment.

"No wonder the cat was getting fat," Titus mumbled as he guided his horse onto the road leading to the Yoders' place. It wasn't that she'd been eating too many mice at all.

He groaned. "Stupid critter came up with a way to get in the house, but hopefully, now that she's had her babies she'll stay put in the barn."

Titus's cell phone vibrated in his pocket, but he was running late and couldn't take the time to stop and answer it now. It would be too hard to hold the cell phone in one hand and control Lightning's reins with the other. He was sure whoever had called would leave a message, so he'd just call them back when he got to work.

Enjoying the early morning breeze and scent of blooming trees along the road, Titus drew in a deep breath and relaxed in the saddle. He'd enjoyed horseback riding ever since he was a boy.

As Titus passed the road leading to the Beilers' store, he thought about Esther and how pleased she'd seemed when he'd invited her to see the monument with him. It might be good to start courting again. Maybe it would help him forget about Phoebe. He still wondered, though, if Phoebe would end up staying in California. It might be best for him if she did. It would be easier than her moving back to Pennsylvania and marrying someone else—maybe even someone he knew.

Feeling a tightness in his throat, Titus forced his thoughts off Phoebe, reminding himself that there was nothing he could do about her decision. He had to concentrate on his life here and hopefully the beginning of a new relationship with Esther.

When Titus arrived at the Yoders', he put Lightning in the corral. He'd just started walking toward the shop when his cell phone vibrated again. He stopped, pulled the phone from his pocket, and said hello.

"Hi, Titus. It's me, Timothy."

"It's good to hear your voice. Was that you who called earlier?"

"Jah. I was gonna leave you a message but decided to try calling again before I did."

"I'm almost at work, so I'm glad you caught me before I went into the woodshop." Titus took a seat in one of the wooden chairs under the maple tree in the Yoders' yard. "How are things going?"

"Not so well." Timothy's voice sounded strained. "Hannah's still not dealing with the miscarriage. She seems to have shut me out. Just sits in the rocking chair with Mindy in her lap, stroking our little girl's face and crying. Hannah's mamm is staying with us for a while, so she's doing all the cooking and cleaning right now."

"I hope things will go better soon."

"Me, too. Mom's tried talking to Hannah, and so has Hannah's mamm, but neither of 'em has gotten very far."

"Maybe you should bring Hannah and Mindy here for a visit. Might be good for all of you to get away for a while."

"We can't do that right now. Dad and I are finishing up planting, and when I'm not helping him, I'm painting for Zach and Arthur. Besides, from what I understand, your place is too small for visitors to stay with you."

"You're right about that. There aren't any hotels close to where I live either. The nearest town with hotels is Hopkinsville."

"It doesn't matter. Even if I could get away right now, I doubt Hannah would come. She's never liked to go very far from home."

"Guess it's a good thing her family lives nearby." Titus glanced up and noticed Isaac heading his way. "I'd better go. The boss is here, and I need to get to work."

"Okay, but keep in touch. Now that you've got a cell phone there's no excuse for not calling."

Titus chuckled. "I'll do my best. I'll talk to you again soon, and I'm still praying for you and Hannah."

"Danki."

Titus had just clicked off the phone and was about to slip it back into his pocket, when Isaac walked up to him wearing a frown. It was the first time he'd seen the elderly man look so stern. "Where'd you get that cell phone?" Isaac asked.

"I. . .uh. . .bought it in Hopkinsville so I could keep in better touch with my family back home."

"Cell phones aren't allowed in our church district." Isaac's bushy gray eyebrows furrowed, making the wrinkles in his forehead more pronounced. "Although I know of a few men who use cell phones anyway, despite what the ministers have decided."

Titus cringed. If cell phones weren't allowed, he'd either have to get rid of his or keep it a secret, which meant he would only be able to use it when other Amish people weren't around. It probably wasn't the right to do, but if others were doing it...

"Why aren't you content to use the phone shanty that's on the property where you're staying?" Isaac questioned.

"What phone shanty? I've never seen one anywhere on the property."

"It's out behind the barn a ways, but since the trailer has been sittin' empty for some time, I guess maybe the phone shanty could be covered with an overgrowth of bushes by now."

"I'll have to look for it when I get home this afternoon." *But even if I find it,* Titus thought, *I'm not sure I'll be willing to give up my cell phone.*

―⁓―

"Looks like my driver's here," Suzanne's mother said, peering out the kitchen window. "I won't be back in time to fix lunch or take it out to the menfolk, because after my dental appointment I have some shopping to do in Hopkinsville, so you'll have to do it."

Suzanne nodded. Since there wasn't much to making sandwiches, she figured she couldn't mess it up too badly. After all, she'd made sandwiches before.

"I'll see you later this afternoon." Mom grabbed her shawl and black outer bonnet, then hurried out the door.

Soon after Mom left, Suzanne went out to the garden to check the bedding plants she'd be taking to the Fairview Produce Auction next week. She noticed Titus talking to

Grandpa, and then the two of them headed for the shop. She wondered if it was hard for Grandpa to go there every day and not be able to do the carpentry work he used to do. Since his fingers didn't have enough strength to hold a piece of wood very long, whenever there was no paperwork to be done, he sat and visited with Nelson and Titus while they worked.

Sure wish they'd let me help out, Suzanne fumed. *If they'd give me a chance, they'd realize that I can do a good job at woodworking, too.*

When Suzanne finished checking the plants, she went out to the barn and fed the cats. As she sat on a bale of straw, watching them eat, her thoughts went to Titus and his dislike of cats. Maybe if Callie stayed at his place long enough, he'd form an attachment to her—or at least build up some toleration.

Suzanne continued to sit, even after the cats had finished their meal and scurried back to whatever place they'd come from. She enjoyed being in the barn, where she could pet the cats, listen to the pigeons coo, and smell the pleasant aroma from the bales of stacked hay.

Her stomach growled noisily, reminding her that it was time for lunch and she needed to go back to the house and make some sandwiches.

When Suzanne entered the kitchen, she found her little sister, Effie, sitting at the table, drawing a picture. "I'm *hungerich,*" the girl said, blinking her eyes at Suzanne. "When's Mom comin' home to fix us somethin' to eat?"

"Not for a while, but I'll fix your lunch."

Effie shook her head. "Think I'd better wait for Mom."

"Sandwiches are easy to make," Suzanne said, taking a loaf of bread from the breadbox. "In fact, you can help."

"Can I make peanut butter and jelly?"

"You can make yours that way if you like, but I'm fixing

tuna fish for everyone else."

Effie wrinkled her freckled nose. "Eww...I don't like tuna. It stinks like fish."

Suzanne chuckled. "That's because tuna is fish."

"Think I'll stick to peanut butter and jelly."

"That's fine." Suzanne set the jars of peanut butter and jelly on the table beside Effie, along with two slices of bread and a knife. "Here you go. Have fun."

While Effie made her sandwich, Suzanne stood at the counter, mixing the can of tuna fish with mayonnaise and relish, which was the way she'd always liked to eat it. When that was done, she slathered mayonnaise on the pieces of bread, then added the tuna and a hunk of lettuce to each one. Next, she put the sandwiches in plastic wrap, placed them in the lunch basket, and added some of Mom's ginger cookies. Then she grabbed a jug of iced tea and turned toward the door. "I'll be back soon, but if you want to eat while I'm gone, that's fine," she called to Effie over her shoulder. "Oh, and don't forget to pray before you eat."

When Suzanne entered the woodshop, Nelson greeted her with a smile. "What'd Mom make for our lunch today?"

"Mom's in Hopkinsville, so I made tuna fish sandwiches."

"There's no vinegar in them I hope," Titus said with a snicker.

She frowned. "Of course not. But I hope you like mayonnaise and relish."

"Sorry about the vinegar remark," Titus said. "I'm sure the sandwiches will be fine."

Suzanne set the lunch basket on Grandpa's desk. "Where's Grandpa? I saw him come to the shop earlier and figured he'd still be here."

Nelson shook his head. "He was tired and went to the *Daadihaus* to take a nap. Didn't you see him come up?"

"No, but then I've been busy, so he might have gone into his side of the house without me knowing it."

"Grandpa's been really tired lately," Nelson said. "I'm worried about him."

"Is he having more pain than usual?" she asked.

Nelson shrugged. "I don't know, but then he's never been one to complain."

The door to the shop opened just then, and one of their English neighbors stepped in. While Nelson spoke to the man about a storage shed he wanted, Suzanne poured some iced tea into the men's cups and set them beside the sandwiches.

"That was a nice party you had for Esther," Titus said, moving to stand beside Suzanne. "She seemed real surprised, didn't she?"

Suzanne nodded. "I think everyone had a good time."

"I know I did. Plan on having a good time tomorrow morning, too."

"What's happening tomorrow?"

"Esther and I are going with Allen and his friend to see the Jefferson Davis Monument."

"Oh, I didn't realize that."

"Figured maybe Esther had told you."

"I haven't seen Esther since Thursday night." Suzanne moved toward the door. "I hope you and Esther will have a good time," she called over her shoulder.

"I'm sure we will."

As Suzanne headed for the house, her insides felt like a twisted rubber band. She was happy for Esther, since she knew this was what Esther wanted. But she couldn't help feeling a bit envious, wishing someone special would take an interest in her.

———

When Titus got home that evening, he put Lightning away

and then went into the house for a drink of water. He'd just taken a glass down from the cupboard when he heard a familiar *meow*.

"Oh no! Not this again!" He hurried into his bedroom. Sure enough, Callie was curled up at the foot of his bed, with all four of her kittens.

"That's it!" Titus snapped his fingers. "I'm going to find out once and for all how that determined cat's been getting in."

Titus spent the next hour searching every nook and cranny for a hole that led to the outside. He was about to give up when he discovered a small hole in his bedroom closet. He ran out to the barn, found some wood to cover the hole, and hauled Callie and her brood back to the barn. When that was done, he decided to look for the phone shanty Isaac had mentioned earlier today.

Sure enough, it was there. . .several feet behind the barn, hidden under some overgrown vines and thick brush.

Titus figured he ought to wait until morning to clear the growth away from the shanty. Right now, he needed to get inside, because from the looks of the darkening sky, they were in for a good rain.

CHAPTER 19

When Titus woke up on Saturday morning, he was glad to see that the sun was shining. He hurried to get dressed, then went to the kitchen and fixed himself a bowl of cereal. When he finished with breakfast, he went out to the barn to give Callie some food and was relieved when he found the cat nursing her kittens inside the wooden box. Apparently he'd taken care of the problem of her getting into the house.

He studied the kittens a few minutes. Two were orange, white, and black like their mother, and two were white with black patches. They were kind of cute, but though they might look innocent and sweet right now, they'd soon grow up and would scratch and bite.

Titus left the barn and went around back to take a look at the inside of the phone shanty he'd discovered the evening before. He quickly cleared away the one vine that was still hanging across the front door of the shed. When he opened the door and stepped inside, it was dark and smelled musty. He brushed away several cobwebs that hung from the ceiling.

He left the door open to give more light and to help air out the shanty. Then he picked up the phone sitting on a rickety-looking folding table. There was no dial tone, of course.

Guess I should probably get the phone service connected, Titus thought, *but I'm already paying for my cell phone, so why pay for both?*

A horn honked, and Titus stepped out of the shanty in time to see Allen's truck pull up in front of the barn.

"I'd like you to meet my friend, Connie Myers," Allen said when Titus opened the truck door and climbed into the backseat of the extended cab.

"It's nice to meet you." Titus leaned over the seat and shook Connie's hand. "I'm Titus Fisher."

She smiled. "Yes, I know. Allen's told me about you." Connie's dark hair was cut short in a curly bob, and her eyes were also dark, like well-brewed coffee. She was pretty but wore too much makeup as far as Titus was concerned. Of course, he was used to Amish women, who wore no makeup at all. . .unless, like Phoebe, they liked to experiment with makeup and jewelry during their running-around years.

As Allen headed down the driveway toward the road, Titus tapped him on the shoulder. "Remember when you said I could invite someone to join us?"

"Yeah."

"Well, I invited Esther Beiler, so we'll need to stop by her folks' store to pick her up, if that's okay with you."

"Sure, no problem. I know where their store is, and it's on our way to the monument."

Titus relaxed against the seat and listened to Allen and Connie's conversation. Actually, it was more Connie doing the talking. Titus wondered if there was anything serious going on between them.

When they arrived at the Beilers' store, Titus hopped out of the truck and went inside. He found Esther behind the counter, waiting on a customer.

"I'll just be a minute," she said, smiling at Titus. "My mamm's in the storage room right now, but when she comes back, she'll take my place at the counter, and then I'll be ready to go."

"That's fine." Titus stood off to one side and waited as Esther rang up the English woman's purchases.

Soon, Esther's mother came out of the storage room. "Your daed's going to stock some shelves for a while," she said to Esther. "So I'm ready to take over for you here." Her blue eyes sparkled as she smiled at Titus. "It was nice of you to invite Esther to go with you today. I hope you'll both have a good time."

Titus nodded. "Allen's been to the Jefferson Davis Monument before, and he said it's pretty interesting."

A horn honked from outside, and Titus glanced out the window. "I think Allen's anxious to go," he said to Esther.

"I'm ready." Esther said good-bye to her mother and followed Titus out the door.

———

Paradise, Pennsylvania

A knock sounded on the back door, and Timothy went to see who it was. He was surprised to find Samuel and his wife, Elsie, on the porch.

"What'd you knock for? Why didn't you just come in like you normally do?" he asked.

"We didn't know if Hannah would be up to company," Samuel said. "So we didn't want to barge right in."

Timothy stepped onto the porch and closed the door behind him. "I'm really worried about Hannah. She still won't say much to me, and she doesn't want to go anywhere or do anything but sit and hold Mindy." He slowly shook his head.

"I'm beginning to wonder if she'll ever be the same."

"Would you like me to talk to her?" Elsie asked. "I had a miscarriage once, so I know how sad she must feel about losing the boppli."

Samuel nodded. "That's right, but God gave us four more kinner after that." He smiled at Elsie. "We're hoping for even more, if it be His will."

When they went inside, they found Hannah sitting in the living room on the sofa, staring at a book she hadn't even opened. The men stood off to one side, while Elsie took a seat beside Hannah. "I know you're sad about losing the boppli," she said, "because I lost one a few years ago, too. But you need to realize that Timothy and Mindy are still here, and they both need you." She touched Hannah's arm. "God knows what He's doing, and if your boppli had lived, he or she might have had some kind of physical problem."

"I. . .I suppose you could be right." Hannah nearly choked on the words.

"The boppli's in heaven now, and that should offer you some comfort," Elsie continued. "Remember, too, that the hardships we experience and the trials we face here on earth will teach us to trust more in God. For the weaker we feel, the harder we'll lean on Him."

Tears welled in Hannah's eyes. "I. . .I know you're right, Elsie, but it's hard not to think about the boppli I lost."

Elsie shook her head. "I understand that, and I'm not at all suggesting you forget about the baby. I just think you need to begin focusing on the family you still have, because they really do need you, Hannah."

"I. . .I suppose so."

Timothy moved over to stand behind Hannah and placed his hands on her shoulders. "We all want to see you getting back to normal."

"I want to get on with life, too." Hannah looked at Elsie and sniffed. "Danki, for coming by and for what you said. I know it's what I needed to hear."

"You're welcome." Elsie took Hannah's hand. "Remember now, I'm here for you, so if you need to talk about this some more, please let me know."

—⁂—

Fairview, Kentucky

Titus tipped his head back and whistled. "Wow, that building's even taller than I thought!"

"It's 351 feet high, to be exact. The site marks Jefferson Davis's birthplace, and it rests on a foundation of solid Kentucky limestone," Allen said as they left his truck and approached the monument. "Another interesting fact is that Jefferson Davis was born here on June 3, 1808, and just eight months later, not more than one hundred miles away, Abraham Lincoln was born." He grinned at Connie. "I've become quite interested in history since I moved here."

"Can we go inside?" she asked. "I'll bet there's an awesome view from the top."

"You're right. There is." Allen pointed across the way. "There's the visitor's center, where we can buy tickets to take the elevator to the top of the monument."

"That sounds like fun." Titus's enthusiasm mounted. Just thinking about going inside the monument had him excited. "Don't think I've ever been in a building so high."

Esther's brows furrowed, and she nibbled nervously on her lip. "I. . .uh. . .think I'd rather wait for you down here."

"And miss all the fun?" Titus could hardly believe she wouldn't want to go up with them. "You've got to go up there and have a look around."

She shook her head. "I. . .I can't."

"Why not?'

"I'm afraid of heights."

"Nothing's going to happen to you," Titus said, hoping to offer her some encouragement. "You can hang on to my arm if you're scared."

Her face paled, and she continued to shake her head. "I'm not going up there, Titus. I'll sit on a bench down here or wait for you in the gift shop."

Titus hesitated a minute, wondering if he should stay with her, but he didn't see why he should miss out on the fun because she was afraid of heights. "Okay, whatever," he finally mumbled. What was the point in Esther agreeing to come along if she didn't want to go up in the monument?

"You look umgerennt," Esther said. "Are you upset because I don't want to go up?"

"No, it's okay. Wouldn't want you to go if you're scared." Titus felt like a heel. He didn't want to hurt Esther's feelings or try to force her to do something she was afraid of, but at the same time, he was disappointed.

"Let's head over to the gift shop and see about getting our tickets," Allen said. "We can also look around and see what they might have for sale."

When they entered the gift shop, Allen paid for his and Connie's tickets, and Titus paid for his. Then he turned to Esther and said, "Would you like me to buy something for you to eat or drink while we're up in the monument?"

She glanced at the small chest freezer across the room. "Maybe an ice-cream bar."

"Sure, go ahead and pick out the kind you like."

When they left the gift shop, Esther took a seat on one of the park benches, and the rest of them followed their guide into the elevator that would take them up the monument.

Once at the top, Titus looked down. He was amazed. He could see for miles around—rooftops of houses and barns, treetops, and the highway spread out below. What had looked so big on the ground looked very small.

"This is great!" Titus exclaimed. "Makes me wonder how small we must look in God's eyes when He looks down from heaven."

"Probably like little specks." Allen laughed. "But God knows each of us by name—even the number of hairs on our head."

Connie frowned. "You two aren't going to ruin the day by talking about a bunch of religious stuff, I hope."

"Talking about God shouldn't ruin anyone's day," Allen said. "I started going to Sunday school when I was a boy, and by the time I became a teenager, I'd given my heart to the Lord."

Connie rolled her eyes, as she pulled her fingers through the ends of her curly hair. "Please keep your religious views to yourself, because I'm really not interested."

Allen opened his mouth, like he might say more, but he closed it and pulled a camera from his shirt pocket instead. "Think I'll take a couple of pictures while we're up here. It isn't every day we get to see a sight such as this." He smiled at Titus. "Maybe if I send a few pictures of the area to Zach, he'll decide to pack up his family and move here, too."

Titus shook his head. "I doubt that. Zach seems content to stay in Pennsylvania with the rest of our family. Hopefully, he and the others will come here for a visit sometime, but I don't think any of them will ever leave Lancaster County."

—m—

Suzanne had spent the morning helping Mom clean house, and by noon she was more than ready for a break.

"Should we make some sandwiches for lunch and eat them outside on the picnic table?" Mom asked.

Suzanne smiled. "That's a good idea. I always enjoy eating outside."

"Would you like to make the sandwiches while I prepare some lemonade?" Mom asked.

"Sure, that's fine."

"Can I help, too?" Effie asked as she skipped into the kitchen. "I think it's fun to squeeze lemons."

Mom smiled and patted Effie's head. "You can squeeze the lemons while I add water and sugar."

While Suzanne started working on the ham and cheese sandwiches, she thought about Titus and the remark he'd made about whether she'd put vinegar on the sandwiches. She knew he'd only been teasing, but it had hurt nonetheless. Still, she couldn't make herself spend time in the kitchen, trying to perfect her skills, when she'd rather be outside doing something else. Besides, with Mom being such a good cook, anything Suzanne ever made would pale by comparison. And since she didn't have a boyfriend and had no hope of marriage, what was the point in learning to cook?

When Suzanne finished the sandwiches, she placed them on a platter and set it on the table. "Is Grandpa in his room?" she asked Mom. "Should I tell him that lunch is ready and we'll be eating in the yard today?"

"I saw him go outside a little bit ago," Mom said. "He said something about a wasp's nest in the barn that needed to be knocked down."

"I'll go out and let him know lunch is ready."

Suzanne left the house and hurried to the barn. When she stepped inside, she didn't see any sign of Grandpa.

"Grandpa, are you in here?" she called.

All she heard was the nicker of the horses from their stalls on the other side of the barn.

Suzanne moved toward the back of the barn, and when she came to a place where a ladder had been set, she halted. There lay Grandpa, facedown on the floor!

CHAPTER 20

Kumme, Nelson! *Schnell!*" Suzanne shouted as she hurried from the barn and cupped her hands around her mouth.

Nelson dashed out the back door of the house. "What are you shouting about? Why do you need me to come quickly?"

"It's Grandpa! He's passed out on the barn floor. I. . .I think he must have been trying to climb the ladder and fell." Suzanne's heart pounded, and her voice shook with emotion.

"Where is he?" Nelson asked as he raced into the barn.

"Over there." Suzanne pointed to the spot where Grandpa lay. "I tried to wake him, but he didn't respond."

Nelson tore across the room, and Suzanne followed. "Grandpa, can you hear me?" Nelson felt Grandpa's pulse. "He's alive, so that's a relief." He picked up Grandpa's false teeth. "Looks like these got knocked out of his mouth when he fell."

Suzanne knelt beside Grandpa, gently patting his face. "Wake up, Grandpa. Please, wake up."

Grandpa's eyes fluttered open. "Wh—what happened? How come you two are standin' over me with such worried faces?"

"I found you here, unconscious." Suzanne motioned to the ladder. "Were you trying to climb that to get to the wasp's nest?"

"Jah. Didn't want any of 'em botherin' the horses while they're in their stalls." Grandpa groaned as he tried to sit up. "Think I must've got the wind knocked out of me when I fell, 'cause I hurt all over. Guess that's what I get for thinkin' my shaky old legs could carry me up the ladder."

"I think we'd better call our driver and take you to the hospital in Hopkinsville," Nelson said.

The wrinkles in Grandpa's forehead deepened when he frowned. "What for?"

"To check you over and make sure nothing's broken."

"The only thing broke is my pride," Grandpa muttered. "Seems like I can't do much of anything these days."

"That's not true," Suzanne spoke up. "You're still doing the bookwork in the shop."

"Bookwork's nothin' compared to what I used to do."

Suzanne knew how much Grandpa liked being in the shop, but she also knew it must cause him pain whenever he tried to use his hands.

"We can talk about this later," Nelson said. "Right now we need to make sure you're okay." He slipped his hands around Grandpa's waist, helping him slowly to his feet, while Suzanne gently held on to Grandpa's arm.

Grandpa winced as he tried to stand. "Oh boy. Don't think I'm gonna be able to walk. My right ankle's sore, and it feels like it's swollen. Same holds true for my wrist."

Nelson lowered Grandpa back to the floor. "I'll go inside and get Russell and Chad. Then the three of us will carry you into the house." He looked at Suzanne. "Run down to the phone shanty and call one of our drivers. Let 'em know that we need a ride to the hospital right away."

—⚏—

Allen had just pulled his truck out of the parking lot at the monument site, when Titus's cell phone rang. As soon as he removed it from his trouser's pocket, Esther's eyebrows furrowed.

Ignoring her questioning look, he clicked the TALK button and held the phone up to his ear. "Hello."

"Hi, it's me, Timothy."

"Hey! Guess where I just came from?"

"Where?"

"Went up inside the Jefferson Davis Monument. It's so high you can see for miles around. If you ever come to visit, I'll have to take you there."

"Did you go there alone?"

"Went with Allen and his friend, Connie. Also brought a friend of mine—Esther Beiler."

"I knew it!" Timothy chuckled. "I knew when you moved to Kentucky that you'd find a girlfriend there. What's she like, Titus? Tell me about her."

Titus's face heated. "We're. . .uh. . .we're all just friends." He couldn't say much with Esther sitting right beside him, still wearing a curious expression.

"How are things with you?" Titus asked. "Is Hannah feeling any better?"

"A bit. Samuel and Elsie were here awhile ago, and talking with Elsie seemed to help her some."

"Glad to hear it."

"It's good that you were able to get a cell phone," Timothy said. "Makes it a lot easier to get a hold of you now."

"Jah." Titus glanced at Esther again, but this time, she looked away.

"Guess I'd better let you go. Just wanted to see how you were doing."

"I appreciate you calling. Be sure to tell Mom, Dad, and the rest of the family I said hello."

"I will. Talk to you later."

After Titus put the phone back in his pocket, Esther looked over at him and said, "I didn't realize you had a cell phone. Did you bring it with you from Pennsylvania?"

He shook his head. "Bought it in Hopkinsville so I'd be able to keep in touch with my family back home."

Her forehead wrinkled. "In case you didn't know it, cell phones aren't allowed in our church district. I'm sure our ministers would be upset if they knew you had one."

The disapproving look on Esther's face made Titus wish he'd left his cell phone at home.

"Since there's an old phone shanty behind the trailer, I'll see about getting the phone there connected," Titus said. *I'll just keep the cell phone for emergency purposes and to call home whenever I need to talk directly to someone,* he silently added.

As Esther turned to stare out the window, Titus thought about her fear of heights. It had really put a damper on his day to have her stay below while he went up into the monument. He wasn't really sure that he and Esther were suited for each other but figured he needed to give her a chance. Maybe after a few more dates he'd feel more comfortable with her and discover that they had a few things in common.

CHAPTER 21

Paradise, Pennsylvania

How's Hannah doing?" Fannie asked when she and Abraham entered Timothy's yard and found him sitting on the porch, with Mindy playing on a blanket nearby.

"She's in our room taking a nap right now, but she's feeling a little better."

"Emotionally or physically?" Fannie asked.

"Both. Samuel and Elsie stopped by yesterday, and Elsie shared a few things with Hannah about the way she felt when she had a miscarriage a few years ago. I think it helped for Hannah to know that someone else understands how she feels." Timothy reached over and patted the top of his daughter's head. "Hannah realizes that Mindy and I both need her, and I think she found comfort when Elsie reminded her that the baby we lost is in heaven."

Fannie nodded and smiled. "I'm glad she's feeling better."

"We wish none of our family ever had to suffer, but unfortunately, everyone must face some trials, Abraham said. "We just need to hold God's hand and let Him lead us through the valleys whenever they come."

151

"You're right about that," Timothy agreed. "On a different note, I think there's something you both should know."

"What's that?" Fannie asked as she and Abraham took seats on either side of Timothy.

"Titus has a new girlfriend." He grinned.

"Already?" Abraham asked before Fannie could respond. "That son of ours sure does move fast." He nudged Fannie's arm and chuckled. "I think he takes after his daed, at least in that regard."

"It's not funny," Fannie said with a huff. "I don't think it's good that Titus has found someone already."

"Why not?" Timothy asked.

"It's too soon after Phoebe." Fannie frowned. "It's not good to get involved with someone so quickly after breaking up. I think Titus needs to give himself some time to adjust to his new job and surroundings before he starts courting again."

"As I'm sure you recall, we fell in love pretty quickly," Abraham reminded her.

"That was different. We'd both been widowed awhile and weren't on the rebound."

Abraham shrugged. "Maybe Titus needed to find someone right away to help him get over Phoebe."

"You could be right," Timothy put in. "This new girl might be a better fit for Titus, too."

Fannie sighed deeply. "If Titus falls in love with a girl from Kentucky and marries her, he'll never move back home."

Abraham patted her arm affectionately. "Let's not worry about that until the time comes."

—⟶⟵—

Pembroke, Kentucky

"Guess it's time to get my horse and buggy ready. Are you

going to the young people's singing with me?" Nelson asked Suzanne as the two of them sat at the kitchen table with Mom, having a glass of cold apple cider.

She shook her head. "I'd better stay here and help Mom take care of Grandpa."

"I don't need your help," Mom said. "Grandpa's sleeping right now, and the pain medication the doctor prescribed will probably keep him sleeping for several hours."

"Even so, I'd rather stay home." Suzanne took a sip of cider and let it roll around in her mouth before swallowing. It was sweet, yet a bit tart—just the way she liked it. When the apples in their yard ripened in the fall, they'd take them to the Beilers' and make more apple cider, using their press. She always looked forward to that.

Mom tapped Suzanne's shoulder. "You need to get out and have some fun. You'll never find a husband if you don't spend time with other young people your age."

Suzanne's jaw clenched. Not this again. She didn't know why Mom thought she had to get married. They knew several Amish women who'd either never been married or were widowed and had chosen not to marry again. *Of course*, she reminded herself, *if I don't care about getting married, then why do I feel envious when others I know find boyfriends and get married?*

"Suzanne, did you hear what I said?"

"Jah, Mom, I heard."

"Are you going with Nelson to the singing or not?"

Suzanne looked over at Nelson. "Won't you be taking your girlfriend tonight?"

He nodded. "I'll be picking Lucy up on the way to the singing."

"Then I shouldn't go. I'm sure you'd rather spend time with her alone than have your sister sitting in the backseat of your buggy, able to hear every word you're saying."

"Won't bother me any," Nelson said with a shrug. "Besides, maybe there'll be some fellow at the singing who'll ask if he can give you a ride home."

"*Puh!*" Suzanne flapped her hand. "Like that's going to happen."

"It might," Mom put in with a hopeful expression.

"Maybe I don't want a ride home in some fellow's buggy."

"Aw, sure you do," Nelson said with a wink. "Every girl wants to be courted."

"Not me." Suzanne shook her head.

"You're only saying that because you haven't found the right man," Mom said. "Someday, when the time is right, you'll fall in love and get married."

Suzanne figured it was best not to argue. She'd stayed up late last night, waiting for Mom and Nelson to bring Grandpa home from the hospital. Truth was, she was tired and had hoped she could go to bed early. If she went to the singing that wouldn't happen. Still, if she didn't go, she'd have to hear about it from Mom all evening.

Suzanne took another sip of cider and finally nodded. "Okay, I'll go to the singing."

—⁓—

"I still can't believe your grandpa was up on a ladder," Esther said to Suzanne after the singing ended and everyone gathered around to visit. "Didn't he know how dangerous that could be? Especially at his age and with his arthritis being so bad."

Suzanne moved closer to Esther on the bench they sat upon. "You're right, he shouldn't have been climbing a ladder, but you know how *schtarrkeppich* my *grossdaadi* can be."

Esther nodded. "Sometimes I think the older people get, the more stubborn they become. My grandma often says that

Grandpa's the most schtarrkeppich man she knows. He's seventy-two years old and still thinks he can keep up with his sons."

"My grossdaadi is the same way," Suzanne said. "Thanks to that fall, Grandpa's right wrist and right ankle are severely sprained, and he has several bruised ribs. Since he's right-handed, he won't be able to do the bookwork at the shop for a while."

"Who'll do it?"

"I told Mom I would. She has enough to do in the house."

"But who's going to sell your bedding plants? Will your mamm have to do that as well?"

"Mom will take care of any customers who come to our place to buy plants, but I'll be responsible for taking the plants to the produce auction."

"Speaking of the auction, Titus and I were over that way when we went to see the Jefferson Davis Monument on Saturday."

"I'd heard you were going. How was it? Did you have a good time?"

"It was interesting to see the monument up close, but I didn't go inside. Only Titus, Allen, and his friend, Connie, took the elevator to the top. I sat on a bench and waited for them below."

"With your fear of heights, I guess you wouldn't have felt comfortable being up so high."

"No, I sure wouldn't." Esther shifted on the bench, and glanced across the room where the young men had gathered. "I think Titus was a little disappointed that I didn't go up, though."

"Did you explain things to him?"

"Jah, but he still seemed disappointed."

"Are you thinking maybe Titus isn't the right one for you?"

155

Esther shook her head. "It's not that. I just wish we could have done something that we both enjoy."

Suzanne bumped Esther's arm with her elbow. "Here he comes now."

—∞—

"I just talked to Nelson, and he told me about your grandpa's fall," Titus said, looking down at Suzanne. "I'm sorry to hear it."

"We were glad he wasn't seriously hurt, because at his age it could have been a lot worse." Suzanne sighed and touched her chest. "For some time now, Grandpa has tried to do things he shouldn't do, instead of calling on Nelson or one of the boys. It really scared me when he fell."

"I'd be happy to help out whenever I can," Titus offered.

"That's nice of you."

Esther looked up at Titus and smiled. "Did you enjoy the singing tonight?"

"Sure did."

"Was it like the ones you've attended in Lancaster County?" she asked.

"Pretty much." Titus glanced at Suzanne, wishing she'd go someplace else. He wanted to ask Esther if he could give her a ride home but didn't want to do it in front of Suzanne.

Just then, Ethan Zook, one of the minister's sons, wandered over. Titus held his breath, hoping Ethan wasn't going to ask Esther if he could give her a ride in his buggy. To Titus's relief, Ethan only stopped to ask Suzanne how her grandfather was doing, and then he headed across the room toward a group of young men.

"It's getting chilly," Suzanne said. "Think I'll get my shawl from Nelson's buggy." She gave Esther a quick smile, glanced briefly at Titus, and walked away.

Titus decided that he'd better take advantage of the opportunity while he could, so he leaned close to Esther and whispered, "I'd like to give you a ride home tonight. If you don't already have one, that is."

She gave him another deep-dimpled smile. "I've had no other offers. Even if I had, I can't think of anyone I'd rather ride home with than you."

Titus grinned. "Great. Just let me know when you want to leave."

"I'm ready to go now, if you are," she said sweetly.

"All right then. I'll get my horse and buggy and meet you over by the barn."

Titus hurried out the door and sprinted across the yard, feeling lighthearted and looking forward to the ride to Esther's house. She was a very pretty girl, and he hoped he'd have an opportunity to take her out again so they could get better acquainted.

As they headed down the road a short time later, Esther remained quiet, while Titus tried to think of something to talk about.

"Are you warm enough?" he asked.

"Jah."

"I hope the buggy seat's not too uncomfortable for you. This is an old buggy, and even though I've reupholstered the seats, they're not as padded as I'd like them to be."

"The seat seems fine to me. I'm just enjoying the peacefulness of the evening."

"You're right, it is peaceful. I think the sound of crickets and bullfrogs singing their nightly song makes it seem that way."

"I agree."

"So what do you like to do when you're not working at your folks' store?" he asked.

Before Esther could reply, a noisy *va-room! va-room!*

shattered their peace and quiet. Titus glanced through his side mirror and noticed a single headlight coming up fast behind them. As the vehicle drew closer, he realized it was a motorcycle. It came right up to the back of the buggy; then pulled into the oncoming lane, as though going to pass. Instead of going around, however, the cycle roared alongside the buggy—so close that Titus could have reached out and touched the young man who was driving.

Suddenly, the motorcycle pulled right in front of the buggy, and the driver slammed on his brakes.

Lightning reared up, and the buggy wobbled.

"Whoa! Steady, boy." Titus pulled back on the reins, in an effort to keep control.

The driver of the motorcycle gunned the engine and tore off down the road. Titus's hands turned sweaty and his heart pounded as he continued to try and calm Lightning down.

A few minutes later, the motorcycle reappeared, coming from the opposite direction. When it roared past this time, nearly clipping Titus's buggy, Lightning went wild. He reared up, kicked his back hooves against the front of the buggy, and took off down the road like an angry bull was chasing him.

"Whoa! Whoa!" Titus hollered.

Lightning kept running; the frightened horse was out of control!

CHAPTER 22

Esther screamed, and Titus's hands shook so badly he could barely hold on to the reins. "Whoa, Lightning! Whoa!"

The buggy vibrated, and Titus wondered if it would hold together under the stress of all the bouncing and shaking around. They hit a bump in the road, and Esther screamed again. "Make him stop, Titus! Make him stop!"

"I'm tryin'," Titus said through clenched teeth. In the five years he'd owned the horse, he'd always been able to get him under control. But then, he'd never had a motorcycle charge after him like this.

When Titus was sure the buggy would flip over, Lightning finally slowed to a sensible trot. Titus glanced in his side mirror and was relieved when he saw no motorcycle headlight. "I think he's gone—must have had enough fun for the night."

Titus guided the horse to the side of the road and handed the reins to Esther. "I'd better get out and make sure this old buggy is okay. Want to check on Lightning, too."

He stepped out of the buggy and examined each of the wheels. Everything looked fine. After Titus had checked his horse over and found him to be okay, he breathed a sigh of relief. *Thank You, Lord.*

"I think that fellow on the motorcycle tried to spook your horse on purpose," Esther said when Titus climbed back in the buggy.

"I believe you're right."

"I don't understand why anyone would do such a thing."

Titus reached for Esther's hand. It felt cold and clammy. "Some people do weird things when they're looking for a thrill, and I'm guessing that fellow thought freaking out my horse was a real kick."

She shivered. "It scares me to think of what might have happened. If the buggy had turned over, we could have been injured or killed."

"But it didn't turn over, and we're fine. I'm thankful the Lord was watching over us and that my horse finally calmed down."

Esther released a lingering sigh. "You're right; we have much to be thankful for."

―⁓―

Arriving home from the singing, Suzanne went straight to the house while Nelson put the horse and buggy away.

"How's Grandpa doing?" she asked when she entered the living room, where Mom sat reading a book.

Mom looked up and smiled. "He's doing okay. Was up long enough to eat a bowl of soup, then soon after that, he went back to bed." She patted the sofa. "Come sit and tell me how the singing went tonight."

Suzanne removed her shawl and outer bonnet and placed them on the rocking chair; then she took a seat on the sofa next to Mom. "It went fine. Quite a few young people were there."

"Did anyone special bring you home?"

Suzanne nodded. "Nelson. He's special."

Mom snickered. "I wasn't talking about your bruder. I was hoping some nice young man would have the good sense to ask if he could escort you home from the singing."

"Well, no one did. Esther got an invite, though."

"From who?"

"Titus. He took her to see the Jefferson Davis Monument yesterday, too." Suzanne smiled. "You should have seen the dreamy look on Esther's face when Titus came over to talk with us."

Mom puckered her lips. "I'd rather hoped it would be you Titus took an interest in, not Esther."

Suzanne shook her head. "It's fine with me if he and Esther get together because I have no interest in him at all."

"Why not? He's nice looking, and from what Nelson and your grossdaadi have said, Titus is a hard worker."

"That may be so, but he's not interested in me, nor I in him." Suzanne covered her mouth and yawned. "Think I'll head upstairs to bed."

Mom gave Suzanne's arm a gentle pat. "Sleep well, and I'll see you in the morning."

As Suzanne climbed the steps to her room, she thought more about Titus taking Esther home from the singing, and a feeling of envy washed over her. It wasn't that she'd wanted Titus to give her a ride home; she just wished someone—even someone she didn't care for that much—would have brought her home from the singing. Of course, she wouldn't admit that to anyone. Let everyone think she was content to be an old maid, because that's surely where she was headed.

—◊—

When Titus woke up the following morning, he'd only been

out of bed a short time when his cell phone rang. When he hit the TALK button, he was surprised to hear Mom's voice.

"Hi, Titus. I've been wanting to call ever since I heard you got a cell phone and was hoping I'd catch you before you left for work this morning."

"You caught me all right. I haven't even had breakfast yet." Titus rose from his seat on the bed. "What's up, Mom?"

"I wanted to see how you're doing."

Titus wandered out to the kitchen and turned on the propane-powered stove. He needed a cup of coffee in order to wake up. "I'm good. How are things with you and Dad?"

"We're both fine, but we miss you."

"I miss you and the rest of the family, too."

"Your daed and I stopped by to see Timothy and Hannah yesterday afternoon."

"How are they doing?"

"Better. Hannah's not quite so depressed anymore."

"That's good to hear." Titus moved over to the sink and filled the coffeepot with water. When he glanced out the kitchen window, he spotted Callie slinking across the grass. *Stupid cat. She ought to be in the barn with her kittens. Sure wish I hadn't gotten stuck with her.*

"I hesitate to bring this up," Mom said, "but I spoke with Phoebe's mamm during the meal after church yesterday."

"Oh?" Titus's head started to pound. He hoped Mom wasn't going to lecture him about Phoebe again.

"Arie's been awfully worried since the last time she spoke with Phoebe on the phone."

"How come?"

"Apparently, Phoebe and Darlene are living in a run-down apartment in a bad part of town. Arie's concerned that it might not be safe. Phoebe's also been running around with some English kids, and from what little Phoebe's told Arie, she believes they do some things our church would not approve of."

"There isn't much Arie can do about it, Mom. Moving to California was Phoebe's choice, and she obviously wants to be on her own."

"I know that, but Arie's also worried that Phoebe might never return to Pennsylvania and the Amish way of life."

"She's probably right about that." Titus set the coffeepot on the stove and took a seat at the table to wait for it to perk. He wished Mom didn't feel the need to talk about Phoebe—especially when he was trying so hard to forget her.

"I'm glad Phoebe moved away, because if she'd stayed, she may have dragged you down."

"Why do you say that?"

"I know how easily you were swayed by her, and I'm glad she's finally out of your life."

Titus's fingers tightened around his cell phone. Thinking about Phoebe living in California was bad enough, but did Mom need to mention that he'd been easily swayed by Phoebe? It wasn't as if he'd let her talk him into doing anything bad. Titus's biggest error was in believing Phoebe when she'd promised to join the church and marry him.

"While your daed and I were visiting with Timothy yesterday," Mom continued, "he mentioned that he'd talked to you, and that you're courting a young woman there."

"Her name is Esther, and we're not really—"

"I'm glad you're seeing someone, because I'm sure it's helping you get over Phoebe. But I hope you won't rush into anything. You need to make sure you know this young woman well before you become serious about her."

"Mom, it's not like I'm going to marry Esther. We just went to see the Jefferson Davis Monument on Saturday, and then I took her home from the singing last night."

"Two days in a row? That sounds like you're getting serious to me."

"We're just friends."

"What's Esther like?"

"She has a pretty face and a pleasant personality." He paused, debating about how much he should tell Mom. He didn't want her to think he was getting serious about Esther when he wasn't sure yet how he felt about her. "I'll let you know if we end up getting serious, but right now I need to go. I have to call the phone company. I discovered a shanty out back, and I need to see about them getting the phone in it up and running, and then I need to head to work."

"If you're getting a phone connected in the phone shanty, does that mean you'll be getting rid of your cell phone?"

"I'm not sure. I'll let you know when I decide."

"Okay, son. Take care, and please keep in touch."

"I will, Mom. Bye." Titus clicked off the phone and drew in a deep breath. He wished Mom hadn't mentioned Phoebe. He wished he could forget he'd ever met the beautiful young woman with shiny auburn hair and sparking blue eyes.

As Titus entered the woodshop that morning, he discovered Suzanne sitting at her grandfather's desk, going over the books. "How's your grossdaadi doing?" he asked.

"He's in a lot of pain, and since his wrist is sprained quite badly, he won't be able to do the bookwork for a while, so I'll be coming in to get it done."

"I'm sure he appreciates your help."

"I only wish I could do more."

"Is there something I can do to help today?" he asked.

She hesitated a minute and finally nodded. "If you can stay after work for an hour or two, there are several chores you could help Nelson and the boys with."

"Sure, no problem."

"Starting tomorrow, I'll be taking some of our bedding plants to the auction, so that will cut into some of my time around here."

"I've seen the auction building, and I'm hoping I can stop by there sometime."

"I'm sure you'd enjoy it. If you come hungry, there's a place to get food there, too."

He grinned and thumped his stomach. "I'm always eager to find places that serve good food."

—\\\\—

Suzanne finished the bookwork, then left the woodshop and went out to the phone shanty to check for messages. Mom's sister Karen, who lived in Michigan, had called saying that she'd be going to the hospital in a few days to have surgery on her back.

Suzanne hurried into the house and gave Mom the message.

Mom turned from her job of doing dishes, and deep wrinkles formed in forehead. "I knew Karen's back was getting worse and figured she might need surgery. I just wasn't counting on it happening so soon. I'd like to go and help out, but with Dad needing more care right now, this isn't a good time for me to be gone." She dried her hands on a dish towel and moved toward Suzanne. "Unless you think you can take over for me while I'm gone."

Suzanne could tell by the look of desperation on Mom's face that she really wanted to be with her sister. But if Mom went away, she'd be responsible for most of the household chores, as well as fixing all the meals. She contemplated things for a few more seconds, then finally nodded. "I'm sure I can manage while you're gone. I just hope no one gets sick from my terrible cooking."

CHAPTER 23

Suzanne's mother left for Michigan the next day, and for the next few weeks, Suzanne's life was a blur. Besides seeing that Grandpa's needs were met, she'd been going to the produce auction once a week, and out to the woodshop to do the books twice a week. She was also responsible for seeing that her younger sister and brother did their chores every day, not to mention being stuck with the responsibility of preparing all the meals. Since Suzanne didn't know how to cook much of anything very well, she knew they'd been eating a lot of soup and sandwiches.

She had been hoping to spend some time in the woodshop, making birdhouses to sell at the auction, but the only time she could work there without anyone knowing was late at night, and by then she was too exhausted. Even though Titus had been helping with some of the chores, Suzanne had more than she could handle.

Since today was Saturday and the woodshop was closed, it would have been the perfect time to do some work there. Unfortunately, she had to be at the auction the first half of the day, and the last half, she'd spend doing household chores and making sure that Effie cleaned her room.

As Suzanne hurried to make breakfast that morning, her head began to pound. How did Mom manage to get so much done and make it look so easy?

"You look *meid* this morning," Grandpa said as he hobbled into the kitchen, using his cane for support.

She yawned and stretched her arms over her head. "You're right; I'm very tired."

"That's because you're trying to do too much and not getting enough sleep."

"There's much to do, and so little time to do it."

"You don't have to do it all, you know. Some of the book-work in the shop can wait until your mamm gets home, and I'm sure Russell would be happy to take the bedding plants to the auction for you."

She shook her head. "Russell doesn't know enough about the plants to answer any questions folks might have. Besides, he'll be busy helping at the dairy farm today."

"Oh, that's right." Grandpa took a seat at the table and frowned as he lifted his right arm. "Wish I could do something to help out, but between my sore wrist and ankle, I'm not much good to anyone right now."

"Once your wrist settles down, you should be able to take over the bookwork again." Suzanne handed Grandpa a cup of coffee and poured one for herself.

"I sure miss working with wood." He blew on his coffee and took a sip. "Guess I should be glad Nelson's willing to take over the business for me, because I'd feel even worse if no one in the family wanted to keep the place running. Woodworking's in my blood, and it pleases me to know that it's also in my grandson's blood."

It's in my blood, too, Suzanne thought. *If you'd just give me a chance I'd prove it to you.*

—⚉—

Los Angeles, California

"What was that, Mom?" Phoebe switched her cell phone to the other ear. "I think we have a bad connection, because I can barely hear what you're saying."

"I'm concerned about you and the company you're keeping. Remember, where you go and what you do tells people what you are."

"I already know that, and I don't need any lectures."

"I saw Fannie Fisher the other day. She mentioned that Titus is seeing—"

"Titus saw what?" The phone crackled, making it difficult to hear what Mom was saying.

"He has a—"

More crackling, followed by a buzzing sound.

"Did you say Titus has something?"

"Jah. Titus has a—" Mom's voice faded, and then the phone went dead.

Phoebe groaned. "Stupid cell phone! I'll bet the battery died, and now I'll have to charge it again."

"You'd better quit gabbin' on that phone and get back to work!" Phoebe's boss called to her from the front of the ice-cream store. "There's a line of customers out here, and your break's over!"

Phoebe returned the cell phone to her purse and left the room where the employees took their breaks. She'd have to talk to Mom some other time.

—⚉—

Fairview, Kentucky

"Sure is a warm day, isn't it?" Titus asked Suzanne when he

arrived at the auction and joined her beside the rows of bedding plants she'd brought to sell.

Suzanne nodded. "Summer's almost here, that's for sure."

"Have you sold many flowers so far?"

"I sure have. Things have been real busy here in the parking lot and inside the auction building, as well."

"I'll have to go check it out. Might bid on some lettuce or strawberries." He grinned. "It may surprise you to know this, but I like to cook."

"That is a surprise. Most men I know don't like to be in the kitchen, unless it's to eat something someone else has cooked."

"There are a lot of things I can't make, but one thing I can cook real well is fish."

She blotted her damp forehead with the back of her hand. "I wish I had the time to go fishing again, but with Mom still in Michigan, there's no time for me to do anything fun."

"How much longer will she be gone?" he asked.

"Probably another week or so. Aunt Karen's surgery went well, and she's getting along okay, but Mom wants to stay and help out until my aunt Mary, who lives in Oklahoma, gets there."

Titus's stomach rumbled, and he held his hand against it, hoping she hadn't heard the noise. "You mentioned the other day that there's a place to get a meal here. Where is that, anyway?"

"It's at the end of the auction building, over there." Suzanne pointed to her left and giggled. "From the way your stomach sounds, you probably need to eat something real quick."

He chuckled, although his face heated. "Think I'll go over there and see what they have to eat. Can I bring you something?"

She shook her head. "Thanks anyway, but I brought my lunch from home."

"Okay. Since tomorrow's an in-between Sunday, and there will be no church in our district, guess I'll see you on Monday morning when I come to work."

She gave a nod.

As Titus walked away, he looked back for a minute. The way Suzanne tipped her head as she plucked a dead bloom off one of the mums reminded him of Phoebe. That same old ache settled over him like a heavy blanket of fog, and he quickened his footsteps. Maybe finding something good to eat would take his mind off Phoebe.

—⁂—

Pembroke, Kentucky

When Titus got home from the auction that afternoon, he decided to give Zach a call and see how things were going.

He took a seat on the front porch and reached into his pocket for the cell phone. It wasn't there, and it didn't take him long to figure out why. There was a hole in his pants pocket.

"That's just great," Titus muttered. He had no idea where the cell phone had fallen, so he didn't even know where to look. If it had fallen out of his pocket on the way to or from the auction, it had probably been run over by now.

Titus thought about going back to the auction to look for it but figured the place would be closed for the day.

Guess I'll head out to the phone shanty and call Zach from there, he decided. He was glad he'd called the phone company last week and had the phone connected. He'd use that until he found his cell phone or was able to get another one to replace it.

Titus stepped into the phone shanty to make the call, turned on the battery-operated light he'd put there, and was about to pick up the phone, when he noticed something he hadn't seen before. There was a hole in the wall, and as he bent to examine it, he discovered an envelope sticking partway out.

He reached down and gave it a tug. The envelope ripped open and he gasped. There was a wad of money inside—a lot of money!

CHAPTER 24

Paradise, Pennsylvania

I'm glad you stopped by," Naomi said when Samuel entered Hoffmeir's General Store.

"Oh, why's that? Are you in need of some business?" he asked with a grin.

She shook her head and swatted him playfully on the arm. "Can't a *schweschder* just be happy to see her bruder?"

"Of course a sister can be happy to see her brother, and a brother can be happy to see his sister." Samuel gave Naomi's shoulder a playful squeeze, glad that there were no customers in the store right now so they could talk.

"Actually, there's another reason I'm happy to see you here today," she said.

"What's that?"

"Abby and I are planning a surprise party for Mama Fannie's seventieth birthday, and since it's still a few weeks away, we think there's enough time for us to get everything done and make it a special event."

He leaned on the counter. "A surprise party, huh? Think you can pull it off without her finding out about it?"

"I hope so. Even though Mama Fannie's not our real

mamm, she does so many special things for us, and we all love her so much." Naomi smiled. "We want to make her birthday as special as we can."

"Who do you plan to invite?"

"All of her closest friends, and our whole family, of course." She pointed at Samuel. "Now that you know about it, would you help spread the word to a few people for me?"

"Sure. Who would you like me to tell?"

"You can tell our brothers Zach, Timothy, Norman, and Jake. I've already told Nancy and Mary Ann. Abby will tell Matthew and also let her brother and his family know. Hopefully, they'll be able to make the trip from Ohio to help us celebrate." Naomi snapped her fingers. "Oh, and we'll have to let Titus know."

"You think he'll be able to take time off from his new job to come?"

"I'm hoping he can. If we have the party on a Friday evening, he'd just need to miss one day of work. If he takes the bus, he should be able to leave there Thursday after he gets off work, and then go back to Kentucky sometime Saturday. I know Mama Fannie would be thrilled to see him."

"Sounds like you've got it covered. Now the only thing left for us to do is figure out a way to keep her from finding out about the party." Samuel smiled. "Think I'll give Titus a call right away so he can see about getting the time off."

—⟶⟶—

Pembroke, Kentucky

Titus didn't know which problem to deal with first: his lost cell phone or the money he'd just found. He drew in a shaky breath and tried to think. He needed to find the cell phone, because if someone else got a hold of it he could end up having to pay for a bunch of texting charges that weren't his.

He also needed to figure out what to do with the wad of

bills in his hands. He counted them, and they added up to ten thousand dollars. He could do a lot with that much money: buy a new buggy or put a down payment on a place of his own— maybe even toward this place if he decided to buy it from Allen. He needed to think about this. Try to figure out what he should do. Could the old man who used to own this place have put the money in there? Could he have even had that much money? If he did, then why had he been living in a run-down trailer, and why hadn't he put the money in the bank instead of the phone shanty?

Guess the first thing I'd better do is to give Allen a call, Titus decided. *Since he owns this place, I'm sure the money's legally his.*

He reached for the phone and punched in Allen's number. It rang a few times; then his voice mail came on.

"Hi Allen; it's me, Titus. I. . .uh. . .found something in my phone shanty and I need to talk to you about it. I lost my cell phone today, so you can't call me on that. You'd better call my number here and leave a message so I'll know when's a good time to call you again."

When Titus hung up the phone, he decided to try calling his own cell number, hoping someone may have found it and would answer the phone.

—※—

Fairview, Kentucky

Suzanne's driver had just pulled into the auction's parking lot at the close of the day, when she heard a phone ring. She looked down and was surprised to see a cell phone on the ground. She hesitated to answer it at first, since she didn't know who it belonged to, but when it continued to ring, she finally bent down and picked it up.

"Hello."

"Who's this?"

"Suzanne Yoder. Who's this?"

"Titus Fisher. Did you find my cell phone, Suzanne?"

Suzanne's mouth opened in surprise. "You. . .you have a cell phone?"

"Jah. It must have fallen out of my pocket. Where'd you find it?"

"It was lying in the auction parking lot. When it rang, I wasn't sure whether to answer or not."

"I'm glad you did, and even more glad that my phone's been found. If you're going to be there awhile I'll come back and pick it up right now."

"Actually, my driver's here, and we're getting ready to leave."

"Why don't you take it home with you, then? I'll come over to get it sometime this evening."

"Uh. . .in case you didn't know it, cell phones aren't allowed in our church district," Suzanne said.

"I've heard that already, but I'm only keeping it for emergency purposes, and to stay in touch with—"

"Our ministers won't be too happy about it if they hear you have a cell phone."

"Are you going to tell them?"

"No, but I think you should. Unless you're planning to get rid of it, of course."

"I don't know. I signed a contract for a whole year, so I'd have to pay a cancellation fee if I discontinue the service."

Suzanne could hear the frustration in Titus's voice, so she decided to drop the subject for now. She'd talk to him more about it when he came over this evening to pick up the phone. "I'd better go," she said. "I need to get home so I can do some chores before I fix supper."

"Okay. See you later then."

Suzanne clicked off the phone and sighed. Didn't Titus care about the rules of their church? Didn't he want to be a member in good standing?

CHAPTER 25

Pembroke, Kentucky

After supper, Titus went out to the phone shanty to call Allen again and was relieved when Allen answered on the second ring: "Walters's Construction."

"Allen, it's me, Titus. I tried calling you before. Did you get my message?"

"I haven't checked messages this evening. I went over to see Connie, because I needed to tell her that I've decided we shouldn't see each other anymore."

"How come?"

"She's opposed to religious things, and since I haven't been able to get through to her about the importance of a relationship with God, I decided to break things off before *our* relationship had a chance to become serious."

"That's probably a good idea."

"Yeah, but I'll keep praying for Connie. It's not God's will that any should perish, so hopefully, she'll see the light someday." Allen paused. "What'd you call about, anyway?"

"I found something in the phone shanty I think you should know about."

"What's that?"

Titus explained about the money and ended it by saying, "I thought you'd probably want to come over here right away and get it."

Allen released a low whistle. "Wow, that's really something. But I'm not the one who put the money there, so it's not really mine."

"What are you going to do about it?" Titus questioned.

"Guess I'll notify the sheriff and see what he has to say. Could be the money is stolen, and if that's the case, I'll have to turn it over to the sheriff. If not, we can split the money. How's that sound?"

"Sounds good to me."

"Maybe if you're still interested in buying the place instead of renting it, you could use the money as a down payment." Allen paused. "Of course, that depends on what the sheriff has to say."

Titus sat, too stunned to say a word. He'd never expected to find any money, much less have Allen make him such a generous offer. No wonder Allen and Zach had remained good friends since they were kids. A friend like Allen was a friend for life.

"You still there, Titus?"

"Yeah. I'm just thinking about the money."

"If you'd rather use your half for something other than the trailer, that's okay. Just thought you might like to own a place of your own."

"I would, but I won't get my hopes up about that until after you've talked to the sheriff."

"That's good thinking. I'll call you back and let you know as soon as I have some answers. In the meantime, you'd better put the money in a safe place."

"I already have. Oh, and by the way. . .Suzanne found my

cell phone. Guess it fell out of my pocket when I was at the produce auction earlier today. I'm heading over to her place right now to get it."

"Okay, great. After I hear from the sheriff, I'll try calling your cell phone. If I can't get you there, I'll leave a message on your voice mail in the phone shanty."

"Sounds good. Talk to you later, Allen."

Titus hung up the phone and went to saddle Lightning. He still preferred traveling by horseback, but when the weather turned colder this fall, he knew he'd have to start using the buggy more. He was about to mount the horse when Callie zipped out of the barn and started meowing at him.

"Oh great," he muttered. "She wants to be fed." Well, he couldn't let her starve; not when she had babies who were dependent on her. He left Lightning tied at the hitching rail and headed to the barn.

—⁂—

Suzanne had just finished chopping some lettuce and tomatoes when Nelson came into the kitchen. "What are we having for supper tonight?" he asked, peering over her shoulder.

"Haystack. That's one meal I shouldn't be able to mess up."

He chuckled and gave her a pat on the back. "You'll learn how to cook one of these days. . .when the right man comes along to motivate you."

She shrugged. "I doubt that's ever going to happen."

"What about Ethan Zook? I saw him eyeballing you at the singing the other night."

"Right. More to the point, he was eyeballing the food. Ethan's already overweight, and if he's not careful, he'll end up fat like our neighbor, Neil Parker."

"Say, whose phone is that?" Nelson asked, pointing to the cell phone lying on the other end of the counter.

"It belongs to Titus. I found it in the parking lot at the auction this afternoon. Guess it fell out of his pocket. He's coming over here sometime this evening to pick it up." She frowned. "Did you know he had a cell phone?"

Nelson nodded. "I told him it wasn't allowed in our church district and figured he would have gotten rid of it by now."

"I don't think he plans to get rid of it. I think he's going to keep it and hopes that none of our church leaders finds out."

"That's not a good idea, but then it's not our place to tell him what to do."

Suzanne dropped her paring knife and put both hands against her hips. "I wasn't planning to tell Titus what to do. He's clearly got a mind of his own."

Nelson frowned. "Is that how you see Titus, as a know-it-all?"

She nodded.

"I think you're wrong. During the time I've been working with Titus I've had a few insights as to what makes him tick."

"And what would that be?"

"He's insecure and doubts himself. I've seen it in the way he questions his abilities to work with wood. Always has to check with me or Grandpa to make sure things are just right. Even then he sometimes seems doubtful about whether his work is good enough, which is lecherich, because he's a skilled carpenter."

She compressed her lips. "Hmm. . . Guess I haven't spent enough time with Titus to see his insecurities." *Maybe it's because I have too many of my own.*

"He seems to have gained a little more confidence than he had when he first started working for us, but he often compares himself to his twin brother." Nelson turned on the faucet and filled a glass with water. "From some of the things Titus has said, it sounds like his twin is very successful and confident. I'm guessin' that Titus feels inferior to him."

"That's how I feel sometimes when I'm around Esther,"

Suzanne admitted. "She's such a good cook and has so many domestic skills. It's no wonder that Titus and some of the other young men in our district are attracted to her."

"Not all men choose a wife because she can cook," Grandpa said as he limped into the room.

"That may be true, but if it's not because she can cook, then it's probably because she has a pretty face or is easy to talk to." Suzanne grabbed the bowl of lettuce and set it on the table. "That leaves me out, because I'm neither pretty, nor easy to talk to. In fact, most men probably think I'm boring."

"That's just not so. You and I have had plenty of conversations, and you're not the least bit boring." Grandpa pulled out a chair at the table and lowered himself into it. "And as far as you not being pretty enough. . .well, that is lecherich! You're just as nice looking as any of the other young women in our community—even prettier, if you want my opinion."

Suzanne smiled. "You have to say those things because you're my grossdaadi."

"I'd say 'em even if I weren't."

Just then Chad, Russell, and Effie entered the room. "Is supper ready yet?" Chad looked up at Suzanne with an expectant expression. "I'm hungerich."

Suzanne smiled and thumped his shoulder. "Everything but the sour cream's on the table, so if your hands are washed, you can take a seat."

"I washed mine." Effie held out her hands for Suzanne's inspection.

"Me, too," Chad and Russell echoed.

"Then have a seat." Suzanne went to the refrigerator and took out the container of sour cream, as well as some salsa, knowing that the men in her family liked to spice up their haystack a bit. After she'd placed them on the table, she took a seat beside Effie.

All heads bowed for silent prayer; then Suzanne passed around the various items so each person could make their own plate of haystack: cooked ground beef, chopped onions, cut-up tomatoes, shredded lettuce, grated cheese, steamed rice, olives, and broken saltine crackers. When all those things had been passed around, she handed Russell the sour cream. He spooned a good-sized dollop on top of his haystack and took a bite. His eyebrows furrowed and his nose wrinkled. "Yuck! What did ya do to the sour cream? How come it's so sweet?"

"What are you talking about?" Suzanne reached over, spooned out some sour cream, and took a taste. "Eww. . . This isn't sour cream, it's whipping cream. I must have mixed up the containers." She jumped up and removed another container from the refrigerator. "This must be the sour cream."

"If Mom was here, she woulda known the difference between sour cream and whippin' cream," Chad said.

"I know the difference, too. I just took the wrong container from the refrigerator." Suzanne didn't know why she felt the need to defend herself. She'd taken plenty of ribbing from her family about her lack of cooking skills, so she should be used to their comments by now.

"At least you didn't mess up the meal this time," Chad said with a smirk. "Last night the chicken and dumplings you made tasted *baremlich*."

Suzanne's face heated, and she cringed. "I'm sorry. I guess you're right; it was pretty terrible."

"Suzanne's doing the best she can in your mamm's absence." Grandpa pointed his gnarled finger at Chad. "Instead of picking apart what your sister does, you ought to appreciate the fact that she's been willing to pitch in and do so many things for all of us."

"Sorry," Chad mumbled.

"When's Mom comin' home?" Effie wanted to know.

181

"Whenever Aunt Mary gets there."

"I hope it's not too long," Chad said. "I want her to make some peanut butter cookies."

"We can buy some of those at the bakery," Nelson said. "In fact, I'll pick some up the next time I'm over that way."

Chad smacked his lips. "Sounds good to me."

The conversation around the table shifted to other topics, and when supper was over, Suzanne ran water into the kitchen sink and added the liquid detergent. She was about to start washing the dishes, when her sleek-looking cat, Sampson, leaped onto the counter and stuck his paw into the soapy water.

"You naughty old cat." Suzanne laughed and flicked some water at Sampson, but he just sat there, batting at the sponge in the sink.

Suzanne dried her hands and picked up the cat. "You're cute, but I really don't have the time for this." She opened the back door, and was about to put the cat outside when she spotted Titus riding in on his horse.

She stepped back inside, picked up his cell phone, and met him on the porch. "I'll bet you came for this." She held the phone out to him.

He didn't take the phone; just stood there, shifting his weight from one foot to the other. Was he embarrassed because she'd found out that he owned a cell phone? Was he worried that she might tell one of their ministers about it?

"In case you're worried," she said, "I won't say anything about your phone, but I do think it's wrong for you to have one when you know it's not approved of in this district."

Titus opened his mouth like he was going to say something, when his cell phone rang. She quickly placed it in his hands.

—⁂—

Without looking at the screen on his cell phone, Titus clicked the TALK button, thinking it might be Allen. "Hello."

"Hey, Titus, it's me, Samuel."

"Oh, hi. How are things with you?"

"Great. How about you?"

"Fine." Titus struggled with the temptation to tell Samuel about the money he'd found but didn't want to say anything in front of Suzanne. Besides, depending on what the sheriff had to say, he might not get to keep any of the money.

"The reason I'm calling is to tell you about the surprise party we're planning for Mama Fannie two weeks from Friday. We're hoping you can come," Samuel said.

"Of course I'd like to come, but I'll have to talk to Isaac first. I'll call you back tomorrow and let you know, okay?"

"That's fine, and I hope he says yes, because I know how much it would mean to your mamm if you were there. She misses you something awful."

"Okay, I'll see what I can do."

Just as Titus clicked off the phone, Nelson stepped out of the house. "I overheard part of your conversation. What is it you need to talk to my grossdaadi about?"

"My family's planning a surprise party for my mamm's birthday," Titus said. "They'd like me to be there for it, but if I went, it would mean I'd have to miss a day or two from work."

Before Nelson could reply, Isaac limped onto the porch. "I think you ought to go," he said.

"But we're really busy right now," Nelson argued.

Isaac shook his head. "Don't forget what you've been taught since you were a boy. God comes first, and then our family. No job's as important as Titus spending time with his mamm on her birthday, so even if there's a lot of work to do in the shop, it can wait until he gets back."

Titus smiled. "I'll try to plan it so I only miss one day of work."

"Take as much time as you need," Isaac said.

"I appreciate that." Titus turned toward the stairs. "Guess I'd better head for home now. It's starting to get dark."

"Good night then. See you in the morning," Nelson said, ducking into the house.

Titus mounted Lightning and headed down the driveway. He'd only gone a short way, when his cell phone rang again. He halted the horse, pulled the phone from his pocket, and clicked it on. "Hello."

"Titus, it's Allen. I wanted to let you know that I spoke to the sheriff, and he doesn't think the money's been stolen because there have been no reports of any robberies or break-ins around here for quite some time. He's pretty sure the money must have belonged to the old man who used to live there, but since the man's dead and has no living relatives, the sheriff said the money's mine to do with as I choose; although he did suggest that I not spend any of it for a while, just in case some new information develops."

"Wow! I can't believe it."

"I meant what I said earlier. I want you to have half the money."

Titus grinned. This was the best thing that had happened to him since he moved to Kentucky. Tomorrow he would hire a driver to take him to Hopkinsville, where he'd meet up with Allen. After he'd given Allen his share of the money, he'd put his own half in the bank. Titus felt that for the first time in a long time, things were really looking up. Not only was his bank account growing, but he'd be going to Pennsylvania in two weeks for Mom's party. He could hardly wait to see everyone.

CHAPTER 26

Paradise, Pennsylvania

I don't see why we have to go out to a restaurant to eat," Fannie complained to Abraham as he helped her into the buggy. "I'd be perfectly happy eating supper at home tonight."

Abraham shook his head. "Not for your seventieth birthday. This is a special day, and you shouldn't have to cook."

"Who says I was planning to cook?" She playfully squeezed his arm. "I thought maybe you might volunteer to do that."

He chuckled. "If I cooked, we'd both be wishin' we'd gone out to eat."

While Abraham went around to the driver's side of the buggy, Fannie reached down, picked up the lightweight robe from the floor, and draped it over her lap. Despite the fact that summer had almost arrived, the evening had turned a bit chilly.

"I wonder what the weather's like in Kentucky right now," Fannie said when Abraham climbed into the buggy and took up the reins.

"I don't know. Most likely hot and humid, same as it's been around here."

"It isn't hot or humid this evening," Fannie said.

"Nope, you're right about that."

"I was hoping Titus might call and wish me a happy birthday, but when I checked our voice mail this afternoon, there were no messages from him." Fannie sighed deeply. "He didn't even send me a card."

Abraham reached over and patted her arm. "I'm sure you'll hear something from him soon."

"I hope so, but I'm not counting on it. We haven't heard from Titus in over a week."

"He's probably been busy."

She sighed again. "You think he'll marry the young woman's he's been seeing and stay in Kentucky for good?"

Abraham shrugged and clucked to the horse to get him moving faster. "Let's just have a good time celebrating your birthday and not worry about Titus right now."

Fannie nodded, but despite her best effort, she couldn't get her thoughts off Titus. She wasn't sure she could accept the idea of any of her children leaving home permanently. *Of course*, she reasoned, *it could be worse. Titus might have run off to explore the English world in California with Phoebe. Poor Arie. How hard it must be, losing her daughter like that. I wonder if Phoebe will ever come home.*

Fannie leaned her head back and closed her eyes as the gentle sway of the buggy nearly lulled her to sleep. She could hardly believe this was her seventieth birthday. Where had the time gone? It seemed like just yesterday that she and Abraham had gotten married.

When the horse whinnied and she felt the buggy turn to the right, she opened her eyes. "What are we doing here?" Fannie asked as Abraham directed the horse and buggy onto the driveway leading to Naomi and Caleb's house. "Are Naomi and Caleb going with us tonight?"

A smile played at the corner of Abraham's lips, but he kept his focus straight ahead.

"Abraham, what's going on?"

No response.

"Abraham, did you hear what I said?"

He gave a slow nod. "They're not actually going out with us. They did ask us to stop by for a few minutes, though. I think they might have a gift for you."

"Oh, I see."

Abraham pulled the buggy up to the hitching rail, secured the horse, and came around to help Fannie down. "Let's use the front door this evening," he said.

She tipped her head back and blinked as she looked up at him. "Now why on earth would we use the front door? We always go in through the back door, and you know it."

His face colored. "Well, it's closer. I mean, the front door's right here."

Fannie slowly shook her head. "I'm not so old that I can't walk around to the back door, you know." She started to head that way, but just then, Naomi stepped out the front door and called, "Happy birthday, Mama Fannie! Come inside a minute; I want to give you something."

Fannie smiled. "We're coming!"

When they entered Naomi's living room, everything was dark. It almost appeared as if no one was at home. Suddenly, a gas lamp was lit and a chorus of voices hollered, "Surprise! Happy birthday!"

Fannie gasped and grabbed hold of Abraham's arm. "You fooled me good on this one."

He laughed. "The reason I didn't want to go around back is because all the buggies are parked out there."

Fannie looked at all the smiling faces that had come to her party: family members and friends alike. She placed her hands against her hot cheeks. "This is just *wunderbaar*, and I was so surprised."

"We have another surprise for you," Naomi said, moving closer to Fannie. She pointed to the kitchen.

Fannie's son Harold; his wife, Lena; and their three children entered the living room.

Tears welled in Fannie's eyes as she stepped forward to greet them. "I can't believe you came all the way from Ohio just for my birthday."

"We wanted to surprise you," Harold said, "and we wouldn't have missed your party for anything."

After Fannie hugged her son and his family, Naomi stepped up to her and said, "There's one more surprise waiting for you in the kitchen."

Just then, the kitchen door swung open, and Titus stepped into the room. "Happy birthday, Mom," he said with a big grin.

"Titus! It's so good to see you!" Fannie's voice caught on a sob as she rushed across the room and gave him a hug. This was, without a doubt, the best birthday she'd had in some time.

—⁓—

The look of delight on Mom's face made Titus even more glad that he'd come home for her party. It felt good to see all his brothers and sisters again, too.

At Naomi's suggestion, everyone moved outdoors, where tables and chairs had been set up in the buggy shed. Several of the women had brought food to share for the meal, and Abby had made a large birthday cake.

"It's sure good to see you," Samuel said, thumping Titus's back. "Since you've been gone, it's been kind of quiet when we have family get-togethers. Some of us even miss all those pranks you used to play."

"If you miss me so much, then you ought to come to

Kentucky for a visit," Titus said.

"I've been thinking about that."

Timothy came up to them, wearing a smile that stretched ear to ear. "I'm sure glad you're here. Seems like old times having the whole family together again." He clasped Titus's shoulder and gave it a squeeze.

"How's it going with you?" Titus asked.

"Okay. Hannah's doing much better now, and it makes me feel good to see her smiling again." Timothy motioned to his wife, who stood across the room, talking to Elsie.

"I'm sure it couldn't have been easy for you either," Titus said.

"No, it wasn't, but Hannah took it much harder."

"Women are more emotional than men," Samuel added, "which means they usually take things harder."

Titus glanced to his left and noticed Phoebe's mother talking to Mom. If Phoebe hadn't gone to California, and the two of them had still been together, she would have probably been here tonight, too. Titus knew Phoebe's mother had been friends with Mom for a good many years, but seeing Arie and Phoebe's dad, Noah, made it difficult not to think about Phoebe and what might have been. Would he ever get her out of his system? Could he forget what she'd done to him? Was he ready to begin a serious relationship with Esther? So many questions raced through his head, but he had answers for none.

—⟅⟆—

Pembroke, Kentucky

Shortly after Suzanne entered the Beilers' store, she noticed Esther cleaning some shelves near the back of the building. *"Wie geht's?"* she asked, stepping up to her.

Esther smiled. "I'm doing okay. How about you?"

Suzanne sighed. "I'd be doing better if Mom would come home. It's getting harder to keep up with all the things that are expected of me, and now that Titus is gone, too, we won't have his help with any of our chores for the next few days."

"Is there anything I can do to help?"

Suzanne motioned to the shelves Esther had been cleaning. "I don't see how you can help me when you're busy working here."

"I'm not always busy in the store, and I'd be happy to help you after I get off work." Esther leaned against the shelf. "I could come by your place after I get done at Titus's place this evening."

Suzanne quirked an eyebrow. "How come you've been going over there?"

"To feed his cats. I told him I'd do that while he's in Pennsylvania."

"What do you mean, 'cats'? Callie's the only cat I know Titus has."

"Callie had kittens. Didn't Titus tell you?"

Suzanne shook her head.

"Maybe he forgot. Or maybe he didn't think it was important."

"That's probably more to the point. I'll bet he was upset when Callie had kittens. I'm surprised he didn't haul her and the kittens over to our place."

"You don't like Titus very much, do you?"

"I don't dislike him, but he does irritate me sometimes."

"I think he's really a nice person, and even though we don't seem to have a lot in common, I hope he doesn't decide to stay in Pennsylvania."

"I'm sure he does have his good points, and I doubt he'll stay in Pennsylvania. He seems happy working in the woodshop with Nelson." Suzanne turned aside. "Guess I'd better get what I came for and head home. I'm sure everyone's getting hungry by now, and I need to get something going for supper."

As Suzanne directed her horse and buggy toward home, she thought about Titus and wondered if he was serious about Esther. *I hope I wasn't wrong when I told her that I didn't think Titus would stay in Pennsylvania. Maybe after seeing his family again he'll change his mind about living here.*

Suzanne smiled. *If Titus were to stay in Pennsylvania, Grandpa would have to find someone to take Titus's place in the woodshop. Maybe then I could convince Grandpa to let me work there. I may not be as fast as Titus, but I think I could do most of the things he does, and probably just as well.*

Suzanne's thoughts were halted when she spotted a beige-colored horse running down the road in front of her, with only a lead rope around its neck. The poor thing was lathered up pretty good and acted like it didn't know where it was going.

Suddenly, it turned and trotted along the edge of the road, smacking into the branch of a tree.

A scream tore from Suzanne's throat as the horse then veered to the right and rammed into the side of her buggy.

CHAPTER 27

Suzanne gripped the reins tighter, guiding Dixie to the left, hoping to get out of the way of the crazy runaway horse. "Easy, Dixie. Easy, girl," she coaxed.

Just then, the horse turned and sped past them again, this time going in the opposite direction. It raced along the center line for a while, then suddenly veered toward the shoulder of the road and darted into the woods.

"Whew!" Suzanne sighed with relief. She was glad the horse was off the road and hoped it would find its way home. "Thank You, Lord," she whispered, "for keeping me and Dixie safe."

—◊◊◊—

Los Angeles, California

"Your cell phone's ringing," Darlene shouted to Phoebe.

"I'm getting ready to take a shower," Phoebe called from the bathroom. "Can you answer it for me?" She didn't want to be bothered with a phone call right now. She'd just gotten home from work and was hot and tired.

A few seconds later, Darlene rapped on the door. "It's your mother. She wants to talk to you."

"Tell her I'll call her back."

"I told her that, but she insists on talking to you now. Said you haven't returned any of her calls for the last two weeks and she's worried about you." Darlene knocked again. "I think you'd better talk to her, Phoebe. It's not right to make your mother worry."

"Oh, all right." Phoebe slipped on her robe and opened the door.

Darlene handed her the phone. "Here you go."

"Hi, Mom. How are you?" Phoebe said as she lifted the phone to her ear.

"I'm fine, but I've been worried about you."

"There's no need to be worried. I'm doing just fine." Phoebe twirled her bathrobe belt around her arm and stared at herself in the mirror. She wished Mom didn't worry so much. She wished Mom and Dad would let her enjoy her independence.

"I've called you several times and left messages, but you never reply. What's going on, Phoebe?" Mom's voice sounded harsh and demanding, making Phoebe feel like a child.

"I've been busy," she muttered.

"Too busy to call your mamm?"

Phoebe gave no reply. Just stepped into the bedroom and flopped onto her bed.

"Your daed and I went to Fannie's surprise birthday party this evening," Mom said.

Phoebe yawned. "That's nice."

"Can you guess who was there?"

"Probably Fannie's family and friends."

"That's right, including Titus."

Phoebe sucked in her breath and bolted upright. "You mean he gave up on his little adventure in Kentucky and moved back to Pennsylvania?"

"No, he just came for the party. He'll be heading back to Kentucky before Monday, no doubt."

"I see."

"I also wanted you to know that Titus has a—"

"I really don't care to hear anything more about Titus, and I was about to take a shower, so I've gotta go. Thanks for calling. Bye, Mom."

Phoebe clicked off the phone and smacked her hand on the edge of the bed. *Why'd Mom find it necessary to tell me about Titus being at Fannie's party? Was she trying to make me wish I hadn't left Pennsylvania so I could have been at the party? Well, whatever the case, it didn't work. Even though things haven't worked out perfectly for me here in California, I'm glad I moved. It's better than having my folks tell me what to do all the time.*

—∞—

Paradise, Pennsylvania

"I'm so happy you could be here for my party tonight," Mom said as she, Dad, and Titus sat in the living room after they'd come home from Naomi and Caleb's. "I just wish you didn't have to go back to Kentucky so soon."

"I need to be there by Monday evening so I can be at work on Tuesday morning. Isaac Yoder was nice enough to let me have a few days off, but I don't want to take advantage of his generosity." Titus thumped the arm of his chair. "Besides, I've got a cat and a batch of kittens to look after now, not to mention my horse."

Mom snickered. "With your dislike of cats? I can't imagine!"

Titus frowned. "It's not funny. I got stuck with a cat I didn't ask for, and then she had kittens I really don't want."

"Who's watching them while you're gone?" Dad questioned.

"My friend Esther."

"Isn't she the one you took to the Jefferson Davis Monument?" Mom asked.

Titus nodded. "I've taken her for a couple of buggy rides, too."

Dad nudged Mom's arm and grinned. "See, I told you, Fannie. Our son's not only learning some responsibility, but he's got himself a new girlfriend, too. I think moving away from home's been good for him, don't you?"

Deep wrinkles formed across Mom's forehead. "I suppose, but he could have learned to be responsible if he'd stayed right here."

"I don't know about that," Dad said. "Some young people do better when they're out on their own."

A rush of heat shot up the back of Titus's neck. He didn't like it when his folks talked about him like he wasn't in the room. It made him feel like a child.

Titus had thought he might tell Mom and Dad about the money he'd found in the phone shanty, but decided against it, at least for now. If he mentioned it, Mom would probably make a big deal of it, and Dad would tell him how to spend the money.

Titus rose to his feet and turned toward the door leading upstairs.

"Where are you going?" Mom called.

"Think I'll go to bed. It was a long bus ride to get here, and I'm tired."

"So soon? But we haven't had a chance to visit that much." Mom patted the sofa cushion beside her. "Come, take a seat, and tell us about Kentucky."

"We can talk to Titus tomorrow," Dad said. "If he's tired, then we ought to let him go on up to bed."

Mom yawned. "Come to think of it, I'm pretty tired myself. I believe all the excitement of the party took its toll on my old body."

"Mine, too." Dad helped Mom to her feet. "When we get

home from church tomorrow afternoon, we can spend the rest of the day visiting, and Titus can tell us all about Kentucky." He smiled at Titus. "And we want to hear more about your new girlfriend. Maybe you can bring her here to meet us sometime."

"Maybe so. We'll have to see how it goes."

"Is she nice? Has she got the skills it takes to be a good wife?" Mom asked.

Titus's jaw clenched. "I'm not thinking about marriage right now, and I thought we were all going to bed."

"You're right." She gave a small laugh.

Titus leaned down and hugged her; then he hurried up the stairs. He didn't know if he'd ever feel serious enough about Esther to bring her to Pennsylvania, and if he did decide to get married, he hoped Mom wouldn't pressure him to move back home.

CHAPTER 28

Pembroke, Kentucky

On Monday morning, Suzanne had just started washing the breakfast dishes when she heard a vehicle pull into the yard. She peered out the window and spotted a van parked outside. A few seconds later, Mom stepped out.

Suzanne dropped the sponge into the dishwater, dried her hands on a towel, and hurried out the back door. Grandpa, who'd been sitting on the porch in his favorite chair, smiled at her and said, "Looks like your mamm's finally home."

Suzanne nodded. "I'm ever so glad." She met Mom on the lawn about the same time as Nelson stepped out of the woodshop.

Mom hugged them both. "Did you miss me?"

"Of course," Suzanne said. "It's good to have you home."

"Most definitely." Nelson grabbed Mom's suitcase. "Here, let me carry that for you."

"How's Aunt Karen?" Suzanne asked as they walked toward the house.

"She's getting along fairly well," Mom replied. "Since my sister Mary's helping her now, I felt like I could come home."

She smiled at Suzanne. "How are the kinner? Have they been good for you?"

"I've had no problems with any of them," Suzanne said honestly. "They all pitched in and helped as much as they could."

"That's right." Nelson nodded in agreement. "The only problem Suzanne had was fixing our meals."

Suzanne jabbed her brother in the ribs. "Come on now. My cooking wasn't that bad."

"Never said it was. Just said you had a problem fixing our meals."

"I didn't have any big problems," Suzanne said. "I just kept things simple, which helped a lot."

"Didn't any of the women from our community bring over some meals?" Mom asked as they stepped onto the porch.

"A few were brought in," Grandpa said before Suzanne could respond. "The rest of our meals were mostly soup and sandwiches, and Suzanne did her best." He looked up at her and winked.

Suzanne smiled. Grandpa always tried to see the bright side of things and look past her imperfections.

"How have things been going at the produce auction?" Mom asked Suzanne when they'd entered the house. "Have you sold much?"

"Things have been busy, and many people have stopped to buy our bedding plants and hanging baskets. I'm certain it'll be just as busy in the fall when our mums are ready to sell."

"I'm sure you're right about that." Mom looked over at Nelson. "How are things going for you and Titus in the woodshop?"

"Business is doing well, but Titus has been gone for a few days, so that's put us a bit behind on some orders. He should be back sometime today and will be at work tomorrow morning."

"Where'd he go?" Mom asked, taking a seat in the living room.

"To Pennsylvania for his mamm's surprise birthday party." Nelson motioned to Mom's suitcase. "Want me to take that to your room?"

She nodded. "Then I'll let you get back to work. We can talk more later."

After Nelson left the room, Suzanne took a seat on the sofa beside Mom. "I stopped by the Beilers' store the other night, and Esther informed me that she's been feeding Titus's cat and his horse while he's gone. She also said that Callie has four kittens, which I had no idea about."

Mom's lips compressed. "I find it strange that Titus didn't mention the kittens. Especially since you're the one who took Callie over to his place."

"That's what I thought, too." Suzanne shrugged. "But then, I don't understand a lot of things about Titus."

—⁓—

When Titus got off the special bus that transported Amish and Mennonites from Lancaster, Pennsylvania, to Kentucky he was near the Beilers' store, so he went inside to say hello.

"It's good to see you," Esther said when he joined her near the front counter. "How was the party? Was your mamm surprised?"

Titus nodded. "She sure was. I think me being there was the biggest surprise of all."

"I'll bet it was hard to leave so soon."

"A little bit, but I knew I needed to get back to work, and I was anxious to see Lightning. How's he doing, anyway? He didn't give you any trouble, I hope."

Esther shook her head. "Not a bit. Callie and her babies are fine, too. Those little kittens are sure sweet. I was going to head over there pretty soon and check on them, because I didn't know what time you might get here today." She smiled sweetly at Titus. "Unless you've lined up a driver to pick you up, I'd be happy to give you a ride home."

"I don't have anyone coming for me, so I'd appreciate the ride."

"I'll run in the back room and tell Mom and Dad where I'm going; then I'll go out and get my horse and buggy."

"I can get 'em for you," Titus offered. "Are they around back?"

"Jah. Ginger's in the corral, and the buggy's parked near the shed."

"Okay, I'll meet you out front in a few minutes."

Eager to get home, Titus hurried to get Ginger hitched to the buggy. When he drove it around to the front of the store, Esther was waiting for him.

"Would you like to drive, or would you rather I did?" she asked.

"I don't mind driving."

"Great. Did you get your backpack?" Esther asked as she climbed into the buggy.

"Sure did. Put it in the back of the buggy before you came out of the store." Titus took up the reins and directed the horse onto the road.

"Did your mamm like the little keepsake box you made for her?"

Titus nodded. "She got a lot of other nice gifts, too."

"Do you think your folks will ever come here to visit?" Esther asked. "I'd like to meet them sometime."

Titus chuckled. "If Mom had her way, they'd come for a visit tomorrow. The only trouble is, there's not enough room in the trailer for them to stay with me right now. Maybe someday, if I should decide to buy the place, I can either add on or build something new."

"I didn't realize you were thinking of buying the place from Allen. Do you have enough money for that?"

"Not right now, but I'm saving up for a down payment." Titus considered telling Esther about the money he'd found but decided it was best if he kept it to himself for now.

Their conversation turned to other things—the weather, more about Mom's party, and Callie and her kittens. When they pulled into Titus's yard a short time later, he was surprised to see a beige-colored horse grazing in the pasture next to the trailer.

"Where'd that horse come from?" he asked Esther.

She shrugged. "I have no idea. It wasn't there when I came to feed the animals last night."

"Hmm. . .guess he must belong to one my neighbors. I'll chase him out of the pasture, and hopefully he'll go back to where he belongs." Titus handed the reins to Esther, grabbed his backpack, and climbed down from the buggy. "Danki for the ride home, and also for taking care of the animals for me."

"You're welcome. See you soon, Titus." Esther hesitated a minute, like she wanted to say more, but then she waved and directed her horse toward the road.

Titus stepped into the barn, and seeing that Callie and her kittens were still there, he felt satisfied. At least they hadn't found a way to get into the house.

Next, he went to the stall where Lightning was kept. The horse whinnied and nuzzled Titus's hand. "Did you miss me, boy?" Titus rubbed Lightning behind his soft ears. "I sure missed you."

After a few minutes spent talking to his horse, Titus headed to the trailer. When he entered the living room, he halted and stood there in total disbelief. The cushions from the sofa were on the floor, all of Titus's books had been pulled off the bookshelf and were strewn about. The rocking chair had been turned upside-down, along with the lamp table and lantern, which was now broken.

He dashed into the kitchen for a look around, and discovered that all the cupboard doors hung wide open, and several dishes lay shattered on the floor.

Titus's next stop was his bedroom, where he found that most of his clothes had been pulled out of the closet and scattered on the floor. Even his mattress had been yanked off the bed and overturned. The whole place was in complete disarray!

"Who could have done this, and why?" he grumbled. "Oh, boy! Think I'd better call Allen right away."

Titus pulled out his cell phone to make the call, but soon realized that his battery was dead. He'd have to go out to the phone shanty to make the call.

He hurried outside, and had no more than opened the shanty door when he discovered that someone had been in there, too. The phone cord had been jerked from the wall and thrown on the floor, and several boards had also been ripped from the wall, and even the floor. What a welcome-home present! First a horse grazing in the pasture that didn't belong to him, and now this. What was going on, anyway?

CHAPTER 29

With heart pounding and head swimming with questions, Titus saddled Lightning and rode out of his yard at a fast pace. When he arrived at the Beilers' a short time later, he quickly tied his horse to the hitching rail and bounded onto the porch. The door opened before he had a chance to knock, and Esther stepped out.

"You look upset," she said. "Is something wrong?"

"There sure is. Someone broke into the trailer while I was gone and made a big mess." He gulped in a couple of deep breaths. "When you came over to feed the animals, did anything look suspicious, or did you see anyone snooping around?"

Esther stood with her mouth slightly open; then she slowly shook her head. "Of course I didn't go inside the trailer, so I don't know how things looked in there. I wonder who would do such a thing."

He shrugged. "I need to use your phone to call Allen. My phone shanty was vandalized, too, and the phone's not working."

"What about your cell phone? Did you get rid of it?"

"No, but I can't use it right now because the battery needs to be charged."

Esther motioned to their phone shanty out back. "Go ahead and use the phone. While you're doing that, I'll go inside and tell Mom and Dad what happened at your place."

Titus hurried out to the shanty and dialed Allen's number. He was relieved when Allen answered right away, and then he quickly explained what had happened.

"What do you think I should do?" Titus questioned. "Do you think the break-in has anything to do with the money I found?"

"I don't know, but I'm going to call the sheriff right now. If you'll wait in the Beilers' phone shanty, I'll call you back and let know what the sheriff wants you to do."

"Okay." Titus hung up the phone. While he waited for Allen's call, he listened to the steady *csst. . .csst. . .csst. . .*of the cicadas as he stared out the open door at a herd of cows grazing in the field across the road. Things had been going along so well until now. What did the break-in mean, and would whoever did it come back?

He popped each of his knuckles and drew in a deep breath, trying to steady his nerves. In all the time he'd lived in Pennsylvania, no one in his family had ever had their home broken into. It was unsettling and made him wonder if things were really as peaceful here in Christian County, Kentucky, as he'd thought them to be. He guessed living in a rural community was no guarantee that a person and their belongings were safe. The world was full of evil, and there was probably no place a person could go where they wouldn't have to worry about crime.

The phone rang sharply, causing Titus to nearly jump out of his chair. He grabbed the receiver on the second ring. "Hello."

"Hi, Titus; it's me, Allen. I talked to the sheriff, and he wants you to head back to the trailer. He and I will meet you there. Don't go inside, though, okay?"

"No, I won't."

When Titus stepped out of the shanty, Esther was waiting for him. "Did you get ahold of Allen?"

"Jah. He called the sheriff, and I'm supposed to meet them both at the trailer."

Her face registered concern. "Do you think that's safe?"

"Don't see why not. I was in the house already, and no one was there."

"Please be careful."

"I will." Titus started walking toward his horse, and Esther followed.

"I was wondering if you'd like to come over here for supper tomorrow evening?" she asked.

"Sure, that'd be nice."

"All right then; we'll see you around six."

"Sounds good." Titus climbed on Lightning's back and rode off.

When he arrived at the trailer, the sheriff was already there. "The place is a mess," Titus said as they entered the living room.

"I see what you mean." The sheriff shook his nearly bald head. "Looks like someone might have been looking for something—maybe that money you found in the phone shanty."

Titus nodded. "I've been thinking that, too."

"I think you ought to stay somewhere else tonight. I'll have some of my men come out, and we'll look for any evidence that might let us know who might have broken into your place."

"Titus can stay with me tonight, and then I'll take him to

work tomorrow morning," Allen said as he entered the trailer. He halted just inside the door. "Wow, they really did a number on the place, didn't they?"

Titus grimaced. "The sheriff thinks whoever did this may have been looking for the money I found in the phone shanty."

Allen nodded. "He's probably right."

"Do you think they'll come back?" Titus asked the sheriff.

"I doubt it, but if they do, I want you to notify me right away."

"Guess you'd better grab whatever you need for the night so we can get going," Allen said. He looked over at Titus. "I haven't had supper yet, and I'm sure you haven't either, so we can stop at one of the restaurants in Hopkinsville before we go to my house."

"That's fine, but I need to feed my horse before we go, and also the cat in the barn. She's nursing a batch of kittens so I need to make sure she's fed."

"Sure, no problem."

When the sheriff left, and Titus had gathered up the clothes he needed, he went out to the barn. After he'd put Lightning away and fed the animals, he noticed that the horse he'd seen in his pasture was still there.

"I don't know who that horse belongs to," Titus told Allen, "but I'm thinking we ought to capture the critter and put him in the barn for the night so he doesn't wander off."

Allen gave a nod. "I'm willing to try if you are."

Titus got a rope from the barn, and then he and Allen headed for the pasture. It took a couple of tries, but Titus finally managed to get the rope around the horse's neck.

"Look there," Allen said, pointing to the horse's flanks. "He has a number painted on his flanks, which makes me wonder if he came from the horse auction near here."

"It's too late to do anything about it tonight," Titus said. "We can call and check on it in the morning."

Allen nodded. "Hopefully before tomorrow's over, we'll have some answers about the horse, as well as the break-ins."

CHAPTER 30

Suzanne had just started hanging out some wash on Tuesday morning, when Allen's truck pulled into the yard. She was surprised to see Titus step out of the passenger's side and follow Allen into the woodshop. Titus almost always rode his horse to work, and it seemed odd that Allen had given him a ride.

Curious to know what was going on, Suzanne finished hanging the laundry and headed for the shop. When she entered the building, she heard Titus telling Nelson about a beige-colored horse he'd found in his pasture when he arrived home from Pennsylvania last night. From the description he gave, it sounded like the same horse that had rammed her buggy.

She stepped between Titus and Allen. "I had a close encounter with a runaway horse the other day. It rammed into my buggy and ran wildly down the road."

"Were you or your horse and buggy hurt?" Titus asked with a look of concern.

"No, thankfully not, but it did shake me up a bit."

"I can imagine."

"I'm wondering if it was the same horse that ended up at your place."

"Could be,"Titus said with a nod. "There's a number painted on the horse's flanks, so Allen put in a call this morning to see if the horse might have been one that was sold at the auction."

"What'd you find out?" Suzanne asked.

"Nothing yet. I'm waiting to hear back," Allen said.

Just then Allen's cell phone rang. "Maybe that's the guy from the auction now. Think I'll take the call outside." Allen pulled his cell phone from his pocket and stepped out the door.

"How was your trip to Pennsylvania?" Suzanne asked Titus. "Was your mamm surprised?"

"She sure was—especially about me being there."

"It's good that you were able to go."

"Jah, but what I came back to made me wish I hadn't gone."

"You mean finding a stray horse in your pasture?"

He shook his head. "That was only part of it. What really upset me was—"

"That was the sheriff," Allen said when he returned to the shop.

"What'd he say?"Titus asked.

Allen frowned. "Guess they didn't find any helpful evidence, but he thinks it would be best if neither of us spends any of the money you found until the sheriff is sure it's not stolen. He also said that you can return home now, but he wants you to let him know if you see or hear anything suspicious."

"What's this about you finding money at your place?" Nelson asked before Suzanne could voice the question.

Suzanne felt a ripple of apprehension zip up her spine as Titus told how he'd found an envelope full of money in his phone shanty, and how the shanty, as well as the trailer, had been broken into and ransacked while he'd been in Pennsylvania. It had been some time since they'd had any break-ins in the area, and the last time it had happened, the whole community had been on edge for many weeks afterward.

"The sheriff thinks someone out of the area may have stolen the money Titus found, and then hidden it in the phone shanty because they were on the run," Allen said.

"But why would they break into the trailer?" Suzanne asked.

"Because the money's not in the phone shanty anymore," Titus spoke up. "Allen and I split the money, and we put it in the bank before I left for Pennsylvania. If the person who put the money in the phone shanty went looking there and couldn't find it, they might have thought the money was in the trailer."

Allen's cell phone rang again.

"Maybe that's the sheriff calling back," Nelson said.

Allen glanced at the phone and shook his head. "It's the guy from the horse auction."

Everyone got quiet while Allen took the call. When he clicked off the phone, he turned to Titus and said, "We were right. The horse was sold at the auction, and it got away before its new owner could get it loaded into the horse trailer. The man's been notified, and he'll be going over to your place this evening to get the horse."

"I hope he gets there before six," Titus said. "I'm supposed to go over to the Beilers' for supper this evening."

I'll bet Esther's happy about that, Suzanne thought.

"I'm sure it'll be okay if he comes while you're gone," Allen said. "He knows what the horse looks like, and I told him you'd put it in the barn."

"Guess that'll be fine then," Titus said. "Since Lightning will be with me, I won't have to worry about the man taking the wrong horse."

—ᘯᗉ—

Paradise, Pennsylvania

"Guder mariye, Mom. I decided to stop by on my way to work to see if you and Dad have heard anything from Titus since he returned to Kentucky," Zach said as he entered the kitchen, where Fannie sat at the table, drinking a cup of tea.

"He called and left us a message when he got off the bus."

"Have you heard anything since then?"

Fannie shook her head. "But he's only been back a day, so I don't expect we'll hear from him again anytime soon. Why do you ask?"

Zach pulled out a chair and took a seat at the table. "Allen called me last night. The trailer where Titus has been staying got broken into while he was gone, so Titus spent last night at Allen's."

Fannie's eyes widened. "That's baremlich! Why didn't Titus let us know about this?"

"Maybe he knew Allen had called me and figured I'd give you the message." Zach shrugged. "Or maybe Titus decided not to say anything because he didn't want to worry you."

Fannie gripped the handle of her teacup so tightly she feared it might break, so she quickly set it back down. "He's right; I'm very worried. If this had happened when Titus was at home, he could have been hurt."

"You're right, but God was looking out for Titus because he was here with us and not in the trailer."

"Have the police been called? Did they catch the person who broke in?" Fannie picked up her teacup again and took a sip, hoping it would help calm her down.

"Allen said he called the sheriff, and the sheriff thinks the person who broke in may have been looking for the money

211

Titus found in his phone shanty."

Fannie nearly choked on the tea in her mouth. "What money? What's this all about, Zach?"

Zach ran his fingers down the side of his face. "I'm not really sure, Mom. Allen just said Titus had found some money, and that they suspect it may have been stolen. If that's the case, then whoever stole the money and hid it in Titus's phone shanty might have come looking for it while he was gone."

A jolt of fear coursed through Fannie's body. She pushed her chair aside and hurried across the room.

"Where are you going?" Zach called when she reached the door.

"Out to the field to speak with your daed. He needs to have a talk with Titus and convince him to come home where he belongs."

—ɯ—

Pembroke, Kentucky

When Titus finished work for the day, Nelson asked if he needed a ride home.

"Guess I do," Titus replied. "Since I rode here with Allen this morning, and my horse is in the barn at my place, I figured I'd have to walk home this afternoon."

"There's no need for that," Nelson said. "I heard Suzanne tell Mom that she's planning to take some of her hanging baskets over to the greenhouse. Guess all the ones they had there have sold, so they need more. Since the greenhouse is on the way to your place, I'm sure Suzanne wouldn't mind giving you a ride home."

"Okay, I'll go up to the house and ask her now. See you tomorrow morning." Titus headed out the door.

He found Suzanne out by the barn, putting a hanging

basket full of petunias into the back of her buggy. "Do you want some help?" he called.

She smiled. "I appreciate the offer, but this is the last one I need to load."

"Nelson mentioned that you'll be going over to the greenhouse, and since it's on the way to my place, I was wondering if you'd mind giving me a ride home."

Suzanne shook her head. "I don't mind. In fact I'm ready to go right now."

"That's great." Titus climbed into the passenger's side of the buggy.

When Suzanne took her seat on the driver's side, he smiled and said, "I appreciate this. I don't mind walking, but I'm tired and still have to clean up the mess in my trailer."

"I'd stay and help, but I need to get these flowers delivered to the greenhouse before they close for the day."

"That's okay," Titus said. "I'll be going over to the Beilers' for supper this evening, and Esther said she'd come over after we eat and help me clean up the place."

"Oh okay." Suzanne glanced at Titus, then quickly looked away. "Uh. . .did you see your ex-girlfriend when you were in Pennsylvania?"

He shook his head. "As far as I know, Phoebe's still in California."

"Oh. I thought maybe she came home for your mamm's party."

"Nope. Just her folks were there."

"Oh, I see."

They rode in silence the rest of the way, and when they arrived at Titus's place, Suzanne halted her horse at the hitching rail. "Mind if I take a look at the horse you found?"

"Nope. Don't mind at all. If his owner hasn't come for him yet, he'll be in the barn where I put him last night."

Titus led the way to the stall where the horse lay sleeping.

"That's the same horse that was running wild on the road," Suzanne said. "I was worried about it getting hit or causing an accident, so I'm glad he found his way to your place where he's been kept safe."

Titus started walking toward the barn door, knowing Suzanne was in a hurry to go. As they both stepped out of the barn, a truck pulling a horse trailer entered the yard. A middle-aged man wearing a cowboy hat got out. "I understand you found my horse," he said, approaching Titus.

Titus nodded. "He's in the barn. I'll get him for you."

"I appreciate you taking care of him for me," the man said. "How much do I owe for your trouble?"

"You don't owe me anything." Titus motioned to Suzanne. "I can't speak for her, though. It was her buggy your horse ran into the other night."

The man turned to Suzanne. "If your buggy was damaged I'd be happy to pay for the repairs."

She shook her head. "There was no damage. It scared me; that's all."

"All right then. Guess I'll get my horse loaded into the trailer and head out. Thanks again for all you've done."

Titus smiled. "You're welcome."

"I understand that Callie had some *busslin*," Suzanne said after the man left with his horse.

"That's right; she had four kittens to be exact," Titus said.

"How come you never mentioned it to me?" she asked.

"Thought I had."

"No. I heard about it from Esther."

"Guess I must have forgot."

"Can I see them?"

"Sure. They're in a box near the back of the barn. Let's go take a look."

Titus led the way, and when they came to the box, Suzanne leaned over and stroked the top of Callie's head. "You have some cute little busslin," she murmured.

"Did you know she was pregnant when you gave her to me?" Titus asked.

Her forehead wrinkled as she looked up at him. " 'Course not. This is just as big a surprise to me as it must have been to you. Besides, you've had the cat for a while now, so she may have found a mate since she's been living here."

Titus frowned. "Don't know what I'm gonna do with the kittens once they're weaned, 'cause I sure don't need five cats hanging around."

"They'd help keep the mice down."

"Maybe so, but I still don't care much for cats, and I don't need five of 'em here, making trouble all the time."

"I'm sure you'll be able to find them good homes." Suzanne picked up one of the kittens and held it close to her face. "It's so soft and cuddly. Makes me wish one of our cats would have a batch of kittens soon."

"You can have one of these if you like."

"Maybe, but I may wait and see if Frisky has any kittens this year first." She moved toward the barn door. "I'd better go, or the greenhouse will be closed by the time I get there. When you see Esther this evening, tell her I said hello," Suzanne called as she hurried out to her buggy.

"I will."

When Suzanne climbed into her buggy and headed down the driveway, Titus turned toward the trailer. *Guess I'd better head inside and get a few things picked up so I can take a shower and get over to the Beilers' by six.*

He hurried inside, and had just finished cleaning up some of the things in his bedroom, when he heard footsteps on the back porch. Thinking Suzanne must have come back, he went to answer the door. Two middle-aged men—one heavyset with thinning blond hair, and the other shorter and stocky with thick, wavy brown hair—forced their way into the trailer.

"We want to know where our money is," the shorter man said, pointing a gun at Titus. "It was in the phone shanty out back, but when we came here lookin' for it, we discovered that it was gone. Have you seen it?"

Titus gulped in a quick breath as he took a step back. "It. . . it was there, but I took it out."

The other man stepped forward and grabbed Titus by his shirt collar. "You'd better tell us where it is, or you won't live to see tomorrow."

CHAPTER 31

Paradise, Pennsylvania

Fannie raced into the field, frantically waving her hands. "Abraham, stop what you're doing! We need to talk!"

Abraham climbed down from the hay mower and cupped his hands around his mouth. "What's that you're sayin'?"

She motioned for him to come over.

"What's wrong?" Abraham asked as he stepped up to the fence. "You look umgerennt."

"I'm very upset. Zach just came by and said he'd talked to Allen, and Titus found some money, and. . .and his place was broken into, and I'm worried that—"

Abraham held up his hand. "Slow down, Fannie. You're talking so fast I can barely understand what you're saying."

Fannie took a deep breath and started over. "Sometime before Titus came here for my birthday party, he found some money in his phone shanty. Then while he was here, someone broke into the trailer and made a big mess." She reached over the fence and clutched Abraham's arm. "The sheriff's been contacted, but I don't think it's safe for our son to be there anymore. You need to call Titus and talk him into moving back home!"

217

"Calm down, Fannie," Abraham said. "I'm not going to do that."

"Why not?"

"Because Titus wouldn't appreciate us treating him like a boppli. Besides, if the sheriff's been notified, then he's probably investigating things."

"That might be so, but Titus could still be in danger."

Abraham rubbed the bridge of his nose and squinted. "You may be right, but you know what, Fannie?"

"What?"

"The way things are goin' in our world today, none of us is ever really safe. We could be hit by a car when we're ridin' in our buggy; we could be struck by lightning while we're out in the fields; we could be—"

"Okay, okay, I get your point, but that doesn't mean I'm not worried about Titus."

"Don't waste your time on worry, Fannie. Pray. Pray that God will keep Titus safe, and that the sheriff will find the person who broke into the trailer."

—◆—

Pembroke, Kentucky

"Now where's that money?" The shorter of the two men glared at Titus, his beady blue eyes unwavering as he pointed his stubby finger at Titus's chest.

"It. . .it's not here in the trailer." Titus's face heated, and a trickle of sweat rolled down his forehead. He couldn't believe this was happening to him.

"Where is it, then?" The heavyset man slammed Titus against the door. Searing pain shot from his head all the way down his back.

"It. . .it's in the bank."

The man growled and punched Titus in the stomach, causing him to double over. "You'd better not be lyin' to me."

"I'm not."

The other man stepped forward and shoved Titus against the small table beside the sofa.

Titus wobbled but managed to keep his balance. *Dear Lord,* he prayed, *help me know what to do.*

"That money belongs to us," the bigger man said. "You've got no right to it!"

Titus knew he needed some help, and he needed it quickly. He groped in his pocket, feeling for his cell phone. It wasn't there. *What'd I do with it? Could I have left it at work today?*

The sound of buggy wheels crunching on the gravel drifted in through the window, so Titus edged closer to the window to look out. *Oh no. It's Suzanne. What's she doing back here?*

"What are ya lookin' at, kid?" the shorter man asked.

Titus jerked his head. "Uh. . .nothing."

The other man grabbed Titus by his suspenders, nearly lifting him off the floor. "Let's go. You're takin' us to the bank, and you're gonna get our money right now!"

Titus didn't think he had the nerve to walk into the bank with these men and withdraw the money, but he figured he didn't have any other choice. He just wished Suzanne wasn't out in the yard. He didn't want her involved in this; she could be in danger.

He jerked the door open and called, "Get out of here, Suzanne! Schnell!"

"Now what'd ya do that for, you stupid kid?"

Titus felt a sharp blow to the back of his head; then his world went dark.

—⁓—

It didn't take Suzanne long to realize that Titus was in trouble.

The heavyset man who'd hit Titus was obviously an intruder. Could he be the same person who'd broken into the trailer while Titus was in Pennsylvania? Could this have something to do with the money Titus had found?

With heart pounding and hands sweating so badly she could barely hold on to the reins, Suzanne got her horse and buggy moving quickly and raced out of the yard. She wanted to stay and see if Titus was okay, but first she needed to get to a phone and call for help. Since the Beilers' place was the closest, that's where she would go.

When she arrived a short time later, she raced to the house and pounded on the door.

Esther answered Suzanne's knock, and she quickly told her friend what had happened.

"Ach, my!" Esther exclaimed. "Now I know why Titus is late for supper. We were beginning to wonder if he'd forgotten." She clasped Suzanne's arm. "We'd better run out to the phone shanty and call the sheriff right now."

When they returned to the house a short time later, Suzanne explained to Esther's folks all that had happened. "I'm worried about Titus," she said. "I'm going back to his place to see if he's okay."

"I'm going with you," Esther put in.

Esther's father, Henry, shook his head firmly. "I cannot allow that, girls. The man who hit Titus is obviously dangerous. We need to let the sheriff handle this."

Suzanne knew Henry was right, but she felt almost sick thinking about what had happened to Titus and wondering if he'd been seriously hurt. She paced back and forth on the Beilers' front porch until she heard sirens heading in the direction of Titus's place and knew it must be the sheriff.

With no thought for her safety, Suzanne darted down the porch steps, untied her horse from the hitching rail, and climbed into her buggy. Taking up the reins, she directed Dixie onto the road.

When she arrived at Titus's place, she saw that the sheriff and several of his men had the trailer surrounded and were calling for those inside to come out.

When there was no response, two of the sheriff's deputies cautiously entered the house.

Suzanne held her breath and waited to see what would happen.

Several minutes went by; then one of the deputies stepped out of the trailer. "There's no one inside except Titus, and he's lying on the floor with his head bleeding. You'd better call for an ambulance right away," he called to the sheriff.

Suzanne's heart pounded as she leaped from the buggy. *Dear Lord, please don't let Titus be dead.*

CHAPTER 32

Suzanne picked up a magazine and thumbed through a couple of pages. She'd been sitting in the hospital waiting room for the last hour, waiting to hear how Titus was doing. Knowing he'd need someone to go to the hospital with him, after the sheriff had called for the ambulance, she'd put her horse in Titus's barn and ridden with Titus.

Someone touched Suzanne's shoulder. She jumped up from the chair and whirled around, surprised to see Esther and her parents.

"We came as soon as we got your phone message," Esther said. "How's Titus?"

Suzanne shrugged. "I haven't heard anything yet, and I'm really worried. What if he's—" Her voice caught on the sob rising in her throat.

"You took a chance going over to his place when I told you not to," Henry said. "You could also be in the examining room right now; not just Titus."

"I. . .I couldn't help it. I needed to know whether he was all right."

"Why'd you go over there in the first place?" Dinah asked.

"I was on my way home from the greenhouse and decided to stop and see if I could help him clean up the mess in the trailer." Suzanne drew in a shaky breath. "I hope Titus will be okay."

Esther reached for Suzanne's hand and gave her fingers a gentle squeeze. "We just need to keep the faith and pray for him."

"Who were those men, and why'd they want to hurt Titus?" Henry asked.

"I'm not sure, but from what I heard the sheriff say while we were waiting for the ambulance, I think it has something to do with the money Titus found in his phone shanty." Suzanne paused for a breath. "By the time the sheriff got to Titus's place, the men were gone. They'd just run off and left Titus bleeding on the living room floor."

Dinah's eyes widened. "If those men aren't caught, they might come back or try to hurt someone else."

"Not to worry," Allen said, stepping into the waiting room. "I just spoke with the sheriff, and the men have been caught. They were found hiding in the woods." He looked down at Suzanne and smiled. "Thanks for letting me know about Titus. How's he doing, do you know?"

She shook her head. "I haven't heard a thing since they took him in."

"I'm going up to the nurse's station and see what I can find out, and then I'm going to phone Titus's brother Zach so he can let his folks and the rest of the family know. I'll be back soon." Allen paused and pulled a cell phone from his pocket. "This belongs to Titus. He left it in my truck this morning. Too bad he didn't have it with him when those men showed up at the trailer. He might have been able to call for help." He turned and hurried from the room.

Suzanne sucked in another deep breath and tried to relax. If she felt this bad about Titus, she could only imagine how Esther must feel.

"Do you think Titus's folks will come here when they get the news?" Esther asked her mother.

Dinah nodded. "I'd travel any distance if one of my kinner had been hurt."

"It would be nice to meet Titus's folks," Esther said, "but not under these conditions."

Suzanne shuddered. She couldn't imagine how horrible it would be for his parents if they traveled all this way only to be told that their son was dead.

Stop thinking negative thoughts, she scolded herself. *Pray, and thank God in advance for Titus's healing.*

—✺—

Paradise, Pennsylvania

Fannie had just sat down on the sofa beside Abraham, hoping to read awhile before going to bed, when the door flew open and Zach rushed into the room, his eyes wide and his face glistening with sweat.

"What's wrong? You look umgerennt. Has something happened?" Abraham asked.

"I am upset. Something pretty terrible has happened." Zach paced the floor for several seconds; then he finally took a seat in the rocking chair across from them and drew in a couple of deep breaths. "I don't want to frighten you, but I just had a phone call from Allen, letting me know that Titus is in the hospital in Hopkinsville."

Fannie dropped her book and sat up straight. "What's happened? Why's Titus in the hospital?"

Zach explained all that he'd heard, and ended by saying,

"Allen spoke with one of the nurses, but she wasn't able to give him any information about Titus's condition."

Fannie jumped up. "This wouldn't have happened if he hadn't moved!" She trembled as she turned to face Abraham. "We have to go to Kentucky!"

Abraham nodded grimly. "You're right. We'll leave right away."

—⚋—

Hopkinsville, Kentucky

Titus moaned and opened his eyes. A middle-aged woman wearing a white uniform stood beside his bed. "Wh–where am I?"

"You're in the hospital." She placed her hand gently on his shoulder. "You have a concussion and a pretty deep gash on the back of your head. You'll have to stay in the hospital a few days for observation."

He moaned again. "No wonder my head hurts so much."

"There's a young man out in the hall who says he's your friend. Would you like to see him?"

"Sure."

The nurse left the room, and Allen entered a few seconds later. A deep frown etched his forehead as he moved toward Titus's bed. "I'm really sorry about this. I should never have let you go home alone."

"It's not your fault. You had no idea the men who ransacked the trailer would come back."

"I've talked to the sheriff, so I know the men have been caught, but I have no idea what happened before the sheriff came. Do you feel up to filling me in?"

"The men have been caught?"

Allen nodded. "After one of them slugged you on the head,

they took off. But the sheriff's deputies caught them hiding in the woods behind your place. They're in jail now, and the sheriff will be questioning them about the money they hid." Allen took a seat in one of the chairs beside Titus's bed. "It's a good thing we haven't spent any of that money, because I'm sure now that it was stolen."

Titus tried to sit up, but it hurt too much, so he lay there with his eyes closed, trying to remember all that had happened. "Everything seems kind of hazy, but I remember getting ready to go to Esther's for supper, and then..." He paused and rubbed his forehead. "Then two men showed up and demanded that I tell 'em where the money was."

"What'd you say?"

"Said it was in the bank." Titus grimaced, as the details became clearer. "One of them shoved me real hard, and the other one said I'd have to take 'em to the bank and get the money. Then I heard a horse and buggy pull into the yard, and when I saw that it was Suzanne, I shouted a warning to her. That must have been when I got hit on the head, because I don't remember anything after that." His eyes snapped open. "Where's Suzanne? Is she okay?"

"She's fine. She and Esther, as well as Esther's folks, are in the waiting room." Allen glanced toward the door. "I think Suzanne was really worried about you, because the sheriff told me that she insisted on riding to the hospital with you in the ambulance."

"Tell her I said thanks."

"If you'd like to tell her yourself, I'll go ask her to come in."

"Maybe later. I'm tired and my head hurts too much to talk anymore right now."

"Okay. I'll leave you alone to rest." Allen stood. "Oh, I forgot to mention. I phoned Zach and asked him to let your family know what happened. I'm sure your folks will hire a driver and come to Kentucky right away."

Titus moaned. "That's just great. If Mom sees me in the hospital, she'll insist that I move back home. Well, I won't do it. Kentucky's my home now, and I'm stayin' put."

CHAPTER 33

Fannie's heart pounded as she and Abraham hurried down the hall toward Titus's hospital room. They'd hired a driver to bring them to Kentucky, and it had taken them over twelve hours to get here. She was not only tired and stiff from riding in the van so long, but she was also apprehensive about what they'd learn when they saw Titus.

"Don't look so glum," Abraham said, as they approached the door. "From what we were told, Titus's injuries aren't life threatening."

"I know, and I'm grateful for that, but it upsets me to know he was hurt by those men, and I shudder to think of how much worse it could have been."

He nodded. "We have much to be thankful for, because the Lord was surely watching out for our son."

Fannie paused at the door, and tears gathered in her eyes. She blinked several times, to keep them from spilling over. "Are you going to help me convince Titus to come back home with us once he's well enough to travel?"

Abraham shrugged. "Let's not talk about that right now.

Let's put on a happy face and say hello to our son."

—ᴍᴍ—

When the door to Titus's room opened and his folks stepped in, he blinked a couple of times. "Mom. Dad. I figured you'd come."

Mom moved quickly to the side of his bed, and Dad followed. "How badly are you hurt?" Dad asked.

"I have a concussion and a gash on the back of my head, but I'll live. 'Course, I have a chunk of hair missing now because they had to shave it in order to stitch up the wound. Guess I'll have to wear my hat all the time until my hair grows back." Titus forced himself to smile. He figured he'd better make light of the situation so Mom wouldn't be too upset.

"Tell us what happened," Dad said as he and Mom seated themselves in the chairs beside Titus's bed.

Titus explained all that had transpired, being careful not to make it sound as frightening as it actually had been.

Mom's eyebrows drew together as she reached for Titus's hand. "You need to move back home. It's not safe for you here."

"The men have been caught, and there's no reason for me to move back."

"Oh, but I think—"

Dr. Osmond entered the room.

"These are my parents," Titus said, motioning to Mom and Dad. "They came here from Pennsylvania because they were worried about me."

"And well they should be." The doctor moved closer to Titus's bed. "I'm going to release you to go home, but only if you promise to take it easy for the next several days."

"Oh he will," Mom spoke up, "because we're going to be there to make sure that he does."

"That's right," Dad said with a nod. "We'll go home with

him and stay until he's well enough to manage on his own."

Titus appreciated the fact that his folks had come, but he was worried about what they would think when they saw the trailer. It was bad enough that the place was so cramped; now thanks to the men who'd broken in, everything was a mess.

—⁓—

Pembroke, Kentucky

"This place is a disaster," Suzanne said to Esther as they worked together to get things cleaned up in Titus's trailer.

Esther wrinkled her nose. "I can't believe those horrible men did this, can you?"

Suzanne shook her head. "What I really can't believe is that they hurt Titus. He did nothing but try to warn me that they were here."

Esther stared at Suzanne. "You like him, don't you?"

"Who?"

"Titus. Who else are we talking about?"

Suzanne focused on sweeping the floor and said nothing.

"I saw how worried you were about Titus the night we were at the hospital."

"Of course I was worried. Titus was hurt, and I didn't know how badly."

Esther set the broken dish she'd been holding on the kitchen table and stepped in front of Suzanne. "Do you like him or not?"

Suzanne looked up. "Titus and I have had our share of differences, but as I've gotten to know him better, I've come to realize that he's really a caring person. Even the way he cared for that runaway horse let me know what type of person he was." Suzanne dropped her gaze to the floor. "I do like him, but only as a friend."

"Would you like to be more than friends? Do you wish you were being courted by him?"

"I know how much you care for Titus, and I wouldn't think of trying to come between you."

"I was interested in Titus at first, but after spending some time with him, I've recognized that we'll probably never be serious about each other."

"Why not?" Suzanne asked, fixing her gaze on Esther.

"We don't have much in common, and he's really not my type. So if you're interested in him, you have my blessing." Esther bent to pick up another piece of broken glass and tossed it in the garbage.

"Are you sure about that?"

Esther nodded. "I don't think he's serious about me, either."

"Well, even if I were interested in Titus, he'd never be interested in me," Suzanne muttered.

"How do you know?"

"Because I look like his ex-girlfriend. Besides, I can't cook, and what man wants a woman who can't cook?"

"I've told you before that I'd be happy to teach you."

"I guess it would be easier to learn from you than Mom." Suzanne sighed deeply. "When it comes to cooking, I've always felt like a failure next to her."

Esther slipped her arm around Suzanne's waist. "You're not a failure. I'm sure you can learn to cook, and if you let me teach you, I'll try to be very patient."

"We'll see." Suzanne glanced out the window. "A van just pulled in. Looks like Titus and his folks are here now."

"Oh great. We're not done cleaning the kitchen yet."

"At least we got the rest of the house picked up, and it shouldn't take us long to finish in here." Suzanne motioned to the few broken dishes that were still on the floor.

"Let's go meet Titus's parents and see how he's doing, and

then we'll finish cleaning in here," Esther said.

They hurried from the room, and Suzanne opened the back door just as Titus and his parents stepped onto the porch.

"I'm surprised to see you both here,"Titus said when they'd entered the house.

"We heard you might be coming home today, so we came over to clean up the house before you arrived," Esther replied.

"That was nice of you." Titus motioned to his parents. "These are my folks, Abraham and Fannie. Mom, Dad, meet Esther and Suzanne."

Fannie and Abraham shook hands with Esther first, saying it was nice to meet her. Fannie acted a little cool toward Esther, though. When she shook Suzanne's hand, she stared at her strangely. Suzanne wondered if there was something about her that Titus's mother didn't like. Could it be because she reminded her of Titus's ex-girlfriend?

"It was nice of you both to clean up the place," Fannie said, directing her comment to Suzanne, "but now that I'm here, I can take over the job."

Suzanne glanced at Esther, wondering if she felt Fannie's coolness.

Esther merely smiled and said, "We're almost done. We just have a few more dishes to pick up in the kitchen."

"Oh, I see. I guess you can do that while we get Titus settled in his room." Fannie glanced around. "This place is so small. Does it even have a bedroom?"

"It's at the back of the trailer, but I'm not going to bed." Titus motioned to the sofa in the living room. "Why don't we have a seat so we can visit awhile?"

Sensing Fannie's hesitation, Suzanne said, "I think Esther and I had better finish cleaning the kitchen, and then we'll be on our way." She smiled at Titus. "You look much better than when I saw you in the hospital. How are you feeling today?"

"My head still hurts, but I'm doing okay."

"Remember now, the doctor said you'll have to take it easy for several days." Fannie put her hand on Titus's shoulder. "That's why your daed and I will be staying to help out and see that you behave yourself."

Titus's face colored, obviously embarrassed by his mother's comment making it seem as if he were a child.

"I guess we'd better get back to work. It was nice meeting you." Suzanne smiled at Titus's parents.

"Nice meeting you, too." Abraham returned her smile, but Fannie only nodded before taking a seat on the sofa beside Titus.

Suzanne moved toward the kitchen. "Are you coming, Esther?"

"Of course." Esther followed Suzanne into the kitchen.

"For whatever reason, Titus's mamm doesn't like me," Suzanne whispered to Esther.

"What makes you think that?"

"Didn't you see the strange way she looked at me? She didn't want to visit with us either."

"She acted kind of cool toward me, too, but I think she's just concerned about Titus and probably thought visiting might make him tired."

"Maybe so." Suzanne pushed the garbage can into the center of the room and started picking up the rest of the broken dishes as fast as she could.

—∽∞∽—

Shortly after Esther and Suzanne left, Mom turned to Titus and said, "No wonder you like it here and don't want to leave."

"What do you mean?" Titus asked.

"That young woman with auburn hair reminds you of Phoebe, doesn't she?"

Titus nodded. "She did at first, but since I've gotten to know her—"

"You're staying in Kentucky because of her, not the other young woman, am I right?"

" 'Course not. Suzanne and I aren't even courting. It's Esther I've gone out with a couple of times, but I'm not really serious about her, either."

"Then why don't you come home?" Mom asked.

"Because I want to start a new life here. I like it in Kentucky, and there's nothing for me in Pennsylvania anymore."

"Your family's there."

"I realize that, and as much as I miss everyone, I need to make it on my own without anyone in the family telling me what to do or how to do it."

"Titus is right," Dad put in. "He needs to make his own way, just like I did when I was his age."

Mom sat with her arms folded, staring straight ahead. After several minutes, she turned to Titus and said, "I have no objections to you making it on your own, but I think you could do that just as well if you were at home."

Titus's jaw clenched. He was too tired to argue, but before Mom and Dad left for home, he'd try to make Mom understand that he wasn't going back to Pennsylvania, and that no matter what she said, he planned to make Kentucky his permanent home.

CHAPTER 34

Y ou two can have my bed tonight, and I'll sleep on the sofa in the living room," Titus told his folks after they'd finished eating a late lunch.

"This place is much too small for even one person to be living in," Mom said. "After looking around, I've discovered a lot of things you need."

"Like what?"

She picked up a piece of paper and a pen she'd found in a kitchen drawer. "I'm going to make a list for you. Let's see now. . .pie pans, a spice rack, rolling pin, mixing bowls, and—"

Titus held up his hand. "I'm not planning to do any baking, Mom, so you don't need to get carried away with that list you're making."

Her forehead creased. "I just thought—"

"In fact, there's really no need for you to make a list at all, because I'm getting along fine with the things I have now."

Mom opened her mouth like she might argue the point, but the rumble of a truck pulling into the yard interrupted their conversation.

"Looks like Allen's here," Titus said, going to the window to look out.

When Allen entered the trailer moments later, they all took seats in the living room.

"I came by to see how you're feeling." Allen clasped Titus's shoulder and gave it a squeeze.

"Other than my head still hurting, I'm doing okay," Titus replied. "Just glad to be out of the hospital and back here again."

Allen smiled. "I also wanted to let you know what I learned today from the sheriff about the money you found."

Titus's interest was piqued. "I'm anxious for you to fill me in."

"We'd like to hear it, too," Dad said.

Allen leaned forward, resting his elbows on his knees. "About a month before Titus came to Kentucky, two men broke into an elderly couple's home in Tennessee and stole their money."

Mom's eyes widened. "What in the world would an elderly couple be doing with that much money in their house?"

"I don't know, but I guess one of the men—Harry's his name—used to do yard work for the couple. When he found out they had a large sum of cash in the house, he and his buddy, Marvin, tied the old folks up and took their money. The two men were on the run, looking for a remote area to hide out, when they saw a sheriff's car and got scared. Then, finding what appeared to be an abandoned trailer, they hid the money in the phone shanty here, and took off, planning to come back to get it when they felt it was safe.

"While Titus was in Pennsylvania, the men returned to the phone shanty to get the money. When it wasn't there, they broke into the trailer and searched for it. Of course they didn't find it there, but they soon realized that someone was now living in the trailer, so they came back shortly after Titus arrived home from Pennsylvania. Of course, we all know what happened after that."

"The money will have to be returned to the couple," Titus was quick to say.

Allen nodded. "That's right, but there's a reward of a thousand dollars for finding the money, so that will be yours."

Titus shook his head. "Now that I know what happened, I can't take that old couple's money. It wouldn't be right."

"I think it would hurt their feelings if you don't accept it. They're very grateful and want you to have the reward."

"Oh, all right," Titus finally agreed.

Mom looked over at Allen and frowned. "I can't believe you'd expect Titus to rent this place from you. It's in horrible shape and hardly fit for a person to live in."

"I feel bad about that," Allen said, "but when I bought the place, I didn't realize it was as run-down as it was. Just bought it for the property as an investment."

"You should have seen it before some of the folks in our community came and helped me clean and do some repairs," Titus said. "It looks much better now. Or at least it did before those men broke in."

Mom wrinkled her nose. "I can't imagine it looking much worse than it does now."

"Well it did, believe me." Titus motioned to the sofa. "All the furniture was worn out, but some of the women covered it with slipcovers."

"Tell her about the hole in the roof and how you fell through, trying to put a patch on it so it wouldn't leak," Allen said.

Deep wrinkles formed in Mom's forehead. "Were you hurt, Titus?"

"Just scratched up my legs a bit. Nothing serious." *Sure wish Allen hadn't brought that up.*

"But you could have been seriously hurt, and I think—"

Allen rose to his feet. "I need to get going. Please let me know if you need anything."

Titus smiled. "I will."

"I'll be by again soon to check on you."

"Thanks, I appreciate that."

Allen told Titus's folks good-bye, and headed out the door.

Soon after he left, Titus heard a desperate-sounding *meow* on the porch. "That must be Callie. She has four kittens to feed, so she's probably hungry and waiting to be fed."

"Tell me where you keep the cat food, and I'll feed her," Mom said.

"Her food's in the barn on a shelf near the box where she has her babies."

"I'm sure I can find it." Mom hurried out the door.

Titus was glad for a few minutes alone to talk to Dad. It seemed like Dad hadn't been able to get in more than a few words with Mom talking so much.

"I wish Mom wouldn't hover over me all the time," Titus complained. "She treats me like I'm still a little boy. Doesn't she realize I'm a grown man now, and I want to live my own life without being told what to do?"

"Don't let your mamm upset you," Dad said. "As I'm sure you know, she's had a hard enough time dealing with you moving from home. Finding out that this place had been broken into and that you'd been hurt didn't help things any."

"Sure hope the whole time you're here she won't hover over me and try to convince me to move back home."

"If she does, I'll put a stop to it," Dad said. He gave Titus's arm a light tap. "I think the fact that you and Timothy are our youngest kinner, coupled with her having had you in midlife, has caused her to worry more about both of you."

"Worrying won't change anything. She needs to give me a

chance to prove myself."

Dad gave a nod. "I agree. Be patient, and give her a little more time to adjust to the idea that you're out on your own."

"So what do you think of the little bit of Kentucky you've seen so far?" Titus asked.

"It's nice. Not nearly so congested with people and cars as what we have in Lancaster County."

"That's one of the things I like about it here," Titus said. "That, and the fact that there are lots of places to hunt, fish, and ride my horse. There's also good, fertile land that can be bought for much less than what you'd pay back home."

"Are you thinkin' of buying some land?"

Titus nodded. "Think I might buy this place from Allen. The trailer isn't much, but there's some acreage with it that could be farmed—if I ever decide to do any farming, that is."

"I'm guessin' Timothy would be interested in farming here, but knowing how close Hannah is to her mamm, I doubt he'd ever move."

"I know what you mean."

"Do you have it in your mind to stay in Kentucky, even if all your family remains in Pennsylvania?" Dad asked.

"That's my plan now, but I guess it could change if things don't work out for me here."

"You mean with your job?"

"That, and whether I'm able to buy this place or not."

"Do you need a loan? Because if you do, I'd be happy to—"

"I appreciate the offer, Dad, but I really want to do this on my own. I'm making pretty good money working for Isaac Yoder, and Allen's offered to let me lease this place with the option to buy."

"That's great." Dad gave Titus's arm another light tap. "Remember now, if you change your mind or need anything, just let me know."

—ᘓ—

When Suzanne entered the woodshop that afternoon, she found Nelson on his knees, sanding some cabinet doors. She stood several seconds, breathing deeply of the aromas in the shop. Most people would have turned up their nose at wood being sanded and cut, but not her. She loved everything about being here, and her fingers itched to create something beautiful from the pieces of wood stacked in one corner of the room.

"Did you need something?" Nelson asked, looking up at her with a curious expression.

"Just came out to see if you needed some help. I'm sure with Titus not being able to work right now you must be getting behind on things."

"You're right, I am. I was going to ask Russell to sand these while I cut some wood, but he's busy mowing the lawn."

"I can do the sanding for you," she said.

He quirked an eyebrow. "You sure about that? It can get awful dusty, and it'll wear your fingernails down."

"I don't care about that. My nails are already worn down from all the gardening I do." She held her hands out to him. "I'd really like to help."

"All right then; here you go." He handed her a piece of sandpaper. "Now make sure you sand with the grain of the wood and not across the grain."

She frowned. "I know how to sand, Nelson. I've watched you and Grandpa do it many times. And don't forget about the birdfeeders I've made."

"A birdfeeder doesn't have to be perfect, but cabinets do." Nelson motioned to the row of cabinets sitting across the room. "Those are being done for a lawyer who lives in Hopkinsville. His wife's real picky, so every cabinet door needs to be done very well."

Irritation welled in Suzanne. Nelson obviously doubted her ability to do a good job. Well, she'd show him how well she could sand! If she did a good enough job, maybe he'd let her do something more than sand a few doors.

CHAPTER 35

On Saturday morning, Titus's folks got ready to head for home. Mom turned tearful eyes on Titus and said, "Please, come for a visit whenever you can."

"I'll try, but with me being off work for the past week I'm sure Nelson's behind on things, and I probably won't be able to get away for some time."

"Maybe you can come home for Thanksgiving or Christmas," Dad said.

Mom bobbed her head. "It wouldn't be the same without you."

"I'll have to wait and see how it goes." Titus peered out the living room window. "Looks like your driver's here."

Mom gave Titus a hug. "Take care of yourself, and call as often as you can so we'll know how you're doing."

"I will." Titus hugged Dad, too. "Have a safe trip, and tell the rest of the family I said hello."

Mom gave Titus one final hug; then she and Dad went out the door.

Titus stood on the porch as he watched his folks get into their driver's van. When the vehicle disappeared, he went inside and stretched out on the sofa with a sigh of relief. He appreciated them staying until he felt better, and he knew he'd miss Mom's good cooking. What he wouldn't miss was her hovering and constant badgering him about moving home.

He closed his eyes and rested awhile, then finally decided he ought to go over to the Beilers' store and talk to Esther. When Titus entered the store, he found Esther standing on a ladder, dusting some empty shelves.

"It's good to see you. How are you feeling?" Esther asked after she climbed down.

"The back of my head's still a little tender, but otherwise, I'm doing okay. I plan to go back to work on Monday."

"Are you sure you're up to that?" she asked with a look of concern.

"Jah. I've sat around letting my mamm wait on me long enough."

"How much longer will your folks be staying?"

"They left this morning."

"Oh, I see."

Titus leaned on the edge of the counter. "I heard there's going to be another singing tomorrow evening. I was wondering if you'd like to go with me."

Esther's face flushed, and she quickly averted his gaze. "I... uh...don't think I'll be going to the singing."

"How come?"

"I'd rather not go this time, that's all."

Titus stroked his chin. *What's going on? It seems strange that Esther's acting so disinterested, when not long ago she was practically flirting with me.*

"Are you sure you don't want to go?"

"I'm positive."

Titus figured it was best not to press the issue, so he said good-bye to Esther and left the store.

Think I'll ride over to the produce auction and see what's going on there, he decided. *I'm not in a hurry to go home and sit by myself for the rest of the day, anyway.*

———ᴍ———

Fairview, Kentucky

Suzanne had just sold four hanging baskets to one of her English neighbors when she spotted Titus heading her way. Her heart skipped a beat. She wished there was something she could do to make him notice her without being obvious. Maybe if she learned to cook as well as Esther did, Titus would see her in a different light.

"Are you feeling better?" Suzanne asked when he joined her by the flowers.

He nodded. "My folks left today, and I plan to be back at work on Monday morning."

"I'm sure Nelson will be glad to hear that." Suzanne figured that, with Titus returning to work and Grandpa taking over most of the bookwork again, Nelson probably wouldn't want her hanging around the shop anymore. She'd have to sneak out there after dark and work on some project of her own, the way she'd done several times in the past.

Titus motioned to the few hanging baskets she had left. "Looks like business is going well for you today."

"It has. In fact, I've been so busy since I got here that I haven't had a chance to buy myself any lunch."

"Would you like me to go inside and get something for you?" Titus offered.

Suzanne smiled. "I'd appreciate that."

"What would you like?"

"A hot dog, a bottle of water, and a bag of chips would be fine." She moved toward her cash box. "Let me give you some money."

Titus shook his head. "That's okay. I'll get it. Think I'll buy myself a hot dog, too."

"Feel free to eat your lunch inside before you bring mine out to me," she said. "Other than the folding chair I brought, there's really nowhere to sit. Besides, it's warm out today, so you'd probably be more comfortable eating at one of the picnic tables inside."

"I'm not worried about the heat or a place to sit, but I'll be back soon with your lunch." Titus hurried away.

When he returned a short time later, he had two hot dogs, a bag of chips, and two bottles of water. "Since you don't have any customers right now, why don't we take a seat in there to eat our lunch?" He motioned to his buggy, parked a short distance away.

She hesitated at first, wondering if she should leave her plants for that long. "I guess I can keep an eye out for customers from there," she finally said.

They took seats in his buggy, and when Titus closed his eyes to offer a silent prayer, she poked his arm and said, "Aren't you going to take off your hat?"

He frowned. "There's still a bald spot on the back of my head, and I'm sparing you the misery of looking at it."

"I'm sure it doesn't look that bad."

"Oh, yeah?" Titus jerked off his hat and turned his head so she could see the back of it.

Suzanne suppressed a giggle. He did look pretty silly with a hunk of hair missing.

"You're not saying anything." Titus turned around so he was facing her again. "It looks baremlich, doesn't it?"

"It's not terrible, but I can see why you might want to keep your hat on. Someone could think you'd faced the mirror the wrong way when you shaved this morning."

Titus's lips twitched, and then he leaned his head back and roared. "I like your sense of humor, Suzanne. In fact, the more time I spend with you, the more I like you."

She felt the heat of a blush cover her cheeks, but oh, it was nice to hear him say such a thing. "I. . .uh. . .like you, too," she murmured without looking at him. She was afraid if she did, he might be able to tell just how much she actually did care for him.

"Guess we'd better pray now so we can eat," Titus said.

They closed their eyes, and after their prayer, Titus told Suzanne the details about the money he'd found and about getting a reward.

"That's great. What are you going to do with it?" she asked.

"I'll probably put it in the bank."

"That sure was a frightening ordeal you went through," Suzanne said as they began to eat.

"It was, and when you showed up at my place, I was afraid for you, too."

A flush of heat cascaded over Suzanne's cheeks once more. It made her feel good to know he'd been concerned about her. Of course, he'd probably have hollered a warning to anyone who'd showed up that day.

"Did you hear that there's going to be another singing on Sunday evening?" she asked.

He drank some of his water and nodded. "I asked Esther if she'd like me to pick her up, but she said she wasn't planning to go."

"Oh? Did she say why?"

"Nope. Just said she wasn't going this time." He blotted his lips with the paper wrapped around the hot dog.

"Will you go to the singing anyway?"

He shook his head. "Probably not. Think I'll stay home and rest."

"Oh, I see." Suzanne hoped the disappointment she felt didn't show on her face. If neither Esther nor Titus would be at the singing, she guessed she wouldn't go either.

———

Los Angeles, California

"I'll be going home at the end of the month," Darlene told Phoebe as they headed down the beach toward the concession stand.

Phoebe halted and whirled around to face her friend. "You never mentioned going home for a visit. Is something special going on?"

Darlene shook her head. "I'm not going for a visit. I'm tired of living here, and I'm going home to stay."

Phoebe frowned. "I thought you liked California. It was your idea to come here, you know."

"I realize that, but I've changed my mind. I miss my family, and living in the English world isn't as exciting as I thought it would be."

Irritation welled in Phoebe's soul. "How am I supposed to pay the rent on our apartment if you're gone?"

"I figured you'd probably go back to Pennsylvania, too."

Phoebe shook her head vigorously. "There's nothing for me there anymore."

"What about your folks and the rest of the family?"

"If I moved back home, they'd be after me to join the church."

"Would joining the church be so bad? At one time, you said you were going to join, remember?"

"Of course I remember, but that was when Titus and I were courting. It's over between us, and he's living in Kentucky." Phoebe started walking again, a little faster this time. "You can go back to the Plain life if you want to, but I'm staying here!"

CHAPTER 36

Pembroke, Kentucky

On Monday morning when Titus entered the woodshop, he hesitated inside the door. It felt good to be back; he'd missed working in the shop, but he was surprised to find Isaac, going over the books. He was even more surprised to see Suzanne crouched on the floor with a piece of sandpaper in her hand, working on a cabinet door.

"Looks like I've been replaced," he said, kneeling beside her.

She shook her head. "Not a chance. I've only been helping out with some sanding because Nelson was getting behind."

"Ah, I see." Titus still couldn't get over how easy Suzanne had been to talk to at the produce auction the other day. When he was with Esther, he had to think of things to say. Since he and Esther didn't have much in common, it was difficult to make conversation.

Pushing his thoughts aside, Titus turned to Nelson and said, "I'd have been back here sooner, but the doctor said I couldn't start working again until today."

Nelson, who'd been staining some of the cabinets, slowly

shook his head. "It's not a problem. We got along okay, although it's good to have you back in the shop."

"That's right," Isaac put in, "and I'm happy to be back at my desk again."

"Now that you're both working here again, Suzanne's help won't be needed, and she'll have more time to do other things," Nelson added.

Suzanne abruptly stood. "I guess if I'm not needed here I'll head up to the house!" Without waiting for anyone's response, she tossed the piece of sandpaper down and rushed out of the shop.

Nelson looked at Titus and shrugged. "What can I say? My sister's been acting kind of strange here of late. But then to me, she's always seemed a bit strange."

Titus couldn't help but notice how upset Suzanne had looked when Nelson said her help was no longer needed. He wondered if she'd rather be sanding wood than doing household chores.

He bent to inspect the cabinet door she'd been sanding and was surprised to see what a top-notch job she'd done. It almost seemed like she'd had experience sanding.

—⁊⁊—

Paradise, Pennsylvania

"Aren't you going to do the breakfast dishes?" Abraham asked when Fannie remained at the kitchen table after breakfast was over. "You've always washed the dishes right away."

"I'm really tired today. I'll do them later."

Abraham frowned. "If you'd go to sleep at night instead of lying awake, worrying about Titus, you'd have the energy you need to get things done during the day." He motioned to the kitchen floor. "Looks like this hasn't been swept for a few days, and I'm gettin' low on clean shirts, so I'd appreciate it if you'd wash some clothes today."

Fannie yawned. "I'm planning to."

"Better not wait too long. I read in the paper that rain's in the forecast."

"Okay." She yawned again and poured them both a cup of coffee.

"Ever since we got home from Kentucky, you've done nothing but worry and fret." He touched her shoulder. "You can worry yourself silly about Titus, but it won't change a thing. Just give your worries to God, and let Him take care of our son."

She gave a slow nod. "I know you're right, but it's hard for me not to think about what those men did to him. With Titus living so far away, I struggle not to be anxious."

"I know, but it's not healthy to worry the way you've been doing. You ought to be more like Abby. *Sie druwwelt sich wehe nix.*"

"What do you mean she doesn't worry herself about anything? Everyone worries about something, Abraham."

"That may be so, but from what I can tell, she worries less than most, and she doesn't let things affect her the way you've done lately." He glanced at the battery-operated clock on the wall across the room. "I'd better get out to the fields, or Timothy will wonder what's happened to me."

"Okay. Don't work too hard, and have a good day."

Soon after Abraham left, Abby stopped by. "You look so tired, Mom," she said. "Haven't you been sleeping well?"

Fannie shook her head. "I've been worried about Titus, and it's hard for me to relax. Every time I close my eyes, I see him lying in that hospital bed with a bandage on his head."

Abby poured herself some coffee and took a seat in the chair beside Fannie. "Can I give you some advice that someone gave me once when I was worrying about things?"

250

"Sure."

"When going to bed at night you should empty the pockets of your mind, because if you go to sleep with worries, it'll drain your energy through the night."

"How am I supposed to empty the pockets of worry from my mind?" Fannie questioned.

"Simply say to yourself, 'I'm putting these worries into God's hands,' and then close your eyes and go to sleep."

"I wish it were that simple." Fannie took a sip of coffee.

"It can be simple if you remember what God says about worry." Abby smiled. "In Matthew 6:34 it says: 'Take therefore no thought for the morrow: for the morrow shall take thought for the things of itself.' And Psalm 55:22 says, 'Cast thy burden upon the Lord, and he shall sustain thee.' " She touched Fannie's arm and gave it a tender squeeze. "You need to do that, Mom. Hide God's Word in your heart and dwell on it until you fall asleep at night."

The tension Fannie had felt earlier began to disappear. "I know you're right, and I appreciate those reminders from God's Word. I do need to remember that our Father's in control, and that He's watching over Titus, as well as the rest of our family."

"Did you enjoy your time in Kentucky with Titus?" Abby asked.

"I certainly did. Just wish we could've stayed longer. I still miss him, you know."

"I'm sure he misses you, too, but it's good that he's making a life of his own and is enjoying his job there, don't you think?"

"Jah. It seems like Titus is becoming more responsible, too—more like Timothy in that regard."

"I just can't get over how much those two still look alike," Abby said, taking their conversation in a different direction. "Why, I'll never forget the time when the twins were bopplin and I got them mixed up while I was giving them a bath.

I ended up bathing the same boppli twice."

"Their personalities are different, though, and that makes it easy for most people to tell them apart."

"I remember once when we got the brilliant idea to tie a ribbon around Titus's ankle so we'd know it was him. That worked fine until I forgot to remove the ribbon when I bathed him. Of course it got soggy and fell off." Abby snickered. "Then there was the time that Leona, being just a young girl herself, came over to see the twins and suggested we put a blotch of green paint on Titus's toe. That worked fine for a while, until the paint wore off."

Fannie laughed so hard that tears rolled down her cheeks. It felt good to find a little humor in something. She'd been much too serious lately. "It's a good thing only one of our twins has moved to Kentucky, because I doubt that anyone there would be able to tell them apart."

Pembroke, Kentucky

Suzanne's mother had gone to an all-day quilting bee, so it was Suzanne's job to make lunch for the men today. Along with the sandwiches and hard-boiled eggs she planned to take out to them, she thought it would be nice to make some butterscotch pudding for their dessert. She'd use a box of the instant kind, figuring it wouldn't be too hard to make.

Following the directions on the box, she took out a metal bowl, the eggbeater, and some milk. Carefully, she measured the milk into the bowl and added the package of pudding.

Her nose twitched. "Yum. This sure smells good. I love the aroma of butterscotch."

When Suzanne placed the beater inside and started turning the handle, the bowl slid across the counter, and some of the pudding splashed out.

"This isn't working out so well," she mumbled, blotting the counter with some paper towels. She'd seen Mom use the eggbeater before, and the bowl had never slid around for her like that.

Suzanne pushed the bowl against her waist and started beating again. *Whoosh!*—the bowl slipped off the counter and fell on the floor, spilling pudding on her dress, down the cabinet, and onto the floor, where it seeped under the cabinet.

"That's just great," she fumed. Not only was the pudding ruined, but she'd have to clean the floor and would need to change her dress.

Suzanne wet the mop under the faucet and started with the floor. When that chore was done, she went up to her room to change.

Several minutes later, she returned to the kitchen, put the sandwiches in a plastic container, took the eggs she'd boiled earlier from the refrigerator, and grabbed a handful of cookies Mom had made yesterday. Then she placed everything in the lunch basket, picked up a jug of iced tea, and headed out the door.

When Suzanne entered the woodshop, Grandpa tipped his head and stared at her strangely. "Weren't you wearing a green dress earlier?"

"You're right. I was."

"Mind if I ask why you're wearing a blue dress now?"

"I had a little accident in the kitchen."

"Why am I not surprised?" Nelson said, rolling his eyes.

"Here's your lunch!" Suzanne placed the basket and jug of iced tea on the workbench with a huff.

"What'd you bring us?" Titus asked.

"Ham and cheese sandwiches, hard-boiled eggs, and chocolate chip cookies."

He grinned. "Sounds good."

Suzanne waited until the men had said their silent prayer. She was about to leave, when Titus picked up an egg and cracked it on his forehead. *Whoosh!*—runny egg spilled out of the shell, ran down his face, and dripped onto his shirt.

"Oh no!" Suzanne grabbed the roll of paper towels near the sink and handed it to Titus. "I'm so sorry."

Nelson slapped his leg and chuckled. "I've heard that raw eggs are supposed to be good for a person's hair, so maybe that runny egg will grow the missing hair back on your head," he said to Titus.

Titus mumbled something under his breath as he wiped the egg off his face; then he turned to Suzanne and said, "Did you give us raw eggs on purpose?"

"No, of course not. I really thought they were hard-boiled. I must have grabbed raw eggs by mistake, thinking they were the ones I'd boiled earlier."

"What made you crack that egg on your forehead?" Nelson asked. "Were you just *abweise*?"

"I was not showing off. I've always cracked eggs that way." Titus looked at Suzanne. "At least the ones I don't think are raw."

Suzanne was so embarrassed, she just wanted to hide. *I'll never get Titus's attention in a positive way if I keep messing up and making myself look bad in his eyes.*

Without waiting for the men to finish their lunch, she turned and rushed out the door.

CHAPTER 37

Los Angeles, California

Phoebe frowned as she stared at her meager breakfast—an overripe banana and a glass of water. It had been four weeks since Darlene had gone home, and Phoebe had been forced to take a second job during the evening at a convenience store in order to pay the rent on the apartment she'd shared with Darlene. The cost of living was much higher in California than it had been back home, and Phoebe's money was so tight that she'd had to cut back on everything and barely had enough to eat. Another frustration was that she didn't have any free time to do fun things such as going to the beach, shopping, or out to lunch. The few friends she'd made while living here all had steady boyfriends, so they couldn't be bothered with her anymore.

It was probably for the best. With two part-time jobs, she barely had enough time to sleep, let alone socialize or do anything fun.

Phoebe stared at the calendar on the kitchen wall and grimaced. It was hard to believe, but she'd been away from home over four months already. When she'd first come to

California, she'd expected her life to be easy and carefree, but things were getting more difficult every day.

She pushed away from the table and grunted as she tossed the banana peel at the garbage can and missed. "I don't care how bad it gets," she muttered. "I'm not about to admit defeat and go home!"

—◆—

Paradise, Pennsylvania

Fannie had just taken some throw rugs outside to hang on the line, when she spotted Arie Stoltzfus's horse and buggy coming up the lane. Except for the Sundays when they went to church, Fannie hadn't seen much of Arie lately. She wondered if Arie had been busy or was just keeping to herself.

"Wie geht's?" Fannie asked when Arie joined her under the clothesline.

"I've been better." From the slump of Arie's shoulders and her furrowed brows, Fannie knew Arie must be upset about something.

"What's wrong?" Fannie asked, feeling concern for her friend.

"I'm worried about Phoebe."

Fannie finished draping the rugs over the line and motioned to the house. "Let's go inside where it's cooler and you can tell me about it. The humidity today is so bad it hurts."

Once inside, they took seats at the kitchen table, and Fannie poured glasses of iced tea. "Are you still upset because Phoebe moved to California?" she asked.

Arie nodded slowly. "But I'm even more upset now because Phoebe's friend Darlene has come home—without Phoebe."

"Oh, I didn't realize that."

Arie took a sip of iced tea and blotted her lips on a napkin.

"This is so refreshing. Danki."

"You're welcome."

Arie sighed as she set the glass on the table. "Not only did my daughter choose to stay in California, but now she's living alone. To make matters worse, she won't answer any of my phone calls, and I can hardly sleep because I'm so worried about her." The dark circles beneath her eyes confirmed that she hadn't been sleeping well. "Short of a miracle, I don't think Phoebe will ever return to Pennsylvania and the Plain life."

"I know it's hard to have her living in another state," Fannie said. "It's been hard for me to accept Titus moving to Kentucky."

"It's different for you," Arie said. "Your son's joined the church and has settled down. My daughter's still going through her running-around years and may never return home and join the church."

Fannie placed her hand over Arie's. "You need to keep the faith and pray that God will touch Phoebe's heart and she'll decide to come home." Fannie couldn't believe she was saying such a thing. The truth was, she'd been glad when Phoebe left—at least until Titus had decided to leave, too. If Phoebe had stayed in Pennsylvania and joined the church, Titus would never have left home.

"It's not so easy to keep the faith," Arie said. "Especially when Phoebe won't answer my calls."

"You and your family weren't living here at the time," Fannie said, "but back when Naomi was a young woman dealing with the guilt of leaving her baby brother on the picnic table when he was kidnapped, she left home for a while, too."

"Where'd she go?"

"Went to Oregon with her English friend Ginny. Abraham was so upset about it, he almost made himself sick. But God answered our prayers and brought Naomi home. You'd never know such a thing had happened now, because she's happy and content and such a good *mudder* to her kinner."

"Oh, I pray that will be the case for Phoebe someday."

Fannie placed her hand on Arie's arm and shared some of the scriptures Abby had previously mentioned to her.

Arie sniffed and swiped at the tears trickling down her cheeks. "I appreciate the reminder and know that I do need to trust the Lord where my daughter's concerned. From now on, I'll try to remember to trust God more and put Phoebe into His hands."

—ᗱᗢᗲ—

Pembroke, Kentucky

Titus had just finished breakfast and was getting ready to leave for work, when a knock sounded on the back door. He hurried across the room to answer it, and was surprised to see Bishop King standing on the porch.

"Can I come in?" the bishop asked.

"Well, I. . .uh. . .was about to leave for work."

"It's important, and I won't take much of your time."

"Of course. Come in." Titus led the way to the kitchen and motioned for the bishop to take a seat at the table.

When the bishop sat down, Titus seated himself in the chair opposite him.

Bishop King cleared his throat a few times, while stroking his full gray beard. "It's come to my attention that you own a cell phone. Is it true?"

Titus nodded slowly. "I use it mostly to keep in touch with my family in Pennsylvania. My brother Zach has a cell phone because of his painting business, so it's easier for me to get ahold of him now, rather than having to leave messages on his or my folks' voice mail."

The bishop tapped his fingers on the table and looked at Titus with furrowed brows. "Cell phones are not allowed in this district. Figured someone would have told you that by now."

A trickle of sweat rolled down Titus's forehead, and he wiped it away. "I did hear that, but I was hoping you might make an exception in my case, since it's hard for me to get ahold of my family."

The bishop shook his head sternly. "There are no exceptions to the rule. You'll have to get rid of the cell phone if you expect to remain a member in good standing."

"But I signed a yearlong contract, and—"

"That's too bad, but I can't allow you to have a cell phone and expect others in our district to adhere to the 'no cell phone' rule."

"I suppose not." Titus drew in a deep breath and sighed. "I don't want to do anything to jeopardize my standing in the church, so I'll stop using the cell phone and pay the fee to disconnect the service."

The bishop smiled and gave a nod. "Maybe you can set up a certain time to call your family each week. That's what many others do, you know."

"Okay, I'll do whatever you say."

—∽∾—

"This bread is sure good, Mom." Chad reached for a slice of banana bread, sniffed it, and then popped it into his mouth. "Mmm. . .it tastes even better than it smells." He smacked his lips noisily.

"Duh net so laut schmatze!" Mom scolded. "You're old enough to know better than to make such a noise when you eat."

"Sorry," the boy mumbled.

"When you become a daed someday, you'll need to set a

better example for your kinner," Grandpa said.

Chad slowly nodded. Suzanne figured becoming a dad was probably the last thing on her brother's young mind.

"This *is* tasty bread," Effie said after she'd eaten a piece. "Danki for makin' it, Mom."

Mom shook her head and motioned to Suzanne. "She's the one who deserves the thanks."

Nelson's eyebrows lifted high on his forehead as he stared at Suzanne with a look of disbelief. "You made the bread?

She nodded. "For the last several weeks, I've been going over to Esther's for cooking lessons."

"Well, that would explain it," Nelson said. "Esther's a really good cook."

"That's true," Mom agreed, "and she has a lot more patience in the kitchen than I do, which is why I'm sure I haven't been able to teach you much, Suzanne."

Grandpa took a piece of banana bread and slathered it with butter. "My daughter has a lot of good qualities, but she does tend to be a bit picky about things—especially when it comes to what goes on in her kitchen."

Mom frowned, but then a smile played at the corner of her lips. "I'm not picky. I just like things done in an orderly fashion. I'll also admit that for me, it's usually easier to do things myself than to wait for someone else to do them. It's a fault I need to work on."

"And I haven't been the best student," Suzanne said. "That's mostly because there are so many other things I'd rather do than spend time in the kitchen."

"Then why the change now?" Grandpa asked.

Suzanne wasn't about to blurt out that she'd decided to learn how to cook so she could impress Titus. That would be embarrassing and no doubt bring on some teasing from her siblings.

"So, how come you've been learnin' to cook?" Russell asked, poking Suzanne's arm.

"I just decided it was time; that's all."

"I'll bet she's interested in some fellow and knows she'll need to be able to cook if she's gonna get him to marry her." Nelson winked at Suzanne.

"Who's the fellow?" Effie questioned. "And when are ya gettin' married?"

Suzanne's face heated, and she stared at the table, hoping no one would realize how embarrassed she was. "There is no fellow, and I'm not getting married anytime soon—maybe never." *But I wish I was*, she mentally added.

CHAPTER 38

For the rest of summer, and into the fall, Suzanne continued to take cooking lessons from Esther and practice what she'd learned on her family. She was getting better at cooking, and even her baking skills had improved. Unfortunately, she hadn't had the chance to let Titus sample anything she'd made, because he and Nelson had been installing some cabinets and doing the trim work on the inside of a new house in Hopkinsville, which took them away from the shop every day. While they were gone, Grandpa continued to do the bookwork and usually spent a few hours every day in the shop to greet any customers who came in.

This morning, Mom had accompanied Grandpa to his doctor's appointment in town, which meant nobody was in the shop. That gave Suzanne the perfect opportunity to sneak out there and work on a project of her own that she'd begun a few weeks ago when no one else was around.

Suzanne entered the shop and lit the gas lamps. Then she pulled out the bedside table she'd started working on from the back of the storage closet, where she'd hidden it under a tarp.

She hummed as she began sanding the legs. The wood felt smooth beneath her fingers, and she didn't even mind the bits of sawdust that blew up to her nose. This was where she belonged—where she felt comfortable and at peace. Even though she'd learned to cook fairly well, she doubted that she'd ever feel this content baking a pie or roasting a chicken. If only her desire to work with wood could be accepted by the men in the family. If she just could make them see how much she loved spending time out here.

Suzanne reached for another piece of sandpaper, and in so doing, knocked a jar of nails off the shelf. The jar broke as soon as it hit the floor, and nails flew everywhere.

"Oh great," she mumbled. "Now I have to waste my time picking all that up."

She bent down, picked up a piece of broken glass, and let out a yelp. Her finger was bleeding, and the cut looked pretty deep and had begun to throb. But a close examination convinced her it wouldn't require stitches.

Suzanne left her work and opened the desk drawer where Nelson kept some bandages. The box was empty. *Guess I'd better go up to the house for a bandage and some antiseptic.*

She grabbed a paper towel from the holder near the sink and wrapped it around her finger. Then she pushed the table back into the storage closet, threw the tarp over it, and hurried from the shop.

—⁂—

Titus and Nelson had finished working at the house in Hopkinsville a little earlier than expected, so they decided to stop at the shop and see if any orders had come in during their absence.

"There's no paperwork on the desk," Nelson said, "but look there." He pointed to some broken glass on the floor. "Looks like Grandpa must have busted a jar sometime today. I'd better get the broom and dustpan from the storage room and sweep it up before one of us gets a hunk of glass stuck in the bottom of our shoe."

"I'll get it," Titus said.

He opened the door to the storage closet and was about to remove the broom, when he noticed what looked like a table leg sticking out from under a canvas tarp. He pulled the cloth back. Sure enough, it was a small wooden table, but it wasn't quite finished. It appeared to be partially sanded but no stain had been added.

Titus bent down and studied the table. It had been finely crafted, with perfectly shaped corners and a small drawer in the front. He was about to drop the canvas back in place when he noticed a bloodstain on one of the table legs.

"Did you make that little table?" Titus asked Nelson when he returned with the broom and dustpan.

"What table's that?"

"The one in the storage closet. It looks like a bedside table."

Nelson shook his head. "Never knew there was a table in there. I wonder if Grandpa made it when he's been out here doing the books. I'll have to ask him about it."

Titus began sweeping up the glass and had just finished when Suzanne entered the shop, wearing a bandage on her finger. *Could she have been here working today? Might she have made the table? No, that's ridiculous. If she could do woodworking that well, Isaac or Nelson would have put her to work in the shop by now.*

"I'm surprised to see you two here so early," Suzanne said. "I figured you'd be working late again."

"We did all we could for the day and decided to come back here to see if any orders had come in," Nelson said.

She glanced at the floor, but said nothing about the broken glass. Maybe she didn't know about it. Maybe she'd cut her finger on something in the house, barn, or outside while doing some chore.

Suzanne looked at Titus and smiled. "If you have no other plans for this evening, we'd like you to stay for supper."

Titus smiled. "I have no plans, and I'd be happy to stay." Truth was, he was tired and hungry and didn't feel like going home to an empty house and fixing himself something to eat—especially not tonight on his birthday, which he hadn't mentioned to anyone. He didn't want them to feel obligated to help him celebrate. If he were still living at home, Mom would have done something special for his and Timothy's birthday. When Titus got home, he planned to call and leave a birthday message on Timothy's voice mail.

A short time later, when Titus entered the kitchen with Nelson, he sniffed the air. Suzanne's mother was a good cook, so he looked forward to the meal. "Something sure smells good in here," he told Verna, who stood near the stove. "What'd you make for supper?"

"Not a thing," Verna said. "I was in Hopkinsville most of the day with my daed. Suzanne fixed the meal."

Remembering some things Nelson had said about his sister's cooking, Titus wondered what kind of a meal he was in for this evening. Well, as hungry as he was, he'd eat almost anything.

—⚬—

As they ate the chicken and dumplings Suzanne had prepared, she couldn't help but notice that Titus seemed to be enjoying himself. He'd had two helpings already, which meant he was either very hungry or liked what he'd eaten.

"How are things coming along with your job at that house in Hopkinsville?" Grandpa asked Nelson.

"Real well. If things keep going as they have, we should be done with all the trim work and doors by the end of the week."

"That's good to hear," Grandpa said, "because the last few days, I've taken a few orders for Christmas gifts."

"Here it is fall already, and I can't believe Christmas is only two and a half months away," Verna said. "It seems like the days just fly by anymore. I don't even know where summer went."

"That's 'cause everyone's been so busy," Russell chimed in.

"You're right about that," his mother agreed.

"This is sure a good meal," Titus said around a mouthful of dumpling. "I'm glad I decided to stay. To tell you the truth, I wasn't looking forward to spending the evening alone either."

Suzanne smiled. "I'm glad you're enjoying it, and I hope you'll like the pie I made for dessert."

His eyebrows lifted. "What kind of pie?"

"Lemon shoofly. It was one of Grandma's favorite pies to bake."

"I've never heard of lemon shoofly," Titus said. "Is it anything like the traditional Lancaster County wet-bottom shoofly pie?"

"It's similar, but we think it's even better," Mom interjected. "The pie has molasses in it, but the addition of lemon juice tones down the molasses a bit."

Titus smiled. "If it's half as good as regular shoofly pie, then I'm anxious to try it."

After everyone had finished eating, Suzanne brought out the pie. "Here you go." She placed the pie, decorated with twenty-three lit candles, on the table in front of Titus.

He blinked a couple of times and looked up at her with a curious expression. "What are the candles for?"

"Happy birthday," she said with a grin.

"How'd you know today was my birthday?"

"Your mamm left a message on our voice mail for you this morning. She said she'd tried to call your phone but got a busy signal, so figuring we'd give you the message, she called here to wish you a happy birthday."

"I'll bet I left the door to the phone shanty open by accident last night. One of the cats probably got in and knocked the receiver off the hook," Titus said.

Suzanne pointed to the pie. "You'd better blow out your candles before they melt all over the pie."

Titus leaned forward and blew the candles out in one big breath. Then Suzanne cut a generous slice and handed the plate to him.

He quickly forked a piece into his mouth. "Umm. . . This is really good. I'll have to get the recipe from you and pass it on to my mamm."

Suzanne sighed with relief. Titus had enjoyed everything she'd fixed for supper this evening, and she was glad they'd been able to help him celebrate his birthday. It had to be hard to be away from family on any special occasion.

After everyone finished their pie and the final prayer had been said, the children went to their rooms, while Grandpa and Nelson retired to the living room for a game of checkers.

"If you're not in a hurry to go home, why don't you stick around awhile and play the winner?" Grandpa said to Titus.

"I appreciate the offer, but I think I'll help Suzanne do the dishes, and then I'd better head for home."

"You like to do the dishes?" Nelson looked at Titus like he'd taken leave of his senses.

"Didn't say I liked to do 'em," Titus replied. "Just said I'd help. Figured it's the least I can do to say thanks to Suzanne for the good meal and for making my birthday special."

Nelson shrugged. "Suit yourself."

"If you two are going to do the dishes, then I guess I'll find a book and read for a while," Verna said.

After everyone else left the room, Suzanne filled the sink

with warm water and added some liquid detergent, while Titus finished bringing the dirty dishes over to the sink. "Would you mind washing while I dry?" she asked Titus. "I cut my finger today, and since I'm wearing a bandage, I don't want it to fall off in the dishwater."

"No problem; I don't mind washing."

Suzanne took out a clean dishcloth and waited for him to wash a few of the dishes and put them into the drainer before she started drying.

"So how'd you cut your finger?" he asked as he sloshed the dishrag over one of the plates.

Suzanne's face heated with embarrassment. How would Titus react if she told him how she'd cut it? Would he think, the way Nelson did, that a woman's place was in the kitchen, not in the shop working with wood?

Instead of answering Titus's question, Suzanne quickly changed the subject, telling him about the young people's gathering that would be held at the Beilers' home on Sunday evening.

"There will be hot dogs and marshmallows to roast around the bonfire," she said. "And plenty of hot apple cider."

He smacked his lips. "Sounds good to me."

"Do you think you might go?"

"Probably. How about you?"

"I'd like to, but Mom doesn't like me to take the horse and buggy out by myself after dark."

"Won't Nelson be going?"

"I'm sure he will, but he'll be taking his *aldi*, and I don't want to intrude." Suzanne stacked the clean plates and set them in the cupboard.

"I'd be happy to give you a ride there and back," Titus said.

She smiled and nodded. "I'll look forward to going."

CHAPTER 39

I'm going outside to enjoy this beautiful autumn weather while I wait for Titus to pick me up," Suzanne told her mother on Sunday evening.

Mom smiled. "It's nice that he's taking you to the young people's gathering. He's obviously interested in you."

Suzanne shook her head. "I think he was just being nice when he offered to take me. Titus and Nelson have become good friends, and he probably figured Nelson needed the chance to be alone with Lucy."

"I don't know about that. I saw the way Titus looked at you when he was here for supper the other night. I really do think he has courtship on his mind."

"I know he's not seeing Esther anymore," Suzanne said, "but Titus and I have had our differences since he moved here, so I'm not sure he'll ever see me as someone he'd want to court."

"Things weren't always good between me and your daed before we started courting, but once he realized I was a woman, and not the little girl he'd gone to school with, he changed his mind real quick."

"This is just one ride. I doubt it means anything more to Titus," Suzanne said as she went out the door.

When Suzanne stepped onto the porch, a gentle breeze caressed her face. The cooler weather they'd been having felt good. She glanced into the yard and spotted a chipmunk poking its head in and out of a pile of brush, while two of her cats chased each other across the lawn.

She directed her gaze to the field where they grew their colorful mums. As much as she enjoyed tending the flowers, it was nothing compared to working with wood.

She thought about the table she'd hidden in the woodshop storage closet and wondered what she should do when it was finished. Should she keep it, sell it, or give it away? The table might make a nice Christmas present for Mom.

Suzanne's thoughts halted when she heard the *clip-clop* of horse's hooves. Titus was here. It was time to go.

—◆—

Titus didn't know why, but he felt nervous with Suzanne sitting on the buggy seat beside him. He'd spent time with her before, but never like this on what felt like a date. As Titus guided his horse and buggy down the road, he wondered if he'd made a mistake offering Suzanne a ride tonight. Would she, and probably some others, think they were courting? Did he want to court her? If tonight went well, should he ask her out again?

"I've been wondering about something," he said, looking over at her.

"What's that?"

"I noticed that you were wearing a bandage the other night, and when I asked about it, you changed the subject."

"Oh, that." She turned her head away from him. "I...uh... cut my finger on a piece of glass."

"In the woodshop?"

"Jah. I knocked over a jar of nails, and it fell on the floor and broke."

"Did you touch something with your bloody finger after that?"

"I touched a lot of things. Why do you ask?"

"I found a small table in the storage closet, with a bloodstain on one of the legs. Figured whoever had cut themselves must have touched the table leg."

Suzanne sat several seconds, without saying a word. She looked over at him and said, "I'm the one who made the table."

He blinked a couple of times. "Are you serious?"

She gave a nod. "I've made some other things, too."

"Like what?"

"Birdhouses and feeders. The table was the first piece of furniture I've made."

"Why was it in the storage closet under a tarp?"

"I didn't want Nelson to see it."

"How come?"

"He thinks a woman's place is in the kitchen." She sighed. "He doesn't realize how much I enjoy working with wood."

His brows furrowed. "It is unusual. I mean, I've never known a woman carpenter before. At least not any Amish women."

"Guess I'm an exception to the rule."

Titus wasn't sure what to think of this. Suzanne was a mystery to him. One day she couldn't cook at all, and the next day she'd made a real tasty meal. One day she was sanding cabinet doors in the woodshop, and the next day she'd made a table—and not a bad-looking one at that.

Suzanne may look similar to Phoebe, he thought, *but she's nothing like her at all. She's got spunk, but she doesn't show off. She's already joined the church, so she's settled and not likely to leave the faith. Maybe I should pursue a relationship with her. I'd better think this over some more.*

They drove the rest of the way in silence. The only sounds were the *creak-creak* of the buggy wheels and the steady *clippety-clop* of Lightning's hooves against the pavement. Titus figured the silence was better, because at the moment, he couldn't think of anything else to say.

—⁂—

When they arrived at the Beilers', Suzanne went to speak with Esther, while Titus put his horse in the corral.

"I was surprised when I saw Titus's horse and buggy come in, and then you stepped down," Esther said to Suzanne. "I'll bet you're happy that he asked you to come with him tonight."

"Shh. Don't make an issue of it," Suzanne whispered. "I think he was only being nice when he offered to take me to and from the singing."

Esther leaned close to Suzanne's ear. "Has he had a chance to taste anything you've cooked since I've been giving you lessons?"

"He ate supper with us the other night and said he liked my chicken and dumplings, as well as the lemon shoofly pie I made in honor of his birthday."

"I didn't know it was his birthday."

"Until I listened to a voice mail message for him from his mamm, I didn't know it either."

"Well, if he enjoyed the meal you prepared, then I think there may be some hope for the two of you."

"I'd like to think so, but I'm not getting my hopes up." Suzanne motioned to the barn, where several young people were heading. "Looks like the singing's about to begin. Guess we'd better head in there, too."

Suzanne and Esther followed the others into the barn, and soon everyone found seats. They sang for over an hour, as their voices lifted in harmony and echoed off the barn walls. Then everyone moved outside to the bonfire Esther's father had started. Suzanne enjoyed the warmth of the fire, and even the smoky smell didn't bother her. She'd always loved sitting around a fire, especially on a chilly fall evening such as this. She gazed up at the three-quarter moon above, wishing Titus would join her at the bonfire, but he took a seat beside Ethan Zook instead and didn't even look Suzanne's way.

I'm sure by telling Titus I like to work with wood I probably ruined any chances I might have with him, she thought. *He probably thinks, like Nelson, that a woman's place is in the kitchen.*

"Are you going to have a hot dog?" Esther asked.

Suzanne shook her head. "I'm not hungry right now."

"At least have some hot cider then. My daed made it, and it's really good."

"Okay." Suzanne was on her way to the refreshment table when a gust of wind came up, and several dust devils whirled in the distance. As the wind increased, it grew so strong that it blew the paper plates and cups right off the table.

"Grab the tablecloth, or everything will go!" someone hollered.

Just then, another gust came up, this one a little stronger than the last, carrying debris from the yard that was quickly caught up in the air. Most of the young people started running for the barn, and someone quickly put the bonfire out so that sparks wouldn't fly. The corral gate flew open, and suddenly all the horses were out, running all around the yard.

Titus and some of the other young men chased after the horses.

"You'd better watch out," Ethan shouted as he raced past Titus. "I think the cover on the Beilers' manure pit just blew off."

Titus stepped back, and—*splat*—he stepped right into the pit.

CHAPTER 40

When Titus woke up the next morning, he was relieved he could no longer smell the putrid odor of manure on his body. He couldn't believe he'd fallen into the Beilers' manure pit while trying to chase down the runaway horses. The pit was only a few feet deep, but when he'd stepped into it, he'd lost his footing and ended up flat on his back.

The stench had been horrible, and he'd held his breath, unable to bear the despicable odor, while Esther's dad hosed him off with water so cold it made his teeth chatter. That hadn't helped much, other than to get most of the manure off his clothes, and he'd taken a lot of ribbing from some of the fellows. Even Suzanne had giggled when she'd seen him standing there, sopping wet. It was kind of funny, now that he thought about it, but at the time, he'd been pretty miffed.

While some of the young men had continued to round up the horses, Titus had gone into the Beilers' house and taken a warm shower. Then Esther's mother had given him a shirt and some trousers that had belonged to Esther's older brother, Dan, who was married and no longer lived at home. Even after the shower, Titus had been able to smell the sickening manure aroma.

It reminded him of the time when he and Timothy were boys and had fallen into a pile of manure when they'd been fooling around. They'd gotten in big trouble with Mom for it, too.

Not wishing to subject Suzanne to sitting beside his smelly body, Titus had asked Ethan Zook to take her home. Then Titus had headed to his place and taken another long shower with plenty of soap and shampoo. It sure wasn't the way he'd intended the evening to go. He'd hoped that on the way home he might talk to Suzanne more about woodworking and see if she'd like him to put in a good word with Nelson about it.

Guess I'd better not say anything to him until I've spoken to Suzanne, he decided as he left his bedroom and headed to the kitchen to fix breakfast. *She might not want me to say anything to Nelson about the table she'd made.*

Paradise, Pennsylvania

Samuel had just entered the kitchen when Elsie, who was stirring a kettle of oatmeal, motioned for him to come over. "I've something to tell you," she said.

"What's up?"

"I was going to tell you this last night, but you came home from work late and fell asleep before I had a chance to say anything."

"Tell me what?"

"I went to see the doctor yesterday. What I've suspected is true. I'm going to have another boppli, and it'll be born next spring."

Samuel slipped his arm around Elsie's waist and pulled her to his side. "That's real good news. Have you told anyone else yet?"

She shook her head. "I wanted to tell you first, and then our kinner and both sides of our family."

275

He smiled. "Think I'll stop by my folks' on the way to work this morning and give them the good news."

Elsie sighed and leaned her head on his shoulder. "I'm hoping we have another boy this time. Then Jared will have someone to play with who's closer to his age."

"That would be nice, but I'll be happy whether God chooses to give us a boy or a girl. The main thing is that the baby's born healthy."

"I agree." Elsie removed the kettle from the stove. "The oatmeal's ready now, so if you'll call the kinner to the table, we can eat and give them our news."

—⁓—

Pembroke, Kentucky

As Suzanne helped Mom with breakfast, she thought about how things had gone last night. Not only had the unexpected wind put a stop to their young people's gathering, but Titus hadn't even brought her home. Of course, he'd used the excuse that he smelled bad when he'd told her that he'd arranged for Ethan to give her a ride, but she wondered if the real reason had something to do with her telling him about the table she'd made.

He'll probably blab to Nelson or Grandpa about what I've been doing, she thought as she placed a plate of buttermilk pancakes on the table. *Maybe I ought to tell them myself and get it over with. But if I do that, they might not let me go out to the shop anymore.* Suzanne got the pot of coffee from the stove. *Or maybe Titus was upset because I laughed when he fell in the manure pit. But then, some of the others laughed, too.*

"Everything's ready now," Mom said, placing a platter of bacon on the table. "Would you please call everyone in for breakfast?" she asked Suzanne.

"Sure."

Suzanne felt a nip in the air as she stepped onto the porch

and rang the bell so those who were outside doing their chores would know breakfast was ready. When she stepped back inside, she cupped her hands around her mouth, and called for Effie to come downstairs to eat.

A short time later, everyone gathered around the kitchen table. After the silent prayer, Mom passed the platters of bacon and pancakes.

Grandpa sniffed deeply. "Ah, I do love the smell of maple-cured bacon." He forked a couple of pancakes onto his plate and poured syrup over the top. "Who made these?" he asked after he'd taken his first bite.

"Suzanne did, while I cooked the bacon," Mom replied.

Grandpa looked over at Suzanne and smiled. "Good job! For a young woman who's always disliked being in the kitchen, you're turnin' into a pretty fine cook." He winked at her. "I've got a hunch it won't be long until you find yourself a husband."

The heat of a blush warmed Suzanne's cheeks. She was pleased that Grandpa liked the pancakes but worried that he might suspect she was interested in Titus. She certainly didn't want him to know that she'd asked Esther to give her cooking lessons in the hope of gaining Titus's approval.

"Say, Grandpa," Nelson said after he'd taken a drink of milk, "do you know anything about the table inside the storage closet in the woodshop?"

Grandpa shook his head. "I saw it there, too. Thought maybe you'd made it."

"Nope, it wasn't me."

"Must have been Titus, then. I'll ask him about it when he shows up at the woodshop this morning."

Feeling a sense of panic, Suzanne balled her napkin tightly into her hands and blurted out, "There's no need for you to ask Titus because I'm the one who made the table."

Everyone turned to look at her, eyes wide and mouths hanging open.

CHAPTER 41

Suzanne held her breath as she waited for the family's response to her confession. What if she wasn't allowed to go in the woodshop anymore? She didn't think she could deal with that—didn't think she could ever stop making wooden things. And it would be unfair if she was asked to give it up.

Grandpa was the first to speak. "I'm not really surprised by this, Suzanne. We all know you've made a few birdfeeders, and I've known for some time that you'd rather be out in the woodshop than doing anything in the house."

"That's true," Suzanne said in a voice barely above a whisper.

"How would you like to help out in the shop during our busier times?" Grandpa asked. "With Christmas sneaking up on us, I'm sure we'll be getting a lot more orders."

"I'd like that very much." Tears welled in Suzanne's eyes. She could hardly believe he'd actually invited her to work in the shop—and it would be doing more than bookwork or sweeping the floor. This was too good to be true.

Nelson looked at Grandpa with a grim expression. "You

can't be serious. Suzanne will only be in the way, and I thought you agreed with me that her place is in the house, doing womanly things."

Suzanne slapped her hand on the table, jostling her silverware. "That's lecherich, and it's old-fashioned thinking! Just because I'm a woman doesn't mean I can't do some things a man's capable of doing."

"I agree with Suzanne," Mom put in. "When your daed was alive and had the dairy farm, I used to help him a lot."

"That was different. Milking cows isn't anything like woodworking, and it's not nearly as dangerous," Nelson said.

"It can be dangerous," Russell spoke up. "I remember the time Dad got kicked by one of the cows and it broke his leg."

"That's still not as dangerous as working with wood." Nelson pointed to Suzanne. "You could cut your hand, smash your finger, or any number of things."

"I'll be careful," Suzanne asserted. "Accidents can happen in the kitchen or even out in the garden."

Nelson gave a nod. "That may be true, but only if you're not careful, and you were obviously not careful when you cut your hand on the piece of glass the other day."

"I was careful. I just—"

Grandpa clapped his hands. "That's enough! Since the shop is still mine, it's up to me to do the hiring and firing. I say Suzanne can help out whenever it's needed." He reached for another pancake. "Now let's finish our breakfast so we can get to work."

—⚹—

Titus had just finished eating breakfast when he heard a vehicle pull into the yard. He glanced out the kitchen window and saw Allen getting out of his truck.

"It's good to see you," Titus said after he'd invited Allen

into the kitchen. "Would you like a cup of coffee?"

"Guess I could have one, but I can't stay long. Just came to give you some good news." He pulled an envelope out of his jacket pocket and handed it to Titus. "It's the reward money you have coming."

"I'd almost forgotten about that." Titus smiled. "I'll put the money in the bank the next time I go to town. May as well let it draw some interest."

"I have some other good news as well."

"What's that?"

"I've been given the opportunity to buy a used, but very nice, double-wide manufactured home. I'd like to move the old trailer out of here and have the new home brought in." Allen took a sip of coffee from the cup Titus had just handed him.

"A newer place would be nice," Titus said, "but I guess that would mean I'd owe you more money every month for rent."

Allen shook his head. "I'll charge you the same as you're paying now, and then if you're still interested in buying the place, you can start making your payments count toward the purchase price."

Titus sat for a few minutes, mulling things over. Finally, he gave a slow nod. "That's what I'd like to do."

"Great. I'll get the papers drawn up and bring them over to you sometime later this week. Within the next couple of weeks, you ought to have a new place to call home."

Titus grinned. "I can't wait for that."

Allen drank the last of his coffee and stood. "I'd better get going. A man who lives in Cadiz wants me to give him a bid on remodeling part of his house."

After Allen left, Titus glanced at the clock. He still had half an hour before he needed to leave for work, so he decided to go out to the phone shanty and call Zach. "Hey, Zach, it's me," Titus said after he'd made the call.

"It's good hearing from you, Titus. How are things?"

"Other than me stepping into a manure pit last night, everything's fine and dandy."

"How'd that happen?"

Titus related the story.

Zach chuckled. "Guess it could have been worse."

"I suppose."

"You didn't have your cell phone in your pocket when you fell in, I hope."

Titus grimaced. "No, but I won't be using it anymore."

"How come?"

Titus explained about giving up the cell phone, and finished by saying, "After the bishop confronted me, I knew it wouldn't be right to keep using the phone."

"I think you've made the right decision," Zach said. "If you had your own business and were away from home a lot, you'd probably need a cell phone. Under the circumstances, I'm sure you can get by using the one in your phone shanty."

"I guess."

A fly buzzed overhead, and Titus swatted at it. He'd be glad when the weather turned colder and there weren't so many bugs to contend with. If Samuel were here, he'd probably have caught the pesky fly in his hand. He'd always been real good at bug catching.

"Say, I heard some good news this morning when Samuel came to work."

"What's that?"

"Elsie's expecting another boppli, and Samuel's sure excited about it."

"That's great. Tell him I said congratulations."

"I will. I'd let you tell him yourself, but he's up on a ladder, painting the trim on a house we need to get finished before colder weather sets in."

"That's okay. You can give him my message. Oh, and I have some good news of my own to share."

"What is it?"

"Allen was here awhile ago, and he's getting me a better place to live—a used manufactured home—to replace the old trailer I'm living in now."

"That should give you more room."

"It will, but the best part is I'm going to apply the rent I'm paying him toward the purchase of the double-wide, as well as the property here."

"That must mean you're definitely planning to stay in Kentucky."

"Jah. I like it here, and I enjoy working in the Yoders' woodshop."

The fly landed on the table beside the phone, and Titus smacked it with the palm of his hand. One less buzzing insect to irritate him.

"Think you'll ever settle down and get married?"

"I don't know. Maybe. Esther and I aren't seeing each other anymore, but I've begun to care for Suzanne. So if things work out between us, I might eventually think about marriage."

"Sounds like you're making some mature decisions. Mom and Dad will be pleased."

"They may be pleased that I'm finally growing up, but probably not so pleased about me buying this place and staying here. I know Mom's still hoping I'll move back home."

"From what Leona's heard from Abby, Mom's doing better with all that. I think she's finally come to realize that you have to make a life of your own, even if it means being away from the family."

Titus smiled. "Guess I won't really understand the way Mom feels until I get married and have some kinner of my own."

"That's true enough. Since Leona and I had Lucy, James, and Jean, I see things differently than I did before they were born."

"Say, Zach, before we hang up, I've been wondering about something."

"What's that?"

"Do you still keep in touch with the man who kidnapped you and let you think he was your father?"

"Sure. We call each other every few weeks. In fact, Jim and his wife, Holly, are planning to come here for a visit sometime next year."

"So you don't hold a grudge against him for what he did?"

"Not anymore. I forgave Jim a long time ago." There was a pause. "Why do you ask?"

Titus ran his fingers through his hair. "I've been thinking about Phoebe lately."

"What about her?"

"I've been nursing a grudge against her long enough. Fact is, if I had Phoebe's address, I'd write her a letter so she'd know I've forgiven her for hurting me like she did."

"You could always ask Mom to get Phoebe's address. From what I understand, Mom and Arie are still friends, so I'm sure Arie would give Mom the address for you."

Titus gnawed on his lower lip. "I'm not so sure about that. Mom and Dad disapproved of my relationship with Phoebe. If I ask Mom to get Phoebe's address, she might think I want to get back with Phoebe."

"Just tell her you don't want it for that reason. Tell her what you told me—that you only want to let Phoebe know you've forgiven her."

"I'll give it some thought, but please don't say anything to Mom about this. If I decide to ask for Phoebe's address, the request should come from me."

"No problem, I won't say a word."

"Thanks." Titus pulled out his pocket watch. "I'd better go, or I'll be late for work. Tell the family I said hello, and don't forget to let everyone know not to call my cell phone number anymore."

"I'll do that. Take care, Titus."

Titus hung up the phone and sprinted for the barn. He needed to feed Callie and her kittens, get Lightning saddled, and head to work. When he got there, he hoped he'd have the chance to speak to Suzanne, because he needed to apologize for not taking her home from the young people's gathering.

CHAPTER 42

When Titus entered the Yoders' yard, he was disappointed not to see Suzanne outside. She was often in the garden or hanging clothes on the line, but not today. He was tempted to go up to the house and ask to speak to her, but he was already late and didn't think he should take the time to stop. Maybe he'd see her at lunchtime or after work. He hoped so.

Titus put Lightning in the corral and hurried toward the shop. When he opened the door, he found Nelson and Isaac in what appeared to be a heated discussion. They stopped talking as soon as they saw him, and he wondered what could be going on. He'd never heard the two of them say an unkind word to each other. Maybe Nelson had been getting after Isaac for trying to do too much.

"Sorry I'm late," Titus said. "Allen stopped by this morning, and then I made a quick phone call before I left home, and I'm afraid it set me behind."

Isaac flapped his hand. "It's fine. You're here now; that's all that matters."

"This wasn't a good day to be late," Nelson mumbled.

"We've got a lot of work that needs to be done, and since Grandpa and I have an errand to run at noon, that'll leave you in the shop alone."

"No problem," Titus said. "I'm sure I can work on whatever needs to be done and wait on any customers who might come in."

"If things get real busy and you need some help, just run up to the house and get Suzanne," Isaac said.

"Sure, and while she's here, maybe she can make a table or two." The sarcasm in Nelson's voice was unmistakable. Apparently he knew about the table Suzanne had hidden in the storage room. Maybe she'd felt guilty about it and had told him the truth.

It's not my place to say anything, Titus decided. *If Suzanne told Nelson about the table she made, she might not have said anything to Isaac. Even if she did, it's best if I don't let on that I know. It might not set well with Nelson or Isaac if they learn that I was the first person Suzanne told.*

—⁓—

"Would you like me to take lunch out to the men now?" Suzanne asked her mother after they finished making some tuna fish sandwiches with zucchini relish.

"I'd appreciate that," Mom said. "I still need to wash another load of clothes."

"No problem. I think I'll put some of my banana bread in the lunch basket, too. They can have that for dessert."

"That's fine. Oh, and don't forget the jug of apple cider in the refrigerator. I'm glad we were able to use the Beilers' cider press to make more, because I opened the only jar left from last season."

Suzanne put everything together and headed out the door. When she entered the woodshop, she discovered that Nelson and Grandpa weren't there and Titus was working alone.

"I brought lunch out for the three of you," she said to Titus, "but it appears that you're the only one here right now."

He looked up from staining a door and nodded. "Nelson and your grandpa had an errand to run and left me in charge of the shop until they get back."

Suzanne frowned. *I wonder why they didn't call me out to help. Maybe Grandpa didn't think they were busy enough for my help today. Or maybe Nelson talked him out of letting me work in the shop.*

Titus motioned to the basket she'd placed on Grandpa's desk. "If you made enough food for three of us, why don't you stay and join me for lunch? I sure can't eat it all by myself."

"Thanks, I think I will." Suzanne took everything out of the basket. Then after Titus washed up at the sink, they took seats on either side of the desk and said their silent prayers.

"I made tuna fish mixed with relish again," she said, handing him a sandwich.

He grinned at her. "That sounds good."

They ate their sandwiches in silence; then Titus leaned forward and looked intently at Suzanne.

"What's wrong?" she asked. "Have I got tuna fish on my face?"

He shook his head. "I was just thinking what pretty eyes you have. They're darker and bluer than I thought."

She felt the heat of a blush spread across her cheeks. "Danki."

"I hope you weren't upset with me for not taking you home last night. With the way I smelled, I didn't think you'd want to sit in the closed-in buggy, holding your nose all the way home."

She chuckled. "You did smell pretty bad."

Titus sniffed his arm and snickered. "It took two more

showers after I got home, but I think I finally got the smell off. I washed my clothes, too, but my shoes are ruined." He shook his head. "Still can't believe how I fell into that manure pit."

"It was awfully dark, and you couldn't see where you were going."

"That's the truth. Sure hope nothing like that ever happens to me again."

"I guess the only thing worse than falling into a manure pit would be getting sprayed by a skunk."

He wrinkled his nose. "That happened to me and Timothy once. We were heading outside to feed the chickens and ran into a couple of skunks in the yard. Before we knew what happened, they let us have it." He waved his hand in front of his nose. "That smell was horrible! It took a whole lot of soap and a good dousing with tomato juice before Mom would even let us in the house."

She laughed. "I guess there are some things from our childhood we'll never forget."

"You're right about that." Titus smiled. "I got some good news this morning that made me almost forget about the manure bath."

"What news?"

"I'll be getting a double-wide manufactured home soon. Allen's having it brought in and will be taking the old trailer out."

"That is good news. The trailer is still in pretty sad shape, and it'll be nice for you to have something better to live in."

He nodded. "Especially since I'm planning to buy the place and stay where I am."

"I'm glad you're staying." She handed him the loaf of banana bread. "Would you like some of this?"

He took a slice and chomped it down. "Your lemon shoofly pie was really good, but so is this. You ought to take some of the banana bread to the produce auction on Saturday. I'm sure folks would buy it when they stop to look at your colorful mums."

"That's a thought. Maybe I will take some banana bread."

He winked at her, and another wave of heat washed over Suzanne. Was Titus flirting with her, or was he just in a jovial mood?

"I thought you might like to know that this morning I told my family about the table I made," she said, changing the subject.

"What'd they say?"

"Mom and Grandpa seemed to understand my desire to work with wood, but Nelson wasn't supportive at all. He got pretty upset when Grandpa said I could help in the shop during busier times. I think he's still convinced that a woman's place is in the house, slaving over a hot stove or scrubbing floors." Suzanne took a piece of banana bread for herself. "If you want my opinion, I think my twenty-year-old brother is more old-fashioned than my seventy-four-year-old grandfather."

"I guess age isn't always a factor when it comes to being old-fashioned." Titus smiled. "I'm glad you'll be working in the shop. If there's anything you need help with, just let me know."

"I appreciate that, and I'm glad to know you don't disapprove."

"Not at all. I think everyone ought to have the right to do what they like best."

"By the way," Suzanne said, "I was wondering what you plan to do with Callie's kittens now that they're fully weaned and getting so big."

"Guess I'd better run an ad in the local paper or put a sign out by the road." Titus reached for another piece of bread. "While I can't say that I've become a cat lover, I have learned to tolerate Callie. But that doesn't mean I want a whole passel of cats hanging around."

"I'm sure if you advertise you'll be able to find them all good homes."

Titus swiped a napkin over his mouth and studied her intently again.

"Now what's wrong?"

"Nothin'. I was just wondering if you'd like to—"

The shop door opened, and Bishop King stepped in. "I need to order some new kitchen cabinets," he said, looking at Titus. "Can you have them done in time for my wife's birthday next month?"

"I think so," Titus said with a nod. "Let's go to the back of the shop, and you can pick out the wood you'd like."

Titus would be busy with the bishop for a while, so Suzanne gathered up the leftovers from lunch and headed to the house. She couldn't help wondering what Titus had been about to say before the bishop came in.

—⁂—

After work, Titus hoped to speak to Suzanne again, but Verna informed him that Suzanne had gone to the Beilers' store. So Titus headed for home, hoping he'd have a chance to speak with her tomorrow, for he still had one question he wanted to ask.

When Titus arrived home, he took care of Lightning, then headed to the phone shanty to call his folks. He was surprised when Mom answered.

"Titus, is that you?"

"Jah. I was going to leave you a message and was surprised when you answered the phone."

"I just came out to the phone shanty to check for messages and heard the phone ring. Did you have a nice birthday? Did you get our card and phone message?"

"I sure did."Titus picked up the pen lying beside the phone and drew a doodle of a cat on the tablet. "Suzanne made my birthday special, too."

"Oh?"

"She invited me to supper and baked a real good pie." He snickered. "Even served it with birthday candles."

"Suzanne's the young woman who looks like Phoebe, right?"

"Jah, but she's really nothing like her. In fact—"

"Your daed and I had another surprise today," Mom interrupted.

"What's that?"

"Samuel dropped by this morning and told us that Elsie's expecting another boppli."

"I already know, and it's good news."

"Did Samuel call you?"

"No, I talked to Zach. He said Samuel had given him the news when he got to work this morning."

"Oh, I see. So how are things going with you?"

"Pretty good. Allen came by this morning, and he's bringing in a used manufactured home to replace the old trailer."

"That's good to hear," Mom said. "I wasn't too impressed with the one you're living in now."

"I haven't been impressed with it either." Titus chose not to mention that he planned to buy the new place. He figured he'd tell Mom about it later. If he mentioned it now, she might become upset and start going on about how she didn't want him living in Kentucky.

They talked about other things for a while, and then Titus finally told Mom the reason he'd called. "I was wondering if you could do me a favor."

"Sure. What do you need?"

"I was wondering if you'd speak to Arie Stoltzfus and get

Phoebe's address for me."

There was dead silence on the other end of the line.

"Mom, did you hear what I said?"

"I heard. I just can't believe you'd ask me that. I thought you moved to Kentucky to get away from everything that reminds you of Phoebe. Now you want to contact her? What's happened, Titus? Are you hoping to get back with her? Are you going to try and convince her to move to Kentucky and marry you?"

"'Course not. It's over between me and Phoebe. I just want to write and let her know that there are no hard feelings and that I've forgiven her for hurting me the way she did."

"Is that all?"

"Jah."

"Well, if that's the case, I'll speak to Arie sometime this week and ask for Phoebe's address."

"Danki, Mom. I appreciate it."

"As soon as I get the address, I'll call and leave the information on your voice mail."

"Okay, Mom. Tell everyone I said hello."

When Titus hung up the phone, he sat a few minutes, wondering if Mom would really ask Arie for Phoebe's address. If so, would Arie give it to her? If she did, what should he write to Phoebe, and what, if anything, would be her response?

CHAPTER 43

Paradise, Pennsylvania

Fannie stared at the phone, trying to figure out what she should do. She'd told Titus that she'd get Phoebe's address for him, and she wanted to believe what he'd said, but the fear of them getting back together plagued her so much, she wasn't sure she could follow through with what she'd promised. Maybe if she let it go awhile, Titus would forget the whole idea.

That wouldn't be right, she told herself. *I said I'd do it, so I need to keep my word, and I need to believe that Titus was telling the truth when he said he wasn't trying to get back with Phoebe.*

With a sigh of resignation, Fannie picked up the phone and dialed the Stoltzfuses' number. It rang several times; then their voice mail came on. Fannie left a message, asking Arie for Phoebe's address, and then she hung up the phone. "There, that's done. Now I can get on with the rest of my day."

———

Pembroke, Kentucky

Maybe I should have asked Mom to get Phoebe's phone number

293

instead of her address, Titus thought after he'd hung up the phone. He shook his head. *No, a letter's probably the best way to contact her. Don't think I could deal with hearing her voice on the phone. It might make me start missing her again, and I sure don't need that.*

Titus left the phone shanty and headed for the house. Callie met him on the back porch, with all four of her brood meowing and looking up at him pathetically. He really should have gotten rid of them by now, but he'd been too busy to run an ad in the paper. He'd have to do that soon, because he didn't want to keep five cats around.

"I know you're hungry," Titus said as Callie brushed her tail against his legs. "Okay, follow me, and I'll get you all some food."

Think I might keep one of Callie's kittens so she has some company, he decided. *I'll take the rest of the cats with me to the produce auction this Saturday and see if I can find them good homes.*

When Titus stepped back outside, he leaned against the barn and inhaled deeply. Fall was definitely in the air; he could smell the leaves that had fallen from the trees in his yard and were starting to decay on the ground. He felt a crisp autumn breeze and heard the chattering of squirrels in a nearby tree. He loved this rural area, where there wasn't much traffic and tourists were few and far between.

He glanced at the old trailer he'd called home for the last six months and smiled. In two more weeks, he'd have a new home; only this one had the potential of being his own. That gave him a sense of belonging like never before.

Think I'll go for a walk before I head inside to fix something for supper, he decided.

—⚊—

As Suzanne headed home from the Beilers' store late that

afternoon, she heard the sound of dogs barking in the distance. Her horse must have heard it too, for the mare whinnied and started to run. Suzanne pulled back slightly on the reins. "Whoa, girl. Not so fast."

To her relief, the barking stopped, and her horse slowed to an easy trot. When she neared the road leading to Titus's place, she was tempted to stop. But what reason would she give for her visit? She didn't want to appear to be pursuing him. If Titus was interested in her, chasing after him would probably turn him away.

"I don't know why I'm thinking such thoughts," she muttered. "Just because Titus has been nicer to me lately, and took me to the young people's gathering the other night doesn't mean he's interested in me."

Suzanne relaxed her grip on the reins and tried to focus on other things. The trees lining the road had lost most of their leaves, and there was a distinctive aroma of fall in the air. Soon Thanksgiving, then Christmas would be here, and there'd probably be plenty of snow on the ground.

Her thoughts turned to Titus again, wondering if he would go to Pennsylvania to spend the holidays with his family. It seemed logical that he would, but if he decided to stay here, she'd ask Mom if they could invite Titus to join them for Thanksgiving and Christmas dinners.

Suzanne's musings were halted when her horse whinnied again and started limping. *Oh great. I'll bet she's thrown a shoe.*

Suzanne brought the horse and buggy to a stop and climbed down to check the horse's hooves. Sure enough, Dixie had lost her left front shoe.

Suzanne hoped if she took it slow and easy that they'd be able to make it home okay. She was about to climb back in the buggy, when a pack of six dogs in various sizes darted out of the woods, snarling, yipping, and growling.

Suzanne hurried for the buggy, but as she was about to put her foot inside, the horse bolted and took off down the road, pulling the buggy behind.

Suzanne chased after it, hollering, "Whoa, Dixie! Whoa!"

The horse kept running, and the pack of dogs headed straight for Suzanne!

Suzanne's chest heaved as she drew in a deep breath and released a primal scream. "Dear Lord, please help me!"

CHAPTER 44

Titus slowed his steps and listened. He thought he'd heard the shrill yapping of dogs. Sure enough, there it was again, followed by a woman's scream.

He stepped out of the woods and hurried toward the sound. "Oh no!" he gasped when he saw several mangy-looking dogs chasing Suzanne down the road behind her horse and buggy.

"Hey!" Titus shouted, waving his hands. "Get away from her, you mangy *hund*!" He glanced around, looking for something to use to ward off the dogs, and was relieved when he spotted a limb that had fallen from a nearby tree. He bent to pick it up and also grabbed a couple of rocks, which he quickly hurled at the dogs.

The dogs barked continuously as they turned away from Suzanne and headed for Titus.

"Run to your buggy, schnell!" Titus shouted, noticing that Suzanne's horse had stopped running and was now standing along the shoulder of the road.

As Suzanne ran to the safety of her buggy, Titus wielded the limb, smacking first one dog and then another. They snarled and yapped, snapping at him, and tearing his pant leg with their sharp teeth. He kicked at one dog and sent it running into the woods.

One of the other dogs turned toward Suzanne's horse and buggy again, but Titus smacked it in the rump, and it took off for the woods, along with three of the others. Just one dog was left, the biggest and meanest-looking one of the pack. Baring its teeth, it lunged for Titus's leg.

Titus hated to hurt any animal, but this could be a life-or-death situation. A pack of wild animals could take a man down, and Titus felt as if he was fighting for his survival. With what seemed like superhuman strength, he charged at the animal with the tree limb, wielding it back and forth as he shouted for the dog to go. One more quick swing with the hunk of wood, and the critter went whimpering into the woods to join his crazed companions.

Titus stood for several terrifying moments, waiting to see if the dogs would return.

When the dogs' barking and yapping faded into the distance, he hurried to Suzanne's buggy and climbed in beside her. Seeing that Suzanne was trembling and sobbing, he pulled her into his arms.

"It's okay. The dogs are gone," he said, gently patting her back.

She continued to sob, wetting the front of his shirt with her tears.

"Look at me now," he whispered. "The dogs are gone, and you're okay."

Tears glistened in her eyes as she looked at him. "Danki for coming to my rescue. I. . .I don't know what I would have done if you hadn't showed up when you did."

"What were you doing out of your buggy?" he asked.

"My horse threw a shoe. I got out to check on her, but

then those horrible hund came charging out of the woods."
Suzanne's chin trembled. "I was never so scared in my life."

Titus tipped her chin up with his thumb and gazed at her
pretty face. Every instinct, every fiber of his being, made him
want to kiss her. But he figured that wouldn't be appropriate,
and he didn't want to scare her off. So instead of kissing
Suzanne, he pulled slowly away and reached for her hand.

—⚬⚬⚬—

"You're not hurt, are you?" Suzanne asked.

"No, I'm fine." Titus pulled up his pant leg. "It's torn, and
there's a welt on my ankle, but thankfully none of the dogs
drew blood."

"I couldn't believe it when those hund came charging after
me like that." Suzanne's voice quavered, even though she felt
much calmer than she had a few moments earlier. The whole
ordeal had left her feeling drained. "I had no idea a pack of
wild dogs was running around here."

Titus frowned. "When dogs are abandoned, they sometimes form packs. Without proper feeding and care they can
become wild and will go after anything that moves. I'm going
to notify the local Humane Society and see if they can trap
those dogs before they end up hurting someone."

A cool breeze blew into the buggy, and Suzanne shivered.
"It scares me to think some child might fall prey to any of
those ferocious animals."

Titus looked over at her with obvious concern. "If you're
too upset to drive, I'd better take you home."

She shook her head. "After my horse threw a shoe, she
started limping. Then when the dogs showed up and started
chasing her, she ran like there was no tomorrow. I'm afraid if
I try to take her the rest of the way home, she might become
lame."

"She won't if we go slow and easy, but I think it might be best if we take her to my place. It's closer, and you can leave Dixie there until you're able to get someone to come out and give her new shoes. As soon as we get the horse settled in my barn, I'll drive you home in my rig," he said.

"That's nice of you." She managed a smile, despite the fact that her eyes still stung with tears. "I've already been gone longer than I'd planned, and I need to get home and help Mom with supper."

"Where were you coming from?" he asked.

"I'd been to the Beilers' store."

Titus gave Suzanne's fingers a gentle squeeze. "During lunch today when our conversation was interpreted by the customer, I was about to ask you a question."

"What were you going to ask?"

"I was wondering if you'd like to visit the Jefferson Davis Monument with me on Saturday. I really liked it when I went before, and I thought it would be fun to see it again before the bad weather sets in."

"Saturday's the day of the produce auction, remember?"

"I was thinking we could go to the monument in the afternoon, after things wind down at the auction."

Hope welled in Suzanne's soul. Titus was asking her to go out with him. That must mean he was interested in pursuing a relationship with her.

He nudged her gently with his elbow. "So what do you say? Would you like to see the monument with me?"

"Jah, I would." *You have no idea how much I would.*

CHAPTER 45

Fairview, Kentucky

Titus had arrived at the auction early on Saturday morning, bringing with him a pet carrier he'd borrowed from Suzanne so he could transport three of Callie's kittens. To his relief, by noon he'd found homes for all of them. It made him feel less guilty about getting rid of the cats, knowing they'd all have good homes. It had done his heart good when he'd seen the look of joy on the face of the little girl who had taken the smallest of the three cats and told her mother how happy she was that she'd come to the auction.

After he'd given the last cat away, Titus stepped into the auction building, where many Amish and English folks had gathered.

"Do I hear fifteen?" the auctioneer hollered as he pointed to a basket full of squash and pumpkins. "Fifteen. . . fifteen. . .yep!"

Titus stayed and watched awhile as various produce items were auctioned off. Then he glanced out the door at the parking lot and noticed Ethan heading toward Suzanne's table, which was full of baked goods. A feeling of jealousy coursed through him, wondering if he had a rival. Maybe he shouldn't have been so hasty when he'd asked Ethan to take Suzanne home last Sunday night. Maybe it would have been better if he'd taken her home himself, even though he'd smelled like putrid manure.

Think I'll head over there now and see if I can tell if anything's going on between those two, he decided.

—◊—

"Heard you had some good banana bread over here," Ethan said, stepping up to the table where Suzanne stood. "Thought I'd better buy some now, before it's all gone."

She smiled. "It has been selling quite well. Almost as well as my potted mums." She motioned to one of the loaves of bread. "How many would you like?"

"Have you got any I could sample?"

"Sure." She handed him a napkin and cut a slice from the loaf she'd been using for samples.

Ethan wasted no time eating it, and when he was done he said, "That was sure good. Think I'll take two loaves."

Suzanne put the bread in a paper sack and handed it to him.

He grinned at her. "If I'd known you had such good banana bread, I'd have been over here sooner."

She smiled. "I'm glad you like it."

Ethan gave her the money and then leaned on the table. "Say, I was wondering if you'd like to go to the next singing with me. Heard there's gonna be another one in a few weeks."

Suzanne glanced to her left and noticed Titus heading her way. "Well, I. . .uh. . .don't know. I might already have a ride."

"With who?"

"I'll have to let you know later, Ethan. I have to keep working here for the next hour, so I really can't talk about this right now."

"Oh, okay." As Ethan walked away, Suzanne couldn't help feeling a bit irritated that he'd never paid her much attention until he'd tasted her banana bread. Was food the only way to a man's heart? Was the fact that she was learning to cook the reason for Titus's sudden interest in her, too, or did he see her for the person she really was?

"Looks like you've done well selling your banana bread today," Titus said when he joined Suzanne by the table.

"It has gone fast." She smiled at him. "Maybe I'll bake more and bring it out to the woodshop for lunch sometime next week."

"That'd be nice." He moved a little closer. "Are you still planning to go to the monument with me this afternoon?"

"Of course."

"Good. We can leave as soon as you're ready."

"I'll probably have to stay here for another hour or so, but after the auction winds down, I'll be free to go."

"Okay." He started to move away but turned back around. "Oh, thought you might like to know that I brought three of Callie's overgrown kittens here today and found homes for all of 'em."

"That's good news. Was Callie upset when you took them away this morning?"

"Not really. I think keeping one cat as a companion for her was a good idea because when I headed out, she and Buttons were sleeping side by side on the porch."

"Buttons?"

He nodded. "I decided to call him that because the little black spot on his head looks like a button."

She smiled. It was good to see the way Titus had learned to like—or at least tolerate—cats.

Just then another customer showed up, looking to buy a pot of mums.

"I'd better let you go," Titus said. "I'll be back to pick you up in an hour."

—∽—

Paradise, Pennsylvania

Fannie stepped into the phone shanty to check for messages, and was disappointed to find none. She thought it was strange that she hadn't heard anything back from Arie yet.

Maybe Arie hasn't responded to my message because she doesn't want me to have Phoebe's address, Fannie thought. *Maybe she thinks I want the address for myself and that I might write something to Phoebe that will cause her never to come back.*

Fannie left the shanty and headed up to the house. When she stepped inside, she found Abraham in the utility room, taking off his dusty work boots.

"Why the worried frown?" he asked, touching the wrinkles in her forehead.

"I just checked our voice mail for messages and can't figure out why Arie hasn't responded to me about Phoebe's address."

"There's a good reason for that," he said, removing his straw hat and placing it on one of the wall pegs. "Arie and Noah aren't home right now. They went to Michigan for her niece's wedding and won't be back until sometime next week."

"Oh, I see." Fannie smiled with relief. "Hopefully, I'll hear something back from her as soon as she gets home."

—∽—

Fairview, Kentucky

When Titus and Suzanne stepped off the elevator at the top of the Jefferson Davis Monument, she gasped. "This is wunderbaar! If I'd known you could see so far, I would have come up here sooner."

"I can't believe you've lived here since you were a girl and have never visited the monument," Titus said.

She laughed lightly and shrugged. "I guess that's how it is with most folks. They travel to other places to see things instead of visiting places close to home."

Titus nodded. "I remember when Harold, my mamm's son from her first marriage, came to Lancaster to visit for the first time. He was anxious to see all the sights in our area—some things we'd never seen ourselves until we went there with him and his family."

She smiled as she peered out the viewing window. "I'm glad you invited me to come here, because it's certainly worth seeing."

Titus was pleased that Suzanne had been willing to go up to the top with him. She obviously wasn't afraid of heights the way Esther was.

"Should we go down now and take a look inside the museum?" he asked. "There are some interesting displays about how the monument was made."

"Sure, I'd like to see that."

They went back down in the elevator, and when they stepped outside, Titus took Suzanne's hand and led the way to the museum. After they'd seen everything there, he bought them both an ice-cream bar.

"This has been fun," Suzanne said as they headed to his buggy a short time later. "I'm glad you invited me."

"I'm glad you came. Oh, there's something I forgot to tell you," Titus said as he helped Suzanne into the buggy.

"What's that?"

"I called the Humane Society, and the man I spoke to said they've had several other calls from people in our area who've seen the wild dogs. They sent someone out to patrol the area and managed to capture the dogs."

"That's a relief."

"It sure is." Titus gathered up the reins. "Guess it's time for me to get you home."

"Would you like to have supper with us again? Knowing Mom, I'm sure there will be plenty of food."

"I'd be happy to stay." Titus smiled. If things kept going this way, he and Suzanne would be officially courting soon. Maybe by this time next year, she might even be his wife.

CHAPTER 46

For the next two weeks, Titus saw Suzanne as often as he could. She'd begun working in the woodshop a few days a week, which gave them more time to visit. To makes things even nicer, Titus had been invited to the Yoders' for supper several more times, and he'd taken Suzanne to the last singing they'd had.

Today, the old trailer would be taken away, which meant Titus would need a place to stay for a few days until the new manufactured home was hauled in and set up. Verna Yoder had invited him to stay at their house and share a room with Russell, which meant he wouldn't have far to go to work each day.

Titus was glad it was Saturday and he didn't have to work in the woodshop, because he still had some packing to do before Allen and the crew he'd hired to move the trailer showed up. Most of Titus's things would be stored in the barn until he moved into the new house, so he'd take only the clothes he needed while he stayed with the Yoders. He planned to take his horse and buggy to the Yoders' later in the day and would come back to his home every evening to check on things and feed Callie and Buttons. Titus had come to appreciate the cats for keeping the mice down, and he had to admit it was kind of fun to watch the two cats play.

As he headed to the kitchen to pack a few more boxes, he thought about the other night, when he and Suzanne had been sitting on her porch, drinking hot apple cider and eating popcorn. Samson, one of Suzanne's cats, had joined them, sitting at Titus's feet, begging to be fed.

Titus chuckled as he remembered how comical it had looked when a piece of popcorn fell on the porch and Samson started batting at it. Then, when the popcorn got stuck on the cat's claw and he'd tried to shake it off, Suzanne and Titus had a good laugh.

Titus smiled as he bent to close up a box of dishes. Except for when he'd been with Phoebe, he couldn't remember having such a good time with any woman the way he did when he was with Suzanne.

He grimaced. *I can't believe Mom still hasn't been able to get Phoebe's address for me.* The last time he'd talked to Mom, she'd said Phoebe's folks had gone to Michigan for a wedding, but surely they must be back by now. At this rate, he'd never get a letter written to Phoebe.

—❦—

As Suzanne headed down the driveway to get the mail that morning, she heard a loud *meow.* She turned and saw Samson, following in her footsteps. This was not unusual for the cat, because ever since he'd been a kitten he'd liked to go for walks with Suzanne.

Suzanne's thoughts went to Titus, and how, when he'd first moved to Kentucky he'd made it clear that he had no fondness for cats.

She chuckled to herself. *I think Callie coming to live with him and giving birth to those kittens changed all that.* Sometimes when people were around someone long enough, they'd begin to see them in a different light. That had certainly been true of Suzanne and the way she felt about Titus. When he'd first come to work in the woodshop, she could barely tolerate him. Of course, she was sure the feeling had been mutual.

Since she and Titus had become better acquainted, she'd quickly discovered how much they had in common, and now saw him in a completely different light. What she'd previously seen as arrogance, she now realized was his way of disguising his feelings of inadequacy. Thankfully, he seemed more sure of himself now, as did she.

She'd come to realize more fully that Titus had a caring attitude toward others. He'd proven that when he'd helped out while Grandpa was recuperating from his fall. Even the way Titus had taken care of Callie and her brood was proof that he cared.

Suzanne looked forward to the time Titus would be staying at their house while he waited for his new home to be set up. She realized that since she and Titus had started courting, she been happier than she ever thought possible. All this time she'd been saying she didn't need a boyfriend and didn't care about getting married, but now that seemed to be all she could think about.

By the time Suzanne reached the mailbox, she'd convinced herself that Titus was the perfect man for her. She just hoped the feeling was mutual.

—⁓—

Paradise, Pennsylvania

When Fannie entered Naomi and Caleb's store, she spotted

Arie talking with Naomi at the front counter. She waited until Naomi had rung up Arie's purchases and placed them in a paper sack; then she stepped up to Arie and said, "It's good to see you. I heard you went to Michigan for your niece's wedding."

"That's right."

"How long have you been back?"

"We got home a week ago," Arie said, avoiding eye contact.

"Did you get the message I left on your voice mail?"

"Jah." Arie's cheeks turned pink as she dropped her gaze to the floor.

"Then why haven't you responded?"

"Let's go outside." Arie motioned to the door. "I'd rather not discuss this in here."

Fannie glanced at Naomi and noticed a look of concern on her face. "I'll be back to do my shopping after I speak with Arie," she said.

Naomi nodded. "Of course. Take your time."

Fannie followed Arie out the door and around back to the hitching rail where Arie's horse and buggy were parked. She waited until Arie had put the paper sack in the buggy, then touched Arie's arm and said, "If you got my message and have been home a week already, how come you haven't replied by now?"

Arie's eyebrows furrowed. "Why would you need my daughter's address? Are you planning to write her because you're still upset that she jilted your son?"

Fannie shook her head vigorously. "Of course not. Titus asked me to get the address for him."

"Titus did? Whatever for? Is he hoping Phoebe will come back to him?"

"I'm sure that's not what he has in mind. He just wants to set things right—to apologize for the ill feelings he's had toward Phoebe and to let her know that he's forgiven her for hurting him the way she did."

Arie sucked in her lower lip and her eyes narrowed. "Is that all there is to it?"

"Jah."

"All right then, I'll give you Phoebe's address, but I won't guarantee she'll answer his letter. For the last several months, she hasn't responded to my phone calls or any of the letters I've written." Arie sighed deeply, and tears welled in her eyes. "Unless God performs a miracle and changes Phoebe's heart, I'm afraid Noah and I will never see or hear from our daughter again."

—⁂—

Los Angeles, California

Phoebe's stomach growled as she hurried down the street toward the ice-cream shop. She'd forgotten to set her alarm and had woken up late, so she hadn't taken the time to eat breakfast. Not that there was much in her apartment to eat, anyway. She had cereal but no milk, bread but no butter, and coffee but no sugar to sweeten it. If she didn't get more hours at her evening job soon, she didn't know what she would do. Between Phoebe's two part-time jobs, she was barely making enough to pay the rent and buy a few groceries. In order to save money, she'd started riding an old bike she'd bought at a pawn shop. It was cheaper than taking the bus to and from work and whenever she went shopping. It didn't matter that the basket on the bike didn't hold a lot, because she couldn't afford to buy much, anyway.

When Phoebe entered the ice-cream shop she knew immediately that she was in trouble because her boss, Toby, stood behind the counter with his arms folded, glaring at her.

"You're late," he growled, nodding at the clock on the far wall. "What's your excuse this time, Phoebe?"

"I. . .uh. . .forgot to set my alarm, and—"

"You've used that line before, and it's gettin' kind of old." Toby pointed to the freezer where the ice cream was kept. "As if your tardiness isn't bad enough, the container of strawberry ice cream was nearly full at the beginning of your shift yesterday, and now it's almost empty. What have you got to say about that?"

She dropped her gaze to the floor. "I. . .uh. . .sold a lot of ice cream yesterday."

"Did everyone buy strawberry?"

"Well, no, but—"

"You think I don't know what's been going on behind my back, or when I'm not here in the shop?"

She gave no reply.

"You've been helping yourself to the ice cream whenever you want, haven't you?"

A lump formed in Phoebe's throat as she nodded slowly. "I. . .I was hungry."

"What's the matter? Have you been forgetting to pack a lunch, just like you've forgotten to set your alarm?"

She shook her head. "I don't have much money, and I—"

"So you think it's okay to steal from me?" His steely blue eyes seemed to bore right through her. "I thought you Amish folks were honest and upright."

A feeling of shame washed over Phoebe. While she no longer dressed in Amish clothes, she'd told Toby when he'd first hired her that she'd grown up in an Amish home in Pennsylvania. She guessed he thought that meant she would set a good example. He was probably right—she should have—but he wasn't the one doing without for lack of money. He didn't have to work two jobs to make ends meet, either.

"I know I just got paid yesterday, but that money's gone already, so I'll pay you back for the ice cream I ate when I get my next paycheck."

Toby shook his head. "There won't be a next paycheck for you, young lady. I've had enough of your deceitful ways." He pointed to the door. "You'd better turn around and head out now, because as of this minute, you're fired!"

Phoebe stood a few seconds, letting his words sink in; then she whirled around and dashed out the door. With only one part-time job, she wouldn't have enough money to pay the rent, much less get food. "What am I going to do now?" she wailed.

CHAPTER 47

Pembroke, Kentucky

When Titus woke up Saturday morning two weeks later, he looked around in amazement. He'd moved into his new house two days ago, and liked it a lot. No more squeaky drawers in the kitchen, bumping into the wall when he got out of bed, or dealing with leaky faucets or a toilet that overflowed. The manufactured home had been well cared for by its previous owners and had plenty of room. It had three bedrooms, one and a half baths, a full-sized kitchen, living room, dining room, and even a utility room where Titus's new gas-powered wringer washer sat. It was nice not to have to haul his clothes to the Laundromat anymore.

Guess I should call my folks and let them know I'm settled into my new home, Titus thought after he'd gone to the kitchen and poured himself some coffee. *Come to think of it, I haven't been out to the phone shanty to check messages since I moved in here. Guess I may as well do that now.*

He added a spoonful of sugar to his coffee, picked up the mug, and headed out the door.

When he entered the dimly lit shanty, he turned on the

battery-operated lantern, making it easier to see. The light on the phone was blinking, so he knew he had at least one message.

Titus took a seat at the table, punched the button to listen to the messages, and leaned back in his chair.

The first message was from Allen, reminding Titus that he'd be coming by later this afternoon to check things over on the house. He said he wanted to make sure everything was working right and that he'd picked up a used bedroom set he thought Titus could use if he had any overnight guests. Allen also said he'd be bringing the paperwork for Titus to sign in order to purchase the house and land.

He smiled. *Now that's good news. Sure wish I'd had the manufactured home with an extra bedroom when Mom and Dad were here. Maybe Mom would have felt better about me living here if she'd seen this place instead of the old trailer.*

Titus listened to the next message. It was from Mom, saying she'd spoken to Arie Stoltzfus and that she'd gotten Phoebe's address for him.

He picked up the pen lying beside the phone and started to jot down the information on his arm, but changed his mind and used the tablet instead. It was time to grow up and act more mature.

Titus stared at Phoebe's address, and his thoughts took him on a journey to the past, remembering how things used to be between him and Phoebe. . . .

"Sure wish I didn't have to sneak over here like this in order to see you," Titus said as he and Phoebe hid in the shadows behind her father's barn. "It's not fair that our folks won't let us court until you turn sixteen."

Phoebe moved closer until her arm was brushing his. "We can court without them knowing, just like we're doing now."

*"Puh! This ain't courtin'," he mumbled. "I want to
take you out for rides in my buggy, bring you home from
singings, take you on picnics and to volleyball games, and
come calling at your house."*

*"We only have another year to wait, and then we
can begin officially courting," she whispered. "In the
meantime, we can keep meeting each other like this, and
our folks will never have to know."*

*"I'd wait forever for you, Phoebe." He lowered his
head and kissed her.*

Titus blinked a couple of times as his mind snapped back
to the present. The past was in the past, and he must look to
the future now—a future that would perhaps include Suzanne
as his wife someday living here in his new Kentucky home.

Titus clicked off the lantern, tore the sheet of paper with
Phoebe's address from the notepad, and stepped out of the
shanty. He'd go back to the house, fix himself something for
breakfast, and write Phoebe a letter. Then, knowing he'd done
the right thing, he could put his focus fully on the future.

—w—

When a sandpapery tongue swiped Suzanne's arm, her eyes
popped open. "Samson, what are you doing on my bed, you
big, bad cat?"

Samson nuzzled her hand with his nose and purred.
Suzanne snuggled him close, enjoying the feel of the cat's
soft, sleek fur.

She turned her head toward the window, remembering
that she'd left it partially open last night—apparently wide
enough for the cat to get in. "You need to go back outside
now," she said.

Pushing the covers aside, she slid out of bed, opened the

window fully, and set Samson on the branch of the maple tree growing outside her bedroom window. He'd used the tree as a way into the house a few times before, so she knew he'd have no problem finding his way to the ground.

Suzanne hurried to get dressed, and when she stepped into the kitchen a short time later, the pleasant aroma of hickory-smoked bacon greeted her, making her mouth water in anticipation.

"Guder mariye," Mom said, turning from her job at the stove long enough to smile at Suzanne. "You look tired. Didn't you sleep well last night?"

"I slept okay once I fell asleep," Suzanne replied. "Just had a hard time turning off my thoughts."

"Thoughts about what?"

Suzanne's face heated. She wasn't about to admit that she'd been thinking about Titus. "Just things, that's all."

"You sure it was 'things' and not someone special?"

Suzanne shrugged in reply.

The bacon sizzled and spattered as Mom flipped it over in the pan. "You don't have to hide it from me, Suzanne. I fell in love once, and I know the signs."

"I do care for Titus," she whispered, hoping no one else in the family could hear their conversation. "I'm just not certain he cares for me."

Mom swatted the air with her spatula. "You're kidding, right?"

Suzanne shook her head.

"During the time he was staying with us, I saw the expression on his face whenever the two of you were in the same room." Mom smiled. "It was the same look your daed had on his face when we were courting."

"What look was that?" Nelson asked when he and Grandpa entered the room.

"The look of love." Mom smiled and pointed the spatula in Nelson's direction. "The same look I've seen on your face whenever you're with your aldi."

Nelson shrugged. "I won't deny it. I do care for Lucy, but I'm not sure it's love I actually feel. Right now, I only see her as a good friend."

"If you're not in love with the girl, you shouldn't be leading her on." Grandpa ambled across the room and took a seat at the table. "You've been courting Lucy for some time now, and she's likely thinkin' she'll be gettin' a marriage proposal soon."

Nelson's eyes widened. "You really think so?"

Grandpa gave a nod. "Would you like my advice, son?"

"Sure."

"If you're not in love with Lucy and don't see her as a potential wife, then you ought to break things off with her now, before she gets hurt."

"I'll give it some thought," Nelson mumbled, his face turning red.

Suzanne was glad the focus of the conversation wasn't on her anymore, but she felt sorry for Nelson, who looked awfully befuddled. Suzanne had thought he and Lucy were getting serious. She couldn't believe how wrong she'd been.

Suzanne glanced at the chair Titus had occupied while he'd been staying with them and winced. *Maybe him courting me doesn't mean anything, either. Maybe he's just spending time with me because he needs a friend.* A lump formed in her throat, and she swallowed hard in an effort to push it down. *Maybe he'll never say he loves me or that he wants me to be his wife.*

—◆◆◆—

Los Angeles, California

Phoebe had been sitting at the table going over the want

ads for the last half hour when she heard a loud knock. She tiptoed from the kitchen and looked out the peephole in her apartment door.

Oh no, it's Mr. Higgins. I'll bet he's here to collect the rent I owe for this month. She held her breath when he knocked again.

"Phoebe Stoltzfus, are you in there?"

Go away. Go away. If I wanted to talk to you, I'd open the door.

Three more knocks, then all was quiet. Phoebe breathed a sigh of relief. She couldn't answer the door, because she didn't have enough money to pay the rent, and without another part-time job, she would never have enough.

Satisfied that she'd escaped a confrontation with her landlord, Phoebe returned to the kitchen. As she moved toward the sink to get a glass of water, her gaze came to rest on the unopened letter lying on the counter. It had arrived two days ago—another letter from Mom, no doubt pleading with Phoebe to come home and join the church.

"Well, I won't do it," Phoebe muttered with a determined set of her jaw. "I'm not going back there. No, never!"

CHAPTER 48

Hopkinsville, Kentucky

As Suzanne sat across from Titus at a table in Ryan's Steak House, she couldn't help but smile. They'd both needed some things at Walmart, so after the woodshop had closed for the day, they'd hired a driver to take them to Hopkinsville. Since they were hungry by the time they got there, they decided to eat supper before they went shopping. Their driver had told them he had a few errands to run and would pick them up in an hour.

Suzanne never tired of spending time with Titus. In fact, the more time she spent with him, the more her heart ached to be his wife. She just wished he'd give some indication as to how he felt about her.

"I can't believe it's November already," Titus said, halting her thoughts. "Seems like just yesterday that I moved into my new place."

"Time has passed quickly," she agreed. "Thanksgiving's only a few weeks away, and then Christmas will be upon us."

He cut another piece of his juicy steak. "Any idea what you might like for Christmas?"

A proposal from you. . .or a declaration of love, she told herself.

"I...uh...don't really know."

"I'd thought about making you something in the woodshop—something you could put in your hope chest, but with you workin' there part-time now, it's hard to make anything without you knowing about it."

Hope welled in Suzanne's soul. He wanted to make her a gift for Christmas, and he'd mentioned it being for her hope chest. Did that mean he had marriage on his mind, or was it just wishful thinking?

"To tell you the truth, I don't even have a hope chest," she said, reaching for the salt shaker and adding some to her mixed green salad.

His eyebrows lifted. "How come?"

"I've never had a serious boyfriend and figured I'd probably never get married, so I didn't see a need to store up things for a hope chest."

"What about me? Don't you consider me your boyfriend? After all, we've gone several places together, and I'm always over at your house it seems."

A wave of heat washed over her face as she slowly nodded. "Jah, that's true."

He grinned and gave her a wink. "I'm glad we got that settled."

Suzanne's hopes for the future soared. While Titus still hadn't said he loved her, and there'd been no mention of marriage, the fact that he'd affirmed that he was her boyfriend, made her think it was just a matter of time until he said the three words she longed to hear most: *I love you.*

Paradise, Pennsylvania

"It was nice of you to invite us for supper this evening,"

Elsie told Hannah.

Samuel bobbed his head. "The fried chicken tastes real good."

Hannah smiled. "I'm glad you like it. My mamm gave me the recipe."

Timothy swiped his napkin across his face. "My fraa's a good cook. There's no doubt about it."

"Is that why you married me?" Hannah asked with raised eyebrows. "Because I can cook?"

" 'Course not." He winked at her and reached over to pat their daughter's head. "I knew you'd give me beautiful kinner, like this little *maedel*."

Hannah wrinkled her nose. "You're just like your twin bruder. . .a big *bloge*."

Timothy chuckled. "And that's why you married me— because you like to be teased."

She rolled her eyes and forked another piece of chicken onto his plate. "I think you'd better eat. It'll keep you out of trouble."

Samuel, being the more serious type, wasn't sure how to take the banter between Timothy and Hannah. Could there be an underlying power struggle going on, or were they just teasing each other?

"Have you heard anything from Titus lately?" Samuel asked.

Timothy nodded. "Last time we talked, he said he's all settled into his new home and liking it a lot. Fact is, he seems to like pretty much everything about living in Kentucky. . . including his new aldi, Suzanne."

"Uncle Titus has a girlfriend?" Samuel's eight-year-old daughter, Marla, questioned.

"So it would seem," Timothy replied.

"I'll bet Phoebe Stoltzfus wouldn't like that if she knew," Marla said.

"Well, she doesn't know, because she's living in California."
Hannah frowned. "That girl was never anything but trouble
for Titus. I don't see what he ever saw in her."

Samuel didn't think this was an appropriate conversation
for his children, so he quickly changed the subject again. "I've
been thinking about making a trip to Kentucky to see Titus."
He looked over at Elsie and smiled. "Don't you think that
would be fun?"

She reached for her glass of water and took a drink. "I don't
know, Samuel. Given the nausea and fatigue I've been having
with this pregnancy, I'm not really up to a trip anywhere right
now. Maybe we could go sometime next year, after the boppli's
born and old enough to travel."

Samuel nodded. "That makes good sense."

Timothy looked over at Hannah and said, "Maybe we
should go with 'em. It would be a fun trip for Mindy."

"There's nothing for me or Mindy in Kentucky," Hannah
said sharply.

"How do you know?" Timothy asked. "You've never been
there."

She gave a decisive nod. "That's right, and I don't want to
go there, either!"

—⁊⁊⁊—

Los Angeles, California

Phoebe yawned and stretched one arm over her head. She'd
just returned home from her job at the convenience store and
was exhausted. They'd had a lot of customers this evening:
some demanding and impatient, and some—like the two
bikers who'd showed up shortly before her shift ended—who'd
given her a hard time because she wouldn't go out with them.

Whatever happened to her dream of starting a new,

exciting life in California? Why was nothing going right for her anymore? The only reason she was still in this apartment was because Charlene, one of her coworkers, had loaned her enough money to cover this month's rent. Phoebe still hadn't found a second job, and she knew she couldn't keep borrowing money forever. If something didn't go her way soon, she'd have no other choice but to move back home.

She flopped down on the shabby brown sofa and thumbed through the mail she'd picked up before she'd headed upstairs to her apartment. There were two advertising flyers, an electric bill she wouldn't be able to pay, and two letters. The first one was from Mom, so she tossed it on the coffee table. When she saw the return address on the second letter, her mouth went dry. It was from Titus, in Kentucky.

Phoebe's fingers trembled as she tore the letter open and read it silently:

Dear Phoebe,

This letter is long overdue, but it's taken me some time to come to the place where I could forgive you for walking out on me. I realize now that I've been hurting myself by hanging on to the bitterness I felt when you broke up with me. God has changed my heart and shown me many things about myself, as well as others, since I moved to Kentucky. I'm a different person—more confident and mature. I'm even buying my own place—a manufactured home on several acres of land.

I also want to ask your forgiveness for anything I may have said or done to hurt you in the past. I still don't understand why you'd want to leave the Amish faith and go English, but that's your choice, and it's not my place to say what's right or wrong for you.

I hope things are going well for you in California and

that you've found happiness in whatever you're doing.
I wish you all God's best.

Most sincerely,
Titus

Tears welled in Phoebe's eyes and coursed down her cheeks. Titus was obviously happy in Kentucky. She was miserable here in California. Titus had forgiven her and wished her God's best. She was bitter and angry toward God, as well as everyone else.

Phoebe wasn't sure when all that bitterness had begun, but she thought it may have started when she was thirteen and her folks had forbidden her to see Titus.

She sat for several minutes, mulling things over; then she gathered up Titus's letter and hurried into her bedroom to pack. God must be blessing her already, because she knew exactly what she needed to do. By this time tomorrow, she'd be on a bus headed for Kentucky.

CHAPTER 49

Pembroke, Kentucky

Suzanne took a seat on the sofa, prepared to embroider the pillowcases she'd made the other day. Even though she didn't have a cedar chest to put the things in, she'd decided that in case Titus should ever propose, she ought to have some things ready for marriage. She would put them in a cardboard box for now.

"What's that you're working on?" Mom asked when she came into the living room and took a seat in the rocking chair across from Suzanne.

"I'm doing some embroidery work on the pillowcases I made."

"For your hope chest?"

"Jah."

Mom smiled. "I'm glad to see that you're taking an interest in more domestic things now and have begun making some things you can use when you get married."

"*If* I get married," Suzanne corrected. "Titus hasn't asked me yet, and he may never ask."

"I think he will. Just give him time. From some of the

things you've told me, I assume that he was hurt badly by his ex-girlfriend when she ran off to California. He might be taking his time before he gets serious again."

"I realize that, but I hope he won't take too much time. I'm not getting any younger, you know."

Mom leaned her head back and laughed. "For goodness' sake, Suzanne; you're only twenty-two. It's not like you're *en alt* maedel."

"I'll turn twenty-three in January, and I feel like an old maid. Many women my age are already married and starting their families by now." Suzanne threaded her needle and stuck it into the cotton material.

Mom started the rocking chair moving, causing it to squeak against the wooden floor. "Esther's a few years older than you. Do you think she's an old maid?"

"I guess not, but she's had several boyfriends. I wouldn't be surprised if she finds someone who wants to marry her soon."

"You need to have patience. And whatever you do, don't say or do anything to make Titus think you're trying to push him. Men want to do the wooing, and we women need to be smart enough to at least let them think they're in control of the situation." Mom stopped rocking and leaned forward in her chair. "Just be yourself, and take an interest in the things Titus likes. Eventually he'll come to his senses and realize he can't live another minute without asking you to be his fraa."

Just then, Effie shuffled into the room, looking a bit under the weather. "Look," she said, holding her arm out to Mom. "I've got itchy spots here and on my tummy, too."

Mom studied Effie's arm and then felt her forehead. "You're running a fever, that's for sure. From the appearance of these bumps, I'd say you've come down with a case of *wasserpareble*."

Effie's eyes widened. "Chickenpox?"

"That's what it looks like to me. Have the pox been going around at school?" Mom asked.

Effie shrugged. "Maybe so. Sarah Beth's been out of school all week, and Brian and his sister Peggy weren't there today, so I guess they might have wasserpareble."

Suzanne groaned. "You'd better stay away from me then, because I've never had the chickenpox, and I sure don't need them now."

—◊◊◊—

Tennessee

Phoebe stared out the bus window, trying to concentrate on the passing scenery so she wouldn't worry about how things would go when she saw Titus. What if he wasn't happy to see her? What if he asked her to leave?

He won't do that. I'm sure he won't, Phoebe told herself. *He said in his letter that he's forgiven me for breaking up with him, and I know how much he cared about me even when I was only thirteen.*

Phoebe put her head against the seat and closed her eyes. Her body felt stiff, and she was tired of sitting on crowded buses with people she didn't know. She'd gotten on the first bus at the Greyhound station in Los Angeles two days ago at seven fifteen in the evening, had made two transfers, and would arrive in Clarksville, Tennessee, by seven fifteen this evening. That was the Greyhound bus station closest to Pembroke, Kentucky, where Titus lived.

When she got to Clarksville, she would get a taxi to take her to Titus's place. It would probably be expensive, but she thought she had enough money. The bus ticket had cost her $209, but she'd started out with $300, which she'd borrowed from Charlene, so she should have enough to pay the taxi driver. She'd promised to send Charlene the money she owed for the bus ticket, as well as the rent she'd paid on her apartment. Unless she found a job, however, she probably wouldn't be able to make good on her word until after she and Titus got married.

Of course, she reminded herself, *the only way Titus will agree to marry me is if I'm willing to join the Amish church. He made that clear after he joined the church himself.* She leaned toward the window, trying to find a comfortable position, more anxious than ever to get off the bus.

I've tried living in the English world by myself, and it didn't work out very well, so I think I'm ready to go back to living the Plain way of life. I just don't want to go home and join the church there, because I'm sure Mom will try to make me feel guilty for leaving home, and Dad will probably lay out a bunch of rules, the way he did when I lived there before. Well, I'm not going back to Pennsylvania. I'm going to start a new life in Kentucky with Titus.

─────ᴍᴍ─────

Pembroke, Kentucky

Titus had gone out to the barn right after he'd done the supper dishes so he could continue working on the hope chest he planned to give Suzanne for Christmas. Since he wanted it to be a surprise, he knew better than to work on it in the Yoders' woodshop. Suzanne spent a lot of time out there these days even when she wasn't helping them work. Sometimes it was to bring the men their lunch, and sometimes just to sit and watch. When she wasn't in the shop, she was in the kitchen, perfecting her baking skills. Titus always looked forward to sampling what she'd made and was impressed with how well she'd learned to cook.

He'd just started sanding the hope chest when he heard a car pull into the yard. It didn't sound like Allen's truck, so he figured it must be one of his English neighbors.

He set the sandpaper aside and headed for the barn door. When he stepped outside, he was surprised to see a taxi parked in his driveway.

When the back door of the cab opened, and a young woman with shiny auburn hair hanging down her back, stepped out, Titus froze. It was Phoebe Stoltzfus! He'd have recognized her anywhere, even without her Amish clothes. The question was, why had she come?

CHAPTER 50

"Phoebe, wh–what are you doing here?" Titus stammered as a trickle of sweat rolled down his forehead. He couldn't believe she was standing in front of him. It felt like he was in the middle of a dream.

Phoebe gave him a dimpled smile—the same smile that used to make his heart feel like melting butter. "I came to see you," she said ever so sweetly.

"How'd you know where I live?"

She tipped her head slightly and snickered. "Your address was on the letter you sent me."

"Oh, that's right." Titus felt like a gibbering idiot. Having Phoebe show up out of the blue had taken him completely by surprise.

"Things didn't work out for me in California, so after I got your letter, I decided to catch a bus and come here to see you."

He shifted from one foot to the other, as his heart began to pound. Seeing Phoebe again had stirred up emotions he thought he'd managed to bury. "I. . .uh. . .guess you'll be heading to Pennsylvania from here?"

"Why would I go there?"

"To see your folks, of course."

She shook her head. "I came to be with you. I want us to start over again."

Titus swallowed hard. "Phoebe, I—"

"So this is your place?" She motioned to the manufactured home behind them.

He nodded, not trusting his voice. The longer she stood there smiling at him, the harder it was to think or even breathe.

"It looks nice. Can I see the inside?"

"I guess so." Titus didn't know what else to do—especially since her taxi had already gone.

When they entered the house, he gave her a quick tour, the whole time feeling as if he were dreaming and unable to wake up. When he'd sent her that letter, he'd never imagined she would come here to see him.

"This is perfect," Phoebe said. "There's lots of space, and even a guest room where I can stay."

He shook his head hard, as reality set in. "Huh-uh. No way! You can't stay here."

"Why not?"

"It wouldn't be right, and you know it, Phoebe."

"But I have no place else to go."

"I'll call my driver and have him take you to a hotel in Hopkinsville."

She frowned, causing tiny wrinkles to form across her forehead. "I can't stay at a hotel, Titus."

"Why not?"

"I have no money for that. I had to borrow money from a friend to pay for my bus ticket here, and I used what I had left to pay for the cab."

Titus didn't know what to do. He felt sorry for Phoebe, just like he had when she was a teenager and used to complain that her dad was too strict. After thinking things over a few minutes, he finally said, "Guess I could take you over to the Beilers' place and see if you can stay with them tonight."

"Who are the Beilers?"

"They're part of my church district, and they own a general store in the area. They only have one daughter still living at home, so I'm sure they must have an extra room."

Phoebe's lower lip protruded in a pout, the way it often had when they'd been courting and she hadn't gotten her way. "Are you sure I can't stay here with you?"

"Of course I'm sure, and I'm surprised you'd even ask."

Her face colored to a deep pink, and she quickly averted his gaze. "You're right, Titus. I don't know what I was thinking."

Titus picked up her suitcase and opened the door. "I'll get my horse and buggy ready, and then we can head over to the Beilers' and see if they'd mind putting you up for the night."

"Do we need to go there right now? We have a lot of catching up to do, so can't we sit here and visit awhile?"

"We can talk on the way over there." Titus hurried out the door, eager to get away from Phoebe so he could think. Being in her presence made him feel befuddled and disoriented, like he'd lost his ability to think or see things clearly.

When he entered the barn to get Lightning, he glanced at the hope chest and winced. What would Suzanne say when she found out that Phoebe was here? How would this turn of events affect his and Suzanne's relationship?

—⚉—

"It feels strange to be riding in a buggy again," Phoebe said as she slid a little closer to Titus on the seat.

"I guess it would. What's it been now. . .nine months since you left for California?"

"I went there the first part of March, so it's been eight months."

He glanced at her, and his gaze came to rest on her faded blue jeans. "I guess you threw away all your Amish clothes, huh?"

She nodded and released a lingering sigh. "I wish I still had them now."

He offered no reply.

"Things were great when Darlene and I first got to California. We shared an apartment and both had jobs. Then all of a sudden she decided to move back home, which left me in the lurch."

"How so?"

"The rent on the apartment was too much for me to pay with the money I earned at the ice-cream store where I worked during the day. So I had to get an evening job working at a convenience store." Phoebe grimaced. "Even with two jobs, it was a struggle for me to pay the rent, utilities, cell phone, and also buy food. I paid the fee to end the cell phone agreement, cut way back on groceries, and starting riding an old bike so I wouldn't have to scrape money together for bus fare." She glanced over at Titus to gauge his reaction, but he kept his focus straight ahead and said nothing.

"One day I was late getting to work at the ice-cream store," she continued. "My boss was really upset and fired me."

Still no response from Titus. Was he even listening to what she was saying, or didn't he care?

She reached over and placed her hand on his knee. "Did you hear what I said?"

"Jah. Just thinking is all, and you're makin' it hard, so please take your hand off my knee."

Her chin trembled as she pulled her hand aside. Titus seemed so distant, as though he wished she hadn't come. "You can't imagine how hard it's been for me," she said, struggling not to give in to her tears. "With only one job, I couldn't make ends meet, and the way things were going, I would have been kicked out of my apartment soon and ended up on the street, begging for money and food."

"Sorry to hear you've been through so much. With things being so bad, I'm surprised you didn't return home."

She shook her head and swallowed against the lump clogging her throat. "I told you before. I can't go back there. Mom would say, 'I told you so,' and Dad would lay down a bunch of rules."

He turned his head and looked at her with a grim expression. "So you came here because you were out of money and had no place else to go?"

She placed her hand cautiously on his arm, hoping he wouldn't ask her to move it, and was relieved when he didn't. "That's not how it was, Titus. When I got your letter, it made me miss what we used to have. I realized that I still cared for you, so I came here, hoping you'd take me back."

No response. Just a blank look on Titus's face. Did he believe her? Did he still have feelings for her? Surely he couldn't have forgotten what they'd once shared.

"I'd like to stay in Kentucky and see about joining the church," she said.

"That's. . .uh. . .not a good idea."

"How come?"

"It's different here, and there'd be a lot of adjustments for you to make."

"I'm good at adapting. I did plenty of that while I was in California." Phoebe leaned close to his ear. "I know I'll have to prove myself, and I hope you'll give me a chance."

He glanced at her, and then looked quickly away. "It's not that simple, Phoebe. You see, I have a—"

She squeezed his arm tenderly. "Remember how much fun

we used to have when we were courting?"

"Jah, but—"

"Remember how you always said you'd never love anyone but me?"

"I did say that, but now I'm—"

"Please don't send me away," she pleaded. "I just can't go home, and I really want to be here with you."

When Titus gave no reply, a sense of desperation welled in Phoebe's soul. Didn't he want her anymore?

A few minutes later, Titus guided his horse and buggy off the road and turned up a driveway. "This is the Beilers' place," he said. "I think it's best if you wait in the buggy while I speak to them."

"Okay," Phoebe said with a nod. Oh, she hoped they would let her stay.

Titus hopped down, secured his horse to the hitching rail, and sprinted for the house.

Phoebe leaned back in the seat and drew in a deep breath to help calm her nerves. She knew she'd taken Titus by surprise, showing up the way she had, and even though he was obviously confused right now, she felt sure that after they spent some time together, everything would work out. She'd make sure it did.

Chapter 51

As Titus lay in bed that night, staring into the darkness, he replayed the events of the evening. He'd explained Phoebe's appearance to the Beilers the best that he could, and they'd graciously agreed to let her stay with them until she figured out what she was going to do. Then he'd said good-bye to Phoebe and hurried back home, feeling the need to be alone so he could think things through.

"What I wish Phoebe would do is go home," he mumbled. "If she stays here, it'll wreck things between me and Suzanne, and I might even weaken and take Phoebe back."

Titus turned onto his side and punched his pillow a couple of times, trying to find a comfortable position. Was it possible that Phoebe had been telling the truth about wanting to live in Kentucky and join the Amish church? Did she still have feelings for him, as she'd said, or was she just in need of a place to stay?

Do I still care for her? Titus asked himself. *Could I have only thought I was falling in love with Suzanne because she looks similar to Phoebe?*

If that were true, and he really didn't love Suzanne, then

he needed to know it now before he asked her to marry him.

I need wisdom in knowing what to do, Lord, Titus silently prayed. *Things were going along fine until Phoebe showed up. I thought I had my future planned out, and I figured Suzanne would be a part of it. I'm not sure about anything right now. Please show me what I should do.*

Titus tossed and turned for another hour until he finally made a decision. Tomorrow morning, before he went to the woodshop, he'd stop at the Yoders' house and speak to Suzanne. He didn't want her finding out about Phoebe from Esther or anyone else in her family. He needed to tell her himself.

—〰—

When Phoebe awoke the following morning, she felt disoriented and out of place. With a feeling of panic, she sat up and glanced around the room. "Where am I?" she murmured. This was certainly not her apartment in California.

At the foot of the bed sat a cedar chest, with the pair of jeans she'd been wearing last night, draped over it. Across the room stood a dresser, desk, and a wooden chair. The only window in the room was covered with a dark green shade.

Her gaze came to rest on her suitcase, lying opened on the floor underneath the window. Suddenly, things came into focus.

Oh that's right. I'm at the Beilers' house. I'm staying in what used to be their oldest son's bedroom.

Still stiff and a bit sore from sitting on the bus so many hours, Phoebe pulled the covers back, clambered out of bed, and reached around to rub the knot that had formed in her lower back. She shivered as she plodded across the cold wooden floor in her bare feet. It sure was chilly here in November. Nothing like the warm balmy weather in southern California.

She slipped into her blue jeans and T-shirt, ran a brush

through her hair, and hurried down the stairs, following the welcoming aroma of freshly perked coffee coming from the kitchen.

"Good morning," she said to Esther, who stood at the cupboard, cracking eggs into a bowl.

"Morning," Esther mumbled in a voice barely above a whisper.

Esther's mother, Dinah, turned from where she stood at the stove and smiled. "Good morning, Phoebe. Did you sleep well?"

Phoebe gave a nod. "I didn't sleep much on the bus ride here, so a good night's rest in a real bed was what I needed."

Dinah motioned to Phoebe's jeans. "If you're going to church with us this morning, then you'll need something else to wear. Esther can loan you one of her dresses, since you look to be about the same size."

"I'd appreciate that." Phoebe glanced over at Esther, but Esther ignored her and started stirring the eggs she'd cracked into the bowl.

"Esther," Dinah said, "why don't you take Phoebe upstairs and see what you have that might fit her while I finish breakfast?"

Esther nodded and set the bowl aside, but her pinched expression let Phoebe know she wasn't too happy about it.

Phoebe followed her quickly out of the room.

"Why'd you really come here?" Esther asked when they entered her bedroom. "Was it to cause trouble for Titus?"

Phoebe shook her head. "Of course not. I came because I care about him."

"I see." Esther went to her closet and took out a plain, dark dress. "You can try this on and see if it fits." She handed the dress to Phoebe and turned to stare out her bedroom window.

"Well, what do you think?" Phoebe asked after she'd put on the dress.

"It looks a little short, but I guess you can let the hem down a few inches."

Phoebe stared down at the dress. "I don't think it's too short."

"That's probably because you're used to seeing the dresses English women wear, which, of course, are much shorter than any of ours."

Phoebe moved over to the dresser and picked up the hand mirror that had been lying there. "Guess I'd better pin up my hair and put a covering on. Have you got an extra one I can wear?"

Esther opened her top dresser drawer and pulled out a white organdy head covering that she handed to Phoebe. "You can wear this today."

"After church is over, I'll probably go home with Titus," Phoebe said, "because we need to talk—to make some plans."

Esther tipped her head. "What kind of plans?"

"Plans for our future. He asked me to marry him once, and now I'm ready to say yes."

Esther's face blanched, and she blinked a couple of times. "You're kidding, right?"

"No, I'm completely serious. I told Titus on the way over here last night that I want to stay in Kentucky and join the Amish church. Once I'm a member, we can be married."

"You really think he's going to marry you after you walked out on him?"

"He told you about that?"

Esther nodded. "It's taken Titus a long time to get over you, and now that he has a serious girlfriend, do you think you can just show up here and expect him to welcome you back like nothing ever happened?"

Phoebe's jaw dropped. "What did you say?"

"I said, do you think you can just—"

Phoebe held up her hand. "No, the part about Titus having a girlfriend."

"Her name's Suzanne, and she's a good friend of mine." Esther took a seat on the edge of her bed and folded her arms. "At first Titus and Suzanne didn't get along so well. I think it was because she reminded him of you."

"In what way?"

"She has the same color hair and eyes as you."

"So what are you saying—that Titus hated me so much that he hated her?"

Esther shook her head. "Hate's a very strong word, Phoebe. Titus is a good Christian, and I don't think he has it in his heart to hate anyone. I think he was so crushed by what you'd done to him that seeing Suzanne, who resembles you in some ways, kept his wounds open for a time."

Phoebe stood as though glued to the floor, not sure what to say. If Titus had a girlfriend, why hadn't he told her so last night?

"There was a time when I thought Titus and I might become a couple," Esther said. "We'd even gone a few places together, but we both realized that we didn't have much in common."

"Oh, I get it now. You want Titus for yourself, so you're trying to make me think he's in love with someone else."

Esther shook her head vigorously. "That's ridiculous. Titus and I are only friends, but Suzanne cares deeply for him, and I'm quite sure he feels the same way about her."

"We'll have to wait and see about that." Phoebe whirled around and started for the door.

"Where are you going?"

"Downstairs. Your mom's probably got breakfast ready by now, and I'm half starved!"

———⁓———

Suzanne squinted against the ray of light invading her room and groaned. Her head pounded, and her throat ached something awful. She hoped she wasn't sick. Pushing the covers aside, she forced herself out of bed.

Shuffling across the room in her bare feet, she stopped in front of her dresser and looked in the mirror. "Oh no," she gasped when she discovered several blistery spots on her face. She looked at her arms. More spots. "Not the wasserpareble!" she moaned.

She needed to let Mom know she was sick and wouldn't be going to church today, so she slipped on her robe and made her way down the stairs. She found Mom in the kitchen, mixing a container of orange juice.

"I'm sick. I've come down with the chickenpox," Suzanne said, touching one of the spots on her face.

Mom's lips compressed as she slowly shook her head. "I'd hoped you were immune to them, but it looks like I was wrong. You'd better go back to your room and get into bed. I'll get a tray and bring yours and Effie's breakfast up to you soon."

"I can't afford to be sick right now," Suzanne said with a moan. "With Christmas coming, we've been getting lots of orders in the woodshop, and my help is needed there."

Mom patted Suzanne's arm gently. "They got along before you started helping, and they'll get along without your help until you're feeling better. Wasserpareble is harder on adults than children, so you'll need to get lots of rest, drink plenty of liquids, and whatever you do, no matter how much the pox might itch, don't scratch them."

A knock sounded on the back door. "Whoever that is, you'd better not let them in unless they've had chickenpox," Suzanne said as she hurried up the stairs to her room.

—⁓—

Titus knocked on the door a second time. A few seconds later, Verna opened the door. "Titus, I'm surprised to see you here this morning. Shouldn't you be at home, getting ready for church?"

"I got up early, hoping I could speak to Suzanne."

"She's upstairs in her room. Both she and Effie are sick with the wasserpareble, so unless you've had them, you'd better not come in."

"Timothy and I both got 'em when we were eight years old, and I've got a few scars where I scratched to prove it." Titus leaned against the doorjamb and pulled in a deep breath, still trying to deal with the tension he'd felt ever since Phoebe had arrived. "If Suzanne's feeling up to it, I really need to talk to her about something."

"I'll go upstairs and see." Verna turned, leaving Titus alone on the porch. When she returned several minutes later, she shook her head and said, "Suzanne isn't feeling up to company right now, and I think she's also embarrassed about her spots."

"She shouldn't be embarrassed in front of me."

"Maybe in a day or two she'll feel well enough to visit with you. Would you like me to give her a message?"

"Uh—no. Guess it can wait until she's feeling better."

"You're welcome to join us for breakfast."

"I appreciate the invite, but I had a bowl of cereal before I left home."

"All right then. I'll see you at the Zooks' for church." Verna smiled and closed the door.

Titus headed for his horse, a heavy weight resting on his shoulders. He needed to tell Suzanne about Phoebe, but maybe it was best that he hadn't been able to do that today. He also needed to speak to Phoebe again. They'd left too much unresolved last night.

CHAPTER 52

Paradise, Pennsylvania

H ow are you feeling these days?" Fannie asked Elsie Sunday afternoon as they sat in her living room with some other women after church. "Is your morning sickness any better?"

"A little," Elsie replied, "but I'm awfully tired most of the time." She rested her hands against her stomach. "Can't remember feeling this way when I was carrying any of my other four."

"It's different with each one," Naomi spoke up. "At least that's how it's been for me."

Abby, who sat on the other side of Naomi, bobbed her head. "With Stella and Brenda, I had no morning sickness at all, but with Lamar, Derek, and Joseph, I sure did."

Elsie smiled. "Guess all bopplin are different when we're carrying them, just like after they're born."

Everyone nodded in agreement.

"Mind if I join you?" Arie asked when she entered the room.

"Not at all. Have a seat." Fannie patted the sofa cushion next to her, and Arie sat down.

"How are things with you?" Fannie asked. "You look meid today."

"I am tired." Arie stifled a yawn. "I haven't been sleeping well for some time, and after the message we discovered on our voice mail in the phone shanty last night, I hardly got any sleep at all."

"Was it bad news?" Abby asked before Fannie could form the question.

"I'm not sure." Arie placed her hands in her lap and clenched her fingers together. "The message was from a young woman named Charlene, who said she was a coworker of Phoebe's. Apparently, Phoebe recently borrowed some money from this woman, and now something's come up and Charlene needs Phoebe to pay her back."

"Is she expecting you to pay the money Phoebe owes?" Fannie asked.

Arie shook her head. "I don't think so. She thought Phoebe would be here and asked that she call her right away."

"But Phoebe's in California, isn't she?" Elsie questioned.

"That's what we thought, but since Phoebe moved to California, she hasn't kept in good touch with us." Arie's chin quivered, and she blinked, as if trying to hold back her tears. "I phoned Charlene back, and when I told her that we hadn't heard anything from Phoebe in several months, she said Phoebe had told her that she needed some money for a bus ticket to Kentucky so she could see a friend."

Fannie sucked in her breath. "Titus?"

Arie gave a nod. "I would assume so."

Fannie's heart began to pound. If Phoebe went to Kentucky and contacted Titus, they might end up together again. Titus was just beginning to make a new life for himself, and if Phoebe influenced him as she had in the past, he might lose his way.

"Charlene said she figured Phoebe would return to Pennsylvania after visiting with her friend in Kentucky." Arie looked over at Fannie, as though struck with a new realization. "Has Titus called you lately? Has he said anything about Phoebe?"

Fannie, trying not to let on about the concerns she felt, shrugged and said, "The last time I spoke to Titus, he made no mention of Phoebe."

"Maybe he didn't know she was coming," Naomi interjected. "Maybe Phoebe decided to go there and surprise him."

A knot formed in Fannie's stomach. Could Phoebe be in Kentucky right now? If so, how would it affect Titus's future?

—✺—

Pembroke, Kentucky

Phoebe didn't know how she'd managed to sit through the three-hour church service that had been held in the buggy shed of a family named Zook. It wasn't the backless wooden benches or even the length of the service that bothered her, though, for she'd become used to that from growing up in an Amish family. What bothered Phoebe the most were the curious stares in her direction. She'd been introduced to a few people before the service began, but most of the others probably wondered who she was, and maybe why the dress she wore was a few inches shorter than those of all the other women who were present.

When the service was over and lunch had been served, Phoebe wandered around, looking for Titus. She was pleased when she spotted him over by the barn, talking to a young man who looked to be about his age. She waited until there was a lull in the men's conversation; then she asked if she could speak to Titus alone.

He started walking toward the area where all the buggies were parked, and then turned to face her. "What's up?"

She glanced around to make sure no one could hear their conversation. "Esther told me that you have a girlfriend. Is it true?"

He nodded.

"How come you made no mention of it last night?"

"I tried to a couple of times, but you kept interrupting me."

"Is she here today?"

He shook his head. "She's at home, sick with the chickenpox."

"Esther said your girlfriend looks like me. Is that also true?"

"She has auburn hair and blue eyes."

Phoebe tapped her foot and gave a slow nod. "Hmm. That's interesting."

"What do you mean?"

"You must still have feelings for me if you picked someone to court who looks like me."

A splash of color erupted on Titus's clean-shaven cheeks. "I didn't care for Suzanne at first because she reminded me of you. Every time I looked at her, I thought of you, and how much you'd hurt me."

"And now?"

"Now it's different. I've gotten to know Suzanne and have discovered that she and I have a lot in common."

"Are you planning to marry her?"

"I don't know; maybe." He sighed. "I've been thinking about it."

Phoebe's hand trembled as she placed it on Titus's arm. "What about me? Won't you give me another chance?"

He shrugged and dropped his gaze to the ground.

She stepped in front of him and looked up so he'd have to see her face. "I told you last night I want to join the Amish church and live here with you. Doesn't that count for anything?"

A muscle on the side of his neck quivered. "I thought I knew what I wanted and was sure I had my future planned out. Now that you're here I'm so *verhuddelt*."

"Spend some time with me, and I promise you won't be confused anymore. Give me a chance to prove myself, and you'll see that you feel the same way about me as you did before."

"Oh, you mean before you left for California and broke my heart?" His tone was clipped, and she could see the hurt on his face.

"Jah, before I left for California." She took a step closer. "Before our folks made so many rules that finally came between us."

—⁓—

Titus swallowed hard and wiped his sweaty forehead with the back of his hand. Being this close to Phoebe, hearing her promising words, made him feel more confused than ever. If only she hadn't run off to California. If she'd just settled down and joined the church while they were both living in Pennsylvania, they'd be married by now—maybe even starting a family. Was it too late for them? And what about Suzanne? Were his feelings for her real, or had he only imagined them, transferring what he'd felt for Phoebe to Suzanne?

"Have you met many people here today?" he asked, feeling the need to change the subject.

Phoebe shook her head. "Just a few. Esther and her mother introduced me to a couple of women before church, and then I met a few more after the noon meal. One of them was Verna Yoder. Is she related to the woman you've been courting?"

Titus's heart raced like a herd of stampeding horses. If Esther and Dinah had introduced Verna to Phoebe, did Verna know Phoebe was his ex-girlfriend from Pennsylvania? If she did, then she'd no doubt tell Suzanne. He couldn't let that happen. He had to make sure he told her himself.

"I've got to get my horse," Titus said, moving away from Phoebe.

"You're leaving already?"

"Jah. There's someplace I need to go."

"Where?"

"I need to speak to Suzanne." Titus hurried off before Phoebe could respond.

—✺—

When Titus arrived at the Yoders' he stood on the porch and prayed for wisdom to know the right words before he knocked on the door.

Isaac opened the door. "Ah, Titus, it's good to see you. You must have taken a detour on your way home from church today."

Titus nodded. "I came to see Suzanne. Is she feeling any better?"

Isaac shook his head. "Not much. Still feverish and dealing with a sore throat. Both she and Effie are covered with spots."

"Since Verna was at church today, I guess you stayed home to look after your granddaughters?"

Isaac grinned. "That's right. Can't do as much as I want to these days, but I'm still able to check on them and see that they get plenty of water and calamine lotion."

Titus smiled, although he had to force it, for the butterflies in his stomach made him feel nauseous. "I really need to speak to Suzanne."

"I'll go see if she's willing." Isaac turned away, leaving Titus on the porch. He returned several minutes later. "She's sleeping, and I didn't want to disturb her."

"Oh, I see."

"Is there a message I can give Suzanne when she wakes up?" Isaac asked.

Titus slid the toe of his boot across the wooden boards on the porch, as he struggled with what to do. Finally, in desperation, he whispered, "I need Suzanne to know that my ex-girlfriend from Pennsylvania is here."

"What's that?" Isaac cupped his hand around his ear. "With you whispering like that I couldn't make out what you said."

Titus motioned for Isaac to step onto the porch. He didn't want to risk waking Suzanne and having her overhear what he'd said. He really wished he could say this to her face so he could explain things to her.

Isaac grabbed his jacket from a wall peg near the door and stepped onto the porch. Then he took a seat in one of the wicker chairs, and Titus seated himself in the chair beside him.

"Now what's this you want to tell Suzanne?" Isaac asked.

Titus repeated what he'd said before about Phoebe showing up, and was just about to say that she'd taken him by surprise, when his horse whinnied loudly.

Titus looked at the hitching rail, and was shocked to see Phoebe climb down from his buggy.

"What in the world?" He leaped off the porch and raced across the yard. "What's going on?" he shouted at Phoebe. "What were you doing in my buggy, and how come I didn't know you were there?"

Phoebe's chin trembled as she looked up at him with tears in her eyes. "When you said you were going to see your girlfriend, I decided I'd better come, too. Since I knew you'd never agree to that, when you went to get your horse, I hid in the back of your buggy."

Irritation welled in Titus, and his hands shook as he held his arms tightly against his sides. "You had no right to do that, Phoebe! What were you thinking?"

Phoebe's tears trickled onto her cheeks, and she started to sob. "Pl–please don't yell. It—it upsets me when you yell."

Titus felt remorse. He'd always been putty in Phoebe's hands whenever she'd turned on the tears. He put his hand on her back and patted it gently. "I'm sorry for yelling, but you had no right to come here uninvited. I needed to speak to Suzanne alone and explain about you being here before she hears it from someone else."

Phoebe sniffed and swiped at her tears. "I thought we could do that together. I thought if Suzanne met me and saw how much you and I care for each other, she'd understand."

Titus stood there, too numb to say a word. Apparently nothing he'd said to Phoebe so far had sunk in. "I'm not sure if I care about you anymore," he said firmly. "To tell you the truth, I'm not sure about anything right now."

—cw—

Roused from her sleep by loud voices, Suzanne forced herself out of bed. Was someone in the yard hollering, or had she been dreaming?

She padded across the room, lifted the shade at her window, and looked down. Her breath caught in her throat, and she grabbed the windowsill for support. Titus stood beside his buggy, and a young woman was next to him—a woman Suzanne didn't recognize but who looked familiar.

Despite the weakness she felt, Suzanne forced herself to get dressed and make her way downstairs. When she peered out the kitchen window, she could see the woman's face. *Oh my. . .she looks a lot like me.*

Suzanne went to the utility room and slipped into a jacket; then she stepped outside. She barely took notice of Grandpa, who stood on the porch, slowly shaking his head. All Suzanne could think about was getting to Titus's buggy and finding out who the woman beside him was.

"Wh–what's going on here?" Suzanne asked when she stepped up to Titus.

His cheeks turned red, and he looked at Suzanne with a kind of desperation. "Uh, Suzanne, this is Phoebe Stoltzfus. She arrived from California last night."

Phoebe nodded. "That's right. I spent the night at your friend Esther's."

Suzanne's vision blurred, and she swayed unsteadily. Then everything faded, and she toppled to the ground.

CHAPTER 53

Titus stood with Isaac, staring down at Suzanne as she reclined on the living room sofa. After she'd fainted, Titus had carried her into the house; then Isaac had put a cold washcloth on her forehead and patted her cheeks. She'd come to fairly quickly but hadn't said a word to either of them since she'd regained consciousness.

"Are you okay?" Titus asked, taking a seat on one end of the sofa near Suzanne's feet. "It gave us a scare when you fainted like that."

"I'm fine," she mumbled.

"Here, drink some of this." Isaac offered Suzanne some water.

She reached for the glass, sat up, and took a sip.

"Would someone bring me some more ginger ale?" a young voice called from upstairs. Titus realized it was Effie.

"Jah, sure. I'll be right up." Isaac excused himself and left the room.

Titus was on the verge of saying something to Suzanne, when she spoke.

"Why didn't you tell me that Phoebe was coming to see you?"

"I didn't know. She just showed up unexpectedly."

"How'd she know where you live?"

"She got my address from a letter I'd written her."

Tears welled in Suzanne's eyes, and she blinked several times, as though trying to keep them from spilling over. "I didn't realize you'd been writing to her all this time. If I'd known I never would have—"

"I haven't stayed in touch with Phoebe," Titus interrupted, his frustration mounting. "It was just one letter, to let her know that—"

"To let her know that you're still in love with her and want her back?"

Titus shook his head determinedly. "No, no. It wasn't like that. I wrote Phoebe to say I'd forgiven her for what she'd done and that I wanted her to know I wished her God's best."

"But you must have given her some encouragement or she wouldn't have come to Kentucky."

He shook his head again. "I didn't offer any encouragement, and I never mentioned the idea of her coming here."

Suzanne lifted both hands in the air. "Well, she must have gotten the idea from somewhere. In all the time you've been living here, she never came to see you before, so why now?"

Titus ground his teeth together. This wasn't going well. "I just told you, when Phoebe got my letter, she decided to come."

"Do you still love her?"

Suzanne's direct question and her furrowed brows made Titus begin to sweat. "No. I don't know. Maybe."

"I figured as much." Suzanne looked away. "She's waiting outside for you, so you'd better go."

"Please look at me, Suzanne." Titus reached over and touched her chin, turning her head to face him. "I'm worried about you. You fainted when you found out who Phoebe was, and I know you were very upset."

"I fainted because I'm weak and sick from the wasserpareble."

"Maybe that was part of it, but I think the shock of seeing Phoebe was too much for you."

She dropped her gaze and stared at the glass, clasped firmly in her hands.

Titus shifted on the sofa, feeling the tension between them. Tension that hadn't been there until Phoebe came on the scene and interrupted his life. "I'd like to stay so we can talk about this some more."

"What's there to talk about? You're not sure whether you're still in love with Phoebe, which means you're obviously not sure about us. Until you are sure, I don't think there's anything left to say." Tears slipped out of Suzanne's eyes and splashed onto her pale cheeks.

Titus wanted to hold Suzanne and reassure her that nothing had changed between them, but she was obviously too upset to talk about this, and right now, he was too confused. He sat for a moment, then rose from his seat and headed across the room. He was almost to the door when he turned and said, "I need some time to think and pray about this. When things become clear, and I come here to talk to you again, I hope you'll listen."

She didn't look at him and gave no reply.

Titus whirled around and went out the door. He hoped he would find the answers he sought before it was too late.

—⁂—

Paradise, Pennsylvania

As Fannie and Abraham sat in their living room that evening, drinking hot cider, Fannie told him about the news Arie had shared.

"I wonder if Phoebe really did go to Kentucky," she said. "And if so, has she found Titus by now?"

Abraham set his mug down and drew his fingers through the end of his beard. "Guess we won't know that until we hear something from him. I'm sure if she showed up, he'd tell us. Don't you agree?"

"I don't know. He knows we never approved of Phoebe, so if they are back together, he might try to hide it as long as he can."

"It won't do any good to worry about it tonight," Abraham said. "We'll just have to wait until we hear from Titus."

"I'm not going to wait on Titus." Fannie pursed her lips. "Tomorrow morning, I'm going out to the phone shanty and call him. When his voice mail picks up, I'll leave a message and set a time for tomorrow evening that he can call when I'll be waiting in the shanty by the phone."

"Do whatever you want, but if you say too much on the subject of Phoebe, you could push Titus away." Abraham drank the remainder of his cider, set his empty mug on the table beside his chair, and stood. "I'm tired. Think I'll go to bed. Are you coming, Fannie?"

"In a bit. I want to sit here by the fire awhile."

When Abraham left the room, Fannie picked up her Bible, which had been lying on the coffee table. She turned to a place she'd marked with a ribbon and read James 1:5, which she'd underlined some time ago: "If any of you lack wisdom, let him ask of God, that giveth to all men liberally, and upbraideth not; and it shall be given him."

Fannie shut the Bible and closed her eyes. *Heavenly Father: Give me wisdom to say the right words when I speak to Titus, and may Your will be done concerning our son's future.*

Pembroke, Kentucky

"I don't see why I have to go back to the Beilers' place right now," Phoebe said as Titus directed his horse and buggy in that direction. "I think we need to talk."

"What good is talking when you don't listen? You've always wanted to have everything your own way."

"That's not true," she said, hoping he would see the sincerity on her face.

"Jah, it is, and you know it."

"Is it wrong because I want you? Is that what you're saying?"

"You say you want me now, but you've said that before—when we were courting. Then you changed your mind and took off for California. Now you're here, and I think it might be only because you have no money and believe you have no other place to go. I'm not convinced you came here because you love me."

"I did come because I love you. Why won't you believe me?" Phoebe's voice sounded desperate even to her own ears. Well, she couldn't help it; she was desperate. Desperate to make Titus understand, and desperate to win him back.

"It's hard to believe someone who's told so many lies," he said, turning his head away from her.

"I wasn't really lying before. I was just confused."

"So you broke up with me and left Pennsylvania because you were confused?"

"That's right. I've been confused and angry with my folks for a long time—ever since they first tried to come between us."

He glanced back at her and slowly shook his head. "If that's your only excuse, then it's a poor one at best. My folks weren't in favor of me courting you either—not even after you'd turned sixteen. But do you see me staying angry at them?"

"I don't know how you feel toward your folks. I only know that I've always felt like I could do nothing right as far as Mom and Dad were concerned, and it makes me angry that they've never wanted me to have any fun."

Titus shook the reins to get his horse moving faster.

She clasped his arm "Are you going to give me another chance or not?"

"I don't know. I need time to think and pray about it."

"How much time?"

"Don't know that either."

"Until you decide, I'll stay at the Beilers' and wait. Dinah said I could stay there for as long as I like."

"You can do whatever you want, but it may be a while before I make a decision." Titus paused and turned to look at her again. "When I do decide, it might not be what you're hoping to hear."

Her heart sank with a feeling of dread. If only she could say or do something to get through to him.

He guided his horse and buggy off the road and onto the Beilers' driveway. "Here we are."

"Are you coming in?" Phoebe asked when he pulled up in front of the house instead of by the hitching rail.

He shook his head. "Good-bye, Phoebe."

She sat a few seconds. Unable to speak around the lump in her throat, she stepped out of the buggy and sprinted for the house. She was fearful that she might lose Titus to Suzanne and didn't know what she could do about it. Should she keep trying to win him back, or should she go home and face Mom and Dad? But if she went home, how would she get there? She'd used the money she'd borrowed from Charlene and didn't even have enough left for a bus ticket.

I just can't go home, she told herself. *I have to stay here and make Titus see that he loves me, and that we're meant to be together.*

CHAPTER 54

On Monday evening, Titus went out to the phone shanty to check for messages. He found one from Mom, asking him to call her at seven o'clock that night. He pulled out his pocket watch. It was five minutes to seven now, so if he stayed in the shanty, he could make the call soon.

While Titus waited, he checked for other messages. Allen had called, saying he was sorry he hadn't been around lately but he'd had a job to oversee in Trigg County and would be over to see Titus as soon as the job was complete.

Titus glanced at his pocket watch again. It was time to call Mom. When he dialed the number it rang just once, and then Mom's voice came on. "Hello."

"Hi, Mom, it's Titus."

"It's good to hear from you, son. I take it you got my message?"

"I did. That's why I'm calling."

There was a pause. Then Mom said, "Is. . .uh. . .Phoebe there?"

"Jah. She got here last week."

Mom groaned. "Oh, dear, I was afraid of that. What's going on, Titus? Why's Phoebe there? Were you in contact with her the whole time she was in California? Are the two of you back together?"

"Please, slow down, Mom. I can only answer one question at a time."

"Then start with my second question. Why is Phoebe in Kentucky?"

"She was down on her luck and didn't have any money. I believe she panicked, thinking she might have to go home."

"Would home be so bad? I don't see why everyone thinks they have to leave home."

Titus tapped his fingers along the edge of the table. *Not this again. Is Mom going to start up about me leaving home?*

"From what Arie said, one of Phoebe's friends loaned her some money for a bus ticket to Kentucky. Did you know she was coming?"

"I had no idea. I was taken completely by surprise when she showed up at my house."

"Have you kept in touch with Phoebe since she went to California?"

" 'Course not. The first and only time I've written to Phoebe was to let her know that I'd forgiven her."

"Did you say anything in the letter that might make her think you wanted her to come there?"

"No, I did not." Titus opened the shanty door to let some cool autumn air in, but quickly shut it again when Callie tried to get in. He didn't appreciate being quizzed like this. He wondered if Mom thought he was lying to her.

"Where's Phoebe staying? I hope not with you."

Titus gripped the edge of the table so hard that his knuckles turned white. Why did Mom have to assume the worst? Didn't she think he knew right from wrong?

"Titus, did you hear what I said?"

"Jah, Mom, I heard. Phoebe is not staying here. She's at the Beilers' place."

"Will she be staying there for good? Are you two getting back together?"

"You're asking too many questions, Mom, and I don't have the answers."

"What do you mean?"

"I mean that I don't know how long Phoebe will be staying, and I'm trying to make a decision about whether I want to give her another chance."

"What? After all that girl has done—stomping on your heart and telling so many lies? I can't believe you'd even consider getting back with her."

"Phoebe says she wants to stay here and join the Amish church. She says she still loves me."

"Do you love her?"

"No. Maybe. I'm not sure. I'm verhuddelt right now."

"I don't understand why you're confused. What about Suzanne? You mentioned some time ago that the two of you were courting."

"We have been, and I thought I was falling in love with her and that she might even be my wife someday."

"Until Phoebe came along, right? Just like always, I'll bet she smiled sweetly and told you a bunch of lies. She probably said those things because she's desperate and thinks she has no other place to go. I don't mean to be judgmental, Titus, but if Phoebe broke your heart once she'll probably do it again."

"You might be right," Titus admitted, "but it's my decision to make, and that's why I'm going to take this week to pray about it and read God's Word for direction. Whatever decision I make, I want it to be God's will for me."

"That's good thinking," Mom said in a more accepting

tone. "I'm glad you're seeking God's will in this, and I'm sure your daed will be, too."

"Did you think I wouldn't seek God's will?" Titus didn't mean to sound defensive, but he'd always felt like he had to prove his worth to his folks, as well as others.

"I just thought—"

"I'm not the immature boy who left home in the spring. I've grown a lot since then, and I'm putting my trust in God these days."

"I'm glad to hear it, and I'll be praying for you as you make your decision."

"I appreciate that."

"I'd better let you go now," Mom said. "Besides, I need to call Arie and let her know that Phoebe's in Kentucky and that I'll keep her posted if I hear anything else."

"Okay, Mom. I'll talk to you soon." Titus hung up the phone and headed straight for the house. He had a lot more thinking and praying to do throughout the rest of this week. One thing he'd already decided was that he wouldn't see either Phoebe or Suzanne until he'd reached a decision. He didn't want to be influenced by anything either of them might say. He would go to work every day and spend his evenings praying and reading God's Word, as he sought the right answers.

—⁓—

For the rest of that week, Titus prayed and meditated as often as he could. On Saturday morning, he took his Bible and went out to the barn, where he could listen to the nicker of his horse and smell the aroma of freshly stacked hay as he spent time communing with God.

Seeking wisdom and a sense of peace, he took a seat on a wooden crate, leaned against the barn wall, and opened his Bible. Philippians 4:11 caught his attention: "I have learned, in whatsoever state I am, therewith to be content."

He pondered that awhile, realizing that he'd been more content since he'd moved to Kentucky than he'd ever been in Pennsylvania. Maybe it was because he was out on his own—away from the pressure of his family to measure up and be more like Timothy. Maybe it was because in this part of Kentucky, life was slower and more peaceful than it had been in Lancaster County. Or maybe it was because he'd gotten to know Suzanne and her wonderful family.

He turned to the book of Proverbs and read verse 30 of chapter 31: "Favour is deceitful, and beauty is vain: but a woman that feareth the Lord, she shall be praised."

Titus compared first Phoebe, and then Suzanne to the description of the woman in the scripture he'd read. Phoebe was beautiful on the outside, and so was Suzanne. But Phoebe's inner beauty was sorely lacking, whereas Suzanne's inner beauty was clearly evident in the things she said and did. As Titus recalled, Phoebe had never feared the Lord or tried to please Him. She hadn't even wanted to join the church, choosing rather to do her own thing and seek worldly pleasures. Suzanne, on the other hand, was a member in good standing in her Amish community, and her Christian attitude and helpfulness toward her family had been obvious to Titus from the beginning—even when he'd shied away from her because she'd reminded him of Phoebe.

For the past week, while Titus had been at work, he hadn't been able to get his mind off Suzanne. He'd seen the shawl she'd left hanging on a wall peg, and caught the sweet smell of the lilac soap she used as he walked by. Whenever Verna had brought lunch out to the men, Titus thought of Suzanne and asked how she was doing. He and Suzanne had become good friends over the last few months, but had he transferred his feelings for Phoebe to Suzanne, or did he care for Suzanne because of the woman she was? Did he still have feelings for Phoebe, or had they died when she'd gone to California?

Meow! Meow!

Titus looked down. Callie brushed his pant leg and looked up as though begging him to pet her.

Setting his Bible aside, he leaned over and scooped the cat into his arms. A few months ago, he'd never have done that. He'd have been afraid of getting scratched or bitten. But Callie had proven him wrong about cats. She was not only a good mouser but had become a good pet, too.

"It just goes to show that a body can be as wrong about a cat as they can about a person," he said, running his fingers through Callie's soft fur.

The cat answered with a *meow*. Then Buttons showed up and got in on the act. Titus petted both cats for a while and then closed his eyes and whispered a prayer. "Thank You, Lord, for giving me a sense of peace about what I should do."

—⟋⟍—

All that week, Phoebe had moped around the Beilers' place, thinking about Titus and wondering what she could do to make him see that she was the right woman for him. She didn't like the fact that he hadn't come over to see her all week. How was she supposed to win him back if they didn't spend time together?

By Saturday, Phoebe was out of patience. Since the Beilers were at their store working and wouldn't have a clue what she was up to, she decided to use one of their horses and buggies to drive over to Titus's place.

She'd just put on a jacket and had opened the back door, when she spotted Titus riding in on his horse. She shut the door behind her and ran out to greet him. "I'm so happy to see you," she said as he tied his horse to the hitching rail. "I was getting ready to come over to your place right now."

His brows furrowed. "I thought I'd made it clear that I didn't want to see you until I'd had time to pray and make up my mind."

"I couldn't wait any longer." She moved closer to him. "Have you made up your mind?"

He nodded. "After much prayer, Bible reading, and thinking things through, it's come clear to me that I'm not in love with you, and that what we used to have wasn't a relationship that would last a lifetime."

Phoebe frowned. This was not the response she'd hoped for. "Titus, I don't think you're—"

He held up his hand. "Please, hear me out."

She compressed her lips and waited for him to continue.

"When I first came to Kentucky, I was all mixed up full of anger and bitterness toward you and struggling with self-doubts about my ability to make a life of my own or do anything right. But I was finally able to move forward with my life."

His jaw quivered slightly. "I believe the Lord has chosen Suzanne for me, and I think the best thing for you to do is go home and work things out with your folks. I'd be happy to give you the money you'll need for the bus ticket to Pennsylvania."

Phoebe shook her head as anger boiled in her chest. "No, thanks. I'm not going back there!"

"Is it because you're afraid to face your folks and admit that things didn't work out as you'd planned?"

She shrugged.

"Since things didn't work out for you in California, did you ever think that God might be nudging you to go home?"

"How do you know He didn't want me to come here? How do you know He doesn't want us to be together?"

Titus touched his chest. "I don't feel a sense of peace or joy when I'm with you anymore. If you're honest with yourself, I don't think you feel any peace or joy with me, either."

Titus's words stung like icy cold raindrops on a windy day. "So you're not going to give us another chance?" she asked, unable to admit defeat.

"No. It's over between us."

She wrinkled her nose. "You're not thinking straight, Titus, and you'll be sorry for this someday."

He slowly shook his head. "The only thing I might be sorry about is that I didn't come to my senses sooner."

Tears stung Phoebe's eyes, and she started to sob.

—⁂—

Titus hated to hurt Phoebe's feelings, but he saw no other way. He just wished he'd seen her for who she was when they both lived in Pennsylvania. She'd never really loved him; he was sure of that now. She'd only cared about her own needs.

Being selfish and self-centered was not the way a Christian should act. Their church taught that a follower of Christ should be humble, not full of pride; obedient to God's Word, not rebellious; kind, not mean-spirited; and always thinking of others, not oneself. Phoebe had never shown any of the Christian attributes. Titus didn't know why he hadn't seen it when they were younger, other than the fact that he'd been blinded by Phoebe's good looks and flirtatious ways.

Suzanne, on the other hand, was everything he really wanted in a woman. She was kindhearted, smart, humble, full of fun, and he was sure she loved the Lord. If she'd have him, he was going to ask her to be his wife.

"I've got to go now, Phoebe. Think about my offer to give you the bus fare home, and let me know if you change your mind." He turned toward his horse.

"Wait a minute! Where are you going?"

Titus said nothing but climbed on Lightning's back and rode away.

—∞—

"How are you feeling today?" Mom asked when Suzanne entered the kitchen.

"A little better." Suzanne went to the cupboard and removed a glass. "But I'd feel even better if I'd hear something from Titus."

"He was in the woodshop every day this week. You could have gone out and talked to him."

Suzanne filled her glass with water and took a drink. "I thought about that, and I could have asked Nelson or Grandpa if Titus had said anything to them about me or Phoebe, but I decided against it. Whatever Titus decides, it'll be better if I hear it from him when he's ready."

Mom moved away from the stove and put her arm around Suzanne. "If you and Titus are meant to be together, things will work out. If he chooses Phoebe, then he wasn't the man God wanted for you."

Suzanne blinked against tears threatening to spill over. "If he chooses her and they stay here in Kentucky, I don't think I could bear it. Every time I'd see them together, my heart would break in two."

"I know it'll be hard, but God will give you the strength to deal with things if it happens that way." Mom smiled. "In Isaiah 66:13 it says that God comforts us like a mother comforts her children."

Suzanne didn't respond. Instead she started setting the table. If Titus ended up marrying Phoebe, she'd accept it as God's will, but she wouldn't stay here. She'd have to find someplace else to live.

CHAPTER 55

After Titus left, Phoebe stormed into the house, dropped to the sofa, and covered her face with her hands. She couldn't believe he had turned her away. When they'd been courting, he'd promised that he'd always love her, but apparently he'd lied. If she couldn't make him see that she'd be better for him than Suzanne, then she had come here for nothing. She'd have been better off in California, living on the street.

Hot tears rolled down Phoebe's cheeks. It was hard not to feel sorry for herself when her whole life was messed up and nothing had turned out the way she'd hoped. Why was it that things went so well for some people, and for others, nothing seemed to work out?

The back door opened and banged shut. Phoebe pulled her hands away from her face and quickly dried her tears on the front of her apron.

"What's wrong, Phoebe?" Esther asked, as she entered the room. "Have you been crying?"

Phoebe nodded slowly and nearly gulped on the sob rising in her throat. "Titus came by this morning. I...I told him that

I love him, but he said he doesn't love me anymore. He thinks he belongs with Suzanne." She sniffed deeply and reached for a tissue from the box on the table beside the sofa. "I can't believe he'd choose her over me. I've known him a lot longer than she has, and the whole time he and I were courting, he kept saying he wanted to marry me and would never love anyone else."

Esther sat down beside Phoebe and reached out to touch her trembling shoulder. "I don't think you really love him. I think you've been using him because you need a place to belong, and he's the person you thought you could turn to in your hour of need."

Phoebe sat with her head down and shoulders slumped. She knew Esther was right but couldn't admit it, not even to herself.

"You need to get your life straight, and in order to do that, you have to give your heart fully to the Lord," Esther said.

"I told Titus that I'd join the Amish church. Isn't that good enough?"

"No, it's not. Being Amish is our way of life, but joining the church is giving your heart to the Lord. You must see yourself as a sinner who needs to be saved, and then joining the church will be your confession of faith." Esther reached for the Bible lying on the table beside the box of tissues. She opened it and said to Phoebe, "Romans 3:23 reads, 'For all have sinned, and come short of the glory of God.'"

Phoebe's tears spilled over onto her dress. "I. . .I know I've done many wrong things in my life, and I wouldn't blame God if He didn't forgive me."

"But you *can* find forgiveness," Esther said, gently patting Phoebe's back. "In 1 John 1:9 it tells us, 'If we confess our sins, he is faithful and just to forgive us our sins, and to cleanse us from all unrighteousness.'"

"I've heard that verse before when I've gone to church with

my family. I just never took it to heart." Phoebe gulped on another sob. "I. . .I want to seek forgiveness and turn my life over to Christ right now."

———ᗯ———

Eager to speak to Suzanne, Titus got Lightning moving at a fast trot. He'd already wasted enough time trying to reason with Phoebe when he should have been at the Yoders', opening his heart to Suzanne. If only, from the beginning, he hadn't been taken in by Phoebe's beguiling ways.

But then, if I hadn't courted Phoebe, and she hadn't run off to California, I wouldn't have come to Kentucky or met Suzanne, he reasoned.

Titus urged Lightning on until the Yoders' house came into view. Then, guiding the horse up the driveway, he stopped in front of the hitching rail. He'd just stepped down from the saddle when Nelson came out of the woodshop and motioned for him to come inside.

Titus secured Lightning and headed up the driveway.

"Are you working here today?" he asked when he entered the shop and found Nelson sitting at his grandfather's desk.

"Jah. I don't normally work on Saturdays, but since Grandpa went shopping with Mom today, I thought I'd take a look at the books and see how we're doing, and then maybe do some sanding on those." He motioned to a set of cupboard doors leaning against the far wall.

"If you needed my help, I could have come to work today." Titus leaned on one end of the desk.

"That's okay. With all you've had on your mind this week, I figured you needed the day off."

"You're right about that. I've been doing a lot of thinking and praying all week."

"Have you reached a decision?"

Titus nodded. He'd shared his frustration and confusion about Phoebe with both Nelson and Isaac this week and knew they'd been praying for him. "I'd like to tell you what I've decided, but I think it's only fair that I discuss it with Suzanne first."

"That makes good sense." Nelson pointed to the ledger. "Don't mean to change the subject, but we have a lot of orders stacking up. I hope we can get them all done before Christmas."

"I think between you, me, and Suzanne working here in the shop we'll be able to get everything done."

Nelson scratched his head. "I'm afraid I haven't been fair to my sister. I've come to realize that she's happy working with wood, and I apologized to her last night. Said I shouldn't have been so narrow-minded about her wanting to do a job I'd thought was only for a man."

"I'll bet she was pleased to hear you say that."

"Jah. Even gave me a hug."

Titus smiled.

"So what'd you come here for?" Nelson asked. "Was it to speak to Suzanne?"

Titus nodded.

"She's up at the house, so go right ahead. She might be resting on the sofa, but you can go in."

"I will. See you later, Nelson." Titus hurried out the door.

He'd only made it halfway to the house when Suzanne's little sister, Effie, came running out of the barn. "Kumme! Schnell!" she hollered, waving her hands. "Something's wrong with Fluffy!"

Titus knew Fluffy was one of Suzanne's favorite cats, so he took off on a run behind Effie. When he entered the barn, he followed her to the stack of hay on the far side of the room. "Where's Fluffy?" he asked.

Effie pointed a trembling finger toward the first stack of hay. "She's behind there."

371

Titus hurried across the room and peered behind the bales of hay. What he saw made him cringe. Poor Fluffy had managed to get herself tangled in a piece of baling twine that had apparently come loose from the hay. The twine was wrapped around the cat's body so tightly that all she could do was roll pathetically from side to side.

There would have been a day when Titus would have hesitated to pick up the cat for fear of getting scratched, but he didn't think twice about helping Fluffy now.

He scooped the cat into his arms and took a seat on a bale of hay. Then he proceeded to untangle the twine, being careful not to frighten the poor critter any more than she was.

"Don't hurt her. Don't hurt my sister's katz." Effie stood beside him, eyes wide and mouth hanging slightly open.

"I won't hurt the cat. I'm only trying to help her." Titus grimaced. "If Fluffy would hold still, it would make things a lot easier."

"I'll pet her head and talk softly to her," Effie said. "Maybe that'll calm her down."

Titus nodded. "That's a good idea. Keep petting her until I get the twine off."

It took some time to accomplish the task, but Titus kept at it until he'd untangled the mess and Fluffy was free. "Here you go," he said, handing the cat to Effie. "That was quite an ordeal, so maybe you ought to get her some water and see if she wants to drink."

Effie said thank you, and holding the cat to her chest, she skipped to the other side of the barn.

Titus rolled the piece of twine into a ball and put it up on a shelf so none of the other cats would end up in a mess like Fluffy had been.

Eager to get to the house and speak with Suzanne, Titus rushed out of the barn. He'd only taken a few steps, when a horse and buggy pulled into the yard. He waited to see who was driving, and was shocked when Phoebe climbed down and secured the horse to the hitching rail next to Lightning.

"Not this again," he mumbled. "What are you doing here, Phoebe?"

"I needed to talk to you, and since I figured you were going to see Suzanne, I borrowed one of the Beilers' horses and buggies and came here."

"I thought I'd made clear the way I feel when I talked to you earlier."

"You did, but I need to tell you what happened after you left."

Titus crossed his arms and tapped his foot impatiently. "What happened?"

"After talking to Esther awhile and listening to her quote some verses of scripture, I realized what a terrible person I've been, and I—I gave my heart to the Lord." She smiled. "From now on, I want to start living for Him."

"Are you saying that to impress me, in the hope that I'll reconsider and take you back, or is this for real?"

"I'm not trying to impress you or get you back. I really did confess my sins and ask the Lord to take control of my life."

"If that's true, then I'm glad for you, but it doesn't change anything between us, Phoebe."

"I understand that, and I didn't come to stir up trouble. I came to say that I'm sorry for everything I've said or done to hurt you. No matter how bad things were for me in California, I shouldn't have come to Kentucky uninvited." She paused and flicked her tongue over her lips. "But I'm really glad I did, for if I hadn't come here, I might never have found a personal relationship with the Lord." She stepped toward him and smiled. It seemed like a genuine smile. "I know what I need to do now."

"What's that?"

"I need to go home and make things right with Mom and Dad. So if your offer to give me money for a bus ticket is still open, then I'll gladly accept it with much appreciation."

Titus could hardly believe Phoebe had found the Lord, but her attitude did seem to have changed, and he was more than happy to give her the money she needed in order to go home. He reached into his pocket and handed her several bills. "I wish you all the best."

"I wish the best for you, too." Phoebe slipped her arms around his waist and gave him a hug. "Thanks for the money. I appreciate it a lot."

—⁂—

Hearing voices outside, Suzanne went to the living room window and peered out. She gasped, shocked by what she saw. Titus and Phoebe stood in the front yard, hugging each other!

"Guess that's all I need to know," Suzanne muttered as she turned away from the window with a heavy heart. Titus and Phoebe were obviously back together. But did he have to hug her right here on their property where Suzanne could see? Was he deliberately trying to hurt her?

Tears coursed down Suzanne's cheeks, and she did nothing to wipe them away. *I was a fool for letting myself fall in love with Titus. He only pretended to like me because I reminded him of her.*

She'd just taken a seat on the sofa, when she heard the back door open. A few seconds later, Titus entered the room.

Suzanne leaped off the sofa and rushed toward the stairs, unwilling to hear what she was sure he was going to tell her.

"Where are you going?" he called.

"Upstairs to my room."

"Please, don't go. We need to talk. I want to tell you what I've decided about Phoebe."

She whirled around to face him. "I already know what you've decided. I saw the two of you outside, hugging."

"It's not what it seems." He moved toward her, and she took a step back.

"How is it then?

"Phoebe came over because she figured I'd be here talking to you—telling you what I'd decided."

"That you love her?"

"No, it's not that at all." Titus motioned to the sofa. "Let's sit down so I can explain things."

Suzanne seated herself on one end, and he sat beside her. "Phoebe came over here to tell me that she's confessed her sins and has found a personal relationship with the Lord," he said, looking at her intently.

"Did she think that would make you see her in a different light and take her back?"

"No, she wanted to apologize for all the things she's done to hurt me, and when she said she wanted to go home to Pennsylvania, I offered to give her the money for a bus ticket. She was grateful and hugged me, that's all."

"I see."

Titus took hold of Suzanne's hand and gave her fingers a gentle squeeze. "I've spent this past week thinking, praying, reading my Bible, and seeking God's will for my life." He smiled at her in such a sweet way that her heart nearly melted. "It's you I love, Suzanne, and if you're willing, I'd like you to marry me sometime next year."

Suzanne blinked. "Are you sure about this? You're not just saying it because you feel sorry for me?"

He shook his head. "I've never been surer of anything in my life. I was verhuddelt when Phoebe first showed up at my place, but my head's clear now, and I realize that the love I thought I'd felt for Phoebe was nothing more than infatuation.

I think I only wanted her because she was a challenge and her rebellious spirit excited me. Now that I've matured and am walking closer to the Lord, I want a woman I can trust—someone who thinks of others, not just herself."

"Do you think I'm that woman?" she dared to ask.

"I know you are." Titus leaned toward her and lowered his head so their lips were almost touching. "Is it all right if I kiss you, Suzanne?"

She nodded. He pulled her close and gently kissed her lips. When their lips parted, he whispered, "I'm so thankful God brought me to Kentucky, and even more thankful He brought you into my life." Then he kissed her again.

—◦◦◦—

That evening, as Phoebe stepped onto the bus, she thought about the things she'd learned during her brief stay in Kentucky. She realized what a selfish person she'd been and realized she needed time to grow and learn how to live her life for the Lord instead of herself. She also needed to seek God's will about His choice for a husband for her. As Esther's mother had said to her before she'd gotten on the bus, "Fulfillment doesn't come from marrying someone, but in a relationship with the Lord."

Phoebe took a seat and closed her eyes. *Help me, Lord, to remember all that I've learned, and when I see Mom and Dad, I pray that they won't criticize or lecture me for leaving, but will welcome me home instead.*

—◦◦◦—

When Titus returned home, after spending the evening at Suzanne's, he went out to the phone shanty to call his folks and leave a message, letting them know that Phoebe was on her way home, and that he and Suzanne were together as a couple.

He was about to make the call when he decided to check his messages first. He discovered one from Mom.

"Something horrible has happened, and we need you to come home right away. Elsie was carrying a basket of dirty laundry down the basement stairs, and she tripped over something and fell." There was a pause, and then Mom started crying. "When Elsie hit the bottom of the stairs, she broke her neck." Another pause. "She's dead, Titus. Elsie and the boppli she was carrying are both dead. The funeral will be in three days, and we hope you'll be there."

Titus sat, too numb to move. All the joy he'd felt over his relationship with Suzanne had been replaced with a deep ache in his heart for his half brother Samuel. Phoebe wouldn't be the only one heading home this week. Titus would be going now, too, only he'd be arriving for a funeral.

When the numbness wore off enough for Titus to think, he picked up the phone and called his folks' number. Then he left a message letting them know that Phoebe was on her way home to her folks, and that'd he be there for Elsie's funeral and would leave as soon as he could secure a ride.

Chapter 56

Paradise, Pennsylvania

When the bus stopped at the station in Lancaster on Monday morning, Phoebe picked up her purse and the book she'd brought along to read and stepped off the bus. She'd just gotten her suitcase from the compartment on the side of the bus, when someone called her name.

She looked to the right, and her heart started to pound. Mom and Dad were heading her way, waving their hands.

"Mom, Dad, what are you doing here?" she asked as they hurried toward her.

"We hired a driver and came to pick you up," Dad said.

"How'd you know I was coming?"

"Fannie told us. She'd gotten a message from Titus."

Mom threw her arms around Phoebe and gave her such a forceful squeeze that it nearly took Phoebe's breath away. When Dad hugged her, too, Phoebe knew without a doubt that her folks were as glad to see her as she was to see them. She felt like the prodigal son in the Bible, returning home after his rebellion, to welcoming arms.

Phoebe explained that she'd come home to stay, had

sought God's forgiveness for her sins, and was ready to take classes so she could join the Amish church.

"I'm so glad to hear that," Mom said tearfully.

"What about Titus? Will he be staying in Kentucky?" Dad asked.

Phoebe nodded. "I ruined things between us when I ran off to California, and now he's found someone else."

Mom put her arm around Phoebe's waist as they walked toward their driver's van. "It obviously wasn't God's will for you and Titus to be together."

"That's right," Dad agreed. "Someday when the time is right, you'll find someone else."

Phoebe didn't answer but kept walking.

"Did you hear about Samuel's Elsie?" Mom asked Phoebe when they reached the van.

"Samuel Fisher?"

"Jah. Elsie was killed on Saturday when she tripped while carrying laundry down the basement stairs. She fell to the bottom of the stairs and broke her neck. Both she and the boppli she was carrying died."

Phoebe gasped. "That's baremlich!"

"You're right, it's a terrible thing," Dad said as they all climbed into the van. "Poor Samuel is not only grieving for his wife and unborn baby, but now he has four kinner to raise by himself."

"Titus must not have known about this when he gave me money for my bus fare home," Phoebe said. "I wonder if he'll come for the funeral."

"Oh I'm sure of it," Mom said. "What brother wouldn't want to be there when someone in his family dies?"

Phoebe's heart went out to Samuel and to all the Fisher family. She knew the days ahead would be difficult for them. It was a good thing they had each other to lean on for strength.

Most importantly, they had the Lord.

She reached over and took Mom's hand. She was thankful that she'd finally seen the light and come home. Families needed each other. She knew that now without a doubt.

—◊◊◊—

Pembroke, Kentucky

"Are you sure you're feeling up to going to Pennsylvania with me?" Titus asked as he and Suzanne climbed into Allen's truck.

"Of course I'm sure," she said, offering him what she hoped was a reassuring smile. "It's been a few weeks since I came down with the wasserpareble, and since my pox marks are mostly gone, or at least crusted over, I'm no longer contagious. If I was, I wouldn't have agreed to come. I'm glad I'm going, though, because I not only want to be there for you, but I'm also anxious to meet the rest of your family."

"I appreciate you coming with me more than you know, and I appreciate Nelson and Isaac letting us both have the time off." Titus looked over at Allen, who sat in the driver's seat. "I'm thankful for your willingness to take us to Pennsylvania, too."

"Wouldn't have it any other way," Allen said as he started the engine. "Besides seeing that you make it home in time for the funeral, I want to be there for my good friend Zach. Want him to know he has my support."

"I'm sure Zach will appreciate that," Titus said. "I think everyone in our family's going to need a lot of support, Samuel most of all. I can't imagine how he must feel right now."

Suzanne thought about the emotional turmoil she and her family had been through when Grandma and Dad had died just a few months apart. They'd needed all the support they could get, and if it hadn't been for family and friends, she didn't think they could have survived the ordeal.

"We may as well relax and try to get some sleep," Titus said, "because it's a long drive between here and Pennsylvania." He chuckled and motioned to Allen. "Except for you, of course. You need to keep your eyes open and on the road."

Allen laughed, and Suzanne smiled. It amazed her that Titus could say something humorous, even though inside he must be hurting.

No wonder I love him so much, she thought as she leaned her head against his shoulder and closed her eyes. *I can't wait for our journey to Pennsylvania to end so I can meet the rest of his wonderful family.*

—ɯ—

Even though Titus had been the one to suggest it, he couldn't sleep. He had too much on his mind.

He looked over at Suzanne, sleeping peacefully with her head on his shoulder. He felt blessed to have found such a special, caring woman.

When Titus first left Pennsylvania for Kentucky, he'd been on a journey to find himself. He'd not only discovered who he was and what he could do well, but he'd learned a lot more. He'd drawn closer to God on this journey, made several new friends he could count on, and had found a woman who loved him unconditionally.

Now a new journey stretched before him. He and Suzanne were traveling together to his home to comfort those in mourning and offer Samuel support and hope. Although the road might be difficult at times, Titus was confident he and Suzanne would make the journey together. Not only did they have each other, but God would never leave them.

Suzanne's Lemon Shoofly Pie

Ingredients for crumb topping:
1½ cups flour
½ cup white sugar
½ cup shortening or butter, softened
½ teaspoon baking soda

Ingredients for pie filling:
1 egg
Zest of 2 lemons
Juice of 2 lemons, strained
2 tablespoons flour
½ cup white sugar
½ cup molasses
¾ cup boiling water

1 unbaked pie shell

Preheat oven to 350 degrees.

Combine all ingredients for crumb topping and work together until they form a crumb-like mixture.

Stir together all filling ingredients until well blended and pour into unbaked pie shell. Sprinkle crumb topping evenly across pie filling. Bake for 45 to 60 minutes.

Discussion Questions

1. Titus suffered from a lack of confidence. What are some reasons a person may lack confidence, and how can he or she gain confidence?

2. What can we do to help a friend or relative who lacks confidence?

3. Titus left home because his girlfriend broke up with him and because he felt he needed to prove himself to his family. Is there ever a time when it's necessary for a person to leave home in order to recover from a broken relationship or to prove themselves?

4. Titus felt inferior to his twin brother, who always seemed to know what he wanted and was able to do everything right. What can a parent do to help their children feel equally important within the family? How can an adult child overcome a feeling of inferiority and stop comparing himself to his siblings?

5. Suzanne also felt inferior and lacked self-confidence when it came to cooking. One of the reasons for this was because her mother was too impatient and made Suzanne feel as if she was a failure as a cook. What are some ways a mother can help her daughter become self-sufficient in the kitchen?

6. Titus's mother had a difficult time adjusting to the idea of Titus leaving home. How can a grown child who leaves home make it easier for his parents to accept and deal with his absence?

7. What are some ways parents can let their grown children know they accept the decision to move away?

8. Suzanne wanted to work in her grandfather's woodshop, but a woman working with wood was looked down upon by some in her family. Why do you think Suzanne's brother was opposed to her working in the shop? Do you feel that some jobs are more suited to men than women? Should a woman be allowed to do a job that a man might normally do?

9. Phoebe was rebellious and didn't want to settle down to marriage or joining the church. What are some reasons some young people are more rebellious than others? How can parents deal with their children's rebellion?

10. How do you feel about the Amish allowing their children to run around and try out the English world? Do you feel it helps the child make a more mature decision about whether they want to join the Amish church?

11. After reading this book, was there anything new you learned about the Amish way of life?

12. What spiritual lessons did you learn from reading *The Journey*?

About the Author

Wanda E. Brunstetter Wanda E. Brunstetter is a bestselling author who enjoys writing Amish-themed, as well as historical novels. Descended from Anabaptists herself, Wanda became deeply interested in the Plain People when she married her husband, Richard who grew up in a Mennonite church in Pennsylvania. Wanda and her husband live in Washington State, but take every opportunity to visit their Amish friends in various communities across the country, gathering further information about the Amish way of life.

Wanda and her husband have two grown children and six grandchildren. In her spare time, Wanda enjoys photography, ventriloquism, gardening, reading, stamping, and having fun with her family.

In addition to her novels, Wanda has written two Amish cookbooks, two Amish devotionals, several Amish children's books, as well as numerous novellas, stories, articles, poems, and puppet scripts.

Visit Wanda's Web site at www.wandabrunstetter.com and feel free to e-mail her at wanda@wandabrunstetter.com.

Coming soon from

Wanda E. Brunstetter

the

HEALING

KENTUCKY BROTHERS · TWO

FALL 2011